THE MEDUSA FOLD

NICK ADAMS

Elliptical
Publishing

For Linda, David & Gale, Bill & Lesley, Rose, Richard and all the staff at the Masons Arms. Thank you all for your love and support through a very challenging period in my life.

PROLOGUE

THE ONE-METRE PLASMA carapace materialised in spiral 107, known locally as the Milky Way. It entered through a remote galactic gateway deep in the recesses of the galaxy's Cygnus arm. The small concentrated and invisible husk of energy immediately dissipated into an undetectable gas cloud.

Katadromiko 26, a fourteen-kilometre long cruiser of the GDA navy, policing the ancient gateway and adorned with the latest in advanced detection arrays, observed nothing.

The alien intelligence passed unseen through the ship's shields and a fraction of a second later, had studied, learnt and recorded every facet, system and operational ability of the giant vessel and its forty-seven-thousand crew, before moving on.

Spreading out quickly to permeate and scrutinise several light hours in all directions it continued towards the heart of the galaxy, patiently searching for a specific system – after ingesting the cruiser's detailed galactic star map, it knew the exact location of its endgame and powered itself in that direction.

The journey lasted almost a local year, during which it visited many systems and worlds en route, inhabited with numerous fascinating humanoid cultures. It enthused and luxuriated in visiting every one, again learning and absorbing, revelling in the intricacies and variety of human evolution throughout this galaxy.

Until finally, shimmying its way through an outer belt of asteroids and dust, the alien arrived in a system within the Orion arm. It contained thirteen planets, eight considered locally as full size and five dwarf, but only one medium-sized inhabited planet, on which it found several differing civilisations. Some could almost be considered modernistic and contemporary and others surprisingly uncultured and extremely vulgar and then everything in-between.

It was rare to have such random and contrasting communities together on one world. When the alien took three-dimensional human form and walked on the planet's surface amongst the populace, it was shocked to discover some areas with enormous affluence surrounded by pockets of abject poverty. It wondered who was responsible for this particular imbalance and why the wealth of the planet wasn't distributed evenly so everyone was comfortable. Neither could the alien understand why it appeared a considerable number of the indigenous races seemed hell-bent on trashing their own planet. It was shockingly incomprehensible.

Terminating the suffering of a few hundred million humans and rectifying a planet's eco balance wasn't the reason for the journey however and, oblivious to any living thing on the planet, the alien settled in to wait.

It had some killing to do and it'd travelled across a large chunk of the universe with revenge on its mind. The alien was three hundred thousand years old, so kicking its heels for

a year, a hundred years, a thousand years was of no consequence; its intended prey was guaranteed to show up here
eventually. Although, the more it thought about things, it
might as well sort out a few problem areas on this planet
while it waited. It would give it something interesting to do.

1

___

Unknown system, Medusa Merger Galaxy

MEANWHILE, many millions of light years away, a creature of a very different species waited and slept, as it had for many millennia on the fringe of the ring belt. As with the other thousand of its brethren surrounding the Vriix's domicile planet, time was of no consequence. The container would only return the custodian to conscious thought, if and when an entity from the conflicting assemblage neared and posed an imminent threat. The container could feel out as far as one hundred light years and constantly plotted the trajectories of millions of entities from both the domiciliary and conflicting assemblages.

The custodian stirred, the fluid temperature slowly increasing and, along with a slight expansion of the container, its major systems gradually became cognisant.

Slowly and one at a time, the custodian extended each

tentacle, testing and reviewing its limits of motion. Once it was sure the indistinctness of the sleep had sufficiently receded, it questioned the breadth of the suspension. Two hundred thousand, one hundred and ninety-six rotations was the outcome. No other custodians had stirred in that time, this was the first time and it was the only one awakened.

It moved on to the detection and was somewhat surprised to find the celestial entity was almost upon it. Wondering why the container hadn't woken it hundreds of rotations earlier, it retraced the entity's path and was puzzled to witness it was actually two sizeable entities, materialising suddenly close in to the system on a trajectory taking them on a gently curving track, straight in and directly towards the fifth planet. Their home world.

Immediately despatching a warning signal back to the planet, the custodian waited for a reply and after the allotted time and no reply had come, it signalled the nearby brethren of custodians. This time it had more luck, as after a short period, it received two hundred and seventeen replies, indicating that they too were now awakened and tracking the two entities. There was a general consensus of surprise that not one of them had received a reply from the planet, but a definite agreement that they would operate as pre-programmed and work in synchrony to deflect the entities.

The custodian, being the first awakened, had all his systems up and operational. So it was his container that undertook the ranging scan of the entities. This was to assess the size and position of the strikes so as to best divert the threat away from the planet. It would have normally been done hundreds of rotations ago, with the custodian containers meeting the entities a long way out, thus reducing the amount of divergence required.

The scan led to another shock for the custodian. As soon as it was undertaken, one of the entities, the largest one, changed course to a heading straight towards the custodian's container.

A contingency such as this, however, had not been planned for. Contact with another sentient race had always been thought of as preposterous, the distances were too great and the ability to exceed the speed of light was considered impossible.

So, the group of custodians now found themselves with a distinct dilemma: stay and greet, or retreat back to the planet. Although, judging by the size, speed and manoeuvrability of the alien container, the distance they'd get if they did flee would be extremely small.

The custodian, quite sensibly, decided to remain where he was, with minimal systems activated and trusting that it wasn't taken as any kind of intimidation or arrogance.

It felt a slight vibration in the flow, indicating its container had just been scanned on multiple wavelengths. The Vriix transmitted a greeting straight at the alien container, a language involving vibrations in multiple colours. Fear was not an emotion that existed in Vriix culture. They had never had any conflict within their society and of course no contact outside their own system. So the custodian felt intrigued rather than nervous regarding the gargantuan container bearing down on it.

It felt a different form of vibration, one that caused it some discomfort. Its container's systems couldn't discern quite what its function was, only that it seemed to be initiating some form of fluctuating sound wave within the container. Extremely uncomfortable for a creature able to detect the sound of a slight colour change many kilometres distant. Quickly reducing the ferocity of the incoming signal, it sent its greeting once more.

The alien container slowed as it approached and the custodian, although not able to fully penetrate some form of field surrounding the vessel, was able to determine its construction was predominantly of ferrous metals. This, it found confusing, as surely the internal fluids would cause the container to corrode.

Seventeen other custodians approached, all of them transmitting the same greeting message using different frequencies. Shortly after, a large panel opened on the underside of the alien container and a sizeable circular mirror motored out from within, turning to face the small fleet of nearing Vriix containers.

It lit up and a beam of intense white light lanced out from the mirror, engulfing one of the Vriix containers. Even through the brightness of the beam, the original custodian witnessed several colours of distress emitted from the lone Vriix inside the struck container, which within a millisecond had vaporised. The internal fluid and custodian instantly boiled away to a faint cloud of vapour that itself swiftly dispersed into nothing.

As the mirror turned to face another of the Vriix containers, they all quickly dispersed back towards the planet at speed. The original custodian dived up and over the giant alien container, thus avoiding the murderous beam, before turning and heading straight for one of the larger asteroids in the planet's ring. It swooped in behind the hulking black rock and hid itself in a narrow crevasse that split the irregular-shaped asteroid's surface. Changing the container's outer colour to exactly match its surroundings, the Vriix custodian shut down its systems, all except fluid environs, and waited.

2

Katadromiko 28, *unknown system, Medusa Merger Galaxy*

HAZZLOU GRUPPS SAT BACK in the captain's chair with one leg draped pretentiously over the right arm of the seat. He stared up at the huge holographic display, not focusing on anything in particular, just thinking and ruminating about where everything had gone so spectacularly wrong.

Three weeks ago, he'd been just hours away from immortality and riches beyond his wildest dreams. His own autonurse, luxury yachts, maybe even his own private island on Panemorfi and girls, lots of girls.

Instead of that, he was stuck on a stolen battle cruiser with a skeleton crew of lazy Klatt, in an uncharted galaxy and the worst thing of all the little girl bitch from hell had taken the captain's suite.

The bruising around his crotch from the stun shot still itched and ached. He rubbed it surreptitiously and got a look similar to raised eyebrows from the nearest systems operator – the Klatt don't have eyebrows, so it was just a look.

'Eyes front,' he snapped, watching as the operator quickly pivoted his head back to the console.

He swore he'd make that sentient computerised witch on the *Gabriel* pay, for the humiliation alone – well, he hoped he would. It wasn't going to happen if they were stuck in this crap hole of a galaxy.

A whole day had passed now since the two ships had sneaked through the Pyli gateway and so far not one habitable planet had been detected. It didn't help that the hastily constructed Klatt ship had serious damage and was slowing them down. Ironic that it was the ship he was on now that had caused the damage.

The *Ice Machine*, as the blue and grey vessel was known in Klatt circles, still had many decks open to space and only one narrow corridor between the bow and stern. They desperately needed to find a spacefaring race capable of conducting the considerable quantity of repairs required. Having to pull the ship in close to the *Katadromiko* to include it in its cloak had proved difficult and would've left a slightly more identifiable trail in their wake when they passed through the galactic gateway.

The damage to the *Katadromiko* however, caused by the *Ice Machine*'s beam striking its hull, was reasonably superficial. The decks in question had been closed off and contained nothing crucial to the ship's operational capabilities.

He watched as they jumped near to yet another system that had a promising planet within.

A shout from one of the array operators snapped him back to reality. He turned and gave the Klatt operator a 'what is it' glare.

'We're being scanned, sir,' he said, nervously.

'What – who by?'

'Some sort of vessel situated on the edge of the asteroid belt, Captain.'

'What sort of vessel?' he asked impatiently.

A slight pause ensued that caused Grupps to become angry.

'I asked you a question,' he snarled.

'Err – liquid, sir,' the operator replied, slowly and anxiously. Most likely waiting for the computer to reassess and produce a more sensible report.

'Have you lost your mind?' said Grupps. 'How can a ship be fucking liquid?'

The operator brought the return into focus on the holomap and pointed at it.

Grupps stared and was about to reprimand the Klatt for his witless suggestion, when there appeared, sure enough, a transparent sphere, that seemed to be a large swimming pool quantity of liquid, hanging there in space, completely unmoving except for an occasional ripple on the internal surface.

'What the fuck are you?' said Grupps, more to himself than the bridge crew.

'There's something in it,' said another crew member.

By now everyone on the bridge had stopped to stare at the anomaly, as a shadowy shape shifted within.

Seconds later, the whole sphere began to change through several colours, fluctuating in intensity.

'Send it a greeting message in a bunch of frequencies,' said Grupps. 'See what that does.'

They noticed the… whatever it was… inside jerk violently as the transmission was sent.

'Well, it certainly received it,' said Grupps. 'Did it understand it?'

'There's more of them, sir,' said the original operator, the *Katadromiko* slowing as the pilot brought the mammoth ship in to five hundred kilometres away. 'Seventeen more, all moving this way and flashing in multicolours too, sir.'

'I don't like this,' said Grupps. 'I don't like this at all.'

'Multiple scans, sir,' the operator called. 'They're all trying different frequencies to penetrate our shields.'

'Will they achieve it?'

'Whether they know it or not, they're on the right track, sir.'

'So, I take it that's a yes then?' said Grupps, giving the operator an exasperated sigh.

'Given time, sir, yes.'

'It's an attack then, that's all I need to know,' Grupps grunted and turned to face the weapons operators. 'Target them with the beam,' he said, pointing at the swarm of slowly approaching spheres, their seemingly random colours changing faster and faster.

The twenty-metre mirror dropped out from its housing in the belly of the vessel. The blinding white-hot beam flashed out and the first of the spheres instantly vaporised. As it targeted the second and another expanding sphere of fluid dissipated into the solar wind, the remaining fleet of spheres turned and fled.

Over the next twenty seconds, all the alien vessels were dispatched before they got no more than a few hundred kilometres.

'Threat eliminated, sir,' said one of the weapons operators.

Grupps nodded and pointed at the planet.

'Pilot, take us in to have a look at that fifth planet,' he ordered.

Its unsuitability quickly became apparent as they passed through the belt and were able to get a detailed footprint.

'Dead desert planet, sir,' came the call. 'A long-dead once ninety percent ocean world, its atmosphere is thin now and average temperature around a hundred and fourteen degrees.'

Grupps rolled his eyes and sighed.

'Another waste of time,' he griped, slumping back into his seat. 'What the hell were they doing defending this dust bowl for anyway?'

He waved a hand irritatedly at the holomap.

'Get us out of here,' he said, standing again and making off towards the main bridge doors. 'Call me when you find a decent fucking planet.'

3

____

The Starship Gabriel, _orbiting Earth, Sol system_

EDWARD VIRR SMILED as he saw Linda's reaction on entering the bridge of the new *Gabriel*.

'Oh, wow,' she exclaimed, her jaw hanging open, as she surveyed the seating spread this time in a semi-circle and the even bigger holomap hanging above. It displayed the Sol system out as far as the Kuiper belt.

'Have a seat,' said Ed. 'You haven't seen the best of it yet.'

Linda slid onto one of the blue leather couches and Ed joined her in the adjacent one and grinned again.

'Okay, Cleo, give her the full show,' he said.

The previously matt black oval ceiling lit up with a three hundred and sixty-degree view from outside: a beautiful blue planet Earth slowly rotating below, a crescent moon off to the left and a million stars glistening in the distance. It went right down to the floor all around, thus giving the impression you were sitting outside and on top of the ship.

Ed noticed Linda's hands suddenly grabbing the sides of her seat, just as he had done when Prota had shown it to him.

'Oh, shit,' she stammered, her eyes on stalks. 'That is utterly wondrous.'

'Isn't it just?' whispered Ed. 'It reminds me of when my parents took me to the planetarium at Fernbank in Georgia when I was ten. It made such an impression on me, I decided there and then I wanted to work in space science.'

'Penelope Drinkwater was my inspiration,' said Linda, Earth's reflection glistening in her eyes as Ed glanced over.

'She was Dewey's co-pilot on the Mars landing wasn't she?'

Linda nodded.

'I was eight,' she said, reminiscing. 'I so wanted to be her when I grew up.'

Ed shrugged.

'You've certainly achieved that and more,' he said.

'Pure luck,' she replied, sounding a little melancholy. 'It could've been any of the NASA pilots that got consigned to your crazy project.'

'Was crazy what you thought at the time?'

'A little, I suppose,' she said. 'Especially after witnessing Andy's childish sense of humour.'

'Hey? I resemble that remark,' said Andy, grinning, as he and Rayl entered the bridge holding hands.

'D'you like our new ride?' asked Rayl, stooping down and giving Linda a hug.

'It's fabulous isn't it?' Linda replied. 'I love the way Cleo's designed the cabins to all our specific personalities and tastes.'

'Yeah,' replied Rayl, sceptically and giving Andy a sly glower. 'Not so sure about the weird motorbike mural on our bathroom wall though,' she added.

'Weird?' inquired Andy, a look of horror on his face. 'That's Valentino Rossi, he's a bloody legend. My mum loved him – used to take me to the British MotoGP to watch him race when I was little.'

'I'm ever so sorry,' said Linda, looking at Rayl sympathetically and squeezing her hand. 'But you did agree to marry him.'

'I know,' Rayl replied, lugubriously. 'I think he caught me on a bad day.'

Andy rolled his eyes at Ed and spoke, quickly changing the subject.

'I understand we're off on a road trip, boss,' he said, sliding into another of the six couches.

'Correct.'

'What mess have the council got for us to sort out this time?' he asked.

'This one's a private charter,' said Ed. 'From Bache and Xutan.'

'Don't tell me – the GDA have run out of ships again?' Andy said, lying back and putting his hands behind his head.

'Kinda,' said Ed, going on to explain how they reckoned Ystolion Flast was the financier behind the whole scheme and with the use of a stolen autonurse, the one-hundred-and-twenty-year-old woman was now hiding in the body of a sixteen-year-old.

'So, they reckon the 28 has escaped destruction for a second time?' asked Rayl, joining the conversation.

'Yeah,' said Ed. 'They also reckon it escaped through the Pyli gateway along with the damaged octaship too.'

'Hmm,' grunted Andy. 'I wondered why that bloody thing hadn't been found.'

'Where did they go to?' asked Rayl.

'The gateway mysteriously opened of its own accord late on in a night period, to somewhere called the Medusa Merger Galaxy,' said Ed.

'How far is that?' Andy asked.

'One hundred and thirty million light years, give or take,' Ed answered.

'Just round the corner then,' joked Andy. 'Best take a packed lunch.'

'What are we supposed to do if we find them?' Linda asked, ignoring Andy's immaturity. 'Surely, even this ship is no match for a *Katadromiko*.'

'Not for a fully operational one, no,' said Ed. 'But you've got to remember a *Katadromiko* has a crew of forty-seven thousand. She's probably got an untrained skeleton bridge crew and little else. The rest of the ship will be deserted.'

'That fucking Skirmat psycho's probably there too,' said Andy. 'Should've killed him while we had the chance.'

'If we come across him, I won't make that mistake again,' said Ed, curling his top lip. 'I've unfinished business with that murdering piece of shit.'

'Where's Phil and Pol, by the way?' asked Linda, glancing over at the tube elevator.

'Phil's helping Cleo install the autonurses from the old ship,' said Ed. 'They're about the only thing that can't be improved upon. He'll be up later.'

'Is he all right about the old ship?' said Linda. 'It was his home for an awful long time.'

'Seems fine,' said Ed.

'I think it has something to do with Prota being involved

in the design and construction of this ship,' said Rayl. 'He immediately feels at home. That, and the fact he had Cleo design his cabin exactly the same way as before.'

'Creature of habit, our Phil,' said Linda, smiling. 'And Pol?'

'Down on the planet, shopping,' said Ed, rolling his eyes. 'I've already had to increase the wardrobe size twice in our cabin,' he said. 'She's gone a bit crazy on clothing since she's been able to buy stuff that fits her.'

'Six-limbed fashion was a bit scarce on Earth, so you can't blame her,' said Rayl. 'And the good news is, I got all my borrowed clothes back.'

'Is Bache coming along this time?' Andy asked.

'He wants to,' said Ed. 'Unfinished business and all that – but the political fallout at the moment is quite severe and he has to be available to give evidence to all the relevant inquiries.'

'Just like here then,' said Andy. 'Did you hear, another African dictator mysteriously went down in a helicopter acci-dent yesterday, along with the majority of his generals. That's two now, or three if you count the unexplained explosion killing the majority of the North Korean leadership.'

'The Russians and Chinese are blaming the Americans and vice versa,' said Ed, shrugging.

'The Brits are blaming the French,' said Linda.

'Ah, that's quite normal,' said Andy. 'We blame the French for everything. They'll retaliate by having a strike and blockading the channel ports to fuck up everyone's holidays. It's a game they've played for decades.'

'Anyway,' said Ed, rolling his eyes at Andy's comments. 'Bache won't be with us this time.'

'He's not likely to be set up for anything is he?' asked Rayl. 'I know what the GDA can be like.'

'Not with ours and Xutan's testimonies, no,' Ed replied. 'But I know he could really do without all this fallout. After all, he retired to get away from the ridiculous political bullshit.'

The conversation stalled for a moment as everyone stared out at the magnificent view. Armstrong Station slowly hoved into view and they watched as the Mars ore freighters, now retrofitted with jump drives, choreographed themselves in and out from the station's docking points, relinquishing their loads of red regolith.

'When are you planning on leaving?' asked Linda, breaking the quiet spell.

'Couple of days,' said Pol, arriving up on the tube lift. 'Just need to confirm and put a deposit on a new home we've found.'

Everyone turned and stared at her.

'You've found somewhere?' said Linda, a cross between a question and an exclamation. She turned to face Ed. 'I thought you said she was clothes shopping?'

Both Ed and Pol nodded and grinned at each other.

'Bloody hell, you kept that quiet,' said Andy. 'What are you buying?'

'A thousand-year-old castle,' said Pol, bouncing up and down, unable to hide her enthusiasm. 'It's amazing.'

'Where?' Andy asked.

'Somerset coast,' said Ed. 'It's even got a fully operational water mill that powers up the storage batteries.'

'The Klatt won't be able to stroll in there and shoot Ed's grandfather clock,' said Pol, chuckling.

'We don't mention the clock,' grumbled Ed. 'Fucking insurance arseholes.'

'Didn't they pay out enough to replace it?' asked Linda.

'Didn't pay out anything at all,' said Pol.

'Damage caused by alien commandos isn't covered, apparently,' Ed sneered. 'Should've said I shot it myself accidentally.'

Ed stood and stretched.

'Okay, everyone, go and sort your shit out – we leave on Friday nine a.m. space time, don't be late.'

4

———

The Starship Gabriel, *orbiting Earth, Sol system*

THE BRIDGE WAS UNUSUALLY quiet as the *Gabriel* slipped silently out of Earth's orbit and accelerated towards designated jump zone three. The view, as all six crew members lay back on their couches, said everything.

No one felt the need to disrupt the glorious spectacle of the beautiful blue planet receding behind them and the moon sliding into view up front. Even at this distance, Artemis base, now covering dozens of square kilometres and home to many tens of thousands of scientists, workers and support staff, could be seen glowing on the planetoid's surface.

Although Earth's climate change was still a thing, it had slowed as the worst of the polluting industries had moved into space and onto the lunar surface.

'Jumping in three, two, one,' said Linda, breaking the silence.

The magnificent spectacle vanished, replaced by a wall-to-wall starscape of non-system outer space, several hundred light years distant.

'Quiet, isn't it?' said Andy.

'What, the jump?' Linda asked.

'Well, everything really,' he clarified. 'The ship itself is so eerily silent. I quite liked the comforting wheeze of the old ship. At least you knew the environmental system was operating and the lighting dimmed ever so slightly, so you knew when the ship jumped.'

'I can make it do that,' said Cleo, materialising in the centre of the holomap on a floating carpet, dressed today as a genie.

'Can I rub your lamp?' said Andy, getting a thump on the arm from Rayl.

Cleo ignored the comment and continued.

'If there are any particular sounds you want for any of the systems around the ship, just ask,' she said, turning to look at Andy. 'I can even make it sound like your two-stroke Kawasaki triple.'

'The seven-fifty with the expansion chambers?' Andy asked, with a hopeful grin.

'Yes.'

'Please don't,' said Ed, giving Cleo an exasperated glance. 'My neighbours in Canterbury never forgave me when you turned up on that thing. Would've been okay, except you had to ride up and down the road with the front wheel in the air.'

'Freakin' awesome,' said Andy, grinning. 'Craziest bike to ever come out of Japan – pride of my collection.'

'I think I'll stick to my clocks, thank you,' said Ed, giving Rayl a roll of his eyes.

'Motorbikes are a bit more exciting,' said Pol.

Ed turned his head slowly to face her.

'I'll pretend you never said that,' he grumbled. 'Last thing he needs is encouragement, he'll be bringing them with him on the ship next.'

Andy and Pol smirked at each other, which didn't go unnoticed.

'You haven't,' said Ed, his eyes wide.

Andy shrugged.

'Might've popped a couple in one of the hangars,' he answered, with a fake contrite expression. 'I hid one on the last *Gabriel* too.'

'And where are you going to ride them, eh?' said Ed, crossing his arms.

Andy shrugged again.

'The hangars are really big on this ship,' he said cheerfully, giving Pol a thumbs up. 'One of them's an off-road enduro bike and anyway, Pol wants to learn to ride.'

Ed looked down at the floor and huffed noisily.

'Well, at least you'll be close to an autonurse when it all goes wrong,' he sighed.

'See,' said Andy, winking at Pol. 'Told you he'd be fine about it.'

Linda opened her eyes for a moment and clapped her hands.

'Okay, people – we don't need everyone on the bridge while we're just rattling between jump points. Even in this ship, it's going to take thirty-nine hours to reach Pyli. Why don't you all go up to the main lounge and relax?'

'The Parisian café you mean,' said Ed, standing and stretching his back.

'It's a modern pub,' said Andy. 'They don't have real ale pumps in Paris.'

'It's more like a Spanish bar,' said Phil, without looking up, until he realised everyone had turned to face him. 'Without the tapas of course,' he added, with a cheesy grin.

'I think it was more, "how would you know", that intrigued us, Phil,' said Ed.

'Ah, well, yes, I did a coach tour down Spain's east coast a couple of weeks ago.'

'A coach tour?' repeated Andy. 'Wasn't that aimed more at pensioners?'

'I'm nearly four thousand years old,' he said. 'How old d'you have to be?'

'He has a point,' said Ed, as everyone chuckled.

'Hey,' said Linda, pointing at the tube lift. 'Go and do your holiday stories somewhere else.'

Ed loitered as they all disappeared upwards through the ceiling on the tube lift.

'It's good to have you back, Linda,' he said, patting her on the shoulder as he passed. 'The *Gabriel* isn't complete without you.'

She looked up with misty eyes and gave him a half smile.

'I missed you guys,' she said. 'I won't be leaving again.'

5

———

The Starship Gabriel, *orbiting Pyli, Metafora system*

'HAVE we got the gateway key loaded into the system, Cleo?' Ed asked, staring up at the holomap. It displayed the familiar triangle of three moons above Pyli and *Katadromiko 7* hanging off their port side.

'We have, indeed,' she answered.

'Good morning, *Gabriel*,' said a bridge officer from the *Katadromiko 7*. 'Captain Trikalon sends his regards. Our drone will return shortly and provide an up to date picture of the other side, please hold.'

'I remember Trikalon,' said Andy. 'He was Bache's first officer on the *12* when we first met. I seem to recall he took a bit of a shine to the real ale I had on the *Gabriel* at the time.'

The drone materialised between the moons, instantly grabbing their attention and transmitted its data to both vessels. The *Gabriel*'s holomap changed to show an expansive starscape on the other side. It revealed the three moons orbiting a barren planet in an otherwise unpopulated system. Its star was a white dwarf, quite some distance away and struggling to illuminate the planet's surface to more than a dull grey half-light.

Ed looked around the semicircle of faces, all gazing up at the vista from a hundred and thirty million light years away.

'Doesn't look very habitable, does it?' said Pol, voicing what Ed was already thinking.

'There's a lotta stars in that view too,' said Andy.

'We've got to remember it's two galaxies colliding,' said Phil. 'There's going to be a lot of stuff going on. A lot of weird gravitational effects pulling this way and that. We need to be careful when plotting jumps within that lot, especially the longer ones.'

'Food for thought,' said Linda. 'Can we make a rule that all jump calculations are given a second evaluation by Cleo before engaging?'

'A very good suggestion,' said Ed. 'If no one has any objection, that becomes bridge policy from now on, until further notice.'

'You'll get no argument from me,' said Phil.

'Good…everyone okay to proceed?' he asked, and on receiving five nodding heads, he opened a channel to the 7.

'Thank you, 7,' he said. 'Data received, hope to see you on our return.'

'Good luck, *Gabriel*, and good hunting.'

Ed nodded at Phil, who immediately accelerated the *Gabriel* out of Pyli's orbit and headed straight out and towards the triangle of space between the three moons. The ship's latest rendition of the Alma drive, or Deviant as it had been named by the designing Theo engineers, was forty-three percent more efficient than the previous design and had the *Gabriel* approaching the gate's threshold in under ten seconds.

'Holy cow,' muttered Andy under his breath as he watched Phil struggling to slow them enough to be within the gate's acquiring velocity.

Phil chuckled as he stood on the brakes.

'The acceleration of this thing is going to take some getting used to,' he said. 'It's so much quicker out of the blocks.'

'Isn't it just?' said Ed. 'I accidentally took out a Chinese military satellite when we brought it back to Earth for the first time.'

'That would've gone down well,' said Linda. 'I didn't hear anything about it, though.'

'We were cloaked,' said Pol, smirking. 'They eventually came to the conclusion it was hit by some errant space debris.'

The conversation lapsed as the gate actuated and the second-hand data on the holomap became real and filled the ceiling above them. Both Rayl and Pol brought all four of the new ship's powerful arrays online and gave the region a thorough full spectrum scan.

Andy, responsible for the ship's defences, cloaked the *Gabriel* and gave the formidable defensive suite a systems check.

'I have a faint jump signature, two point six million kilometres away,' said Rayl.

Ed raised his eyebrows at Phil. Understanding the gesture, Phil had the ship with throttle buried, heading towards the echo. Even with the slight delay in acceleration and braking at the other end, it only took twenty-nine seconds.

'Ah-ha,' chirped Pol. 'They jumped into a system forty-one light years distant.'

'Are they there?' asked Ed, looking at the system now winking in red on the holomap.

Rayl shrugged.

'If they're still cloaked, we need to be in system at least and I'll need to go there to see if there's a trace of an outward-bound jump.'

'Cleo, can you—'

'Checked and approved,' she said, before Phil could finish the question.

Ed pointed at the red flashing icon.

'Go there.'

They materialised in another empty system, with another onward trace that, once again, they followed.

'Well, this is getting monotonous,' grumbled Andy, after several hours and the ninth jump. 'What the hell are they looking for?'

'Probably a humanoid society,' said Cleo, appearing inside the holomap, who today seemed to be going through an Edwardian phase, with a long, frilly, pinched at the waist dress and a huge flowery hat. 'Somewhere they can affect repairs to the ships and maybe recruit some crew. If you notice, every system they jump to has a goldilocks planet somewhere within.'

'A what?' asked Pol, glancing up at Cleo.

'Not too hot and not too cold,' said Ed, before Cleo could answer. 'A planet that could possibly sustain carbon-based, oxygen-breathing life forms.'

'Ah, okay,' she said, not looking too convinced.

'Hmm,' grunted Rayl, staring avidly at her scan results.

'Is that a "hmm", you agree with what I just said, or is it a "hmm", I've found something?' asked Ed.

'Both,' she replied, not looking up. 'But I might have something in the next system.'

'What d'you mean by something?' Ed asked.

'A small reading that's suspiciously like weapon residue.'

Ed nodded at Phil.

'Get us over there, but at a distance,' he cautioned. 'Don't want to jump into the middle of someone's war zone.'

They all glanced up to watch the holomap as it updated when they materialised inside the next system. Phil had brought them in behind the star, before taking a wide loop around, so they could take a more concentrated look from a hundred million kilometres away.

'Whatever happened here, is now over,' said Rayl. 'There has definitely been some recent gun play here however, in the vicinity of that desert planet with the rock-strewn ring system.'

'Any wreckage?' asked Ed.

'None.'

'What the hell were they firing at then?' Andy asked.

'Might've been weapons testing,' said Phil. 'Perfect place with all these rocks around.'

'Yeah,' said Ed, slowly, sounding unconvinced. 'Take us over there quietly and carefully. I want to see that planet and its rings up close.'

Phil didn't hurry this time and brought the *Gabriel* in at point four light, gradually decreasing velocity as they approached.

'Someone was waving an asteri beam around here not so long ago,' said Rayl.

'How long?' Ed asked.

'Within twenty-four hours,' she said. 'Another day and the traces would be gone.'

'Oh!' exclaimed Pol, suddenly, creating a momentary silence on the bridge as the other five turned to stare at her.

She looked up at the row of expectant faces.

'There's something weird going on on one of those rocks,' she said.

'In what way?' Andy asked.

'Small area of liquid.'

'What, like water trapped inside the asteroids?' Ed asked.

'No, on the outside.'

'Can't happen,' said Andy. 'It would boil off in seconds.'

Pol shrugged, and transferred her readings onto the holomap, panning in on one specific rock. It was one of the larger asteroids and had a deep crevice down its length. A lump of something sitting within the fissure was shaded red.

'From the cameras, it looks the same as the surrounding rock faces,' said Pol. 'But it isn't and it's kinda spherical.'

A dark shadow moved slightly within the anomaly.

'There's definitely something alive in there,' said Rayl, bringing her array around and into play too.

'Can you define a shape?' Ed asked.

The image phased through several unfocused shadows as she took the array through its repertoire of frequencies. Until one suddenly flicked into sharp definition.

They all sat back in their seats, staring at the creature hanging centrally in the bubble of liquid.

'Fuck,' said Andy. 'Never thought I'd see one of those in space.'

'What is it?' asked Pol, looking between the image and those each side of her.

'A cephalopod,' said Linda, speaking for the first time in a while. 'My college roommate did her dissertation on octopi for her masters in marine biology.'

She turned to Pol.

'They're solitary creatures that live in Earth's oceans, apparently highly intelligent.'

'This one's in bloody space,' said Andy. 'Unless it was put here by someone else, we must assume it's a bit more intelligent than we thought.'

'Send a standard greeting signal,' said Ed. 'And perhaps a drone to have a closer look.'

6

Vrixx container, asteroid crevasse, above Vrixxion

THE CUSTODIAN REELED, as again, a beam of painful sound waves penetrated the container. As before, it reduced the ferocity of the waves, only this time it didn't send a greeting back.

This time it remained mute and motionless, hoping that the third smaller alien container would simply move on. Unfortunately, it detected a small entity emitted by the alien, that accelerated straight towards it. Believing this to be a missile of some kind, it darted out of the crevasse and began dodging randomly through the asteroid rings. The escape attempt didn't last more than a few seconds, as its container mysteriously slowed, then stopped. No matter what the custodian tried, its container was strangely held immobile by an invisible force.

It watched, staying completely motionless as the alien

container neared, seemingly able to nudge aside the smaller rocks and asteroids with some unseen influence. For a sentient lifeform unused to feeling any kind of trepidation or fear, the custodian did detect a certain discomfort in being manipulated in this fashion. Deciding its best course of action was inaction, it decided to play dead and remain completely inert.

As the alien container slowed and stopped only a few hundred metres away, a large back-lit rectangular doorway materialised on its flank. The custodian dared not move a tentacle as its container was dragged first towards, then through a strange permeable, vibrating barrier and inside the much larger alien craft. Shocked to discover the inside of the container was hollow and dry, it flinched as its normally spherical container plopped down on a hard surface and squashed down into an oval shape, under the influence of some kind of gravitational effect.

It noticed the atmosphere had changed once inside the craft, similar to what was above Vriixion's home liquid.

Perhaps they only fill the areas they need, it thought, continuing to remain absolutely still.

Expecting the space to fill with liquid at some point, the custodian was astonished as three quad-tentacled aliens entered the dry space, seemingly without any form of breathing apparatus. Equally shocking was the way they seemed to be able to perambulate quite dextrously on the lower two of their tentacles.

As the aliens neared, the custodian found it somewhat difficult to remain inert, when its natural instinct was to recoil from such a frighteningly hideous life form.

It twitched involuntarily as the up to now bright luminescence within the space began to change through many dull hues and at the same time, bright colours. Complete gobbledegook to the custodian, but it did wonder if this was some kind of communication attempt and their colour language was different. The three dry aliens didn't seem to be making any aggressive moves. Perhaps this really was an attempt to talk, although it could detect the same sound vibrations on its container's hull as before coming from them, only this time much fainter and less uncomfortable.

It made its mind up to send a message back and see what effect that had.

'I welcome new alien visitors to our world. We offer no threat,' it flashed.

The reaction from the aliens was immediate. They all moved towards each other, slapping a tentacle above themselves, before waving both upper tentacles at the custodian.

It thought about this for a moment. Was this reaction a good one or were they dismayed or even affronted at its communication attempt?

The aliens had resumed their previous positions, as the message it had flashed was flashed back to it. After a little more thought, it came to the conclusion that the aliens were trying to learn the language and most likely needed it to communicate more so their container's artificial brain system could learn and adapt.

'I colour more,' it flashed. 'I am custodian eight one nine from the planet Vrixxion. We know ourselves as the Vrixx. Myself and my thousand allies are the custodians or deflectors from the conflicting assemblage.'

It stopped flashing for a few seconds as it thought, before deciding it had nothing to lose by asking and added, 'Why did your other ships attack us?'

The aliens began conversing with each other again using

their peculiar sound waves and waving their upper tentacles. The custodian jumped suddenly as a fourth alien materialised next to the others straight out of the atmosphere. It was so surprised it involuntarily inked and the interior of the container went instantly black.

Castigating itself for the premature bodily function, it hoped the act wasn't taken as an insult, as it most definitely would on its home world. As the fluid cleared again, following an emergency flush, it adopted a contrite and apologetic pose by crossing its tentacles in front of itself.

A message was flashed back to it, once they could see each other again.

'*Nut atac usse.*'

The same line repeated several times, as the custodian tried to make sense of it.

Does it mean, 'Not attack us' *or*, 'Not us attack' *or even*, 'Attack us not?' It mulled the possible meanings for a few moments before coming to a decision and flashing a reply.

'If not your allies, then who attack us and why?'

The reply came quicker this time.

'Bud alliens, evaydyng kepture. Wee arre on pesyutte.'

The Vrixx cringed at the bad colouring, but pretty much understood what the aliens were trying to say. The first aliens were bad, we are good and in pursuit to capture them.

'The bad aliens destroyed seventeen of my allies. This form of crime is unknown to us,' it flashed, feeling a little more confident now, as it reasoned its imminent death was less likely now the situation was clearer.

'Thay destroyed menu thousinds uf ower allies tuu,' the aliens coloured, before continuing. 'Cann wee asck yu a qeestion? Whiy arr yu awl owt hure?'

'We are kept here in deep sleep to be able to deflect any

dangers away from our home planet below. We have been here for over two hundred thousand rotations.'

This time the reply took a little longer, but when it came, the shock of what the custodian was told, almost caused it to ink again.'

7

Forward port hangar, the Starship Gabriel, *unknown system*

ED, Andy, Linda and Cleo waited patiently, watching the large octopod as it floated motionless for a while. It hadn't moved a tentacle since they'd asked why an ocean-based life form was protecting a dry, barren, desert planet.

A holographic image of the red-coloured planet below rotated slowly, hanging above the two parties.

'My scans indicate the planet's oceans dried up around a hundred thousand years ago,' said Cleo, her words automatically flashing in colour around the hangar for the benefit of their guest.

'This true is not,' the octopod eventually coloured back. 'Vrixxion planet of oceans.'

'When was the last time you scanned your own planet?' Linda asked.

'Not placement since,' it coloured. 'All eyes outwards are facing.'

Ed noticed the *Gabriel* turning as the stars outside began moving. Cleo ushered them to one side as the planet below became visible through the hangar's huge main doorway.

'See for yourself,' she coloured, waving at the ochre orb almost filling the space.

Cleo detected the alien's scanning system reaching out through the atmosphere barrier and downwards. When it shut off again shortly after, the alien floated motionless and silent for several moments. Even the watching humans, unaccustomed to observing an octopod, could clearly see it had withdrawn within itself and become slightly smaller. Just the very tips of its tentacles twitched randomly.

'Fourteen billion,' were the only two words it coloured, slightly weaker in brightness than before.

'I'm so sorry,' replied Ed, realising as with the others, it was stating how many of its kin had once thrived in the oceans below. 'We will do everything we can to help find you and your allies a new home.'

'Other planets habitable are none,' it coloured. 'Container unable for travel interstellar.'

'We will help,' said Linda, moving around the alien's ship to face what she hoped was its front. 'We have ocean planets where we come from that don't have any risk of a galactic conjoining.'

The octopod seemed to jump slightly at the realisation of what Linda had said.

'How avoid conflicting assemblage?' it coloured. 'You cannot travel at another galaxy, distance impossible.'

'Actually, it is,' said Ed, waiting as his words were converted into colours.

The Vrixx went quiet and still again for a few moments, its two eyes independently flicking over the four of them.

'You from galaxy distant?' it coloured slowly, almost as if it didn't believe them.

'We are,' said Ed.

'Distance?' it asked.

'One hundred and sixty-three million rotations of your star at light speed,' interrupted Cleo. Doing the calculation using Vriixion's slightly quicker orbit of its sun.

The creature suddenly jetted around its misshapen sphere, stopping abruptly just the other side of the pliable and see-through hull nearest them. Six of its tentacles spread out, the suckers growing large as they attached themselves to the inside wall membrane.

They all took an involuntary step back as it loomed over them, except for Cleo, who stood her ground. The Vriix's large eyes swivelled between them once more.

'Journey length?' it flashed brightly, its confidence seemingly growing.

'Instantaneous,' Cleo continued. 'Through an ancient alien gateway a few light rotations away.'

The Vrixx studied Cleo for a moment, before releasing itself from the hull and jetting back to the centre of the sphere.

'I know you're having doubts,' said Linda. 'But everything Cleo has said is true. The conjoining of these two galaxies has only just begun and will take many millions of rotations. There will be a lot of turmoil, with stars and systems colliding. We can get all of you away from that danger and provide a safe home in a stable galaxy.'

'Your ship is large,' it coloured. Cleo's translating

program was getting better at the language all the time. 'But unable to fit almost a thousand of our containers.'

'That is true,' said Andy. 'But there is a ship that can.'

All eyes turned to face him.

'The *28*,' he said, shrugging.

Cleo tilted her head to one side.

'He's right,' she said. 'If we can retake the *Katadromiko* without too much damage, it would be big enough to get all the surviving octopods back to the Milky Way.'

'The what?' asked the Vrixx.

Ed smiled and looked over at Cleo.

'Can you show our Vrixx friend some ocean images from Earth, Cleo?' he asked.

The holomap image changed to a three-dimensional undersea view somewhere on a pretty coral reef. Multi-coloured fish flicked in and out of the coral, until an octopus, disturbed by the diver making the recording, shot up and out across the camera's view.

The Vrixx jumped back, before squirting its way quickly across to the hull nearest the images and pressing its eyes up against the membrane.

'This is the ocean,' it coloured. 'You've been here before.'

'No,' said Ed. 'These are images from our home planet and that is what we know as an octopus and is about ten times smaller than you. But as you can see, almost identical.'

'How can that be?' it asked. 'You're from a galaxy millions of light rotations away.'

'Long story,' said Linda. 'A race of aliens we know as the Ancients who originally built the galactic gateways – they spread our human DNA around as they went and it seems they may have done it with other species too.'

The Vrixx looked back at the images of the octopus swimming along the sea floor, settling into a depression before changing its colour to match the background.

'Did they help you in developing your extraordinary technology?' it asked.

Ed gave Linda a wide-eyed 'be careful what you say' glance. She gave him a barely discernible nod in return.

'They are one of the smartest non-human life forms on our planet,' she said. 'But they didn't evolve into the larger fully sentient beings that you became here.'

The Vrixx swam down to them again.

'Is this where you propose for us to re-establish?' it asked.

'Not there,' said Ed. 'There are better worlds, that are almost all ocean.'

'We would also need to get authorisation from the ruling council in our galaxy,' said Linda.

'You have a galactic council?'

'We do, yes.'

'How many sentient races does it govern?'

'Over sixteen hundred.'

Cleo changed the holomap to show images from multiple worlds. Cities, oceans, forests, glaciers, space stations, ships, animals and lakes, flicking from one to the next.

The octopod looked up and watched transfixed, with just the odd twitch from the tips of its tentacles again. Eventually it brought its gaze back down to the four humans.

'We thought we were alone in the universe,' it coloured.

'If it's any consolation, so did we until quite recently,' said Andy. 'We've only been members of the council for four of our rotations.'

'I'm going to need to communicate with my allies,' it

coloured. 'They will have no idea of the disaster that has come to pass.'

Cleo ushered the other three away from the sphere, before turning back to face the Vrixx.

'You are free to leave and contact your friends,' she said, the multicolours of the translation flashing around the hangar.

Ed stepped forward before the octopod could react.

'We will come back for you when we've concluded our mission and find you that new home,' he said.

The sphere lifted silently from the hangar floor as Cleo released the tractor beam securing it. Reforming into its natural spherical shape, it moved towards the door. It stopped abruptly before it exited and turned to face the small group huddled next to the hangar exit.

'Would I be able to accompany you on your travels while you're here?' the Vrixx asked.

'Concerned we won't return for you?' Ed asked with raised eyebrows.

'No, it's not that,' it coloured back. 'I trust you on that front. It's just...' The octopod hesitated, its tentacle tips twitching. 'Our technology is limited and as a race, we're hugely inquisitive and I would...'

'Like to see some stuff?' said Andy, interrupting.

The Vrixx jetted its way over to the hull membrane nearest them and suckered itself to the hull.

'Yes...could I?'

The three humans looked at each other, before turning to Cleo.

'Is that okay with you, Cleo?' Ed asked. 'It's you that has to secure our friend's vessel down here safely.'

'It wouldn't be a drama,' she said.

'Fantastic,' coloured the Vrixx, releasing itself from the

hull and jetting around the sphere three times at breakneck speed.

'Wow,' said Andy. 'You can really get a shift on when you want to.'

It stopped and faced him.

'Even with our size and intellect, we still had predators in the ocean to watch out for.'

Ed walked forward and put his hands on his hips.

'If you're going to be coming along with us, we really ought to know your name?' he asked.

'13647918502,' it coloured back.

'Oh dear,' said Linda, puffing out her cheeks and rolling her eyes. 'That's so easy to remember.'

'I think we're going to have to provide you with a shorter name,' said Ed. 'One we can remember.'

'Please don't take offence,' said Linda. 'But are you a male or female of your species?'

'Female,' she coloured back.

'Oona,' said Cleo, before any of the others had time to think.

'Oona the octopus…sounds good to me,' said Ed, looking round at the other two, who nodded their approval. 'Okay, from now on we will address you as Oona. So long as that's acceptable to you?'

'It is,' she coloured. 'Oona will return shortly.'

The sphere rotated and, apart from the buzzing of the atmosphere shield, it left the hangar silently, under its own steam.

8

___

Katadromiko 28, *unknown system, Medusa Merger Galaxy*

THE FOURTEEN-KILOMETRE BATTLE cruiser dropped into the unnamed system behind one of two moons orbiting the next promising-looking planet. This was the third that day and the seventeenth since they had arrived in the Medusa galaxy.

The blue Klatt octagonal ship winked in fifty kilometres away, still showing the damage inflicted by the attack above Paradeisos. They'd managed to secure the ship and section off the worst areas, but you still required a vacuum suit to get to the rearmost compartments of the vessel. Not that it mattered a great deal, as the majority of the personnel had been transferred over to the *28*, leaving a skeleton crew to man the bridge.

Back on the *28*, Captain Grupps was slouched across his raised bridge chair. He was bored, and after all the previous unsuitable planets, he wasn't paying much attention anymore.

His ears pricked up when he heard the words 'oxygen-based atmosphere' and 'humanoid population'. Looking up at the large holographic image of the planet as it appeared above them all, he was pleased to see large landmasses surrounded by oceans, clouds, green areas and brown mountainous regions.

Standing suddenly, he pointed at the planet.

'Cloak the ship and take us in for a closer look,' he ordered. 'Are there any signs of space technology?' he added, turning to stare at the array officers.

'No, Captain,' one of them said, without looking up. 'No ships, no space stations and no satellites.'

'Well, it's no good to us if they're still in the fucking stone age,' he grumbled.

'They have atmospheric aircraft achieving Mach 2, sir, and ground vehicles capable of three hundred kilometres an hour.'

'Hmm, do they?' he grunted. 'Show me what they look like.'

The operator must have hacked into the planet's web network, as multiple random images of tall humanoids with varying skin tones circled the bridge.

'Excellent,' said Grupps, sounding almost cheerful for the first time. 'Multicultural is what we want, strangers will be less likely to stand out. Find the most common language and get the computer busy updating our translators. I want them to think we're just from another region when we first venture down. Also study their culture and laws, we don't want to be arrested for something stupid as soon as we land.'

Thirteen hours later, Grupps, along with four of his previous protection detail – he couldn't use any of the Klatt crew as they looked just too alien – sat in the cockpit of one of the *28*'s many heavily armed marine landing ships. He'd found the planet's largest city and seat of government. He'd had clothes produced that wouldn't look out of place in this region's inner city environment with pockets sewn inside them to conceal their technology and weapons.

They watched as the two Klatt pilots took the cloaked landing ship out into space and dropped quickly into the planet's upper atmosphere. The four antigrav drives screamed their familiar symphony of disapproval as they descended into the darkness. They had deliberately chosen the dark early morning, as few would witness their insertion trail and, if it was observed, it would most likely be mistaken for a shooting star.

Once the firework display flashing past the front screen had dissipated, they could see the lights of differing-sized towns and cities below. It was the one on the coast next to the mouth of a large river they required. A grid of lights stretched inland from the ocean for several kilometres right from the sea front and stretching across both banks of the river.

The pilot nodded and turned the ship as Grupps pointed to the city in question called Faitten Yiss. It was seemingly not only the administrative capital of the planet, but a large industrial region too. Perfect for what Grupps wanted. Another reason he liked this particular town was a collection of small islands just offshore, of which all except two were deserted and an ideal location to land a cloaked ship.

'Four minutes,' the pilot informed them.

Grupps stood and beckoned the other four to join him downstairs in the main cabin. A small troop landing inflatable awaited them. Its original matt black finish had been sprayed over with a more friendly shade of blue, in an attempt to make it appear a little less military. Checking the electric motor was still fully charged, they picked the boat up and waited by the rear door. The antigravs' bellow reached a crescendo as the ship flared and crunched down on the ocean side of one of the uninhabited islands. Its rear door powered quickly down, creating a ramp onto a coarsely pebbled beach.

The five of them trotted down the slope, stumbled on the pebbles with the weight of the inflatable and crouched once they were clear of the ship. The rear door immediately closed, the antigravs spun up again and the shuttle lifted, tracking sideways across to the highest part of the island, where it would land and wait on permanent standby.

The scans had said the island was deserted, but they still remained motionless for a few moments. There were two moons visible in the sky, one on the eastern horizon and the other almost directly above, providing just enough ambient light to see by.

Once Grupps was happy they'd disembarked unnoticed, he gave the command to launch the boat. Knowing there were homes on the island to the right of them, they went left. The almost silent electric motor dropped into the light choppy swell and purred its way around the landmass, following the line of the beach at about fifty metres out.

As soon as they cleared the back of the island, the lights of the town came into view, stretching left to right almost as far as you could see. Grupps knew the dense concentration of lighting at the water's edge on the western side of the river estuary was the main marina. Scans had shown it was crammed with an amalgam of vessels of all shapes and sizes in a kaleidoscope of colours. Perfect for five supposed boat crew to disappear in a small blue tender.

It took them almost an hour to creep in close to the marina entrance. Grupps slowed the little inflatable and skirted wide, coming in under the shadow of the six-metre-high breakwater. He knew there were invisible beams across the entrance to alert someone or other when vessels came and went. He didn't want to disturb those, but because of waves in bad weather the lowest beam was over a metre above the high water mark. They all lay flat as he steered inside as close to the wall as possible and once in, quickly motored into the lines of vessels, again keeping in the shadows as much as possible.

There were many tenders from other bigger boats attached to the ends of each jetty, and after pulling up the motor, Grupps cruised in alongside one of them and they tied up.

The first rays of dawn glowed between the islands, reflecting off the tops of the tall glass tower blocks nearby in the centre of the city, bathing the marina in a crimson glow. The occasional local busied themselves with early morning chores on their vessels as they wandered by. The occasional nod, which they returned with a wave was the only reaction to their presence. Other than that, they were content to discover no one was giving them a second look.

The main reason Grupps had chosen this route in was of course the ability to have the cloaked shuttle somewhere nearby where it was unlikely to be bumped into; that, and the town's free automated monorail system which came out as far as the marina and gave them easy access to all areas of the city.

A shining metal spiral staircase took them up to the

monorail station, where the first train of the day awaited the start of its daily routine. This had been anticipated and they were thankful to see a sprinkling of other passengers doing the same.

Finally, after a short wait, the doors beeped and closed. The short three-coach train hanging from its overhead gantry quickly accelerated and headed away from the sea towards the river and city centre.

9

City centre, Faitten Yiss, the planet Yiss

THEY REMAINED alert as they decamped the train deep in the city, watching for any sign that they were being observed. Seeing nothing, Grupps led them onto a raised walkway that continued at the same height as the monorail and appeared to enable you to completely navigate the town without actually descending to ground level.

At regular intervals, more of the spiral staircases waited to take you down and in some cases up to elaborate entrances into shining buildings stretching away above. They found moving around on this planet easy as the gravity was roughly a third lighter than on Dasos.

The city was slowly coming to life around them and Grupps wanted to find the building he sought before too many people were around. He could see the huge gold-windowed tower block ahead and headed straight for it.

Yiss Gard Vey was the widest and tallest building on the planet and housed the planet's government chamber along with all the administrative offices, including that of the Adjutant General.

Grupps led the small party down a back street behind the building to where the vehicles entered down a ramp and through heavy metal gates. He stopped them in the shadow of the building opposite to avoid the cameras before calling the *28*.

'In position,' was all he said.

'Ninety seconds,' came the reply.

Making sure they were under cover, they waited. They didn't hear the detonation, but they certainly witnessed the result of the powerful EMP device as it detonated over the centre of the city. The buildings around them suddenly went dark along with the street lighting and the sound of ground traffic from the main thoroughfare not far away also ceased.

'Let's go,' said Grupps, heading out across the street. 'Keep your personal shielding on too,' he added.

A huge boom, followed by an intense and prolonged crashing sound, echoed from nearby and had them ducking as they ran.

'Must have been an aircraft over the city,' said Grupps.

They all kept one eye on the sky as they approached the government building's vehicle entrance. While the others shielded him, Grupps drew his laser weapon and melted the lock mechanism of the heavy gate. Once inside they pushed the gate shut and proceeded down to the dark garage level, using the lights on their weapons to illuminate the way to a central stairwell. *Spiral stairways seemed to be in fashion on this planet*, he thought, as they wound their way slowly up the green marbled steps. They met a couple of people going in the opposite direction using the glow from something they held in their hands. Surprisingly they paid them no attention at all.

Grupps had to stop and catch his breath every ten floors or so. His detail knew to keep their mouths shut, but in reality they were all glad of the rest themselves. Floor ninety-seven was their target as research had dictated this was where the Adjutant General resided.

As they finally arrived and Grupps leant against the wall panting, one of the detail cracked the double doors a centimetre and peeked through. He squinted as daylight blinded him and he had to wait for his eyes to adjust.

'Large floor-to-ceiling window illuminating an empty corridor, sir,' he reported. 'Eight single doors and one fancy double door at the far end.'

'That'll be the one,' Grupps answered. 'I'm surprised there's no security.'

'It's early, sir,' said another. 'Perhaps there's no one here yet.'

'I think it's just too easy,' said a third, holding up his weapon. 'I expected to have to use this well before now. After all, this is the office of the administrative leader of half the planet. There doesn't seem to be any security at all.'

'You worry too much,' mumbled Grupps. 'They have engineering facilities here that can manufacture the ship parts we need. Getting that Klatt ship and the *Katadromiko* back into full battle readiness is all I care about.'

Seemingly now recovered from the exertion of the climb, Grupps pushed open the doors and strode confidently into the corridor. The bright daylight assaulted his eyes, as he blinked his way towards the big double doors at the far end. He discovered the doors were locked when he arrived and as with the gate below, he melted the mechanism with his laser weapon on a low setting.

The office, as he expected, was large and plush and empty. The walls were panelled with a light wide-grained wood, most likely indigenous to the planet. Minimalist furniture with an industrial twist loitered sparingly around the space. Grupps thought it gave the room a boutique hotel vibe, but it was the window that really caught his attention.

The whole of the back wall was smoked glass overlooking one of the main thoroughfares heading north out of the city. He could see lines of stationary vehicles left stranded in the middle of the carriageways after the EMP detonated. A large fire a few hundred yards further up the road belched black smoke up into clear morning sky. He stared at it confused for a moment, before realising it must be the site where the aircraft they heard coming down ended up.

'Why aren't the people moving?' asked one of his detail from behind him.

He stared down at the cars again. A lot of the drivers and passengers in the vehicles had got out when the pulse had killed their electrics. He hadn't noticed it before, but the man was right. None of the people were moving. They were all frozen in time and resembled shop mannequins.

'What the fuck?' he mumbled under his breath.

'Makes it look like a model doesn't it?' said a strange male voice behind them.

All five of them spun around, their weapons coming up, to find a young man with long dark hair reclining nonchalantly in a chair beside the door they'd entered through. He wore a dark grey suit that didn't give the impression of being the usual attire endemic to the planet.

Grupps was convinced he hadn't been there as he walked

through. The man smiled and raised his hands as if surrendering before speaking again.

'Put your weapons away, gentlemen,' he said, dropping his hands back into his lap. 'You can't use them here.'

'Where the fuck did you come from?' Grupps demanded. 'And why is no one moving out there?' he added, jabbing a finger towards the window.

'Oh, I just paused everything so we could have an undisturbed conversation, Hazzlou,' said the stranger, shrugging.

'Paused everything?' Grupps demanded. 'How could you possibly do that? Who are you? And how do you know my name?'

'So many questions,' the stranger sighed. 'I'll attempt to keep the answers as simple as possible.' He stood – well, more floated upwards out of the chair – into a standing position. Firstly, I like to be known as Tartarus…I'm what you regard as one of the Ancients.'

'That's crap,' said one of Grupp's detail, striding towards the stranger, raising his weapon to pistol whip him.

He stopped suddenly, his arm still raised, a snarl frozen on his face. The others looked on with puzzled expressions.

'You really should keep your dogs under control,' said Tartarus, extending a finger and pushing the frozen figure over. He clattered to the floor, remaining in the same position as if a toppled action figure.

Grupps gaped at the man on the ground and for virtually the first time in his life, was quite unsure of what to do.

'Kneeling before one's god always goes down well,' said Tartarus, recognising Grupps's hesitancy.

'I don't kneel before anyone,' Grupps snapped back.

Tartarus's face clouded, he clicked his fingers and all four of Grupps's detail vanished. It startled him as he involuntarily took a step back, before gravity began rising around him. Grupps fought it but the increasing weight of his own body eventually forced him down to his knees.

'Now that's a little more respectful, isn't it?' Tartarus quipped, with a sly grin.

'What have you done with them?' Grupps asked through gritted teeth as the weight bearing down on him continued.

'Ah, they're just hanging around somewhere,' said Tartarus, glancing at the window.

Grupps's neck muscles strained as he managed to turn his head to follow Tartarus's gaze. The four men were suspended in mid-air outside the ninety-seventh floor window, their terrified and pleading expressions staring back at Grupps, their screams muted by the thickness of the glass.

'Let's have a little game of truth or death,' said a grinning Tartarus.

10
___

The bridge, Starship Gabriel, *unknown system*

IT HAD TAKEN Oona fourteen hours to gather all the other Vrixx and relay the information. There had been a lot of discussion and argument regarding trusting the dry humanoid creatures. But one thing that couldn't be denied was the loss of their home planet's oceans. They were never going to be able to return there and they certainly didn't have the technology or means to travel the interstellar distances required to find another ocean planet within their galaxy.

Putting their faith and the future existence of their race in the hands of these strange aliens was a huge risk, but totally unavoidable. It was that or inevitable extinction. Once Oona had replayed the ocean images she had recorded from the *Gabriel* to her allies, the few dissenting voices within the group quickly melted away. The final consensus of opinion was that Oona would indeed travel with the aliens on their mission to secure the bigger intergalactic vessel, and the remaining Vrixx would return to their previous non-cognisant state and wait for her return.

'Are your friends happy with the current state of play?' asked Ed, on Oona's return to the *Gabriel*'s hangar.

'I wouldn't use the word happy,' coloured Oona. 'But we are in agreement. They will sleep until our hopeful return with the large vessel.'

'Hopeful return?' inquired Ed.

'Remember we witnessed the size and power of those two ships. This one is considerably smaller. Your enthusiasm and confidence might make a bit of difference, but there are a considerable number of my allies that honestly don't expect to be woken ever again.'

'We'll just have to prove them wrong then, won't we?' said Linda, joining the conversation.

'This ship does have a few surprises they don't know about,' said Ed, 'starting with its very existence and the fact we're on their tail. By now they're most likely believing they're away and clear.'

'How do you intend on taking such huge vessels?' Oona coloured. 'They must have a crew of thousands and you're only five.'

'That's just it,' said Linda. 'They should have a crew of thousands, but they don't. Over ninety percent of the ship will be deserted, with a skeleton crew on the bridge and only a small fraction of the systems manned.'

'It's damaged too,' said Andy. 'They're most likely trying to find a humanoid race somewhere to press gang some more crew and with engineering technology advanced enough to effect repairs to the ships.'

'If we can get to them before they do that, it will make our job considerably easier,' said Ed.

'Then, don't let me hold you up,' coloured Oona, swimming over to the inside of her hull. 'I would like to see what's going on though,' she added, the sultry human female voice Cleo had programmed into the translator for Oona echoing around the hangar in time with the changing colours.

As Linda and Andy left the hangar, a holographic display, identical to the one on the bridge, appeared next to her ship along with Cleo herself.

'I have connected the audio from the bridge for you too,' she said. 'You'll know what's going on and be able to interact with us as if you're a member of the crew.'

'You're very generous and trusting,' said Oona, her eyes swivelling to gaze at the holomap interpretation of her own system.

'Don't get me wrong,' said Cleo. 'You won't have access to the ship's systems and our technology is off limits too. It'll be up to the council on our return to decide what you're entitled to have in the way of scientific upgrades.'

'I understand fully,' she said. 'Your council represents bipedal human races in your galaxy, not water-based eight-tentacled ones, so I imagine it will require a bit of negotiation.'

'Most likely,' admitted Cleo. 'But don't let that concern you. We'll all be with you when the time comes.'

'You little diplomat, you,' chuckled Ed, as he and Cleo left Oona and made their way through the corridors to the tube lift.

'I have every file on human diplomacy ever produced,' said Cleo, swishing today's clothing choice of a long flowing red summer dress inside the tube so it didn't snag as they whipped up to the bridge.

'You have every file on everything there's ever been,' said Ed. 'Sometimes your capabilities are quite scary.'

'What's scary?' Andy asked, glancing up as Ed and Cleo popped up inside the domed bridge.

'Your bloody hearing, that's what,' Ed grumbled, as he sat and reclined on his control couch.

'He was referring to me having an intimate knowledge of everything,' said Cleo, folding her arms and looking smugly at Andy.

'You're female, so it goes without saying,' said Andy, rolling his eyes at Phil.

'And don't you forget it,' quipped Rayl, punching her husband on the arm.

'Ow,' he yelped, giving Ed an anguished expression while rubbing his bruised bicep.

'Don't look to me for backup over your sexist comments,' said Ed, deliberately not getting eye contact. 'You fight your own wars.'

Pol giggled and snorted, causing everyone to chuckle.

'Is everyone ready to continue the search?' Ed asked, when silence returned.

'It's ten p.m. ship time,' said Cleo. 'You lot go get some sleep. I'll continue to follow the trail and watch over things.'

Ed glanced around and didn't see anyone looking disagreeable to the offer.

'The slightest abnormality, you wake me straight away,' he said, pointing at Cleo.

'Aye aye, cap'n,' she said, throwing him a mock salute before disappearing.

11

Office of the Adjutant General, Faitten Yiss, the planet Yiss

'THE RULES ARE, I ask questions and if I think you're lying, one of those men stains the pavement below,' said Tartarus, his eyes flicking towards the four men screaming and flailing on the other side of the glass.

Grupps, still straining from the weight of the increased gravity, grunted and nodded.

'What d'you want to know?' he asked, struggling to keep his head up.

Tartarus strolled slowly across the office, picked a framed photograph off the large desk and studied it for a moment before placing it back down. He turned towards Grupps, clasping his hands behind his back.

'What are you doing here?' he demanded, suddenly and making Grupps jump.

'Looking for somewhere to repair our two ships,' said Grupps, through gritted teeth.

'One of those ships is a *Katadromiko*,' said Tartarus. 'Where the hell are the crew? Those things have personnel numbering in the tens of thousands. Why can I only find a skeleton bridge crew?'

'We stole it,' said Grupps.

Tartarus eyed Grupps suspiciously and flicked a finger towards the window. One of the four men disappeared suddenly downwards.

'No, no it's true,' Grupps pleaded, as the man's screams faded below.

Tartarus waved a finger again and the man reappeared, his white face a picture of absolute terror.

'You stole a *Katadromiko* cruiser from the GDA?' he said. 'Not possible.'

'We faked an imminent core containment breach,' said Grupps. 'They abandoned ship and had it jump into clear space where we boarded it.'

'Didn't they want it back when it didn't detonate?' Tartarus asked. 'They would also have the override code to kill the ship's systems.'

'We faked the explosion with a large drone and changed the code.'

'You are a resourceful little bastard aren't you?' Tartarus said, looking at Grupps with renewed respect.

Grupps suddenly jumped upwards and emitted a sigh of relief as the heavy gravity bearing down on him was released.

'And what about the other ship full of what looks like lizard men?' said Tartarus, continuing with the questions.

'They're Klatt,' said Grupps. 'Not members of the GDA.

The ship was used in an attempted internal coup between rival Klatt clans.'

'I see,' said Tartarus. 'And how did the damage come about?'

'The GDA intervened along with a pain in the arse called Edward Virr.'

Tartarus looked startled and took a step back at the mention of the name.

'Edward Virr is alive?' he asked, staring at Grupps with wide eyes.

'Well, yes, we kinda involved Virr from the start by kidnapping him to keep the GDA busy while the coup took place.'

'I take it as you're here, the plans went awry.'

'Virr is a slippery character,' said Grupps, almost spitting out the words.

'You can say that again,' Tartarus grumbled under his breath.

'You've been to our galaxy?'

'Not recently,' he replied. 'But it seems it's time I did.'

Grupps stared at the man with renewed interest.

'Why is it I think I've seen you before?' he asked. 'Did you used to have shorter hair?'

'Oh, you mean like this?'

Tartarus waved his hand across his face. The long dark hair was replaced with a much shorter blond style and he suddenly looked twenty years older.

Grupps stared wide-eyed. He closed his mouth with a clop when he realised it was hanging open in astonishment.

'You,' stuttered Grupps, pointing at Tartarus and falling back hard on his backside. 'You're Xavier Lake!'

Lake smiled, reclined back into the chair by the door and put his hands behind his head.

'Give that man a cigar,' he said. 'Your detective skills are shining through.'

Grupps felt a swell of pride in his chest and then hated himself for it.

'Weren't you supposed to be killed in some other galaxy somewhere, while being pursued by…'

Grupps thought for a moment.

'That's why you baulked when I mentioned Edward Virr isn't it? You blame him for everything that happened.'

'Well, technically his finding out the truth about the crew of the 37 saved my life and without him chasing me across two galaxies, I wouldn't be the person I am or have the power I have now.'

'But you still hate him?'

'With an obsession. I had thought he was dead though. This changes things.'

'Then, we have something in common,' said Grupps, gaining a little confidence. He nodded towards his men still hollering ninety-seven floors above the pavement.

Lake followed his gaze and waved a finger. The four men reappeared inside the office, collapsed on the floor and backed away from Lake with terrified expressions on their faces.

'Weren't there two of you?' Grupps asked.

'Ah, you mean Mr Herez.'

'Is he not here?'

'Back home,' said Lake. 'A complete new look, billions in the bank and most likely having a ball.'

'He didn't get this…godlike upgrade then?'

'No.'

'How did it happen to you?'

'I ask the questions and my next one is, who's the young girl sitting in the captain's chair on the cruiser?'

Grupps thought about lying, but changed his mind after having visions of hitting the pavement below at terminal velocity.

'She calls herself Noilstoy Salft,' he answered, shrugging. 'But in reality she's Ystolion Flast, wanted by the GDA for multiple murders and fraud stretching back over eighty years.'

'Eighty years?' Lake marvelled. 'She doesn't look a day over eighteen.'

'Rumours are she has some sort of eternal youth drug,' said Grupps, rolling his eyes. 'I reckon it's a load of crap and in actuality she's just a granddaughter or something. Nobody can look like that at a hundred and twenty years old, drug or no drug. But she pays amounts of money I couldn't possibly earn in a hundred lifetimes of GDA salaries.'

'Hmm,' grunted Lake, thoughtfully. 'I like your motivation, Mr Grupps. I take it you intend to return to the Milky Way so you can enjoy all this money?'

'Shit, yes. It's not worth a damn out here.'

'That's good,' said Lake, grinning. 'In that case I have a proposition for you.'

12

The bridge, Katadromiko 28, *orbiting the planet Yiss*

Noilstoy Salft glanced up impatiently as a junior officer approached her raised captain's dais and cleared his throat.

'What?' she snapped.

The young man took an involuntary step back, caught himself and stood rigidly to attention.

'Erm, Grupps is back, ma'am,' his eyes nervously flicking left and right so as not to stare at her.

'I can see that on here,' she sneered, holding up her tablet and glaring at the officer.

'Erm…'

'Stop saying "erm",' she barked, interrupting and rolling her eyes. 'You're a bridge officer not a deck hand.'

'Yes, ma'am, sorry, ma'am…'

'Get on with it,' she growled when he hesitated again, the exasperation clear in her tone.

'Grupps has a guest who'd like a word, ma'am.'

'Oh, he does, does he?' she said. 'Well, they'll just have to wait won't they?'

'No, he won't,' boomed a voice from the main bridge doors.

She spun her chair round violently, to find an embarrassed-looking Grupps strolling across the bridge alongside a smartly dressed middle-aged man.

'Grupps,' she bellowed. 'You know very well, nobody enters my bridge without my express permission.'

Grupps flinched, stopped where he was and averted his eyes. The newcomer, however, strode on, fixing Salft with a malevolent glare.

'Who the fuck d'you think you are, strutting onto my bridge unannounced?' she spat.

'More to the question,' he said, stepping up onto the dais and looming over her, 'just who the fuck d'you think *you* are attacking my planet without any justification?'

'I don't have to answer to you,' she replied. 'Security, get this man off my bridge and teach him some manners.'

Nobody moved, nobody came. She stood suddenly and went to push the man off the platform. Her outstretched arms seemed to meet an impenetrable force a few centimetres away from him. The next thing she knew, she was being forced to her knees by a great weight bearing down on her. She gritted her teeth and forced her head up to stare at the man.

'Who the fuck are you?' she managed to force out, finding breathing and talking exhausting.

'Four gee's can be a bitch, can't it?' he said, looking down at her with a fake sad expression.

He circled her, tapping his chin with a forefinger. She tried following him around her, but found it made her neck ache. Giving up, she just faced forward and stared at the floor.

'To answer your question, my name is Tartarus—'

'He used to be Xavier Lake,' called Grupps, interrupting him.

Lake curled his lip and raised a hand. Grupps levitated off the floor, hit the ceiling with a crack and flew backwards into the bridge wall, staying spreadeagled against the bulkhead, two metres off the floor.

'You speak…when you're invited,' Lake sneered.

Turning back to Salft, he smiled the smile of a predator about to devour its prey.

'Now, where were we, young lady?' he said, reverting back to his calm and slightly chilling voice.

'Aren't you the one they charged with murdering the crew of that cruiser?' Salft asked, not even attempting to look up anymore.

'If you know that, then you'll also know it was a fucking lie,' he growled back at her through clenched teeth. His knuckles turned white, the lighting on the bridge flickered and a few sparks fizzled out from nearby electrical consoles. If he didn't have the attention of everyone on the bridge before, he certainly did now.

Nervous eyes peered from behind control panels, the sudden awkward silence in the room only disturbed by the faint electrical hum of the consoles and the whisper of the environmental vents high above.

Lake closed his eyes and took a deep breath, the sudden flash of anger dissipating as quickly as it had come.

'We may be able to be beneficial to each other,' he said, in the same calm tone he'd used before, as if nothing had just happened.

'I'm all ears,' she croaked, her arms beginning to wobble. Even though she was in the body of a healthy teenager, four gravities soon become difficult to manage.

She finally collapsed forward as her arms gave way, smacking her face on the floor.

'Oops a daisy,' said Lake, patronisingly.

Salft almost levitated off the floor as the local gravity around her returned to normal. She sighed, coughed and pushed herself back up into a sitting position with a grunt.

'Well?' she asked, half-heartedly, glaring up at him for the first time in a while. 'Whatever it is, I don't imagine I have much choice anyway.'

'Ah, don't be like that,' he said, the acerbic smile returning. He rubbed his chin thoughtfully and stepped back down from the platform.

She emitted a squeak as she found herself lifted into the air and dumped unceremoniously upside-down onto the captain's chair. While she righted herself and readjusted her clothing, Lake spoke again.

'You need your ships repaired, don't you?' he said, raising an eyebrow. 'And perhaps a few more crew?'

'Tell him yes,' called Grupps, still stuck to the bridge wall.

'Ah, Mr Grupps,' said Lake, turning to face him. 'I forgot you were still hanging around.'

Grupps slid down the wall and crashed into the floor head first. He stood up slowly, rubbing the top of his head and grimaced at Lake before speaking.

'He wants the Klatt ship,' he said.

'Really…and what do we get in return?' Salft asked.

'Your lives,' Lake replied, shrugging. 'Oh, and a repaired ship and full complement of crew.'

Salft eyed Lake sceptically, like you would a door-knocking politician.

'Why the hell would you want that thing?' she asked. 'It's designed to do just one job.'

'Create a permanent ice age on any habitable planet it's fired at, yes, I know,' replied Lake. 'It's perfect.'

Salft glanced around Lake and across at Grupps, who was nodding enthusiastically.

'Okay,' she said, looking back at Lake. 'It's yours. I never could trust those smelly reptiles anyway.'

Lake smiled and closed his eyes, then started waving his arms around as if he was conducting an orchestra.

Salft, with an incredulous look on her face, glanced over at Grupps, who replied with a shrug.

'Woah,' shouted one of the bridge crew, a look of shock written on her face as she held her hands up above the console. She eventually noticed everyone had turned towards her.

'The damaged decks are all coming back online,' she said. 'They're just sort of self-replicating back as they were.'

Lake opened his eyes again and exhaled.

'There you go,' he said. 'All right as rain.'

'How did you know what went where?' asked Salft.

'The blueprints are in the data core,' replied Lake, holding his hands out wide. 'Piece o' cake.'

'You found the plans in the data core that quickly?'

'I read and ingested the entire core in less than a thousandth of a second when you arrived in orbit,' he said. 'You can't keep anything secret from me.'

'Captain, the Klatt vessel's reporting it's repaired and fully operational too,' came a call from below.

Salft looked back at Lake and raised her eyebrows.

He winked back and nodded.

'How fucking good am I, eh?' he said smugly and turned to walk away. 'Have fun with your fully operational battle cruiser,' he added. 'I have to go now.'

'What about our crew?' Salft asked.

Lake stopped, turned and pointed at the holomap.

'There's a planet down there with a couple of billion people…help yourself.'

Then he vanished along with Grupps.

13

———

The Starship Gabriel, *unknown system, Medusa galaxy*

Ed was awoken from a dream about pepperoni pizza growing on trees by Pol shaking his arm vigorously.

'Eh…what is it?' he mumbled.

'It's Cleo,' she whispered. 'She's found the *28.*'

'Shit, really?' he said, blinking the sleep out of his eyes and sitting upright. 'Fuck, that was quick.'

He dressed as quickly as he could and made his way up to the bridge. Phil was already there studying the results of Cleo's scans.

'Don't you ever sleep?' Ed quipped as he slid into his control couch.

'I had a snooze last year, so I'm wide awake,' replied Phil, with a smirk.

'What have we got?' asked Ed, glancing up at the holomap as Phil brought up an image of a distant system and panned in on one planet in particular. It was an indistinct image at this range, but close enough to distinguish its blue colour and the fact it appeared to have an atmosphere.

'See for yourself.'

Phil pointed at a red icon sitting a few hundred kilometres above the surface that read, *STATIONARY OBJECT, FOURTEEN KILOMETRES BY TWO KILOMETRES, IDENTITY UNKNOWN.*

'Could be a small moon,' said Ed.

Phil shook his head.

'It's not orbiting,' he said. 'It's sitting stationary relative to a point on the surface.'

'Phil is correct,' said Cleo. 'It's the right size for a *Katadromiko* and its holding station, which proves it's powered.'

'Where's that Klatt octaship thing though?' asked Phil. 'If the ship we can see is the *28* then it can't be far away.'

'It could be cloaked,' said Andy, as he and the girls arrived on the bridge together and took their seats.

'But why one and not the other?' asked Phil.

'Can we jump in behind the star without being detected?' Ed asked.

'We wouldn't be detected by the *Katadromiko*, but if we don't know where the other one is then it's a bit of a gamble,' said Cleo. 'Although, the chances of them scanning the star at that precise moment are extremely low.'

Ed stared at the holomap for a moment before making a decision.

'Plot the jump,' he said.

'Already done,' Phil replied.

'And checked,' said Cleo.

'Okay, go there and let's have a closer look at that ship,' said Ed, leaning back on his couch and crossing his arms.

They all squinted as the bridge lit up with the brightness of the star only a few million kilometres away. Phil brought the *Gabriel* out from behind it and they all watched closely as the holomap updated.

'*Katadromiko* class cruiser confirmed,' said Cleo. 'Oh, that's odd.'

They all looked up, waiting for Cleo to explain her consternation.

'What is it?' Ed asked.

'It's fully intact and operational,' she said.

'How have they managed to repair it so quickly?' said Linda. 'The report I read stated it had multiple deck breaches on its port side from blocking the beam.'

'Are we sure it's the *28*?' asked Pol.

'It is,' said Cleo.

'That's impossible,' said Andy. 'They've only been here a few days. It would take several months in a fully kitted shipyard to repair the damage that ship had.'

'Perhaps they found a way to fix it on the move,' said Rayl.

'What with?' said Andy. 'You'd need considerable raw materials to replace the missing decks which they didn't have and to make matters even harder, they only had a skeleton crew.'

'Perhaps they used the raw materials from the octaship,' said Phil. 'That could be the reason it's missing, and they used the Klatt crew to do the work.'

'No way,' said Ed. 'They just haven't had the time. As Andy said, barring divine intervention, you really would need a shipyard to achieve that level of repair.'

'What about that planet?' asked Pol. 'Has that got the resources?'

'No spacefaring capability,' said Cleo. 'Although, their technology is reasonably advanced and easily capable of building vehicles to escape the atmosphere, for whatever reason, it looks as though they haven't bothered. But that's not the really surprising thing about this place.'

'And that is?' Ed asked.

'There's only one language on the entire planet.'

'Well, that's not unusual,' said Andy. 'In GDA space there are loads like that.'

'Yeah,' said Cleo. 'But on this planet they're speaking English.'

'WHAT!' echoed around the bridge, as everyone had the same reaction.

When the cloaked *Gabriel* had got closer, Cleo was able to tap into the planetary broadcasts and display them on the bridge. As they watched, images of a reasonably modern human society played out across the holomap.

'I don't believe it, we're a hundred and thirty million light years away from our galaxy and to me, that looks just like the UK,' said Andy. 'Even the architecture is eerily similar and with the multicultural society down there, any of those towns could be London or Manchester or Birmingham and they're speaking fucking English.'

'He's right,' said Linda. 'How can that be?'

'They're crewing the cruiser from the planet's population too,' said Cleo. 'Regular shuttles are bringing personnel up from the surface and they're not returning.'

'Voluntarily or press ganging?' Ed asked.

'Unknown,' said Cleo.

'What's press ganging?' asked Pol.

'I was wondering that too,' said Rayl.

'Brutal British Navy recruitment from the seventeenth and eighteenth centuries,' said Ed. 'Groups of sailors called press gangs would roam around coastal towns and grab able-bodied men off the street to man the British fleet of warships.'

'I take it they didn't get many volunteers in those days?' said Linda.

'Hardly surprising when you consider the conditions onboard the ships,' said Andy. 'It was pretty harsh.'

'And you think this might be what they're doing down on the planet?' said Phil.

'It's a possibility,' said Ed. 'We need to find a way to disable that ship. Judging from what Bache has said about that spurned woman, I'd hate to think what she'd be capable of with a fully operational and fully crewed *Katadromiko*.'

'Its shields are preventing us from seeing anything onboard,' said Rayl. 'I don't want to get too penetrative, just in case they detect the intrusion.'

'They're not cloaked, so they're not expecting any trouble,' said Andy. 'We need to get aboard somehow to have a shufti.'

'Have a what?' asked Pol.

'A dekko, a butcher's,' replied Andy, shrugging.

'He means a look,' said Rayl, rolling her eyes. 'He does this to me all the time.'

'Ah, okay,' said Pol. 'Why don't you say that then?' she asked, giving Andy a shrug in return.

'Force of habit, old fruit,' he replied, giving Ed a wink.

'Andrew, shut the fuck up,' said Rayl, glaring. 'And do something useful, like thinking of a way to get aboard that ship undetected.'

'Yes, dearest, I shall acquiesce,' he said, pulling a silly expression.

'I think I might have an idea,' said Ed quickly as he noticed Rayl clenching her fists. 'Cleo, can you warm up the *Cartella*?'

14

The Cartella, *preparing to land on Planet Yiss*

CLEO DROPPED the *Cartella* down quietly in a corner of an airfield just on the outskirts of Faitten Yiss. She'd avoided the comings and goings of the *28*'s shuttles that were busy on the other side of the field nearest the terminal buildings. The almost continual racket from their antigrav drives covered the noise of the *Cartella* as it plonked itself down outside a run-down hangar about a kilometre away.

'Keep the *Cartella* close,' said Ed, scratching irritatedly at the beard he'd had grown quickly in the autonurse to disguise his appearance. 'At least for the time being. Once we're recruited and on board a shuttle up to the *28* there's not much you can do.'

'Don't you dare take any unnecessary risks,' called Pol, from the *Gabriel*.

'Don't worry,' said Andy. 'He's with me.'

'And that's supposed to reassure me is it?' said Pol, with the sound of Linda scoffing in the background.

Andy was about to issue a rebuttal, but kept quiet on seeing Ed shaking his head in the background.

They jumped down from the airlock and made off around the paved trackway that skirted the perimeter fence towards the hustle and bustle across the field.

'Unusual for Rayl not to read you the riot act about taking risks,' said Ed, as they walked.

'Ah, yeah. She just gives me "the look" now,' he answered, making inverted commas with his fingers. 'That's even more scary.'

A fine drizzle began to fall as they were about halfway and they were forced to cover their ears as a shuttle took off straight over the top of them.

'Noisy bastard,' grumbled Andy, glaring up at the ship and then having to wipe the rain from his eyes. 'Reminds me of a barbecue I went to years ago.'

'What, with the rain?'

'No, my friend's parents' garden was on final approach to Heathrow. Your conversation was drowned out every ninety seconds and all the burgers and hotdogs tasted like they'd been marinaded in avgas.'

'Delicious,' said Ed.

'They were too.'

'So long as they weren't flushing out the toilets as they went over,' joked Ed.

'Hmm,' grunted Andy. 'Thinking back, they did have particularly healthy-looking roses.'

Ed chuckled before grimacing and scratching his beard again.

'I fucking hate facial hair,' he moaned. 'I should've just

worn glasses with a hat.' He looked over at Andy, who'd gone for designer stubble and a baseball cap on backwards.

'What you gonna say when someone asks who the San Antonio Spurs are?' he asked, nodding at the logo on the hat.

'A team from another galaxy,' he replied. 'They'll just think I'm being whimsical and…'

He stopped talking and gestured towards a ground vehicle leaving one of the terminal buildings that had turned abruptly in their direction.

'I'll do the talking,' said Ed. 'And remember, we're ground crew on a break.'

'This is where we find if these overalls Cleo knocked up are convincing or not.'

'Keep your hands in your pockets and look bored,' Ed mumbled as the open-top vehicle approached.

'They're Klatt,' whispered Andy, as the small truck circled around them and pulled up facing back the way they'd come.

The two uniformed Klatt soldiers inside clambered out and stood blocking their way.

'Just where d'you think you're going?' one of them snapped through a translator hung around his neck.

'We're on a break,' said Ed.

'Stretching our legs and getting a bit of fresh air,' Andy added.

The soldiers glanced at each other with expressions of bewilderment.

'You're in breach of the curfew,' the soldier growled.

It was Ed and Andy's turn to look at each other in puzzlement.

'What curfew?' Ed asked.

The soldier looked surprised, shook his head and seemed to be studying what they were wearing for a second.

'You work on aircraft?' he asked.

'Yeah,' they both said in unison.

The two soldiers looked at each other again and smirked. The talkative one pulled a weapon and waved it towards the truck.

'Get in,' he demanded, as his partner also produced a hand weapon and side-stepped around them to block any avenue of escape.

'Okay,' said Ed, leading Andy up onto the open back of the vehicle.

The talkative soldier holstered his weapon and drove, while the other one stayed with them in the back, covering them with his.

'Can we go via the café?' asked Andy, with a hopeful grin. 'I haven't had my mid-morning espresso.'

The soldier just stared at him and Ed gave him a dig in the ribs.

'The Klatt don't do humour,' he whispered. 'Trust me, I know.'

It only took the truck a couple of minutes to reach the first of the terminal buildings. Another shuttle screamed in over them as they arrived and clunked down on the hard standing. The drizzle had stopped now and as soon as the vessel's rear door powered down a line of nervous-looking people filed out from the terminal, splashed their way through the puddles and boarded the ship.

The soldier driving the truck went inside, saluted and spoke to another more senior Klatt officer. Ed could see him gesticulating in their direction as a short conversation took place and he soon returned and drove the truck up to the shuttle's lowered ramp. They were both searched and stripped of any possessions, not that they had much on them for just this reason.

'In there,' the soldier ordered, pointing to the shuttle's cargo bay.

They both jumped down from the truck and shuffled up the ramp, squeezing in and taking a seat on the floor with all the others. The truck pulled away as the ramp powered up.

'All aboard for London Victoria,' Andy mumbled as the scream of the antigravs reached fever pitch and the ship lifted back off the pad.

'I think I might have been right about the press ganging,' whispered Ed, glancing around at the terrified faces nearest them.

'Where are you from?' asked a woman next to him, who didn't seem to be as scared as some of the others.

'A long way from here,' said Andy.

'Indeed,' she said. 'I can tell by your strange accents. Have you any clue to where they're taking us? The rumour is they want us for food.'

Andy scoffed and shook his head.

'It's not for food,' he said. 'It's to crew a large starship.'

'What, like in space?' she said in astonishment. 'We're going into space?'

'Uh, huh,' Andy grunted.

The conversation hadn't been missed by those closest to them, so this revelation quickly rippled through the seated passengers. Followed by a crescendo of wailing and terrified cries.

'What's your name?' Ed asked.

'Callon,' she replied, confidently.

'You don't seem as frightened as some of the others?' he asked.

'I have a terminal illness,' she said. 'I didn't tell them that, so what can they do to me?'

'Oh, crap,' said Andy, as his eyes met Ed's. 'Whatever happens when we get up there try and stay with us,' Andy whispered in her ear.

'Why?' she asked.

The sudden silence as the antigravs were shut down caused more consternation amongst the passengers.

'We're up,' said Ed.

'You didn't answer my question,' said Callon, switching her gaze between the two of them.

'You're just going to have to trust us,' said Ed.

'And for your sake, you must,' said Andy. 'Stay close, we might just be able to help with your health problem.'

15

———

The captain's suite, Katadromiko 28, *orbiting Yiss*

Noilstoy Salft finished reading the daily ship reports and turned off her desk screen with an impatient flourish. She stood, crossed to the bedroom and began preparing herself for bed. She despised having to do any of the mundane administration involved in the day-to-day operation of the starship. Since Grupps had annoyingly disappeared with Xavier Lake in the Klatt ship, she had no one trustworthy enough to rely on to do it.

She entered her cabin's large bathroom and undressed, admiring her slim feminine eighteen-year-old body in the mirrored walls. She smiled at the reflection before adopting a more lugubrious expression.

Leaving the autonurse behind had not been part of the plan and she couldn't think of anything worse than getting old and frail again. She stared once more at her reflection and promised herself once this cruiser was fully crewed and operational, retrieval of her autonurse took priority over any revenge ambitions on the GDA – although it sounded like Lake had some aspirations of his own along those lines.

Retiring to bed, she adjusted the gravity down slightly and quickly fell asleep. She dreamt of a handsome young man making love to her on a silk-curtained four poster bed. It overlooked a pair of wide open double doors giving onto a pure white sandy beach, with the sound of waves lapping serenely on the shore and the shrill mournful call of sea birds high above.

When she awoke early at the start of the next day period, she was surprised just how much of the dream she could remember. Normally her dreams, although vivid at the time, had become vague echoes once awake and all the detail evaded her.

This, however, was as though it had really happened, just a few minutes ago. She was sure she could still smell the sea, but peering around the darkened room, there was no handsome young man, no double doors and no beach or sea birds. Just the soft glow of the floating holographic star map showing their location.

She shrugged, almost disappointed. Sex had been something she hadn't thought about for a very long time, even with this body.

An hour later, she marched purposefully onto the bridge, noticing immediately that several more of the control consoles were now manned. She raised her eyebrows at the duty pilot, silently asking for an update.

'Crewing at twenty-seven percent, Captain,' he said, recognising the cue. 'Another ten days and we should be over forty percent and we can begin training drills.'

She stopped next to him and stared out across the bridge.

'How long will that take?' she asked curtly.

'Er…a few weeks, ma'am, probably,' he replied, nervously.

'A few weeks?' she snapped, dropping her eyes down and glowering at him.

The pilot swallowed apprehensively.

'None of them have been in space before, ma'am.'

Salft exhaled with a wheeze.

'Lake,' she hissed through clenched teeth. 'Bastard would've known that.'

'We've started training pilots for the fighters already, Captain,' said the navigator, leaning back in his seat.

Salft walked past him and slapped his head, knocking him back upright again.

'And how many are reasonably competent and ready to fly, eh?' she demanded, stopping and staring back at him.

'Fourteen, ma'am,' he said, not meeting her gaze.

'Fourteen, ma'am,' she repeated, mimicking his nervous Dasos accent. 'And how many operational fighters do we have in the hangars?'

'Three thousand six hundred and eighty-seven,' he said, slowly, keeping his face front.

She continued her glare for a few long seconds, before huffing and stepping up onto her raised platform and raising her voice so everyone in the room could hear.

'This vessel will be fully operational in seven days,' she thundered. 'Anyone who has a problem with that is welcome to leave the ship via the nearest airlock. Have I made myself clear?'

A few half-hearted 'Yes, ma'ams' floated across the room.

'I said…have I made myself clear?' she screamed.

This time a resounding chorus of 'Yes, ma'am,' echoed around the bridge. She nodded, turned and pointed at the pilot.

'What's your name?' she demanded.

'Lieutenant Harglam, Captain,' he said, his eyes wide with worry.

'Consider this a field promotion,' she said. 'As of now, you are First Officer Harglam and second in command of the ship. You have seven days.'

Salft jumped down from the platform and marched off the bridge, leaving over fifty crew staring at a shocked Harglam, some expectantly, but most sympathetically.

16

Hangar 67, Katadromiko 28, *orbiting Yiss*

THE SHUTTLE CLATTERED DOWN HEAVILY on the hangar's deck, causing some of the armed guards to fall over and a crescendo of added wailing from the already frightened passengers.

'Fuck me, I don't think Linda would be very impressed by their piloting skills,' griped Andy, gritting his teeth and glaring towards the front of the spacecraft. 'That was more crash than landing.'

'I don't believe they have many experienced pilots,' replied Ed. 'Or experienced anything for that matter.'

'What happened to the original crew of this ship then?' asked Callon, raising her eyebrows at Ed.

'Cutting a long story short, they stole the ship while the crew were elsewhere,' Ed replied.

'Who are *they*?' she asked.

Ed looked at Andy, wondering how best to answer that one.

'Enemies of our ruling council and the owners of the vessel,' said Andy, as Ed nodded in agreement.

The noise of the ramp lowering halted the conversation and immediately they were ordered to stand by the rifle-bearing guards. They were quickly filed off into the cavernous hangar. Rows of frightened wide-eyed faces peered around nervously, especially at the gaping hangar door that appeared to be open to space. Another shuttle entered, fizzing as it passed through the invisible atmosphere barrier. This brought gasps of disbelief from the new arrivals as they shrank back away from the entire wall of open space.

'How the hell does that work? And how is there gravity on here?' asked Callon, staring at the doorway, then at her feet.

'We'll explain later,' said Ed, whispering in her ear. 'Most importantly, when they ask you what your job was, tell them you're an aircraft engineer and look confident.'

'I don't know anything about aircraft,' she said, taken aback. 'I'm a restaurant manager.'

'Don't worry,' said Andy. 'We'll cover for you, just tell them that and stay close.'

She stared at them dumbfounded for a second, before they were ordered across the acres of hangar floor and through into a wide corridor.

Ed watched closely, trying to get his bearings. He'd been on several *Katadromiko* cruisers before with Bache Loftt, but so far hadn't seen anything to give him a clue as to where on the huge ship he was.

They joined the back of a queue that snaked up the corridor to a tube station. Callon stood on tiptoe and squinted down the line.

'Are we going on a train?' she asked, incredulously.

They both nodded.

'The ship's too big to walk around,' said Andy.

'How big is it?' she asked, turning to face them while walking slowly backwards.

'Fourteen kilometres,' Andy answered.

Her eyes widened and she stopped abruptly, causing Ed and Andy to bump into her. They'd reached the tube train entry and before she could say anything, one of the soldiers overseeing the loading of the trains grabbed her arm and bundled her onboard. The other two followed without assistance, finding they had to stand, crammed in like sardines. Once the carriage was completely full, the soldier leant in and entered the destination on the keypad. He whipped his arm out before the door swished shut and they were off, accelerating quickly away to allow another carriage to take its place.

The journey went on for ten minutes, then twenty minutes, until twenty-five minutes after leaving the hangar deck the carriage finally stopped and the door disappeared into the bulkhead once more.

'You weren't kidding with the size of this ship were you?' she mumbled, as they piled out into a wide corridor overlooking the ship's central atrium. 'Gods alive!' she exclaimed, almost drowned out by the cries of astonishment from the other passengers as they witnessed the spectacle stretching away from them.

They had disembarked at one end of the central atrium

about thirty decks up from the apparent ground level. As it was almost two kilometres wide and over ten long, you'd be forgiven for believing you were in a huge cavern on a planet, rather than in the middle of a starship.

Ed and Andy had seen this many times on several different *Katadromikos*. Each ship's central atrium had been designed slightly differently and Ed noticed this one had a distinct tropical theme, with beaches, lakes and areas of rain forest-type jungle. The sound of artificially created waves lapping on the sandy beaches reached him, along with several different caws and squawks from communities of parrots flitting through the treetops.

'Keep moving, you're not on bloody holiday,' shouted one of the soldiers, gesticulating down the passageway.

They were led into one of the many refectory areas and ordered to sit at the long communal dining tables.

Over the next hour they were split into groups relative to their previous occupations and skills. Ed and Andy made sure that they and Callon were selected into an engineering group. They were taken aft on the tube again to the main engineering section. There were fourteen of them, nine male and five female. They had an unremovable plastic bracelet sealed around their right wrists. These, they were informed, were their only form of identification and would also gain them access to their relative areas of work and personal cabins.

Ed knew they would also work as a location detector. He searched around with his DOVI and found they were reasonably simple to deactivate. Useful if they wanted to be anonymous and go anywhere undetected.

'Easily manipulated,' whispered Andy, discovering the same thing for himself.

A dull clang like two saucepans being hit together resonated from somewhere distant on the ship, followed shortly after by shouting out in the corridor. Ed couldn't make out what was being said as the speaker's translator was too far away, but the Klatt soldier guarding the door suddenly stiffened and appeared anxious. He brought his weapon up and waved it around the room nervously.

'Was that an explosion?' asked Andy.

Ed didn't answer as he was concentrating on decommissioning the soldier's rifle as quickly as possible.

'Linda, can you hear me?' he transmitted once he knew they weren't going to get shot accidentally.

'No, she can't,' replied Cleo. 'But I can.'

Ed noticed Andy jerk upright and raise his eyebrows. He'd obviously received Cleo's message too.

'If you can, why can't Linda?' Ed asked.

'Because the interior of the *28* is shielded from the *Gabriel* and I'm on the *Katadromiko* with you,' she replied.

'Fuck, really?' Andy blurted out loud, getting a questioning stare from Callon and a couple of others within earshot. 'How did you get aboard?' Andy asked, reverting to his DOVI.

'I downloaded a copy of myself into one of the shuttles as it came up from the surface.'

'Was that bang something to do with you?' Ed asked.

'Just a little distraction to keep them busy and prevent the ship going anywhere,' she replied. 'In a moment do exactly as you're told.'

'What are you on abou—' The door crashing open interrupted Andy mid-sentence.

The soldier guarding them suddenly snapped to attention

as a senior Klatt officer marched into the room, looked around and made straight towards Ed and Andy.

'You two, come with me,' he ordered, turning and heading straight back to the door. 'Carry on,' he said to the nervous soldier as he passed and exited out into the corridor.

They both sat there gaping at each other and then at the open door.

'What did I just say?' said Cleo, to both of them.

They shrugged, stood and beckoned Callon to come with them, quickly joining the officer outside the door.

'Who's she?' he asked. 'I said just you two.'

'She's part of our team and where we go, she goes,' said Ed, glaring at the Klatt officer.

'Cool banana,' he said, spinning on his heel and striding aft towards the tube stop. 'Follow me.'

'What's cool banana mean?' Callon asked, as they made off in pursuit.

Andy was grinning from ear to ear.

'It means he's not what he appears to be,' he whispered as they hurried along.

Piling into an already waiting tube carriage, the officer looked up at the green light on the camera and waited until it winked out.

Callon gasped as the Klatt officer morphed into a young woman, who smiled at her.

'What the…'

'Ah, yes, can we introduce Cleo?' said Ed, lowering Callon back into a seat as her legs seemed to give way.

'How?…who?…erm?' was all she could manage.

'Long story,' said Cleo. 'The condensed version being, I'm the sentient computer from their ship,' she pointed at Ed and Andy. 'Using this ship's excellent quality holo emitters.'

'You have a ship too?' she asked, her gaze swapping between Ed and Andy.

'We need to get you onto it as soon as possible,' said Andy, raising his eyebrows at Cleo. 'Late-stage terminal cancer, we need her in an autonurse quickly.'

'Absolutely,' said Cleo, adopting a thoughtful and resolute expression. 'Leave it with me.'

The bridge, Katadromiko 28, orbiting Yiss

SINCE THE EXPLOSION in the aft waste disposal unit, activity on the bridge was frenetic. Salft had gone apoplectic and ranted at them for a good ten minutes.

She now sat in the captain's chair with a face like a sulky teenager, which ironically matched her appearance, her eyes menacingly sweeping around the room from person to person, trying to find someone to blame.

'All evidence suggests it was just a build-up of methane due to lack of maintenance, ma'am,' one of the engineering officers told her nervously.

'Absolute fucking rubbish,' she screamed back. 'This ship has more than fifty waste disposal facilities – why would the only one adjacent to the central navigation node be the one to explode, eh? Answer me that!'

She jumped down from the captain's raised dais and strode over to loom over the officer who'd spoken.

'It was deliberate bloody sabotage to cripple the ship,' she hissed in his ear. 'Now find the fucking culprit and allow them to walk home.'

She lashed a pointed finger up at the planet on the large holomap slowly rotating above them, before storming off the bridge and returning to her cabin.

All the crew knew full well the new crew members from the planet would have absolutely no knowledge of the ship's design or systems layout. Besides, the whole section of the huge vessel where the waste disposal unit concerned was situated had been shut down and deserted since they stole the ship. The camera footage confirmed no one had been even remotely close.

Nervous eyes swept around the bridge; none of them wanted to issue the order that would get a couple of innocent people thrown out of an airlock.

Suddenly, relief from this scenario came in an incongruous fashion. Another remote waste unit exploded, followed shortly after by a third. Both, again, in completely deserted and random areas of the ship.

Salft was sent the video evidence and finally conceded that it might indeed be a lack of maintenance causing the problem and ordered the engineering team to drop everything and check all the remaining units.

'How many crew do we have now?' she asked Harglam as she returned to the bridge.

'Thirty-two thousand, ma'am,' came the reply.

'Pilots?'

'Four hundred and eleven.'

'You've trained four hundred pilots in a few hours?'

The first officer grimaced and stared at the floor.

'If they can successfully exit the hangar, circumnavigate the ship twice and land back inside without hitting anything, they're considered trained, ma'am.'

She continued staring at Harglam for a few moments, deciding whether he was being flippant or just brutally honest. Deciding on the latter, she nodded.

'Just make sure they know how to use the weapon systems too,' she said. 'We're going to need all our defences fully operational when we get back into GDA space.'

It was Harglam's turn to nod. He spun his seat back to his console with a look of relief on his face.

'Ma'am?' a timid questioning voice said from behind her.

Salft spun round to find a young female officer with a trembling arm hanging half raised, as if she wasn't quite sure whether she wanted to involve herself or not.

'What is it?' Salft growled, exhaling impatiently.

'I think there's something strange going on in the computer system.'

'In what way?'

'Well, it's kinda like a lot of computing power being utilised in peculiar areas, ma'am.'

'Explain?'

'Erm – holo emitters using considerable energy in remote closed down corners of the ship.'

Salft's eyes widened.

'Camera footage in those areas?' she asked.

'No, ma'am,' she answered. 'Wherever it occurs the cameras become non-operational.'

'Shit,' grumbled Salft. 'We could have a hostile AI loose on the ship. It could also be responsible for the explosions. Orchestrate a ship-wide systems purge, default absolutely everything,' she said, stepping back and turning to glare at the array officers.

'Have there been any anomalous readings out there recently?' she snapped, waggling a finger at them. 'No matter how small, I want to know about it right now.'

Three heads shook in unison, but the fourth and furthest away officer was sat bolt upright staring at his panel.

'What about you?' she barked, her eyes zeroing in on the hapless crewman.

Suddenly becoming aware that Salft was addressing him, the officer's face went pale. He glanced over at her, the worry evident in his sallow expression.

'Erm, well, yes,' he stuttered. 'There w-was a slight power fluctuation on one of our shuttles earlier, ma'am.'

'Explain?'

'Err, the shuttle's onboard navigation system lost its course and began drifting,' he said. 'The pilot had to do an immediate system reboot and manually reset the course. He mentioned that the system seemed to be overwhelmed with data for a few seconds and it caused an overload in the navigation.'

'That's how it got aboard,' she said, speaking more to herself. 'But from where?'

She swept her gaze over the other array operators and raised an arm to garner silence. 'There's a fucking cloaked ship out there somewhere,' she snapped. 'Find it and destroy it. It'll give our new weapons operators and fighter pilots something to practise on,' she added, giving the weapons offi-cers a malevolent scowl.

A sea of anxious faces began glowing red as they turned back to their screens and the bridge lighting reduced to a dimmer crimson hue. The huge ship changed onto a war footing and went on the hunt for the suspected nearby clandestine vessel. Distant sirens echoing in from the outer corridors went silent as the outer bridge blast doors sealed, replaced by the subdued hum of the electrical systems and the whispered hiss of the overhead environmental ducts.

18

Section 37, Deck 191, Katadromiko 28, *orbiting Yiss*

'I'LL BE as fit as a butcher's dog with all this walking,' moaned Andy. 'Isn't there a café round here I can get a nice steak dinner? I'm starving.'

'Rare with French fries and a nice chasseur sauce,' added Ed.

'No, it has to be a pepper sauce,' replied Andy.

'Shit,' said Cleo, suddenly.

'No, it's never had that effect on me,' said Andy, glancing at Cleo questioningly.

'They know I'm here,' she said. 'They're purging all the ship's systems.'

As she spoke, the lighting changed to a reddish hue and an alarm sounded.

'Can't you hide in a corner somewhere and pull the shutters down?' asked Ed.

'I'm going to load myself into one of the military vessels in hangar—'

As well as being cut off mid-sentence, her hologram disappeared, leaving Ed and Andy alone in a corridor on deck 191.

'Is she dead?' Callon asked, a horrified expression clouding her face.

'No,' said Andy. 'Just deactivated, don't worry.'

'Where's the nearest tube station?' Ed asked.

'Cleo said we can't use those and especially not now they're actively looking for onboard threats. They'll definitely spot train movement with deactivated cameras, we need to find—'

A grinding noise behind them stopped the conversation as they both spun round. The bulkhead blast door back to section 38 was slowly closing.

'Run,' shouted Ed. 'There's food in that section, I don't know about this one.'

They sprinted back, squeezing through just before it sealed and a winding noise followed by a clunk signalled it had locked.

'Are we able to open these?' Ed asked, as he noticed Andy had his eyes closed.

'Not a chance,' Andy replied, opening his eyes again and shaking his head. 'The ship's on a war footing, everything is closed up and doubly shielded to repel any attempt at boarding.'

They both glanced up at the nearest camera together.

'What about them?' Ed asked.

Andy shook his head again.

'Look casual and stroll back to the food station,' he said. 'There might not be a full English breakfast waiting for us, but it'll be better than the crap we'll get if they catch us.'

The section canteen was one of the smaller ones as the area they were in was more orientated towards engineering than accommodation.

'Is it just me, or has it got colder?' Andy asked, as they wormed their way through the tables and approached the food dispensers at the back of the room.

'At a guess, they've rerouted power from here to shields and weapons,' said Ed. 'We knew these sections were unmanned.'

'Either that, or they know we're here and they're going to vent the section to space.'

'What?' said Callon, looking scared again.

'O ye of little faith,' said Ed. 'Since when have you become such a gloom and doomer?'

'Since you, Pol and Linda got yourselves killed, that's when.'

'Yeah, okay, fair point. But remember we're just three completely anonymous locals here, no one knows our true agenda or identity.'

'That's actually not quite correct, Mr Virr,' said a new voice from the doorway.

They spun around to find a smiling young girl they both recognised leaning nonchalantly against the door frame. Eight Klatt soldiers filed past her with weapons in the shoulder and covered the two of them.

'Oh shit,' said Callon, shrinking behind Andy.

'Scylla, or should I address you as Ystolian Flast?' asked Ed.

'Whichever you prefer,' she said. 'I take it by your presence here, it's your ship, the *Gabriel*, that we're searching for?'

'Search away,' said Andy. 'You won't find it.'

'I don't need to now,' she said, a malevolent grin crossing her lips. 'I have you three. I take it your friend here is another member of your crew?' she added, leaning to one side to see behind Andy.

'She's from Yiss,' said Andy. 'Just tagged along…she's nothing to do with this.'

'My crew won't jeopardise the *Gabriel*'s safety for us,' said Ed, changing the conversation away from Callon. He noticed Andy had his eyes closed too.

'It's no good, Andrew,' said Salft. 'Remember I spent time with you guys, so I know all about your Theo mind control abilities. I think you'll find my associates here are locally shielded, so trying to disable their weapons will prove a little difficult.'

Ed glanced at Andy as he reopened and rolled his eyes, receiving a small shrug and a barely discernible shake of his head.

'So, what's the plan with this thing then?' said Ed, waving an arm to indicate the ship. 'Going to use it to murder a load more people perhaps?'

Salft stared at Ed, pulled a sad expression and shrugged.

'You have a very low opinion of me, don't you?'

'Should I not?'

Her face clouded.

'You didn't have your husband of forty-three years murdered by a corrupt oppressive regime,' she hissed.

'That was like twenty to thirty years ago,' said Ed, adopting a puzzled expression. 'And if what I remember from

Bache Loftt is correct, it was your granddaughter that killed him shortly after he'd nuked an entire colony over a mining claim and wiped out a destroyer together with its crew, with the intention of blaming the Klatt for the atrocity. The GDA had absolutely nothing to do with your husband's death.'

Ed noticed a couple of the Klatt soldiers flinched and sneaked a look at her out of the corner of their eyes at the mention of that nugget of information.

'It was Loftt's fault and he's GDA,' she spat.

Ed and Andy glanced at each other, incomprehension written all over their faces, until Andy turned back to Salft.

'No, he wasn't,' he said. 'Bache hadn't even joined up then. He was just a seventeen-year-old kid that got muddled up in the whole fiasco by being in the wrong place at the wrong time.'

'You're just splitting hairs,' she growled. 'The GDA are responsible. In fact, the GDA are pretty much responsible for everything. You can't as much as fart in that galaxy without them interfering in some fashion or other. They've had their day and it's time for them to go. The galaxy deserves a true leader. Someone with some youth, foresight and—'

'Some imperious dictator like you, you mean,' said Andy, crossing his arms and glaring accusingly across the room.

Salft clenched her fists, sneered and half turned back to the corridor before changing her mind and turning back.

'If you thought it was going to be me with one ship overthrowing the GDA, then you're wrong,' she said with a smirk. 'I believe that's being taken care of by someone else. I'll just return after the fact and pick up the pieces. Shame you won't be alive to see it.'

'What are you talking about?' Ed asked.

She grinned back menacingly.

'Take all three to the brig,' she ordered. 'I need them alive until we have their ship. Stun them if you have to.'

19

Hangar 119, Katadromiko 28, *orbiting Yiss*

Sergeant Di'Grat entered hangar 119 and peered around the cavernous expanse. Rows of military assault ships stretched away for several hundred metres in front and to the left of him.

'Where are you detecting the electrical field?' the Klatt sergeant asked over his communicator as he strolled into the first row of ships.

'Go left and into the middle,' the electronic voice crackled in his ear.

He moved left and followed the wall purposefully down the ranks of heavily armed vessels, until he reached about halfway to the far end and turned right between rows of assault ships to his right and larger freighters to his left.

'Keep going straight and perhaps a little more left,' the

voice instructed him. 'It's probably just a ship left powered up from the last systems check.'

He jinked left one row, now having freighters on both sides, and continued forward.

'You're getting close, about another thirty metres.'

He slowed down and examined each ship closely as he passed. The darkness in each cockpit signalled for him to move on to the next.

'You should be right on top of it,' the voice instructed.

'There's nothing here,' he said. 'All the ships are dark and—'

He suddenly found himself knocked flat on his back. He sat up looking puzzled and straightened his helmet, which had luckily taken the brunt of the impact.

'Are you still there?' the voice inquired.

'Affirmative,' he said. 'I just walked into some sort of invisible field.'

Getting up, he inched forward again with one arm stretched out, soon finding the unseen barrier that tingled slightly as his fingers ran across it. As he traced the field with his hand, it led him around the nose of a freighter and down its port side.

'It's one of the ship's shields that's activated,' he said.

'Can you see anything inside?'

'Negative.'

'Can you get inside to deactivate it?'

He shook his head at the stupidity of the question.

'Did you really just say that?' he replied, the irritation evident in his voice.

'Oh, right, yes,' said the voice, trying not to sound embarrassed. 'Can you give me the ship's designation? It should be on one of the rear winglets.'

Di'Grat walked on and peered up at the lettering painted on the fuselage.

'DAH1194C,' he read out loud.

'Stand back while we look up the deactivation code for that vessel,' the voice instructed.

He walked back down the side of the ship and waited about fifteen metres away from the front airlock, stretching an arm out periodically to check if the shield was still activated. Thirty seconds later, his fingers found no obstruction and he jumped at the sudden clunk and loud whine as the rear cargo doors began powering open.

With an irritated glare at the airlock in front of him that hadn't opened, he walked back to the rear of the ship again. Drawing his sidearm as a precaution, he leant around the bulkhead and peered inside.

The freighter's cargo deck was stacked high with wrapped military equipment sitting on auto trundles waiting to be unloaded to support the marines in the gunships.

'See anything inside?' the voice asked.

'Negative,' he replied. 'Can you see anything untoward on the cameras?'

'They show the ship to be clear. Can you make your way to the cockpit and shut everything down?'

'Roger that,' he said, slowly climbing the ramp and checking behind the piles of freight, not quite trusting their assurances that the ship was safe.

He worked his way forward through the cargo bay and up the stairs leading to the cockpit. Finding nothing, he relaxed a little and searched around for anything activated that shouldn't be.

'The co-pilot's console is glowing,' he said.

'Are you in the cockpit?' the voice asked.

'Affirmative.'

'That's odd, we can see the cockpit on the camera and you're not there.'

Two things happened in the next five seconds.

A cough behind him caused him to spin around. His eyes widened as he came face to face with himself.

The exclamation of "what the fuck" didn't actually reach his lips as sudden unconsciousness had him slumping into the arms of his doppelgänger.

His double removed his helmet and donned it himself, just as the voice questioned him again.

'Did you copy that?'

'Yes, I did,' the doppelgänger said in exactly the same voice. 'The cameras might have got stuck in a loop or frozen or something. Give me a minute.'

He dragged Di'Grat's unconscious body into a storage locker, closed and locked the door, then reached up and tapped one of the camera lenses.

'That's it,' the voice said. 'We can see you now, Sergeant, it must have been a bad connection.'

'Roger that,' the doppelgänger said, walking to the co-pilot's seat and shutting down the activated systems.

'How did you know how to do that?' the voice asked, in a surprised tone.

'Oh, err — I did some flying courses a while back,' he lied, castigating himself for the stupid error.

'What, on GDA ships?'

'It's all pretty similar,' he said, hopefully. 'Most of our ship technology is stolen from the GDA anyway. Can I close the ship up now?' he added, trying to change the subject as quickly as possible.

'We'll do it from here,' the voice replied. 'Exit the ship the way you came in and continue with your duties.'

He made his way quickly back through the vessel and strode purposefully back towards the door Di'Grat had entered by. Once he was a good distance away from the hangar and in a camera dead zone, the sergeant's doppelgänger morphed into an exact copy of the young Salft. Stopping to admire herself in the glass wall of a decommissioned water feature, Cleo stared back at herself, grinned, and continued on towards the rear of the ship to find Ed and Andy.

'How are you two getting on?' she transmitted.

Surprised to get no answer, she stopped and buried herself into the ship's systems, searching for her friends.

20

The bridge, Klatt octaship, re-entering the Milky Way

'THEY'LL HAVE a cruiser permanently stationed at the exit to the gateway,' said Grupps, without looking up from the control panel. 'There's no way of avoiding it detecting us.'

'Actually, it might not,' said Lake, casually reclining on the captain's chair with one leg over the arm and waving a hand nonchalantly in the air as if swatting away a fly. 'Their array could suffer a temporary glitch just at the wrong time. Wouldn't that be handy?'

Grupps glanced up at Lake, not quite sure if he was being facetious or not. When Lake's expression didn't so much as flicker, he decided Lake must actually have the ability to engineer such an outcome.

'Two minutes to gateway jump,' came the call from the navigator sitting off to the right, catching Grupps's attention away from Lake.

'You better be right about this,' Grupps muttered. 'We're no match for a fully operational *Katadromiko*.'

His head suddenly became incredibly heavy and clunked down on the edge of the control panel. He struggled but found he couldn't move his arms either.

'You seem to require constant reminders of my abilities, young sir,' said Lake, not even looking in Grupps's direction. 'You worry about getting this ship cloaked and off towards Dasos as soon as we're through the gate. Let me deal with the cruiser.'

Grupps's head sprang up as the invisible force holding him ceased without warning. He turned his head and scowled at the captain's chair but thought better of saying anything.

'Thirty seconds to gate,' the navigator informed them.

Grupps looked up at the huge holomap that showed the ship closing rapidly on the triple moons parked in orbit around the small planet.

'Stand by,' came the call from the pilot. 'Jumping two seconds after gateway emergence.'

He watched the local Medusa star map haze away and a different field of stars move into focus, including a huge cruiser sitting only a hundred thousand kilometres away. But, no sooner had it loomed into focus, it vanished again, the stars changed around and they were instantly many light years away from the intergalactic gateway.

Grupps turned to stare first at the array officers, who shook their heads, and then up at the captain's chair. Lake shrugged and adopted a rueful, told you so smile.

'You seem surprised, young Grupps,' he said, stretching and yawning.

'I really have no idea how you just did that and to be honest, I really don't care,' said Grupps. 'So long as you can get me to an island on Panemorfi with a new identity and shitload of cash, I'll do whatever you want.'

'That's the idea,' said Lake, standing up. 'And talking of islands, I'm going to lie on a beach with a large cocktail right now. Let me know when we're approaching Dasos.'

'Where the hell are you going to find a beach on this ship?' asked Grupps, as Lake stepped down from the captain's dais.

Grupps thrust his arms out backwards to cushion the fall as his chair vanished. But it wasn't the bridge floor he'd expected his backside to meet, as he sank into something soft. He looked down between his legs to discover he was sitting on soft sand. Raising his gaze, his jaw gaped as he found himself on a beautiful beach of light golden sand. Palm trees rustled above in the light breeze and an ocean lapped gently about twenty metres in front of him. He looked right and found Lake reclining on a beach chair sipping from a bright blue cocktail.

'You see, Grupps – if I want a beach, I get one.'

'Where the fuck are we?' Grupps mumbled, as a beautiful girl clad in the skimpiest bikini strode over and handed him a similar drink.

'My imagination,' replied Lake, sliding his hands behind his head and staring out to sea. 'You know, I really fancy some fried chicken. How about you, Grupps? Would you like some?'

'What's fried chicken?'

'Ah, of course, you're not from Earth. Let's just say it's one of life's great pleasures.'

Grupps lay back on the sand, took a sip from his drink, which he found to be delicious, and nodded.

'Bring it on,' he said. 'If it's as good as this blue drink, I'll give it a go.'

21

The Starship Gabriel, *close to Yiss, unknown system*

'LINDA,' Phil called, from the *Gabriel*'s bridge. 'You're gonna want to see this, bring the others too.'

It was five in the morning ship time on the *Gabriel* as everyone gathered on the bridge bleary-eyed and a little dishevelled.

'What's up, Phil?' Pol asked, yawning as she exited the tube lift.

Linda noticed the expression on his face was not that of a happy man. He pointed at their couches.

'We have a communication from the cruiser,' he said, once they were seated.

'Judging by the look on your face, it's not an invitation for breakfast,' said Rayl.

'See for yourself,' he said, touching one of many floating icons hanging in front of him.

A holographic image of a smiling young girl materialised above them.

'Oh shit,' said Linda.

'Scylla,' said Rayl, almost spitting the name. 'Or Noilstoy Salft, or Ystolion Flast, or whatever she's calling herself today.'

'Hello, *Gabriel*, wherever you may be out there,' Salft began. 'I'm impressed you got your ship repaired so expeditiously after its little adventure on Paradeisos.'

'Patronising bitch,' grumbled Rayl.

'She doesn't know about the new ship,' said Linda.

'Sending Edward and Andrew to board the ship from the planet was a great plan,' Salft continued. 'Great plan, until they got caught.'

The image hazed for a second before reforming into Ed, Andy and an unknown girl sitting at a table looking decidedly miserable, their hands secured to their chair arms.

'Fuck,' muttered Phil, causing the other three to glance at him in surprise. It was extremely rare to hear him swear.

'Who's she?' asked Rayl, pointing to the girl sitting next to Andy.

'Absolutely no idea,' said Linda. She turned back to the hologram as Salft merged back into focus.

'Your sentient computer also cleverly sneaked aboard too. Cleopatra, I believe you call it, if my memory serves me right. Well, she can't help them or you either. We purged all the ship's systems back to their default settings, so I wouldn't be relying on that to save the day.

'Ah shit.' This time it was Pol's turn to swear.

'If you want to see these three alive again,' Salft's smiling image continued, 'then you'll uncloak your vessel within one hundred kilometres of this ship, turn off your systems and shields and allow us to tractor you in. This includes shutting down and purging the sentient computer from the core. We will then board the ship and transfer you all down to the planet's surface. You have my word no harm will come to you. You have two hours to comply. Oh, and by the way, remember I know about the chip in their necks. A crypti, I believe you call it. There'll be no rebirthing this time I'm afraid. Two hours, tick tock.'

Salft's grinning persona faded, replaced by the three-dimensional system map from before.

The four of them sat silently and stared into space for a few moments, before Pol spoke nervously.

'D'you think she'll do it?' she asked.

'Between her and her late husband, they've murdered thousands,' said Linda. 'I don't think three more would be a problem for that bitch.'

'I still want to know who that girl is,' said Rayl. 'Salft seems to think she's with them.'

'What do we do?' asked Phil. 'We can't just hand over the ship.'

Linda adopted a thoughtful expression and glanced around at the others.

'As I mentioned before, she doesn't know about this ship. She's expecting the old *Gabriel*. Why don't we give her what she wants?'

Linda looked up at the ceiling.

'Cleo, are you able to reproduce a copy of the old ship like you've done in the past?'

Cleo appeared, unsmiling, this time dressed in a black ninja suit.

'As you know, it takes almost all my computing power,'

she said. 'But if it aids in that bitch's downfall, then I'm all for it.'

'What happens when they try and board it though?' wondered Phil.

'That's where it gets a bit tricky,' said Cleo. 'However, if we're planning on rescuing the boys, it really needs to be done before they get to that stage. I can recreate parts of the old *Gabriel* in reality, but not all of it. Ninety percent of it will still be holographic and able to fool their array, but certainly not solid enough to dock a vessel to.'

'Okay,' said Linda. 'We need to get Ed and Andy off that ship while Salft still thinks she's won. Any suggestions?'

'Where's the tractor beam emitter on that cruiser?' Phil asked.

'There are four,' said Cleo, as an image of a *Katadromiko* appeared above them with four large nacelles flashing in red.

They all stared at the slowly rotating hologram for a moment until Phil spoke.

'The two emitters halfway down the sides of the ship,' he said. 'They're right next to hangar entrances.'

'Yeah, so?' said Rayl, raising her eyebrows.

'To operate a tractor beam,' he continued, 'you have to make a hole in your shields and it needs to be wide enough to allow for the beam to track around.'

'Ah, I see where you're going with this,' said Linda. 'You think we could sneak in through the hole and into the hangar?'

They turned and looked at Cleo.

'Is that possible?' Pol asked, before anyone else.

'In a small ship it's technically possible, but touch that tractor beam and it'll lock on to you, cloaked or not,' she said, shrugging. 'You wouldn't be able to escape from that thing by jumping either, it'd rip the ship apart.'

'Are the shuttles small enough?' asked Rayl.

'Questionable,' said Cleo.

'The *Cartella*'s smaller,' said Phil. 'That could squeeze through.'

'Are you volunteering to pilot?' asked Linda, giving Phil a sideways glance.

He shook his head slightly and looked at Cleo.

'I think she might be a better bet,' he said. 'She has a reaction time infinitely quicker than mine.'

Cleo smiled.

'Be like going home,' she said.

'What d'you mean?' Pol asked.

'Cleo was the sentient computer in the *Cartella* before she took over the *Gabriel*,' said Linda.

'Oh, I see.'

'Who's coming then?' asked Cleo, changing the conversation back to the problem at hand.

'I'll go,' said Rayl, surprisingly quickly. 'I want to find out who that girl is.'

Linda and Phil's eyes met. They'd both seen how Rayl reacted when a pretty girl was anywhere near Andy.

'I'll go too,' said Pol, unaware of Rayl's jealous streak.

Linda nodded and looked up at Cleo.

'Are you sure you can handle both the fake *Gabriel* and piloting the *Cartella*?' she asked.

'Probably,' she answered, scrunching her face up and looking sheepish.

'Probably isn't the answer I was expecting from a computer,' said Linda. 'Can you do it or not?'

Cleo nodded.

'I'd appreciate one of you taking over the *Cartella* once you're inside the hangar though,' she said, looking between Rayl and Pol.

'I'll do it,' said Rayl. 'You'd better sort us out with some uniforms of some kind before we go too. We won't get far on that ship dressed like this.'

22

The bridge, Klatt octaship, en route to Dasos

GRUPPS HAD RUN through almost everything the Klatt food dispenser could produce, but much to his displeasure, nothing got remotely close to what he was looking for. He sniffed the lumpy mush the machine had just produced, wrinkled his nose and pushed the container straight back into the waste chute, muttering under his breath.

'You won't find any fried chicken in that thing,' said Lake, materialising sitting at one of the tables.

Grupps jumped, smacking his head on the front of the dispenser.

'Shit,' he grumbled, rubbing his forehead. 'Can't you give me some warning before you do that? And how did you know I was looking for chicken?'

Lake smiled and shrugged.

'You dispatched a whole chicken in one sitting yesterday. Call it an educated guess.'

'I take it you want me for something,' Grupps continued, impatiently.

'Indeed,' said Lake, cheerily. 'We're only one jump away from Dasos. I want you on the bridge orchestrating the firing sequence.'

'What about the planetary defence satellites? They'll rip this ship apart when we lower the shields to fire.'

'I'll deal with those.'

'You'd better – and what about any naval ships in the vicinity?'

'Ditto.'

Grupps nodded and made his way towards the door before turning back to Lake.

'You're not thinking of jumping in close to Dasos are you?' he asked. 'It's the busiest area of space in the whole galaxy. The chance of jumping onto another ship, especially in something this big, is frighteningly high.'

Lake adopted a lopsided grin.

'Okay, okay, I know,' said Grupps, turning to leave again. 'You'll deal with that too.'

There was a hum of anticipation on the bridge as Grupps arrived. The murmur of conversation ceased as he strolled across the room and mounted the captain's dais. A mix of human and Klatt personnel made up the bridge crew. They all knew from experience to keep quiet and their heads down whenever Grupps was present.

He turned and pointed at the Klatt officer manning the

main beam weapon control console.

'Begin charging the beam,' he ordered.

'Yes, Captain,' came the reply. 'Nine minutes to firing optimisation.'

'Optimal beam period for the planet?' he asked.

'Sixty-seven seconds, sir,' the operator stated.

Grupps winced, knowing the ship would be completely unshielded for that length of time.

'I hope Lake knows what we'll be up against,' he mumbled under his breath. 'We'll be a sitting duck.'

'Stop whinging and get on with it,' Lake's voice boomed around the room.

Grupps eyed the small door on the right-hand side of the bridge that led directly to the captain's hangar. A small Lathraia class personal yacht sat in the small space, permanently ready to fly, containing enough GDA currency to last him ten lifetimes. He knew he could be up, out and jumped away in around twenty-four seconds if the shit hit the fan and he thought he might take a stroll in the direction of that door once the beam was deployed.

The nine minutes to power up the beam seemed to take an age, until finally the controller glanced up at him and nodded.

'Weapon optimised and ready to fire, Captain,' the Klatt officer said, licking his lips and sounding overly excited at the prospect.

Grupps turned and glared at the officer, but realised he was of the Klatt Spleeta clan and was most likely relishing inflicting revenge on the GDA for thwarting their recent coup attempt. So, he decided not to reprimand the man.

'Time to Dasos jump?' he asked, turning to face the navigator.

'Two minutes, Captain.'

'At what distance?'

'Fifty thousand kilometres, Captain,' the navigator stated. 'Oceanside and beam weapon orientated towards the atmosphere.'

'Excellent,' Grupps said, spinning back to face the beam weapon controller. 'Stand by to drop shields and fire on my order.'

The bridge was completely silent now except for the navigator counting down to the jump.

'You'd better have the area clear,' Grupps shouted up at the ceiling as the count dropped to one second.

The huge overhead holomap suddenly lit up with the sudden close proximity to a large planet and several thousand ship movements. Grupps braced himself, but no collisions transpired. Lake had apparently been true to his word and wriggled them into a clear section of space.

'Shields down and fire,' shouted Grupps, pointing both index fingers at the beam officer.

The eight white flames of light radiated from the octaship's arms, hitting the lenses at the rear of the vessel. They arrowed out from the ship and inwards, before becoming one massive purple-edged column of light flashing into the planet's upper atmosphere.

'Planetary defences locking on and firing,' called an array officer, his face white as a sheet. 'In three, two, one...'

For the second time the holomap lit up above them. Not with traffic this time, but with large explosions. Dozens of them, all around the planet.

'Captain!' exclaimed the array officer. 'The planetary defence platforms, they've all exploded.'

'What, all of them?' demanded Grupps, staring up at the holomap aghast.

There were one hundred and seventy-two such platforms surrounding Dasos. They were huge five-hundred-metre spheres packed solid with the latest technology heavy space weapons.

The shrapnel from these, everything from the size of a rivet to a medium-sized ship burst outwards, puncturing and pulverising everything in their path. In the first few moments hundreds of ships ceased to exist and they themselves became more exploding and flying debris.

'Fuck me,' shouted Grupps, his eyes on stalks as the maelstrom of complete destruction spread out around the entire planet.

'Thirty seconds to weapon shut down,' called the beam officer, as a massive donut of blackness grew menacingly and expanded out from the beam's contact with the atmosphere. Spreading with alarming speed, it already had a quarter of the planet shrouded in stormy blackness.

Grupps realised Lake was protecting the octaship. Anything that came in their direction with an impact trajectory seemed to just dissipate or veer away. Nothing collided with the hull at all.

He inched his way across the bridge nearer the hangar door. Even though Lake had kept his word so far, Grupps wasn't convinced he wanted to leave a ship full of witnesses to him being there and responsible for this catastrophic attack.

'Twenty seconds to weapon shut down,' came the call as Grupps slipped unseen through the side door and ran down the corridor towards the small hangar and his prepped ship.

All around the Klatt vessel the obliteration continued. Satellites that controlled the recognised spaceways were wiped out, causing many ships that had narrowly escaped being hit by debris to run into each other in their haste to get away. Some, but not many, managed to execute an emergency jump and escape the cataclysmic event. It was the middle of the night space time, so most vessels had only a skeleton crew on the bridge and those that were on duty were tired, had their feet up and were relying on the automated systems to take them to their destinations.

Things were not much better down on the planet's surface. The larger chunks of debris that didn't completely burn up in the upper atmosphere came crashing down at many thousands of miles per hour. The planet-based laser cannons did their best to target the incoming storm of wreckage, but soon became overwhelmed with the sheer weight of targets.

In the capital, Kentro, entire tower blocks were felled and craters, some hundreds of metres across, exploded outwards as the detritus rained down. It was late evening, so most of the casualties died in their own homes without even knowing what hit them.

Seventeen GDA ambassadors ironically debating exorbitant defence budgets, together with their relative entourages, were killed when the huge council chamber took a direct hit from what was actually not a huge piece, but was big enough to cause the entire roof of the building to fall and bury everyone inside.

Power failures swept the planet and in places the darkness was complete. The areas under the beam's spreading storm clouds suffered even more. Winds of over a hundred and eighty miles per hour smashed homes and infrastructure alike. Hailstones the size of bricks rained down, pulverising and killing indiscriminately. Only those in extremely strong buildings survived relatively unscathed. But with the temperature dropping thirty-five degrees in a matter of minutes along with the power failures, they weren't going to believe they were the lucky ones for very long.

Vasi Stathmos space station, the biggest station in GDA space, permanently situated two thousand kilometres above the capital, was similarly in a lot of strife. Although it had a defensive shielding system similar to a ship, the sheer quantity and size of some of the impacts overwhelmed the apparatus and it failed within minutes, allowing multiple strikes directly onto the hull, causing countless depressurisations and complete deck shutdowns.

The Kordoni or space elevator connecting the station to the surface took many hits until one was big enough to completely sever the string. The elevator carriage, although low enough in the atmosphere to avoid burning up as it fell, was still high enough for it to be a terrifying several-minute plummet to certain death for the hundred and sixty-five passengers and crew. It impacted two hundred and eleven kilometres west of the city in an orchard of green calopie fruit, followed by hundreds of kilometres of the wide cable snaking down in its wake and smashing anything in its path across kilometres of countryside and one small town.

The longterm space station commander Yorge Stak'oui had the biggest day of his career, narrowly avoiding losing the immense station with its millions of personnel when it attempted to drop out of space. With multiple power and system failures including most of the manoeuvring thrusters, he had to blow airlocks and vent sections of the station to push the vast construction high enough to evade the pull of the planet.

It didn't stop a considerable number of the station's residents from panicking and completely ignoring the repeated warnings over the tannoy from launching almost half of the lifeboats – only for most to be destroyed, the majority within seconds by the massive quantity of flying detritus and wreckage travelling at huge velocities randomly around the entire planet. Of the few that did make it to the surface, some crashed because they had unknowingly acquired damage on the way down, and the ones who did land safely had the storms and temperatures of minus twenty to contend with.

Back on the bridge of the octaship, the beam weapon was finally shut down, its job now done, and the operator smiled as his panel reverted back to a standby mode. He glanced over at one of the weapons and defensive officers and nodded that it was okay to re-energise the ship's shields. Unfortunately, Grupps had been right to doubt Lake's commitment to their safety. The officer in question thought he had all the time in the world to casually reach up and touch the relevant icon to engage the shields. Unbeknown to him their protection had ceased at the same time the beam was shut down and the first impact hit the ship hard.

It was just plain bad luck that it hit and penetrated the main engineering section at the rear of the ship, severing several power supplies to critical systems, one of which was the shields.

Now completely vulnerable, it was only a matter of time before the vessel would suffer the same fate as so many others in close proximity to the doomed planet. Fourteen seconds later, as the ship absorbed multiple impacts, it dismantled itself, the screams of the crew quickly extinguished by the incoming vacuum of space.

23

The captain's hangar, Klatt octaship, above Dasos

GRUPPS LEAPT up the steps and through the open airlock, punching the door close toggle as he passed and thumping his backside down in the pilot's seat. He immediately realised he'd done the right thing, as a lump of something crashed through the hull right in front of him, causing his ship's struts to screech across the floor as the hangar vented. The debris disappeared on through the opposite hangar wall and deeper into the Klatt vessel.

Glancing at the huge hole in the outer wall, he surmised it would be suicide to try and fly out of the hangar before jumping, so he reached up, braced himself and hit the emergency jump icon innocently flashing away top right of the control panel.

He hadn't realised he'd also closed his eyes and held his breath, as when nothing happened, he reopened one eye and checked the scene out of the front screen. He exhaled noisily and gratefully as he witnessed a sea of stars and not the interior of a doomed ship.

'Fucking outrageous,' he muttered to himself, as he set the navigation computer with the co-ordinates for the Trelorus system. 'I think I'm going to enjoy retirement,' he said out loud this time, glancing and grinning at the huge stack of GDA credits piled up on the co-pilot's seat.

The star field outside slewed around as the small ship turned and began powering away towards the next jump zone.

24

Cartella, *hangar 87*, Katadromiko 28

THE RUSE WAS WORKING. The *Katadromiko*'s tractor beam had locked onto the fake *Gabriel*. Cleo had made the outer hull the correct size and as solid as possible so as to ensure the tractor beam operator's telemetry didn't look out of place. Once the beam had locked on, Cleo had hurried the cloaked *Cartella* through the reasonably stable but narrow gap and once inside the shields, had been able to override the hangar door.

Rayl had quickly taken over control of the small ship and as fast as she dared, buzzed through the atmosphere barrier and entered the large space, while Cleo reinitiated the door, hopefully before anyone noticed.

As Rayl expected, the large space was deserted of personnel but crammed full of various vessels. She knew from previous experience that right at the back of these hangars there were service bays that would be both clear and close to the rear hangar exits. She chose the left-hand one, setting the ship down as quickly as possible and shutting down the noisy antigravs.

They had no time to waste and didn't wait to see if their entrance had gone unobserved. Cleo had provided them both with basic GDA marine armour, so donning their helmets with the darkened visors lowered, they jumped down and rapidly made their way to the hangar rear exit door.

'This way,' said Rayl in the genderless electronic voice the helmet microphones produced, and pointed right as they entered the corridor.

'You were correct,' said Cleo over the helmet speakers. 'They're being held in the main security bureau on deck 149.'

The tube took them straight to the deck in question. They turned right as they exited the carriage and paused to look out over the huge central atrium stretching away fore and aft.

'Never ceases to amaze me the size of these things inside,' said Pol, watching a flock of multicoloured birds squabbling for space in a palm tree below.

'Keep moving,' whispered Rayl. 'Someone might notice us acting weird.'

The security station was a hundred and thirty metres up on the right. They both checked their weapons were on a stun setting and moved purposefully through the front entrance.

They were confronted by a single human guard sitting at the reception desk, who glanced up from his screen as they entered.

'What can I do for you two?' he asked, raising his eyebrows.

'We're to pick up the prisoners and escort them to the bridge,' said Rayl, sounding as officious as she could.

'Which prisoners?'

'Virr and Faux,' she said, stopping directly in front of the desk in an attempt to intimidate the guard.

He nodded and adopted a slight grin.

'They're in suite three,' he said, pointing to a door opposite. 'I'll deactivate the door field. Go straight in, they're all yours.'

They crossed the room and as the shimmering door field disappeared they entered the secure room. It didn't take them long to realise their mistake – the room was empty and the door field reactivated as soon as they were inside.

'You just make it too easy,' said a familiar voice from outside the room.

Salft appeared from one of the other rooms and stood outside the door, her arms folded and a smug expression on her face.

'Shit,' Rayl said under her breath.

'Can't be many left aboard your ship now?' said Salft, patronisingly. 'That feisty girl, Linda and the Theo coward, Philip, if my memory serves me right.'

Rayl levelled her weapon and pointed it at the door field.

'Go right ahead,' Salft chuckled. 'All weapons are automatically deactivated inside any of the secure suites.'

Rayl clicked the pistol to full power and pulled the trigger. The weapon beeped, but did nothing more.

Salft tilted her head to one side and grinned.

'Oops, didn't take my word for it then?' she scoffed. 'Might as well make yourselves comfortable, I have a ship that's becoming more likely to be mine by the hour and I don't mean that ridiculous holo image you tried to fool us with,' she continued. 'Oh, and thanks for the *Cartella*, that'll provide me with a nice little runabout.'

'I think Cleo might have other ideas about that,' said Pol.

'Ah, I don't think so,' she said. 'We'll just purge that box of annoying sparks from the system, same as we did here.'

'Are you sure about that?' said a voice from the main doorway.

Salft spun around at the sound of the voice. A Klatt sergeant stood just inside the threshold holding a laser rifle.

'What's the meaning of this, Sergeant?' she demanded.

The guard at the desk had drawn his weapon unseen. He raised it and fired at the Klatt soldier in one swift movement.

The lethal bolt went straight past the soldier and impacted the door frame. It exploded in a shower of sparks and panelling. In the second that the guard shielded himself from the door frame shrapnel, the sergeant fired in return, knocking the guard off the back of his seat. He impacted the wall behind, slid to the floor and remained there, unconscious.

The sergeant turned his weapon towards Salft and fired again. This time the stun bolt went straight through her and hit the wall behind with a crack, leaving a slight burn mark.

Salft disappeared into thin air, causing the sergeant to swear, before he morphed back into Cleo in her black ninja suit.

'Cleo, it's you,' called an excited Pol. 'Get us outta here.'

Cleo trotted over behind the desk, stepped over the unconscious guard and deactivated the door field.

'She was a fucking hologram too,' said Rayl. 'We need to get off this deck fast – can you do anything about the cameras and sensors, Cleo?'

'I can,' she said. 'The whole deck is dark at the moment, but if I do that everywhere we go, they'll know exactly where we are. They're getting quick at purging the systems as well, so I can't hang around in any system for any length of time.'

'You're present in the *Cartella* too,' said Pol.

'Oh, that's good,' she said. 'That's one place they can't get me.'

'But what about this version of you?' Rayl asked.

'I just have to be vigilant and keep on the move,' she said. 'Before we go on and just in case they get me, there's a strangely shielded area in a hangar near the bridge. I can't penetrate it, so it might be where they're holding the boys and the new girl.'

'What deck's it on?' Pol asked.

'Two…'

Cleo vanished.

'Bollocks,' said Rayl.

'Was that deck two or two hundred and whatever?' Pol asked.

'Most likely two hundred odd?' said Rayl. 'As it's near the bridge. We need to get out of here fast.'

They sprinted to the damaged door and peered left and right; the wide corridor was empty.

'Go right,' said Rayl. 'I think there's an emergency stairwell not too far along.'

They left the smouldering door frame and stink of burnt plastic behind, hurried down the corridor to the stairwell door and yanked it open. Inside, a spiral stairway led up and down.

'Which way?' Pol asked, turning to Rayl.

'The bridge is on deck two forty and there are two hangars on each side of the ship adjacent to it, if I remember rightly,' said Rayl. 'I used to visit my mum on the *Katadromiko 47* and got to know the layout of these ships quite well.'

'Okay, up then,' said Pol and quickly began the long

climb as the sound of shouting and boots clattering along the corridor sounded behind them.

'She was very pretty wasn't she?' said Rayl, out of the blue as they climbed.

'Who?' asked Pol, looking confused.

'That strange girl next to Andrew.'

'Yeah…I suppose so,' Pol replied, confused and glancing over her shoulder at Rayl. 'What's that got to do with anything?'

25

The Starship Gabriel, *close to Yiss, unknown system*

'Stop it,' said Phil, glaring at Linda across the bridge.

'What?' she said, exclaiming in surprise and staring back like a deer caught in headlights.

'Tapping your bloody foot. It's really irritating.'

'I'm nervous,' she said. 'Why haven't we heard anything?'

'Give them time, it's only been a couple of hours.'

'What's that?' asked Linda, pointing to movement from near the bridge area of the *Katadromiko*.

'It's a military gunship,' said Phil. 'One of the big ones.'

It powered away from the bigger vessel, heading out away from the planet and into empty space.

'Where the hell do they think they're going?' Linda wondered.

The gunship vanished as it jumped.

'Well, that's weird,' said Phil. 'Jump was embedded too.'

A sudden huge flash on the holomap had the two of them shielding their eyes.

'What the hell was that?' shouted Linda, squinting up at the holo image as her sight gradually returned.

'Shit,' said Phil, frantically hitting icons and backing the *Gabriel* quickly away from an expanding concussive wave front approaching them extremely rapidly. 'It came from the *Katadromiko*,' he said, glancing at Linda, his face ashen.

The *Gabriel* shuddered as the wave passed through. Phil had managed to get them away to a reasonably safe distance so the shields could absorb the majority of the shock.

They watched in horror as the realisation of what had just happened dawned on them. The huge fourteen-kilometre vessel had been split in two and the sudden released atmosphere from the central atrium had rammed the two sections apart with a massive decompression surge. The two enormous halves of the *Katadromiko* were already kilometres apart, both spinning randomly and gradually succumbing to the planet's gravitational pull.

'Oh, fuck no,' screamed Linda, her mouth hanging open in shock.

'Shiiiit,' shouted Phil, as he reversed the *Gabriel*'s trajectory as fast as possible and accelerated back towards the planet. 'I don't know which section they're all on.'

'Both, I think,' said Cleo, appearing on one of the empty couches. 'The shields have understandably failed and I can detect Pol and Rayl in the rear section. Ed and Andy were in a hangar near the bridge in the front section, where that gunship came from.'

'Are…the…girls…conscious?' Linda asked between sobs, her head in her hands.

'No, but one of me is,' said Cleo.

'Whereabouts?' Phil asked.

'Front section.'

'Can you get to the hangar?'

'I'm already there.'

'Are they okay?'

'The hangar's empty, the boys are no longer on the ship. That's why I can't detect them.'

Phil glanced across at Linda.

'The gunship that jumped away,' he said. 'They must've been aboard.'

'Well, at least we know they're probably alive,' said Linda, wiping the tears from her eyes. 'D'you think the bitch from hell was on that gunship too?'

'Of course she was,' said Cleo. 'She would always have an escape plan for any scenario.'

'Something serious must have happened to warrant sabotaging the bigger ship,' said Phil. 'A mutiny or something amongst the crew would do it.'

'There's nothing we can do about the boys at the moment,' said Linda, pointing at the tumbling rear section. 'But we must try and get to the girls. Can we stabilise that section to give us more time?'

'I don't think our tractor beam has the power to stop it dropping into the atmosphere,' said Phil, shrugging. 'But we might be able to alleviate some of the tumble and give them a chance of getting off.'

'Can you get over there?' Linda asked, staring at Cleo.

'Most systems are down, including the holo emitters,' she said, pulling an apologetic face. 'But if we can address that tumble, I can fly over and with a bag full of temporary emitter grenades, work my way towards them with a couple of skin suits.'

'You'll need an operational airlock,' said Linda. 'I'll see if I can find one.'

'I'm gonna need to try and stabilise the wreck first,' said Phil. 'That's not going to be a walk in the park.'

'I'll give you a hand in a second,' said Linda. 'We've got more than one tractor beam on this ship.'

Two huge thirty-four metre emitters motored out from their concealed housings as the *Gabriel* approached the tumbling rear section. The odd lifeboat occasionally jettisoned out from the six-kilometre lump of doomed vessel before arcing around towards the planet.

'How long have we got?' Phil asked, glancing nervously at Cleo.

'My calculations indicate the rear section will begin dropping into the upper atmosphere in around ninety-eight minutes,' she answered. 'The front section about seventeen minutes after that.'

Phil and Linda both turned their heads toward the front section to witness a constant flurry of lifeboats spewing out from the slowly tumbling wreck.

'The majority of the crew must have been up front,' said Phil. 'Just as well, as the inertial dampers seem to be still partially operational, allowing people to move about and get to the lifeboats.'

He brought the *Gabriel* within tractor range and held position while they both grabbed hold with the hugely powerful beams. Their eyes met before both glanced up at the ceiling as a sickening groaning came from the bones of the ship.

'This is testing the structural integrity,' said Linda, raising her eyebrows and wincing as the *Gabriel* juddered alarmingly.

'Well within acceptable limits,' said Cleo. 'The wreck's spin has alleviated by three percent too.'

'Is that all?' Phil said, pulling a pained expression.

'Keep the beams at full torque,' said Cleo, nodding. 'The effect will increase as the rotation lessens. I estimate I could get aboard in approximately seven minutes.'

Another loud creak followed by an even louder crack made Linda jump.

'Will we have a ship in one piece in seven minutes?' she asked, staring at Cleo nervously.

'It's just the hull bedding itself in, nothing to be alarmed about,' came the reply, although Linda did notice a slight tone to Cleo's voice that indicated she wasn't quite convinced that what she was saying was entirely true.

Linda kept her stare on Cleo, who smiled a nervous smile back and promptly disappeared.

'Hey, where d'you think you're going?' Linda called.

'For a little walk,' Cleo's voice boomed back.

'Oh…right…yes,' Linda answered, wincing at Phil, who shrugged in return.

'I think you'll be able to enter through this airlock here,' said Linda, as the holomap panned in to the wreck and an undamaged door began flashing red. It disappeared every few seconds as the wreck's spin took it out of sight, but the reduction in the speed of rotation was quite obvious now.

'Can you match the spin with the *Gabriel* please, Phil?' asked Cleo. 'And keep the main array concentrated on that airlock. Linda, can you continue to reduce the rotation, it'll make it easier for the girls to don their suits when I get to them.'

Neither of them answered, just nodded and did as requested.

Linda gasped as Cleo materialised just outside the *28*'s airlock. She found it quite shocking to see a human figure floating in space without any suit or protection of any kind.

Cleo stabilised herself in relation to the wreck and approached the exterior door control, which thankfully illuminated as she touched it. A couple of seconds later the outer door swept lazily upwards into its housing. Cleo floated one of her grenades inside, watched it sail towards the inner door before bursting and distributing several self-adhesive holo emitters around the inside of the airlock. She turned and nodded back towards the *Gabriel* before floating inside. The door quickly closed behind her.

Phil and Linda's eyes met again.

'Now we wait,' said Phil, the stress evident on his face.

'I hope she's got time to find them,' said Linda. 'It's a hell of a long walk through that wreck to get to them and then if they're injured they've still got to get back to the airlock.'

'She'll get to them and carry them off if necessary,' he added, trying to keep the worry out of his voice as he noticed the anxiety on Linda's face.

26

GDA marine gunship, location unknown, Medusa Merger Galaxy

ED WAS THOROUGHLY FED UP. He could tell Andy was pretty pissed too by the expression on his face as he snored quietly in the corner. Quite what he was dreaming about he didn't know, but he was sure it wasn't free beer in the pub.

They were both convinced they were being dragged to an airlock earlier, but were surprised as they were bundled aboard a marine gunship sitting menacingly in the captain's hangar near the bridge. Callon hadn't been brought with them, which was a little worrying. That had been several hours ago and the lighting in the small, hastily emptied ammunition store they had been unceremoniously dumped into had dimmed a couple of times, signifying the small ship had jumped.

Andy opened an eye and grunted as he shifted his seated position on the hard floor.

'Who booked this fucking hotel?' he mumbled. 'The food better be an improvement on the sleeping arrangements.'

'Don't put money on it,' Ed said in reply while stretching his back. 'The guards are human here too, so that means only one thing.'

'Ah…crap.'

'Precisely, although they look Dasonian and their food isn't quite as bad as the cat food the Klatt seem to prefer.'

'We might not get fed at all,' said Andy, sitting up and yawning. 'They might be just disposing of us somewhere remote.'

'She wants the *Gabriel*,' Ed replied. 'At the moment, that's what's keeping us alive.'

'The girls wouldn't trade us for the ship though would they?'

'Shit no…they all know better than that.'

'Why d'you think we left the *28* and why didn't Callon come with us?'

'Now, they are both very good questions,' Ed agreed, shrugging. 'I'm sure—'

The door burst open and four human guards entered, followed by the young Salft just as the lighting dimmed again, indicating another jump.

'Virr, come with me,' she ordered, as one of the guards unlocked the cuffs securing him to the shelving and resecured his hands with plastic ties.

'What about me?' said Andy, attempting to stand and getting pushed roughly back down again.

His question was met with silence.

'Hey,' he shouted, as the entourage filed out of the room,

dragging Ed with them. 'I asked you a question.'

Ed tried to turn and give Andy a reassuring nod, but was quickly shoved straight and forward as the door slammed shut behind him.

'What d'you need me for?' he asked as they made their way across the main crew and equipment deck and up the steps to the cockpit.

Again, silence.

The leading guard pointed at the co-pilot's seat, into which he was pushed and his hands secured to the seat arms. Salft strolled around him and leant against the control panel to face him.

'You're going to relay a message in a moment,' she said. 'You're going to read exactly what's on the screen, and any deviation whatsoever will result in your friend going for a walk outside.'

She paused for a second and stared at Ed to let the threat sink in.

'Are we quite clear on that?'

Ed nodded.

'I think I know you well enough to know you're not bluffing,' he said. 'What's the message and who's it to?'

Salft looked over at the pilot.

'Are we alone?' she asked.

'I have no evidence of any other vessels, cloaked or otherwise in the vicinity, ma'am,' he said, nervously.

Salft nodded slowly.

'For your sake, you'd better be right,' she whispered, before turning back to Ed. 'In a moment we're going to re-enter the Milky Way and you're going to speak to the captain of the vessel guarding the gateway.'

'To do what?'

'You'll see when you read it.'

'If I don't practise I'll sound wooden and he'll smell a rat.'

'Smell a what?'

'Earth expression,' Ed explained. 'It means he'll be suspicious.'

Salft moved to one side and pointed at a screen on the console where a message flashed up. Ed read the text and nodded.

'I get the gist of it,' he said, lifting his arms up to illustrate the plastic restraints securing his wrists to the arms. 'You might want to remove these before he sees me too.'

Salft nodded at one of the guards, who cut the ties off. Ed sat rubbing his wrists and rereading the message.

'I'll personalise the text a little,' he said, giving Salft a quick glance. 'If I read that word for word, it'll sound a bit weird and I've met the captain before, so he'll expect a little banter, especially from me.'

Salft stared back, her dark eyes boring into him suspiciously.

'If you try anything to warn him, I will space your colleague,' she growled. 'Do you understand me, Virr?'

'Completely.'

Salft nodded slowly without taking her eyes off him and Ed knew he had to tread very carefully in the next few minutes, or risk his best friend's life.

The starfield glowing through the front screen blurred as the gunship jumped and then quickly reformed in a different order. The pilot turned the ship, bringing a familiar formation of three moons into sight. He slowed the vessel and turned his head towards Salft.

'In position for galactic transfer, ma'am,' he said.

Salft nodded and raised an eyebrow at Ed.

'You know what to do, Virr. Don't forget what I said about your friend.'

She turned to gaze out of the front screen and pointed at the moons.

'Go,' she ordered, not bothering to look at the pilot.

The ship accelerated and twenty seconds later the starfield changed abruptly this time. The cockpit became suddenly brighter as the reflected light from Pyli swathed them with its blue radiance. The holomap chirped a warning chime and flashed up a red icon as the *Katadromiko* cruiser was detected. A stern voice boomed out from the cockpit speakers as they were immediately hailed.

'Unexpected GDA gunship, please explain your arrival?'

'Hello *Katadromiko 7*,' said Ed, in the friendliest voice he could muster. 'This is Edward Virr, could I speak to Captain Trikalon please?'

A pause ensued before a minute later a different voice spoke.

'Edward, this is unexpected, especially in that vessel?' the new voice said, as an image of a short middle-aged bearded man appeared above them.

'I'm sure it is, Captain, and it's good to see you again,' Ed replied, as an image of him sitting in the co-pilot's seat was returned.

'I take it as you're in a gunship registered to the *28*, that you've managed to find it and repossess the vessel?' Trikalon said, smiling.

'Indeed,' said Ed, grinning back as authentically as he could manage. 'I need you to do something for me.'

'Absolutely, what do you need?'

'Can you contact Commander Bache Loftt and request he

meets me for an important and private conversation? It's of life-threatening proportions and I'll meet him halfway at these co-ordinates.'

A position in a lifeless system halfway between Pyli and Dasos was transmitted by the gunship pilot. Ed could see Trikalon glance over at the location and nod slightly.

'I'll do what I can,' he said, returning his gaze to Ed. 'Although, we're having a bit of trouble getting any reply from Dasos at the moment. We sent a fast drone after getting no reply, but that failed to return too.'

'Okay, if you could send another one straight away to Commander Loftt with our request, we'll go and wait at the meeting location,' replied Ed.

'Will do, Edward.' Trikalon turned and spoke to another member of his crew. 'It's on its way shortly,' he said, looking back at Ed again. 'Is Andrew there with you?' he asked.

'No,' Ed replied. 'You know him…he won't go anywhere that doesn't have his favourite cold lager.'

Ed noticed the smile on Trikalon's face slip slightly, but quickly recover, followed by an almost indiscernible nod.

'Ah, yes,' he said. 'I'd forgotten about that. Give Commander Loftt my regards when you meet.'

The Captain's holo image disappeared and Ed turned to Salft.

'Happy now?' he asked. 'I hate lying to people.'

Salft's stern expression never wavered as she stared at him for a moment.

'What is cold lager?' she asked, her eyes boring into him.

'Earth beer,' said Ed, as casually as he could. 'It's Andrew's favourite. It made a legitimate excuse why he's supposedly not here.'

'Hmm,' she grunted, eyeing him suspiciously.

Andy jumped as the cell door burst open. He'd been dozing.

'I didn't order any room service,' he quipped, as the three guards bundled in. One of then unlocked him from the shelving as another secured his hands behind his back.

'Come with us,' the third ordered, as he was roughly pushed out the door. He turned to glare at the guard who'd pushed him.

'Face the front,' the guard spat and pushed him again.

'I'm going to tell your mum of you,' Andy muttered under his breath.

They took him up to the cockpit, where he saw Ed sitting in the co-pilot's seat and Salft watching over him. She stepped in front of Ed as he entered so he couldn't see Ed's face. But not before he noticed one of Ed's hands drop to his side with his fingers firmly crossed.

'What's your favourite Earth beer?' she demanded before he had time to settle or say anything.

'Oh…err,' he mumbled, deliberately not getting eye contact as he thought about the crossed fingers. 'Lager,' he said, quickly enough to avoid suspicion and hoping it was the right answer. 'Cold fizzy lager…yum, yum.'

Salft sighed noisily and nodded her head towards the door.

'Take them back and set a course for the rendezvous location. We have preparations to make.'

'Why didn't Callon come with us?' Andy blurted, as the guards led them away.

'You told me she wasn't a member of your crew,' she answered. 'She remains on the *28*.'

Salft smiled inwardly at her clever pun.

27

Flyer station, east of Kentro City, Dasos

THE SNOW WAS over a metre deep in places as Commander Bache Loftt waded his way towards the flyer's terminal building. The hat he wore did little to keep the almost horizontal flakes whipping around in all directions from stinging his eyes. He rued his completely unsuitable choice of footwear as he stumbled towards the reception area, although he hadn't anticipated his vehicle getting stuck two kilometres into a five-kilometre journey.

Finally heaving the snow-drifted doors open just wide enough to slip inside, he paused to tip the slush out of his shoes and winced as he had to slip the soggy things back on again.

The receptionist, who knew him well, gave him a sympathetic expression and shook his head slowly.

'Sorry, Commander,' he said, shrugging. 'I'm afraid it's been a wasted journey. Nothing's going up in this.'

An explosion nearby had them both ducking as another lump of wreckage came down from above at supersonic speed and debris rattled around the walls of the building.

'Shit,' said Bache, as he glanced nervously back at the door. 'That was the closest one yet.'

'D'you know what the hell's going on?' the receptionist asked. 'Are we at war or something or is it a meteor shower?'

'I wish I knew,' Bache replied, slipping his hat and gloves off and slumping into one of the chairs lining the wall. 'Communications are down for some reason. It could be a meteor storm that's caused a problem with the satellites, but where the hell has this stupid weather come from? I was hoping to get to naval headquarters and find out.'

'I thought we had a foolproof planetary defence system that could eliminate a threat from anything like this,' said the receptionist. 'We would have had several months' warning about a rogue meteor shower, wouldn't we?'

'In theory, we should've had years of warning about that,' said Bache, scratching his chin and the more he thought about it, he realised it was the most unlikely scenario. 'The objects entering the atmosphere can only be debris of some kind.'

'D'you think that's where the satellites have gone?'

'It certainly explains the lack of communications,' agreed Bache. 'But if we were under attack they couldn't possibly have got them all. There are thousands of them.'

'Well, there's a lot of something hitting the ground,' said the receptionist, and just to emphasise the point another boom of an impact sounded in the distance.

They both glanced at the windows as the flash was even brighter than the whiteness of the snow piled up outside.

The sudden scream of heavy antigravs overhead had them both out of their seats as a large dark shadow dropped down and settled on the flyer pad to the right of the building. When they reached the windows it was almost impossible to see what or who had landed. The antigravs churned up the powdery flakes and, mixed with the already falling snow, it was a complete whiteout.

Gradually, the vague outline of a shuttle of some kind materialised as the engines died down to a low rumble. Two shadowy figures hunched against the storm approached the building, their faces obscured by helmet visors.

'Well, at least someone's brave enough to fly in this crap,' mumbled Bache, as he recognised the GDA marine winter issue uniforms. He moved over to the door and pushed as the leading marine pulled to brush the snow to one side enough for them to enter.

'Morning, Sergeant,' said Bache, noticing his rank. 'I'm hoping you have some idea as to what the hell is going on?'

'Ah…Commander Loftt,' the newcomer said, flicking his visor up, and a look of relief appeared on his face. 'We have orders to find you and take you straight to Bithgurt, sir.'

Bache nodded and raised his eyebrows at the receptionist.

'Must be serious if they've warmed up that facility,' said the receptionist, returning Bache's glance with a ruminative expression and a shrug.

Bache nodded. 'Shit and fan come to mind,' he mumbled, replacing his hat and gloves.

'Shit and what, sir?' the marine asked.

'Earth expression, son,' he said. 'Don't worry, just lead the way.'

Bache waved a goodbye to the receptionist as the pair of marines quickly escorted the Commander back out into the snow and across to the waiting military shuttle. Its antigravs were already beginning to rise from idle.

Bache felt his cheeks glow as he moved into the sudden and surprising warmth of the shuttle's interior. The airlock closed quickly and the vessel rose up off the pad as soon as his backside hit the couch. He knew the emergency military underground facility at Bithgurt was only to be used in extreme emergencies, one of which was an imminent planetary invasion.

'Either of you two know what the hell is going on?' Bache asked, looking between the two marines.

'Sorry, sir,' said one. 'We're honestly as much in the dark as you.'

'Whatever it is, it's pretty damn serious,' said the other. 'They've recalled absolutely everyone who's off shift or on leave in every one of the services.'

'Hmm,' grunted Bache, his brow furrowing. 'That hasn't happened since the Trelarix incursion back when I was your age.'

Bithgurt was only ten minutes' flight time from Kentro City and Bache soon felt the shuttle begin to descend and the tone of the antigravs change from a scream to a low bellow. Watching the feed from the forward-facing camera on the bulkhead monitor, he hoped the pilot knew what he was doing in this almost complete white-out. He wouldn't have any of the automated flight aids with the satellites out of action. He'd be relying instead on the feedback from the vessel's array providing a continuously updated holo image replayed in front of his eyes on his helmet visor. Bache had flown like this several times in the past and knew it took a hundred percent concentration.

A gentle whine from the unfolding struts below followed

by a reassuringly insubstantial thud had him exhaling the breath he hadn't realised he was holding. Both airlock doors hissed open, allowing a freezing wind to pervade the cabin, dragging with it a flurry of snow that melted immediately on contact with the shuttle's floor.

A human shape appeared, also wrapped from head to foot in marine issue winter fatigues. A grimacing face peered out from within, one that Bache recognised.

'Captain Hoo, it's been a long time,' said Bache, unfastening his belt and standing.

'It has, Commander,' Hoo replied, reaching in and shaking Bache's hand. He stepped back down the steps to allow Bache to exit the shuttle. 'It's good to see you. I wish it was in less serious circumstances though.'

'I take it you have some idea as to what the fuck is going on?'

'I do…come with me.'

He led Bache quickly across the landing apron and through a low disguised carboncrete doorway leading to a stairway which descended into semi-darkness, only illuminated by soft blue panels at each landing.

Bache lost count of how many floors they descended before the stairs ended in a metal doorway. Hoo entered a code into a recessed keypad and the heavy door ground ponderously into the wall on the right. They stepped into an elevator, allowing the door to close again in its slow lumbering way. Bache felt the floor drop and he became almost weightless as the lift descended at alarming speed.

'How deep is this place?' he asked after glancing around and failing to find any indication of how far down they were going.

'Three kilometres,' replied Hoo. 'Well, to the uppermost level anyway.'

Bache raised his eyebrows and as they descended he wondered what it would take to attack and destroy such a facility so deep in solid rock. He turned to face the door again as he felt his weight increase considerably as the elevator began slowing quite brutally. The door reopened into a wide corridor of plain carboncrete lit from above by dull red glow panels. A small group of four people loitered in the corridor and turned as the door slid away into its housing.

The leading figure Bache recognised immediately.

'Madam Vice President,' he said, stepping out of the elevator and bowing his head slightly.

A slight smile crossed Vice President Milne's face, quickly dissipating into the stern and somewhat worried expression from before. She stretched out a heavily ring-bedecked hand and shook Bache's hand firmly.

'Commander Loftt, thank you for coming and I do appreciate we didn't give you much choice, but as you will shortly see, it was a necessity. Follow us, please. I need your expertise and advice.'

She turned and marched off, closely followed by her entourage of three.

Bache smiled inwardly as he hurried forward to keep up with the group. It'd been a long time since he'd heard Milne's broad Scolainian accent and it reminded him of an interesting few days he'd had a long time ago.

28

The rear section of the doomed Katadromiko 28

THE INNER AIRLOCK door powered slowly open, obviously struggling with only the drastically reduced emergency power available. Cleo clicked forward, her magnetised boots helping to keep her on the flooring rather than spinning around in the corridor in which she found herself.

She tossed another grenade as far up the corridor as she could and made her way quickly forward. Keeping her holographic density as thin as possible to allay some of the centrifugal effects of the wreck's spin proved helpful as she followed the signal to Rayl and Pol.

She discovered the emitters had a range of around a hundred metres, although every time she rounded a corner she had to deploy another grenade. She chose a stairway to take her up to the level she needed and invented a new trick of pulling emitters off the walls and ceiling as she went and re-sticking them further along. It saved her rapidly depleting stock of grenades.

A sudden shout from above surprised her as a uniformed Klatt soldier hanging onto the handrail with one hand and trying to point a weapon with the other blocked the way forward.

'Who are you?' he shouted. 'And how are you able to move around?'

Cleo stopped and stuck an emitter on the ceiling so she could proceed.

'What's that?' he called. 'Have you boarded the ship? Are you to blame for all this?'

The muzzle of his rifle swayed around as he tried desperately to get a bead on Cleo, but the ever-changing inertia made it impossible.

'I'm here to help,' she said, calmly. 'The ship has been sabotaged. You need to get to a lifeboat.'

'That's rubbish,' he raged. 'I'd be executed for abandoning my post.'

He fired. The shot went well wide but hit one of the emitters, which caused Cleo's holographic image to flicker.

'You're a fucking hologram,' he shouted, his eyes wide and a look of shock on his face.

The shots came thick and fast now as he panicked. Some of them would have hit the mark but of course sailed straight through Cleo and struck the stairwell walls.

'I'm so sorry,' said Cleo, pulling a laser pistol out of her bag, checking it was on stun and hitting the soldier square in the chest with a single bolt.

He slumped and began bumping around the walls, floor and ceiling with the spin of the ship. Cleo threw a grenade past him and ducked under him, quickly continuing as time was now getting short.

She reached the level she needed, grenaded the corridor and hurried six hundred metres along to another stairwell door. She swore when she found it was locked. Banging suddenly coming from the other side surprised her and, clicking the pistol to full power, she stepped back, hunched down and fired at the lock mechanism. Turning the weapon back to stun, she kept it focused on the door.

The banging, which had stopped, recommenced and with the mechanism now compromised, the door soon burst open. A body flew through and landed in a heap on the corridor wall opposite and began a slow roll around, following the spin of the ship. Long thin human hands hanging onto the door frame came into view, followed by a grimacing Pol.

'Fucking hell,' she yelled. 'What in the name of shit is going on around here?' Then she saw Cleo and her eyes widened. 'Where the fuck have you been?' she demanded. 'I've got bruises on my bruises and Rayl hit her head on the stair rail.'

'No time to explain,' said Cleo. 'We need to get off this ship. Put these on and pick up Rayl.' She threw her a pair of the magnetic shoes.

'What happened?' Pol asked as she donned the shoes and grabbed Rayl.

'Sabotage,' said Cleo. 'Quickly, come this way. The ship is about to drop into the atmosphere.'

'Oh shit,' said Pol, carrying Rayl over her shoulder and swaying her way back towards the other stairwell following Cleo. 'Did they blow up engineering or something? We heard the bang.'

'Something like that,' said Cleo, as she made much better

time now she didn't have to pause every so often to throw another grenade.

'Can you hear me? Have you got them?' called Linda from the *Gabriel*, interrupting them. 'The internal shielding just failed on the rear section, we can see where you are now.'

'We're on our way,' said Cleo. 'Have two autonurses prepped.'

'Oh no, are they in a bad way?' called Phil.

'I'm not so bad,' said Pol. 'But Rayl's unconscious.'

They reached the first stairwell and headed back down. The soldier was still out for the count and Cleo scooped him up and carried him along with them.

'What are you taking him along for?' asked Pol, giving Cleo a puzzled look.

'It was me who stunned him. I can't leave him to die,' she snapped, returning Pol's look with a determined stare.

'Ah, okay,' she replied, knowing it was against Theo programming protocols for any of their sentient ships to purposely take life.

They reached the lower level where the airlock was and scooted along the corridor as fast as they could stumble with their burdens.

'Be quick,' called Linda. 'Only seven minutes to go. We're right outside.'

Cleo stopped at the deck's lifeboat, opened the door and bundled the soldier inside. She slammed the door closed, uncovered the emergency launch toggle and sent it on its way.

They continued, quickly reaching the airlock. The inner door was still open and they flew inside.

'Put one of these on,' said Cleo, giving one of the Theo suits to Pol. 'I'll dress Rayl.'

'Oh, fuck,' said Pol, holding up the pad you would normally stand on to allow the liquid suit to form around you.

Cleo's eyes widened as she realised Pol's dilemma. One of the soldier's laser bolts must have hit the bag; the suit pad had a neat hole punched through it. She looked at the other suit and that was damaged too.

'Oh, fuck, indeed,' she said.

'What do we do?' Pol asked, her face etched with worry.

'Four minutes, guys, hurry up,' called Phil, not realising the problem.

Cleo glanced up the corridor.

'Come with me,' she said.

'But the lifeboat's gone now,' Pol exclaimed.

'The one I'm thinking of hasn't,' said Cleo, running back up the way they had come only seconds earlier.

Pol followed her after heaving Rayl up onto her shoulder again.

Cleo stopped at another door facing inward, peered through its circular window, nodded with satisfaction and pressed a big blue button recessed into the wall.

'That's no good,' cried Pol. 'That's the internal tube train.'

Cleo turned to her and grinned.

'Got a better idea?' she said, throwing a grenade inside the tube carriage as the door opened slowly under the emergency power.

Pol shook her head and followed her aboard, laying Rayl down on a seat.

'Where are you guys?' Phil called. 'You need to get out now, right this minute.'

'Get ready to catch a train,' said Cleo, pressing the code for a station in the front section of the ship.

The carriage moved away from the station gradually, both Pol and Cleo urging it forward as it slowly began to pick up a bit of speed.

'A train?' repeated an obviously confused Phil. 'What are you on about?'

'Just get the *Gabriel* around to the severed end and be ready with the tractor,' Cleo said.

'Oh, shit…you're not doing what I think you're doing, are you?' called Phil. 'Is that carriage airtight?'

'I don't know,' she replied, her eyes meeting Pol's. 'We'd better hang onto something just in case.'

'What d'you mean, severed end?' asked Pol, as she pinned Rayl against the seat and wrapped her arms around its frame.

'The ship's in two pieces,' Cleo replied. 'We're going to pop out into space, where the *Gabriel* can grab us.'

Pol's eyes widened as they both turned to stare at the front of the carriage.

'What if there's debris blocking the tube?' said Pol.

'We've just got to hope there isn't,' Cleo replied, noticing Pol's knuckles going white as she gripped onto the seat even tighter.

The carriage had by now picked up all the speed it could with the limited amount of power available. A sudden judder and a bang from underneath made them jump, followed by another crunch, a succession of knocks, ending in a loud scrape down the opposite side to the door, a huge bang, then the lights went out.

Weightlessness followed along with a sudden silence, quickly replaced by a faint hissing that grew in intensity as the structure of the carriage was subjected to stresses far in excess of its design remit.

They were suddenly jerked violently downwards and Pol lost her grip on the seat. The light from the planet below glowed through the door's circular window, flinging shadows randomly around the interior as the carriage continued spinning. Her arms flailed around helplessly as she floated down the length of the carriage, finally crashing into the front seats, closely followed by Rayl.

Pol noticed it was getting suddenly very cold and her breathing was becoming laboured.

'Don't hang about, Phil,' she called. 'This thing's leaking like a sieve.'

'Hang on…hang on,' shouted Phil. 'Nearly there.'

A loud buzzing, followed by a steady bright white light and a final crunch, that had the three bodies in the carriage thrown around for the last time as everything went still and quiet, except for a slight hissing of air coming into the carriage this time.

'Is everyone all right in there?' called a voice from outside.

Pol stood up on the carriage wall. It had settled on its side on the *Gabriel*'s hangar floor. She limped over to Rayl's body lying awkwardly nearby and turned her onto her back, cradling her head.

'Wait a second,' said Cleo, disappearing from the other end of the carriage.

Pol shielded her eyes as a bright white beam from inside the hangar cut a rectangular section of the roof away, allowing Pol to see out across the hangar to find an agitated octopus peering at her from inside its liquid sphere.

'Are you all right?' asked Oona again, the multicolours of

her words turning the hangar into a disco as they were translated. The tips of her tentacles flicked nervously as she pressed one of her eyes against the inner wall of the sphere.

'I hope so,' said Pol, as she attempted to pick Rayl up once more, before slumping forward and passing out herself.

29

*Bithgurt Subterranean Command Centre, near Kentro,
Dasos*

BACHE WAS LED deep into the facility using another elevator
and an underground train. He was eventually led into what
seemed like a central command room. Over twenty officers
sat at consoles facing inwards and a huge hazy holographic
image of Dasos and the surrounding system hung above
everyone, rotating slowly. The room reminded him of a
scaled-down *Katadromiko* bridge.

'What's up with the holomap?' he asked, as they stopped
and Milne turned to face him.

Her expression turned melancholy as she gazed up at the
out-of-focus and ill-defined image floating above.

'We have no space-based arrays at all,' she said, despon-
dently. 'This is all we can get from what's left of the old
quickly recommissioned land-based arrays.'

'What about the fleet navy ships in orbit?' Bache asked. 'There's always several dozen here at any one time.'

Bache noticed the naval officer to Milne's left flinch as he said it.

'All gone,' she said. 'Well, as far as we know.'

'Gone?' demanded Bache. 'Gone where?'

Milne glanced and nodded at the naval officer as a cue for him to answer the question.

'Err…as far as we know, sir, they're all destroyed,' he said, averting his eyes and staring at the floor awkwardly.

'What…all of them?' Bache asked, in astonishment. 'Who the hell could do that? And what about the huge planetary defence satellites? No one could get by those monstrous things.'

The naval officer puffed out his cheeks and pulled a pained expression.

'Also…all destroyed,' he said, continuing to stare at the floor.

'So, I take it the planet's defenceless?' Bache said, turning to look at Milne. 'Do we have any idea who we're up against?'

Milne turned and nodded at a nearby console operator.

'This is the last clear image we have before everything went dark,' she said.

Immediately the holo image became crystal clear. The familiar scene of Dasos from space swarming with traffic appeared; hundreds of ships in neat controlled lines snaking in all directions and the unmistakable ring of massive defence satellite spheres lurking menacingly and encircling the planet.

Suddenly a large blue and grey octagonal ship jumped straight into the middle of the melee. Miraculously avoiding hitting anything, it almost instantly unleashed a beam of purple light into the planet's atmosphere. Bache watched mesmerised as the defence satellites activated, but before they could lock on and fire they all exploded so violently, he had to avert his eyes.

When he'd blinked away his blindness, he looked back at a scene of utter devastation, quickly escalating outwards as the sheer volume of shrapnel engulfed everything, including the satellites providing the images. The quality of the recording gradually deteriorated before dropping out completely and reverting back to the grainy image from before.

'Holy crap,' said Bache, his shoulders slumping. 'I recognise that blue ship as the Klatt vessel that tried to attack Paradeisos, which explains the crazy weather. But what I don't understand is how they orchestrated the simultaneous destruction of the defence satellites. I saw no other ships.'

'We were hoping you might be able to shed some light on that,' said Milne.

'I have no idea,' he said. 'The recent rout of almost the entire Klatt fleet meant they couldn't have done it with cloaked ships sneaking up on us. Even that would've been next to impossible with our level of detection systems. It could have been a very elaborate mission of sabotage though. But how in hell's name did they even get close to them, let alone affix explosives to a hundred and seventy platforms without anything going awry?'

'Or someone else entirely was the culprit,' Milne interjected. 'The Klatt ship could've been a diversion, or it was an inside job.'

Bache nodded and looked around the room.

'Are all the senior naval personnel en route here?' he asked. Milne and the naval officer exchanged a quick glance.

'Erm…no,' said Milne. 'There was a Gerousia Council meeting, including all senior naval officers, on *Katadromiko 3* at the time of the attack.'

Bache's eyes widened.

'Where was the *3*?' he asked, already afraid of the answer.

All three standing in front of him glanced upwards.

'We've heard nothing,' said the officer.

'Who was on board?'

'Everyone except me from the Inner Gerousia Council and every serving senior naval officer in the fleet,' said Milne. 'Hence, why we need you.'

'I'm supposed to be retired,' said Bache.

'Well, consider yourself un-retired and I'm instigating an emergency field promotion of you to Admiral of the Fleet. What's left of it anyway.'

'Ancients alive…I think I need to sit down,' said Bache, sitting heavily on the nearest empty chair and placing his head in his hands. 'I grew through the ranks with most of those people. Some of them were my best friends…I can't believe they've all gone. Are we sure the *3* was destroyed?' he said, glancing up and around at the circle of control room staff.

He was met by a sea of contrite faces.

'There's nothing big enough in system to be a *Katadromiko*, sir,' said a voice from the left-hand side. 'A few vessels that were fairly distant when the attack happened have survived relatively intact. But they're having to remain at a distance to avoid the massive quantity of debris flying about.'

'What about Vasi Stathmos station?' Bache asked.

'From what we can tell,' said Milne, 'it suffered quite severe damage to its outer decks and will continue to do so until the planet's gravity tidies up a bit. The Cordoni has been completely destroyed with no survivors on the carriage descending at the time.'

'How many ships were lost?' he asked, not looking forward to the answer.

'At the last count, three hundred and nine naval vessels and around fourteen hundred civilian ships.'

Bache exhaled noisily and rubbed his chin.

'Many survivors?' he asked, this time not even bothering to look up, knowing the answer was going to be pretty awful.

'A lot of the lifeboats that actually managed to launch were taken out or damaged by the weight of wreckage surging about, sir. Some made it down unmolested, but we don't have any numbers yet because of the storms harrowing most rescue attempts.'

'Do we know where that Klatt ship is now?'

'It was destroyed, sir.'

'What?' exclaimed Bache, this time turning to face the officer in question. 'How did we manage that?'

'We didn't, sir. It was also wrecked by the flying debris. It seemed to have some sort of impregnable field around it while the beam weapon was in operation and as soon as it was shut off the shrapnel cut it to pieces.'

'You mean it used its own shields and then they inexplicably failed?'

'No, sir. Its shields were inoperable while the beam was employed, but it suffered zero hits during that period.'

'Then what or who the fuck was protecting it? This is getting weirder all the time,' he said, standing up and pacing slowly back and forth. 'Based on the evidence so far it almost certainly wasn't a Klatt-sponsored operation; the majority of their fleet had been decimated. Their remaining handful of vessels were spread around the galaxy and to be honest, they're not that smart. The most likely culprit is that bloody Flast woman. We know she had access to that ship the last time we saw it. In fact, Edward Virr is in another galaxy searching for her now along with that Klatt ship and the missing *28*.'

'Sir,' said a new voice from the far side of the room.

Bache turned towards the voice and tilted his head to one side.

'Sir, we've just had a drone jump in system from the *7* out at the galactic gate.'

'And?'

'It's from Captain Trikalon, sir,' the officer said, turning to read something on his screen. 'He has a message from Edward Virr.'

'Talk of the devil… Play it,' ordered Bache, pointing up at the holomap.

Everyone turned as an image of the *7*'s bridge filled the space. It was grainy but Bache recognised his old first officer staring down at them.

'This is a message for Commander Loftt from Edward Virr,' he said. 'Captain Virr has just returned through the gate in a marine gunship registered to the *28*. He has requested a meeting with Commander Loftt at this location as soon as possible.'

The co-ordinates of an empty system a few thousand light years away flashed up on a secondary hologram underneath Trikalon.

'Although, I believe you might want to listen to the transcript of our conversation first,' Trikalon continued, giving the impression he was concerned with something said in the exchange.

Bache listened to Ed's voice instructing Trikalon to send the drone and when it came to the part about Andy's favourite beer being cold lager, he pursed his lips.

'Virr is under duress,' he said. 'There is subterfuge at play.'

'How d'you know that?' Milne asked, speaking for the first time in a while. 'I heard nothing in that conversation that aroused any suspicion.'

'Andrew Faux hates cold lager.'

'What is that?' Milne asked.

'A type of Earth beer.'

'And from just that, you know this is a trick?'

'Oh, yes,' said Bache, confidently. 'Ed was being scripted, probably with a gun to his head. That last bit wasn't and it was intended for me.'

He turned and raised his voice to make himself heard around the whole room.

'Where is the nearest *Katadromiko*?' he asked, surveying the sea of expectant faces staring back at him.

'*K21*,' said a voice from right in front. 'Be here in six hours, sir.'

'Who's the captain on that ship?' he asked.

'Captain Mye,' said the same voice.

Bache felt his heart miss a beat at the mention of the name, followed by a little trepidation. 'I need to be on it and away to that location the minute it arrives,' he said.

'Impossible,' said Milne. 'We need you here…I need you here and we need that ship and its resources to aid in the disaster relief here.'

'Absolutely not,' said Bache, getting a few raised eyebrows around the room for talking so impertinently to the new president of the GDA. 'Madam President, with all respect,' Bache continued, 'I believe the answer to what is going on here is on that gunship.'

'You could delegate someone else,' she said.

'I was specifically requested to go there,' said Bache, looking up at the location still hanging above them. 'And I think I know why.'

30

GDA marine gunship, rendezvous location, Milky Way

ED HAD BEEN BROUGHT up to the cockpit again, much to Andy's chagrin. You could still hear him swearing halfway across the ship. Salft was stood in the corner and nodded at the co-pilot's seat again.

Ed sat and exhaled noisily.

'What is it this time?' he asked, impatiently.

'I want you to talk to your friend.'

'Which one?'

'Loftt.'

'He came?'

'Of course he came…you asked him to.'

'I might be a friend, but he's a retired senior GDA commander with probably better things to do.'

'You underestimate yourself,' she said, with a wry grin. 'I

want you to glance over at this monitor here,' she added, pointing to a screen on the wall next to her.

An image of the inside of the port airlock appeared. Someone was tossed inside and the inner door closed, trapping them in. Ed looked on in horror as he realised it was Andy. His frightened face glanced up at the camera and mouthed something. There was no sound, but Ed could lip read some of the swear words.

'A little extra incentive for when you chat to Loftt,' she said. 'Any warnings and I hit this icon here.'

Her hand hovered over the flashing outer airlock control.

'You won't need to do that,' said Ed, making sure he got eye contact with her.

'Large vessel…the *Katadromiko 21* just jumped into the neighbouring system, ma'am,' interrupted the pilot.

'Tell him you want to meet privately in a hangar of his choice,' she ordered, nodding at the pilot to open a channel.

'This is Edward Virr calling *Katadromiko 21*, do you copy?' he said, in as friendly a voice as he could muster in the circumstances.

'Greetings, Captain Virr,' said an unfamiliar voice. 'This is Captain Mye, we'll be with you in a few minutes.'

Bache couldn't help but notice a look of shock on Salft's face at the mention of the *Katadromiko* captain's name.

'Hello, Captain Mye,' he said, wondering what had troubled Salft. 'Could I have access to a hangar for my meeting with Bache?'

'Commander Loftt will meet you in hangar 37, rendezvous in nine minutes, Mye out.'

As soon as the communication was severed, a cacophony of sirens sounded around the cockpit, quickly silenced as all power was suddenly lost and the ship went very dark and silent. Ed looked up and out of the front screen as all the visible stars vanished.

'What the fuck?' shouted Salft. 'What did you do?' she screamed at Ed, stabbing at the now dead airlock control. 'You bastard, you warned them somehow.'

Salft promptly disappeared and Ed realised she'd been a holographic image all along. Without warning, bright white light from outside the gunship illuminated the cockpit as the small vessel was dragged inside the *Katadromiko* by a powerful tractor beam.

The two Klatt soldiers stood by the door looked at each other and then at Ed.

'I'd surrender if I were you,' he said. 'There'll be a dozen armoured marines coming up those stairs in a moment and their rifles won't be dead.'

They both glanced down at their weapons and without another word, placed them on the floor at their feet. The pilot sighed and dropped his hands into his lap.

'The bitch abandoned us,' he sneered. 'So much for retiring rich then.'

'Where is she?' Ed asked.

'On the other gunship,' the pilot mumbled.

'Oh shit, there's two of them?' Ed blurted.

Now he was free to use his DOVI, he called the *Katadromiko*'s bridge and let Captain Mye know.

'She's gone,' Mye answered. 'We detected a faint embedded jump signature from just outside this system's space.'

'Ah fuck…she's got away again,' Ed muttered under his breath.

'Is that you swearing up there, Edward?' said a familiar voice from the stairwell.

Ed smirked and spun the chair around to see Bache's grimacing face appear around the door bulkhead.

'Ah, there you are,' he said, stepping inside and frowning at the two Klatt soldiers with their hands behind their heads. 'Oh, dear,' he added. 'Your friends don't look very happy. Much like the ones sitting downstairs with a nuclear warhead in a box.'

'She had a nuke?' Ed said, a look of shock on his face.

'Yeah…looks like one from the *28*'s inventory. It was in a wheeled box… They were told to push it down the rear ramp when we let you land in the hangar and then jump away before it went bang.'

They looked at the pilot, who was nodding slowly.

'Only thing was…it had a motion detector on one of the wheels,' he said. 'It would've gone bang as soon as it was moved.'

'That lying bitch,' growled the pilot.

Ed shrugged.

'You're certainly learning about her the hard way, aren't you?' he said, raising his eyebrows at Bache, who rolled his eyes in return.

A stream of expletives from down the stairs caused them to grin at each other.

'I take it your guys have just released Andrew?' chuckled Ed. 'He's not a happy bunny.'

'Being chained to a shelving rack for three days would've strained my sense of humour too,' said Bache. 'And can I say the lager comment was a stroke of genius.'

'It was all I could think of at the time,' said Ed, puffing out his cheeks.

'What was?' said Andy, grumpily as he entered.

'Your love of lager,' said Ed, standing to give his friend a hug.

'Yeah…fucking fizzy piss…what the hell was all that about anyway?'

'Is everything okay over there, Commander Loftt?' a familiar voice asked.

Bache smiled, walked to the co-pilot's console and touched the transmit icon.

'All secure, Captain Trikalon,' Bache answered. 'You can depart back to the gateway in your own time and thank you for following and providing backup.'

'You're welcome, returning to station, *Katadromiko 7* out.'

The cockpit was quickly full of marines tasked with escorting the pilot and the Klatt soldiers away to cells in the detention centre. The nuke, now made safe, was secured in one of the ammunition bunkers aboard the *21*.

Ed, Andy and Bache made their way the short distance to the bridge, where a slightly miffed Captain Mye awaited them.

'You brought a bloody live nuke aboard my ship,' she growled as soon as they entered, staring at Ed.

Bache held his hands up in a placating manner.

'To be fair, Captain, they didn't know about the weapon and the EMP beam had disarmed it anyway.'

'That bitch is as twisted as her bloody husband was,' said Mye, glowering.

Ed remembered something about his last minutes with Salft.

'Did Salft know you or something?' he asked. 'I saw a look of shock on her face when you introduced yourself.'

Mye glanced at Bache fleetingly, before turning her attention back to Ed.

'He obviously hasn't told you,' she said, nodding at Bache and sitting back down on the captain's chair. 'It was me that killed her husband…my grandfather.'

'You're her granddaughter?' exclaimed Ed, turning to meet Bache's gaze.

'Fucking hell,' blurted Andy. 'Remind me not to piss you off.'

'Hence the look of shock,' said Bache. 'She'd set this up to get revenge on me and in that moment, realised she would be killing her own granddaughter too.'

Mye nodded and shrugged.

'Probably couldn't believe her luck…are we going after her?' she asked, turning her attention to Bache again.

'We need to get back to the Medusa galaxy,' said Andy. 'Make sure Phil and the girls are okay and reclaim the *28*.'

Bache rubbed his chin thoughtfully.

'I promised the new president I'd bring the *K21* straight back to aid in the Dasos disaster relief,' he said. 'I kinda have to with my new promotion.'

'What disaster?' asked Ed.

'What promotion?' asked Andy.

31

The Starship Gabriel, *close to Yiss, unknown system*

LINDA RUSHED DOWN to the medical suite in the middle of the night period, after Cleo woke her to say that Rayl was waking up in the autonurse. She arrived barefoot and wrapped in a bathrobe to find Rayl sitting up and scowling at Phil.

'Where's that stupid husband of mine?' she moaned, swivelling her head to glare at Linda as she approached. 'Don't tell me…he's in the pub?'

Phil and Linda's eyes met briefly.

'He escaped the *28* with Ed and probably Salft in a gunship before it exploded,' Linda answered.

'Oh…right…are my parents here? I want to go home now.'

Phil tapped away on the autonurse for a few seconds. Rayl looked at the two of them with a confused expression for a moment before sinking back down and closing her eyes.

'I feel so tired,' she whispered, before her mouth dropped open and she snored lightly.

'Concussion,' said Phil. 'She did have a serious knock on the head.'

'Just as well Andy's not here then,' said Linda. 'He'd be freaking out.'

'Hmm,' grunted Phil. 'The autonurse has sedated her and as with any brain injury it can only do so much. Time and rest are the best solution at the moment.'

'I'm concerned about her asking for her parents when they're both long dead, though,' said Linda, pushing some of Rayl's hair off her face and stroking her forehead gently.

'Memory hiccups is a symptom,' Phil admitted, placing his hand on Linda's shoulder. 'We have a decision to make,' he said. 'Do we stay here a while and help the locals sort out the mess below? Or pursue Ed and Andy?'

'How's it looking on the surface?' Linda asked, squeezing Phil's hand and making for the door.

'The front section of the *28* luckily went down in a remote uninhabited area, but the massive impact still pushed a vast quantity of dust and crap into the atmosphere that'll take a decade or two to normalise. It will certainly drop the average temperature by a few degrees, but that's something the remaining population can probably cope with, judging by their level of technology. It's the rear section that went down in the ocean that concerns me more.'

'Did the tsunami make landfall?' Linda asked, as she walked.

'About two hours ago, all along the western side of the main landmass.'

'How big was it?'

'Around twenty-two metres.'

'Oh shit…is it bad?'

'Went inland up to nine kilometres in places. The smaller communities were wiped clean and five larger cities were overwhelmed and are severely compromised. It's receding now but to be honest, there's not much we could do to help them with this ship anyway.'

'The gunship jumped away back towards the galactic gate,' said Linda, as they arrived on the bridge and slid into their couches. 'Perhaps the best thing is to pursue the boys and let the GDA know there's a humanoid planet that needs assistance here. They're much more geared up to help in a situation like this.'

'We still need to find a solution to help our friend in the hangar and her colleagues,' said Phil.

'A solution…that's funny,' said Cleo, appearing on one of the empty seats, dressed for some reason as a Viking warrior. 'Well, are we staying or going? I need to plan my wardrobe.'

Linda glanced over at Phil and raised her eyebrows.

'It's your final decision,' Phil said, placing his hands in his lap, and staring back expectantly. 'Of course, Salft has left a trail for us to follow. She's only kept the boys as a bargaining tool to get her hands on this ship.'

'We'd better not disappoint her then,' said Linda, nodding at them both.

'Disappoint who?' asked Pol, stepping onto the bridge and yawning.

'She who cannot be named,' said Cleo.

'Ah, the psycho bitch from hell,' said Pol, still blinking the sleep from her eyes. 'Am I allowed to shoot her?'

'Indeed,' said Phil. 'Even I probably could as I don't consider her a human being.'

'We need to organise transport and a new home for Oona

and the surviving Vriix too,' said Pol. 'I know what it's like not having a home to go back to.'

'I concur with that,' coloured a voice from the hangar.

'Don't worry, Oona. We haven't forgotten you,' said Linda. 'I'm sure the GDA will have somewhere for you guys to call home.'

'It would be a dream for us to be in an ocean again after all this time and rebuild our society in a safe environment,' she added.

'Well, I think the decision's made then,' said Phil, glancing around at the other three. 'Home it is.'

'Take us back to the gateway, Cleopatra,' said Linda, pointing at her. 'And don't spare the diesel.'

'Plotted and on our way,' she said, as the lighting dimmed slightly, signalling the first jump, and the journey home had begun.

32

Near the Ecuadorian border, Amazonas department,
Colombia, Earth

NEFERUPTAH THE SEVENTEEN had been enjoying herself since she had arrived on the planet known locally as Earth. She was spending her time rectifying some of the mistakes made by this young, naive, but fascinating humanoid race that one of her colleagues had most likely spawned many thousands of years ago.

She materialised herself in a corridor of a large mansion in the Amazonas department on the southern border of Colombia. She had taken on the appearance of a nineteen-year-old girl, six foot one, with legs that went on forever and long straight black hair. She'd discovered this was one of the best ways to get attention and intimidate males on this planet. Quite why this civilisation had evolved with the male of the species controlling almost everything was beyond her. Especially the whiter skinned variety. They seemed to believe they were a cut above the rest, but in reality the majority she'd come across, especially in senior positions, were in fact extremely stupid and selfish.

She was wearing a pencil-thin navy blue dress that perfectly accentuated her legs and curves. The colour-coordinated stilettos made her even taller and generally freaked the males of this planet out, although, she found them ridiculously uncomfortable and couldn't quite understand why the females chose to wear them at all.

The door she wanted was unlocked, but she already knew that. She also knew there were four males inside. The first was Benedicto Macaria, the undisputed king of the Colombian drug cartels. He sat behind a huge wooden desk, cluttered with local carvings and photos of his family. Behind him was a pair of huge arched leaded glass doors. They were open and led out onto a fourth-floor balustraded balcony, some thirty metres above a stone courtyard below.

The second male sitting opposite Macaria was Tommaso Valtti, eldest son and heir to the Sicilian Valtti family's organised crime empire. His aging father now too old to travel had sent him in his place to strike a new deal to replace the European imports previously handled by the late Gastotti family. Quite how the entire Gastotti family of twenty-three had managed to die in a fire at their Tuscan villa had never been answered. The ensuing enquiry by the Italian authorities had been short and not particularly thorough.

The last two males, standing a couple of metres either side of Macaria, were his personal armed bodyguards, conciliating to Benedicto's acute paranoia of impending doom.

All four turned as she entered the room. The two bodyguards instantly revealed large handguns and pointed them at her.

She smiled and closed the door behind her.

'Who the fuck are you?' snapped Macaria, looking quite taken aback that a complete stranger was able to enter his private office, seemingly unchallenged by his small army of security personnel.

'I'm Neferuptah,' she said, still beaming. 'The Seventeen.'

Macaria must have had a panic button, as the sound of running feet out in the corridor reached them. The two bodyguards circled the massive desk and approached her from the front as the sound of the door handle rattled behind her. Macaria looked confused for a moment as the rattling of the door handle quickly ceased, becoming banging and shouting instead.

'What the fuck did you do to that door?' he asked.

Neferuptah glanced over her shoulder and shrugged, as the two bodyguards reached her and both pointed their weapons at her head.

'I melted the lock mechanism,' she said.

Valtti burst out laughing and looked back at Macaria.

'We own a lock factory in Milan,' he said, still chuckling. 'We might have a little side business there too.'

Macaria ignored him.

'Get her out of here,' he thundered. 'And keep her alive. I want her before she's fed to the pigs.'

The two bodyguards went to move forward and grunted, dropped their outstretched arms and both their handguns clunked onto the floor. They remained rooted to the spot no matter what they tried.

'What are you doing?' Macaria bellowed at them. 'What are you waiting for?'

He went to stand up, but felt an unseen force push him solidly back into his chair.

'What the fuck?' he whispered, finding it difficult to talk.

'Let me explain,' said Neferuptah, bypassing the body-guards and sitting on the edge of the desk. 'You're going to die today and the illegal fortune of currency you've amassed is going to feed millions of starving humans on this planet.'

The banging from outside the room irked her. She waved a finger and it stopped. Complete silence ensued.

'What gives you the right?' Macaria forced out, his malevolent eyes never leaving her.

'What gave you the right to think you could rape me and feed me to the pigs?' she answered. 'I believe that was your intention.'

'What are you?' he spat, shaking with the effort.

'One of the Ancient creators, little human,' she said. 'I think you know us as God on this planet. Quite why you refer to us in the singular, I have no idea.'

Macaria's eyes flicked to Valtti.

'What about him?' he grizzled.

Valtti's eyes hardened, as he too had found himself held by an unbreakable force.

'Ah, yes…the Valttis, I'm quite looking forward to a trip to Sicily,' she said, looking over Macaria's shoulder and out the open double doors. 'Lovely view…it's a shame this house has to burn down, it's actually rather pretty.'

Flames suddenly sprang up around them, quickly igniting the surrounding soft furnishings. Macaria began making child-like keening noises and shaking with effort, trying desperately to get away from the spreading fire. Valtti sat still and just glared at her.

'You have no idea, lady,' he snarled. 'They will find you and it will take days for you to die.'

Valtti's eyes almost bugged out of his head and his mouth dropped open as Neferuptah morphed into an exact copy of him. She reached forward, wrenched his wedding ring off his finger and slipped his wallet out from the inside of his jacket.

'I don't think so, do you?' she said, using Valtti's voice. 'Disposing of your family will be easy and for the sake of this particular human race, quite necessary.'

'You're Lucifer himself,' he hissed.

'No,' she said, changing back into herself and grinning. 'I believe that award goes to men like you…'

She stopped abruptly and suddenly stared out of the window. A tell-tale tickle out on the edge of the system caught her attention and anticipation washed over her.

'Hmmm,' she grunted, as if tasting something delicious. 'I have to go…I believe an old friend is coming to visit.'

She disappeared and as the mansion was completely engulfed in flames, dozens of muffled screams from within went unanswered and unaided.

33

The bridge, Katadromiko 21, *Medusa Merger Galaxy*

CAPTAIN MYE WATCHED as the huge vessel winked into existence within the familiar three moons above the barren unnamed planet in the Medusa Merger Galaxy. Admiral Loftt had agreed to take a fleet of the *K21*'s smaller ships back to Dasos to aid in the relief. Leaving the *Katadromiko* free to take Ed and Andy back to find the *Gabriel*, recover the *28* and bring the surviving Vrixx back to the Milky Way to restart their society.

'You've been given the co-ordinates of Yiss,' she said, looking over at the navigator. 'Take us there as quickly as possible.'

The navigation officer nodded.

'Estimated travel time of forty-nine hours, Captain,' he said, locking in the first jump and giving the pilot the green light.

'Where are our two guests?' Mye asked.

'Grissom Café on level 216, Captain,' came a voice from the back row of bridge crew.

'Okay, call me if you need me,' said Mye, striding towards the main bridge doors.

She took the train across the ship and down to level 216, walking towards the café while admiring the view down the atrium. The many Hygrenthis trees were in full bloom, with their bright scarlet flowers and pungent citrus scent pervading the huge void. She smiled as she noticed a group of children running and playing in the shallow stream meandering down the nine-kilometre length of the atrium. It never ceased to amaze her just how big the vessel actually was and how sobering it could be knowing how many souls she was responsible for. Her smile slipped a little and she chastised herself for allowing the occasional niggling doubt in her own abilities to raise its ugly head.

The café wasn't busy and she could see Virr and Faux sitting alone in a semi-circular blue fake leather booth against the back wall. They both grinned as she approached.

'Care to join us, Captain?' Andy asked. 'It's his round,' he added, pointing at Ed.

'What are you drinking?' she asked, stooping down to join them in the booth and glancing at their drinks.

'It's beer from Regg'taa,' said Ed.

'Kinda got the taste for it on Krix'ir a few years ago,' said Andy.

'It came in handy!' said Ed, with a smirk.

'Shut up, you,' griped Andy, glancing at the slightly lighter colour of his right hand. 'You can't palm me off with that lame joke.'

'Boom-tish,' added Ed, as Mye looked on with a bewildered expression.

'Sorry, Captain…private joke,' Andy said, looking contrite.

'Hmm,' she grunted. 'Bache did warn me about your warped senses of humour.'

'Did he?' said Ed. 'His is certainly getting weirder as time goes on.'

'I noticed,' she said, tilting her head to one side. 'I've got you to thank for that, have I?'

'Only a little iddy widdy bit,' said Andy.

She shook her head and glanced towards the door.

'The kids out there in the water are more mature than you two.'

'You're welcome,' said Andy.

A waitress arrived and she ordered Dasonian tea and judging by his expression, it was not to Andy's taste.

'This planet, Yiss,' Mye said, changing the subject. 'Do I understand you find it remarkably similar to your home planet?'

Ed and Andy both cringed a little and exchanged a shrug.

'I know it sounds an impossibility,' said Ed. 'But, in the short time we were there it was a bit déjà vu.'

Mye's brow furrowed.

'What he means is, it felt like an exact copy,' explained Andy. 'The architecture, the multicultural society, the vehicles and the most ridiculous thing of all, they spoke English.'

'I mean, how the hell can that happen in another galaxy over a hundred million light years away?' said Ed, holding his hands out wide.

'The Ancients have a lot to answer for,' said Mye, leaning back as her tea was delivered.

'Maybe,' said Ed. 'But, I do have a weird feeling we're missing something. It's just too similar, like England the sequel.'

'When we get there, we need to find Callon,' said Andy. 'She'll be able to tell us more and anyway, we need to get her into an autonurse as soon as we can like we promised.'

'That's assuming we can get aboard the *28*,' said Ed. 'We don't yet know if it's still at Yiss, or for definite why Salft abandoned it.'

'You mentioned to Bache that you heard a lot of weapon discharges just before you were hurried onto the gunship?' said Mye.

Ed nodded.

'Yes, it all started when we were very quickly moved up near the bridge,' said Andy. 'We noticed our guards were suddenly no longer Klatt, but members of her personal security force, who seemed nervous and had their weapons up at all times.'

'The Klatt contingent must have had enough of her and mutinied,' said Mye. 'She must have had the gunships parked in the captain's hangar and ready to fly at a moment's notice as a precaution.'

'She certainly wouldn't have survived this long without making sure she had a back door exit ready to go,' said Ed. 'But…I'm surprised she left a bunch of pissed off Klatt with a fully operational *Katadromiko* though.'

'Hmm…that is a sobering thought,' said Mye, blowing on her tea. 'We need to be wary if it's still there. She might have left it booby trapped.'

'The Klatt have had plenty of time to sort that out if she did,' said Andy.

'Yeah,' said Ed, tilting his head to one side. 'But remember, the Klatt are not the sharpest tools in the shed.'

'True,' said Andy, nodding. 'Their IQ barely reaches room temperature.'

Mye spluttered taking a sip of tea, followed by a fit of coughing as it went down the wrong way.

'Don't make me laugh like that,' she said, after recovering her composure and mopping her mouth with a napkin. 'My crew are watching.'

***

Almost two days later, they made the last jump behind the star in the Yiss system, as it was now known. Captain Mye had called Ed and Andy up to the bridge and they all stood staring up at the huge holomap as it updated. The cruiser cloaked and emerged from the shadow of the star.

There was a sea of disappointed faces around the room as it became apparent there was no ship in orbit around Yiss.

'Cloaked?' Andy asked, turning to face Mye.

The Captain glanced over at her group of array officers seated to her right.

'No evidence of a cloaked vessel, ma'am,' came the reply.

'I'm getting debris and explosive residue emanating outwards from the planet, ma'am,' said another operator, raising his hand.

'Oh, shit,' said Andy. 'She didn't ignite the core did she?'

'No,' said Mye, reading information flashing up on her personal screen. 'One side of the planet would've been decimated if that was the case.'

She turned back to the array team.

'Was it multiple detonations as in a space battle, or just the one?' she asked.

'The evidence suggests it was just the one, Captain. But quite a big one.'

'How long ago was the detonation?'

'Reading the distance the furthest debris has travelled, I would estimate around thirteen days, ma'am.'

'That's almost exactly how long since we left,' said Ed. 'Put out a call for the *Gabriel*, the girls might still be around.'

'The debris field make-up is consistent with a GDA vessel, Captain,' said a third operator.

'Shit,' mumbled Andy. 'I hope the *Gabriel* wasn't too close.'

Ed gave him a look out of the corner of his eye.

'Cleo has the reactions of a gazelle,' he said. 'There's absolutely no evidence of any Theo-based debris I take it?' he added hopefully, turning to face the array team.

'You're correct in that assumption, sir,' one of them said.

Andy breathed out noisily, having been holding his breath.

'Perhaps they've gone looking for us and we've passed them on the way here,' said Ed.

The Captain asked for a wide band communication channel to be opened.

'Starship *Gabriel*, this is Captain Mye of the *Katadromiko 21*, are you receiving me?' she broadcast throughout the system.

No reply was forthcoming.

'Starship *Gabriel*, I have Edward Virr and Andrew Faux on board. They would very much like to converse with you.'

Again, no reply came.

'Take us into a high orbit around Yiss, please,' Mye instructed the pilot.

'Yes, ma'am.'

'Array team, scan that planet within an inch of its life. I want to find that ship.'

'Do you think they might've tried to land it?' Andy asked.

Mye read something on her screen before answering.

'Judging by the amount and make-up of the debris field, I'll wager the central atrium was compromised,' she said, solemnly.

'Holy crap,' said Andy, turning to face Ed. 'That would've been catastrophic…a decompression that vast could blow the ship in two.'

Mye looked at the array team again.

'We're looking for a possible crash site,' she said. 'Maybe two,' she added, giving Andy a worried glance.

'Found one, Captain,' a nervous voice called.

'Inhabited area?' she asked.

'No, ma'am…quite remote. But the impact has pushed up a lot of dust that will most likely affect the planet's average temperature for some time.'

'I have tsunami damage along the western edge of a major landmass, Captain,' said a second officer.

'Any cities along that coast?'

'Several, ma'am. One of which is the capital.'

'I'm getting a load of small vessel readings on the surface, ma'am,' said the first officer. 'Most likely landed lifeboats.'

'I hope Callon was in one of those,' said Andy.

'So do I,' said Ed, puffing out his cheeks. 'So do I.'

34

The Oval Office, White House, Washington, Earth

PRESIDENT ALASTAIR JAMES thanked his Chief of Staff as he left with a nod, leaving him alone in the Oval Office with his thoughts. He glanced around as he sat behind his desk in the big leather chair and sighed. His eight-year tenure as the fifty-first president of the United States of America would come to an end in a few days. The new President Elect, James Rucker, had surprised everyone by becoming the Governor of New Hampshire only twelve months ago and then throwing his hat into the presidential race only at the last minute.

Not only had he shocked the political world by making the last two candidates, he then went on to surprise the entire planet by taking sixty-seven percent of the national vote in the biggest election turnout in American history.

Alastair liked him too; not only was he ex-NASA, he was the ex-commander of Armstrong Station and had aided Jim

Dewey when he first became the Earth Ambassador to the GDA. It was a running joke now with the media, that if you didn't have James somewhere in your name, you might as well not turn up.

He looked up at the picture on the wall of Armstrong Station with the USA clearly visible below. It had been there since his first day in office and he reminded himself to delegate one of the staffers to take it down before he left. It would look just fine on his study wall in Maine. He puffed out his cheeks and glanced down at the stack of files his Chief of Staff had brought in for him to read and sign.

'Not long to go now,' he said to himself, opening the first and pushing the others to one side.

'You're right,' said a strange voice from within the office, making him jump; he hadn't heard anyone come in. 'You haven't got long at all,' the voice continued.

A stranger stood up from behind one of the high back leather chairs facing the fireplace and turned to face him.

'Who the hell are you?' President James asked. 'And how on Earth did you get in here?'

'Magic,' said the stranger, although James did find him vaguely familiar.

'Do I know you?' he asked, pressing the hidden panic button under his desk.

'Yes, you do,' the stranger answered. 'And it's pointless pressing that little red button. I disconnected it.'

James tried to stand, but found himself held in the seated position by some unseen force.

'Don't want you wandering off now do we?' said the stranger as he disappeared from the fireplace and reappeared sitting on the corner of the President's desk.

'Fuck,' blurted James, as he recoiled at the shock of the

stranger materialising right in his face. 'You're a hologram,' he added, once he'd regained his composure. 'How can that be? There are no holographic projectors permitted within this building.'

'Ah, well, you see, I'm not actually a hologram,' said the stranger, a baleful grin washing across his face.

'Wait a minute!' exclaimed James, squinting at the disrespectful man sitting on his desk. 'You're Lake…Xavier Lake. Aren't you supposed to be dead?'

Lake nodded and pulled an enigmatic expression.

'Rumours of my demise were grossly exaggerated,' he replied, swinging his legs under the desk like a petulant schoolboy. 'In truth, I became the most powerful Earth human in the universe.'

'I see,' said James. 'And I imagine, considering your past record, you're not going to use these newfound abilities for anything beneficial to the human race?'

'Ah, now, that's where you're wrong,' said Lake. 'I'm absolutely no threat to Earth or indeed the human race. I'm only a threat to those who wronged me in the past.'

'And you consider me to be one of them?'

'Well, now you come to mention it, I do seem to recall a missile being fired at me from one of your stealthy spacecraft. I'm sure that order must have come direct from this office… am I right?'

James remained silent.

'I thought so,' said Lake, tilting his head to one side and raising his eyebrows. 'It's kinda something you don't quickly forget, or forgive, when someone tries to murder you.'

'So, you're here to kill me are you?' James asked.

'Ah…you didn't get this job by being stupid, did you?'

'You were guilty of more than one murder, multiple

counts of industrial espionage and God only knows what else that we didn't know about. If you'd been in this office, you would've made the same decision.'

'Possibly…but I wasn't and you were,' Lake snapped. 'I don't know about you, but where I come from, when someone tries to murder you…you feel a little indignant and it tends to work out better if you get them before they finally succeed.'

'You think I'm still trying to have you killed?' said James. 'Up to a moment ago, I thought you were already dead and you were away scot-free.'

James stared at Lake for a moment.

'You were in a galaxy hundreds of light years away, with it seems powers that most can just dream about. You could've done anything, gone to any number of a million worlds…but you chose to come all the way back here just to kill me. That's bullshit. I think you miss this place…you were homesick, weren't you?'

Lake grinned, but James likened it more to a wolf baring its teeth.

'I think this conversation is coming to a conclusion,' Lake sneered, balling his hands into fists.

'Oh dear,' said James. 'Hit a nail on the head did I?'

'Any last requests?'

'If you're expecting me to beg for my life, you're going to be disappoi—'

James stopped suddenly as he found he couldn't breathe. The force holding him down in his seat lifted him up, smacking his knees painfully on the edge of the desk. He hung there in mid-air, his lungs burning with the need to breathe, when he noticed there was someone else in the room, a female, standing behind Lake.

Lake saw James's eyes staring over his shoulder and as he began to turn his head, a voice spoke and Lake's expression dropped.

'Put the man down, Xavier,' the girl said.

James fell the eight feet back onto his chair with a crash and frantically sucked in air as he found he could finally breathe again. He winced with a pain in his shoulder as he sat up, rubbing his bruised knees and peering over the edge of his desk.

Lake went as white as a sheet as he faced the newcomer. The President had no idea who she was, but he silently thanked her for saving his life. She was a stunning-looking woman, quite young, wearing white robes with gold trim and a black and gold headdress. She stood bolt upright with her arms folded across her chest, glaring menacingly at Lake.

'Neferuptah, dearest,' he said, unable to disguise the anxious tone in his voice. 'How delightful to see you again.'

'Don't you dearest me,' she spat. 'You lying, cheating, murdering piece of excrement.'

'You know him well,' muttered James, his face peering up from behind the desk.

She ignored the comment and slapped Lake hard across the face. The crack of the strike made James jump and jarred his shoulder, sending waves of pain through his arm and chest.

Lake was hit so hard he flew sideways, toppled off the other side of the desk and landed in a heap in the middle of the President's seal woven into the carpet.

'You disappeared,' Lake bleated. 'I thought you'd just moved on.'

She shook her head slowly.

'I'm one of the original twelve, Xavier,' she said,

sounding irritated. 'There are certain powers we have that I didn't pass on to you and one of those is the ability to know when someone is lying.'

'But you're here and you're fine,' he said, trying to stand but seemingly unable. 'I was just disposing of that bastard, Virr.'

Neferuptah laughed, rolling her eyes at James.

'I've done a bit of research since I've been here and to use an Earth term, "waiting for your sorry arse to turn up,"' she said, the smile vanishing. 'It seems you lied about just about everything. You, it seems, had broken out of a human jail using a secretly built starship, and as for you convincing me that Edward Virr was responsible for the deaths of two of my colleagues, that turns out to be a complete work of fiction. This planet hadn't even left their own solar system when they were killed, let alone having galactic travel. It seems Virr aided in the hunt for the Moguls, who apparently are the real killers, and is considered a bit of a hero round here. Quite the opposite to you...dearest.'

She spat the last word and glanced over at James.

'I must apologise for my lack of judgement, Mr President,' she said, her voice softening. 'Even gods, as you like to call us, make the odd error. Giving this human godlike powers was the biggest mistake of my existence.'

'You'll get no argument from me,' said James, grimacing and struggling up back into his leather chair.

Lake suddenly let out a roar of effort, as if he was lifting a heavy weight. He struggled up into a stooped standing position, bared his teeth at both of them, and disappeared.

'Dammit!' exclaimed Neferuptah, staggering back slightly. 'Bastard's been working out.'

'He hasn't escaped has he?' James asked.

Neferuptah furrowed her brow and promptly vanished too.

James retried the emergency button. This time four members of the Presidential Protection Division burst in through two doors with guns drawn. Once they'd cleared the room and surrounded the President, James spoke softly.

'Someone summon my doctor, I think I've broken something.'

35

The bridge, starship Gabriel, *the Prasinos system, Milky Way*

'HOLY MOLY!' exclaimed Phil, as he jumped the *Gabriel* into the Prasinos system.

It'd taken a few days for them to reach the home system of the GDA back in the Milky Way. They'd thought it strange there wasn't a *Katadromiko* guarding the gateway as they went through. Now they found out why, as the holomap updated above them.

They had conformed to the warnings by jumping into the system a much greater distance from Dasos than usual, in temporarily set up jump zones on the outer edge.

'Ah, crap,' said Linda. 'Look at all that shit flying around. How are we going to find a way through all that?'

'Dasos is completely covered in clouds and storms,' said Pol, zooming in on the home of the GDA. 'It's bloody cold and windy down there.'

'You'd think they'd have more ships cleaning up all this debris,' said Phil.

'I think the debris are the ships,' said Pol. 'Judging by my readings it's all bits of navy and domestic vessels.'

'What the hell happened here?' asked Linda. 'To do this amount of damage would've taken a sizeable enemy fleet and where are those bloody huge defence platforms that surrounded the planet?'

'Destroyed too,' said Pol. 'There's lumps of them everywhere.'

They watched for a while as the few dozen naval ships returning from around the galaxy had been hastily assembled into some sort of defensive screen around their capital planet. Between them they'd managed to staunch the flow of all but the smallest flotsam from dropping into Dasos's gravity well.

'The damage on the surface is extensive,' said Pol. 'The massive change in climate must be down to that Klatt octaship thing they were going to use on Paradeisos. Perhaps we need to find that and destroy it.'

'No need,' said Linda, studying her screen. 'It destroyed itself, it says here. After utilising its beam on Dasos, all the shrapnel cut it to pieces.'

'They didn't think that one through did they?' said Phil, shaking his head slowly.

Linda put a call out for Commander Loftt. It only took him ten minutes to reply.

'It's Admiral of the Fleet Loftt now,' came a tired but familiar voice. 'Are Ed and Andy aboard?'

'I was kinda hoping they were with you,' Linda replied in a disappointed tone.

'They went back to the Medusa galaxy to find you a few days ago,' he said.

'Oh,' she said. 'We must have passed somewhere on the journey here. Congratulations on the new job by the way. I thought you were retired.'

'All the GDA senior naval officers were lost, along with half the council members in various places.'

'The President?' Phil asked.

'Lost too,' said Bache. 'Vice President Milne is now the new President.'

'Ah, I think I've met her,' said Linda. 'She has a strange accent from…err…'

'Scolain.'

'That's it,' she said, now recalling the conversation. 'A beautiful but cold planet somewhere distant if I remember right.'

'Indeed, it is,' Bache confirmed.

'If you managed to rescue Ed and Andy, have you got Salft in detention now?' she asked, changing the subject.

Linda noticed the slight delay in the answer to her question.

'No,' came the eventual and gritty reply.

'She's dead?' asked Pol, looking hopeful.

'No…unfortunately not,' said Bache. 'She was in a second gunship that no one knew about.'

'Shit,' mumbled Linda.

'Did she have something to do with this?' Phil asked.

'We have no idea,' said Bache. 'But with her and her late husband's record, it's something we can't rule out. I have, as of yesterday, persuaded the President to sign a termination on sight order for Salft.'

'Oh, joy,' said Linda. 'I certainly won't hesitate the next time.'

'Nor will anyone under my command,' said Bache.

'May we invite the Admiral of the Fleet to dinner later?' Linda asked.

'I thought you'd never ask,' he said, his usual cheerful tone returning. 'I much prefer the menu choice on a Theo ship than the naval emergency ration packs we're having to endure down here.'

'Is the food situation bad?' asked Phil.

'All crops destroyed planetwide,' he said. 'We're having to bring in everything fresh from all the local systems and of course the freighters have to be escorted by a navy ship through all the debris.'

'Do you want us to come down to pick you up?' Linda asked.

'No, you stay right where you are,' he said. 'Don't want to scratch that new ship of yours, Ed would never forgive me. I'll have a destroyer bring me up to you in three hours.'

'We'll be waiting and the wine will be chilled,' Linda answered, with a slight smirk.

At the designated time, the *Gabriel* extended one of its new automated docking tunnels, which the destroyer *Jasslayn* was able to orient onto one of its airlocks. The two vessels bonded together with a field similar to that used to seal in the atmosphere of a hangar.

Bache bounded across, the gold braiding on his new uniform glinting under the bright white light of the tunnel and the *Gabriel*'s airlock. He particularly liked that the artificial gravity field on the *Gabriel* extended out into the tunnel too and negated the need to wear gravity boots for the crossing.

He grinned as the inner airlock opened and Linda met him with a hug.

'Ah...I've missed these,' he said, pulling her in close.

'I take it none of your junior officers hug you very often,' she said, chuckling.

'No,' he replied. 'Everyone's shit-scared of me now.'

'Well, come on in,' she said. 'Cuz you know we're not.'

They all gathered on the top deck of the *Gabriel*, a room known as the blister lounge. As with the previous ship, it was a large circular space set up with a bar, several food replicators and comfortable red leather Chesterfield-style seating. Right in the middle a circle of couches was arranged underneath the huge domed carbon glass ceiling, giving anyone lying on these a panoramic view of the heavens. Cleo was also able to project anything she wanted onto it from any of the exterior cameras or the array in two-dimensional or holographic forms.

This evening they all stared up at an image of Dasos. Not the usual gleaming blue planet everyone was accustomed to, but a grey ball with hundreds of lightning flashes every second circling the entire celestial body. Occasionally, flashes above the planet caught their eye as gunners on naval ships zapped larger lumps of debris that might not burn up in the atmosphere.

'There must be something that can be done,' said Linda. 'Don't you have some of that terraforming technology that can sort this mess out?'

'Unfortunately not for this,' said Bache. 'If it was a barren inhospitable world, yes...if it was affected by radiation, yes. But turning a perpetual winter into a more temperate one, no, we have nothing for that at present. We do have people working on it though.'

'If a beam was able to rearrange your climate to colder one, surely there must be a way to reverse that beam's effect to warm instead?' said Phil.

'That's exactly what they're trying to work out,' said Bache. 'But the ship was destroyed and without being able to study the technology and kinda reverse engineer it, they're having to start from scratch.'

'Won't they have the plans for that ship at the yard it was constructed in?' said Linda. 'We know where that is too.'

Bache rubbed his chin and thought about that for a moment.

'I don't think they'd be very keen to give those up,' he said. 'There are galactic agreements relating to intellectual property and so forth. It would take years of wrangling in the courts to get those plans into our hands and there's always the possibility we don't.'

Linda glanced across at Pol and Phil, and a slight smile crossed her lips.

'But if they accidentally came into our possession for some inexplicable reason…we would be forced to hand them over to the authorities for safe keeping,' she said, tilting her head to one side and turning to Bache with sad eyes. 'And then you'd have to return them to the rightful owners.'

Bache smirked.

'Quite right…we would,' he said, nodding slowly. 'After a day or so. Do you think that's likely?'

'Stranger things have happened,' said Cleo, materialising next to Bache and giving him a wink.

36

Marine landing ship, above Yiss, Medusa Merger Galaxy

ED SAT amongst a troop of marines on one of *Katadromiko 21*'s marine landing vessels. He wrinkled his nose as the strong odour of oil, sweat and farts wafted around the cabin.

Captain Mye had agreed to provide the soldiers and ship to descend down to the surface to see if they could find Callon. They'd made her a promise and they intended to keep it. Andy had decided to remain on the *K21* and oversee the search using the ship's powerful arrays. They weren't sure what sort of reaction they were going to get, hence the troop of marines.

Ed watched though a small porthole on the opposite side of the cramped troop seating area. The orange glow and sparks of atmospheric entry were soon replaced by a dark grey mist flashing past the small window and he knew they were in amongst the ash and dust thrown up by half a

Katadromiko hitting the surface at many times the speed of sound.

He was wearing the same clothes as the last time he visited. Two of the soldiers had been kitted out in similar attire, so they could mingle without drawing too much attention, although the small arsenal of weaponry they carried did make them appear a little overweight.

Ed felt the ship begin its deceleration and the scream of the antigravs increased tenfold. He pulled the ear phones hanging behind him over his head, which dulled the racket considerably.

'Two minutes,' came the call from the cockpit.

The three of them in civilian clothes prepared themselves. The inner airlock door beside them powered away into its housing and Ed readied himself with his hand over the harness release.

They'd chosen to be dropped off two kilometres from what appeared to be a hastily assembled crisis centre inland from one of the major cities. It was also in the vicinity of the densest group of lifeboat landing spots from the front section of the *28*, and if Callon had managed to get in a lifeboat, then this was a good place to start.

Ed grunted as the troop carrier turned sharply and thudded down on solid ground. The outer airlock door motored upwards, he released his harness and quickly followed the two marines through the door.

It was dawn and the noisy ship screamed upwards again, quickly disappearing into the greyness and then heading north up to their standby zone on a nearby deserted mountain top. Ed could just see the glow of lights on the opposite hill through a copse of trees and because of the mission briefing, knew this was their destination.

Even though it was the warm season on this part of the planet, it was shockingly cold with the dust-laden atmosphere blocking the stars' heat. It had been getting gradually cooler for many days now.

He noticed the newest growth of green vegetation around the wooded area they were passing through was drooping and turning brown. Ed knew a considerable percentage of the planet's flora and fauna wouldn't endure the sudden change, leaving the human population who managed to survive the tsunami and extreme cold with problems of starvation.

He secured his coat up to his chin, pulled up his hood and donned a pair of marine issue gloves he'd thankfully grabbed before they left the *K21*. He followed the two marines as they trudged silently through the sagging trees. They were fully aware that any locals they met this time might not be overly welcoming to strangers from above.

Once they reached the road leading to the crisis centre, they joined an almost continuous stream of refugees silently lumbering up the hill. No one seemed to pay them any attention as they slipped into the column of misery. The occasional vehicle passed by. Most were military, but one was a civilian van of some sort, completely packed with people, their faces avoiding eye contact as they crawled slowly by.

'You might want to split up from the other refugees,' said Andy, in Ed's ear, using his DOVI. 'The military are scanning everyone who enters the relief area.'

'What are they scanning for?' asked Ed.

'Not completely sure, but they're removing knives or anything resembling a weapon.'

Ed relayed the information to the marines and they decided to saunter into the trees lining the road one at a time as if to relieve themselves, but not reappear.

Once they were sure they hadn't been followed, the marines upped the pace, took them about two hundred metres away from the road and turned to run parallel with it. Twenty more minutes had them on the periphery of the camp and they circled around the large site to the rear. There was a hastily cleared area all around the site patrolled by the occasional military vehicle. Beyond that was a sea of tents and prefab buildings, some still in the process of construction.

They waited until it was clear, stepped out and began doing stretching exercises as if they were supposed to be there. Gradually manoeuvring themselves closer to the tents, they'd got over halfway before a vehicle bounced its way around the outer track and stopped. The soldier driving the military jeep glared at them.

Ed wandered over with a smile on his face. It had been decided he would do the talking as neither of the marines spoke English. They remained where they were doing sit-ups and star jumps.

'Morning,' said Ed, sounding perhaps a little too cheerful.

The soldier ignored the greeting and demanded to know why they were outside the containment line.

'That's the tree line isn't it?' Ed quizzed.

The soldier rolled his eyes and pointed.

'No, the tent line,' he snapped. 'Get back inside.'

'Okay, sorry,' Ed replied, beckoning to the other two.

'Where's that accent from?' the soldier asked, as Ed turned to leave.

'Vellum-Dar,' he answered, remembering the name of one of the more remote towns.

'Is it fuck,' he said, with suspicion creeping into his voice. 'I have cousins there and they don't speak anything like that.'

He picked up something that looked like a microphone

and went to speak, keeping his eyes firmly on Ed. This turned out to be his big mistake as Ed was unarmed, but one of the marines who'd been listening in to the conversation through his translator wasn't and had idled around to the other side of the jeep. The soldier never got the chance to say anything into the microphone, as he jerked around in his seat, his eyes staring straight ahead in shock. He slumped over the wheel as the stun shot knocked him unconscious, the marine hastily reholstering his weapon and sliding into the vehicle on the opposite side. Ed didn't waste any time. He opened the door on his side, pushed the soldier over into the middle, jumped in and surveyed the controls.

'Can you operate this vehicle?' the marine asked, as his colleague clambered into the back.

'Yeah, I think so,' said Ed, finding the hand brake and letting it off.

'There's a tablet over here,' said the marine in the back. 'But the language isn't Ellinika.'

Ed steered the electric vehicle in between the tents and stopped again.

'Give us it here,' he said. 'It'll be in English.'

Luckily it wasn't password protected and he was able to flick through the menu and find what he was looking for.

'They're keeping anyone from the lifeboats separate,' he said. 'For their own safety. There are lynch mobs looking for anyone to blame and they're not holding back.'

'Where are they containing them?' the marine in the front asked.

'Separate camp east of here.'

'How far?'

'Two kilometres.'

'Can we get there in this?'

'I think so,' said Ed, glancing over at the unconscious body. 'We need to lose him though, the vehicle's too small to hide him.'

'Most of these tents here are still empty and he'll be out for a good two hours.'

'Be quick,' said Ed, checking there was no one around.

Finding an empty tent nearby, Ed parked the jeep with its door right up close to the entrance and they slid the sleeping soldier inside. Ed exchanged jackets and hats with the soldier, so when he was driving the jeep he appeared legitimate.

'Let's go find this camp,' he said, as they bundled back aboard the vehicle and set off around the perimeter.

37

The bridge, starship Gabriel, *the Exoplismoi system,*
Milky Way

'THE SALFT YARD IS THAT ONE,' said Cleo, as one of the dozens of platforms orbiting Sidero began flashing red.

The *Gabriel* had jumped into the Jagnorite system behind the star, was now cloaked and heading at point nine light straight towards the planet of the same name.

'There doesn't seem to be much going on there,' said Pol, bringing a holographic view of the construction platform into focus above them. 'The main doors are open and there's nothing being built in there.'

'I believe the GDA had it shut down and sealed up as a crime scene,' said Linda.

'Correct,' said Cleo. 'They left a skeleton crew on board to keep the giant platform in its designated orbit and to protect its assets from poachers.'

'What, like us you mean?' quipped Linda, raising her eyebrows at Cleo.

Cleo smirked and then took on a more serious expression.

'Hmm…that's interesting,' she said. 'There's no shielding whatsoever on its computer core. I can just stroll in and rummage around.'

'What…wait, Cleo,' said Linda, looking alarmed. 'That doesn't sound right.'

'Oh…oh…no…that's not righhhtttt…'

Cleo's hologram phased in and out a couple of times, wearing a look of surprise on her face before she disappeared completely.

'Cleo?' said Pol.

'CLEO!' shouted Linda.

'I'm taking over control,' said Phil, his hands frantically whizzing around and touching icons to take manual control of the ship.

'That's weird,' he said, stabbing at the same icon with increasing impatience.

'What's wrong?' Pol asked, craning her neck to see what he was trying to do.

'The ship seems to be locked on a trajectory straight at and into the platform,' he said. 'I'm not able to override it for some reason.'

'Did Cleo programme it?' Linda asked, the worry evident in her voice.

'No, I don't think so…the course was altered after she disappeared,' Phil answered, meeting her gaze with a concerned expression of his own.

'Oh crap,' muttered Linda, bringing the ship's controls up in front of her and also failing to gain control over the vessel.

'Who the hell is doing that?' said Pol.

'It's impossible,' said Phil.

'It was a trap,' groaned Linda, folding her arms across her chest and glaring at the hologram of the platform. 'Leaving their system completely unshielded suckered us in. Somehow, someone has the Theo construction codes for this ship.'

'I can hazard a guess,' said Phil, rolling his eyes. 'Salft.'

'Salft!' exclaimed Pol. 'Why would it be her?'

'We already know she raided Paradeisos a while back for the autonurse,' he said. 'What's to say she didn't help herself to few other things while she was there?'

'But that was years before this ship was built,' Pol interjected.

'You would only need the Theo base coding and a really fast cryptohak,' he said, shrugging.

'A what?' said Pol.

'It's a machine that can run billions of permutations in a fraction of a second. You do have to be inside the core to be able to use it though,' said Phil. 'That's what the trap was for.'

'And Cleo blundered straight in,' said Linda, shaking her head.

'She wasn't to know,' said Phil. 'We tend to forget she's still very much a youngster.'

They all looked up at the holomap as the tone from the alma drives dropped to a deeper tone, indicating the ship was slowing. They watched as the ship was piloted down the length of the huge platform, turning abruptly at the far end and entering through the massive doors that began closing immediately once the stern had passed.

'What do we do?' asked Pol, glancing around at the others.

'Your guess is as good as mine,' said Linda. 'They'll have access to the cameras, so it's pointless trying to hide.'

'Quite right,' said a new voice, booming around the bridge.

A beaming young girl they all recognised materialised in the centre of the room.

'Told you it was her,' mumbled Phil.

'How very astute of you, Theo,' she said, in a condescending manner. 'You hadn't told me you had this wonderful new supership either, had you? What's that excellent Earth term I heard someone use the other day, "winners are grinners."'

'Patronising arse wipe,' spat Linda, glaring at the newcomer.

'Now before you all start getting aggressive and abusive, I want you to remember I can vent this ship to space if I so wish. Believe it or not you're all still valuable to me…so I want you to make your way over to airlock fourteen on the starboard side. There you will find an attached umbilical with four of my friendly ambassadors waiting to escort you into the facility. Needless to say, don't turn up with any hastily concealed weapons or there will be a price to pay. I believe you're all intelligent enough to know what that might be.'

Salft turned, achieving eye contact with all three of them.

'Make sure you bring the fourth one from the medical centre too,' she said, pointing downwards.

'But she's under sedation,' said Phil.

'All the better,' said Salft with a shrug. 'That's one of you that's less likely to play up.'

'Bitch,' Linda muttered under her breath.

Salft chuckled and raised her eyebrows at Linda.

'I've been called much worse, young lady,' she said. 'But I'm still smiling and this is my ship now.'

The three of them sat and stared into space for a while after her image disappeared, until Linda threw her arms up in despair.

'Well, we'd better go and get Rayl,' she said, dejectedly. 'Nothing we can do about any of this today.'

They all wandered over to the tube lift and disappeared below decks.

38

Military vehicle, Yiss, Medusa Merger Galaxy

THEY SPED around the perimeter of the camp in the small electric jeep and approached the main entrance slowly and casually. Ed drove with his elbow rested on the door as if he didn't have a care in the world. Most of the traffic was pedestrian and going in the other direction.

'Where d'you think you're going?' an obviously higher ranking soldier shouted at them as they reached the bottleneck of the entrance.

He stomped up to the jeep door as Ed was forced to stop by the throng around the gate.

'The other camp,' said Ed, jabbing his thumb in the direction they had to go. 'These two are from one of the lifeboats and we don't want them found by this mob.'

'Uh, right,' he grunted, peering over Ed's shoulder. 'Come straight back though, we're bloody undermanned as it is.'

'Yes, sir,' he said, hoping he hadn't made a faux pas with the man's rank.

'What did you call—?'

A way ahead presented itself and Ed didn't hesitate. Flooring the throttle, he whipped through the temporary gap in the human traffic and turned immediately left. He glanced across to see the soldier scowling in his direction before he was swallowed in a surge of gesticulating people again.

'I think we got away with that one,' he said, driving up the track as fast as the jeep would go. 'I imagine this next camp will be a harder nut to crack.'

They followed the trail for a few minutes before concealing the vehicle deep in the woods; it might come in handy later.

'Andy, do you have eyes on the smaller camp?' Ed asked privately via his DOVI.

'Yep…this one's smaller but fully fenced and only about fifty tents and a couple of permanent buildings. I think it has two separate areas, it looks like one for human and one for the Klatt prisoners.'

'Any clues as to where we should head for?' he asked, as they tramped quietly through the trees.

'It's fenced as I said, and the trees run right up close to the fence, especially at the rear of the camp; they almost overhang there,' replied Andy. 'The human section is at the front though, so you'd have to cut through two lots of wire and negotiate the Klatt prisoners if you went that way and…oh!'

'Oh, what?' Ed said.

'They've just dragged a Klatt prisoner out of one of the tents and shot him.'

'They're blaming the aliens for everything,' said Ed. 'It's what would happen on Earth after all.'

'You're getting close now, you might want to slow down,' said Andy. 'Go round the back of the facility and approach from the far side. They're obviously not expecting anything to come at them from that direction as the terrain gets very steep there. Make sure you go more than halfway down that side before breaking in to avoid the Klatt zone.'

'Okay, will do.'

'Have you got something to get through the wire?' Andy asked.

Ed confided in the two marines. One of them rummaged inside his coat and produced a rather vicious-looking pair of snips. He grinned and raised his eyebrows.

'I think we've got that covered,' said Ed, giving the marine a nod.

Once they could see the wire through the trees, they turned left and crept around the perimeter to the far side. They stopped abruptly as something in the trees ahead caught their attention.

'There's something up ahead outside the wire,' he said to Andy.

'One of the lifeboats,' he replied. 'There's no one there, it's safe to pass.'

Creeping by the abandoned and scorched craft, Ed looked up and could see the gap in the branches it had crashed its way through in its attempt at a safe landing. Its landing struts had sunk into the soft leaf litter, causing it to topple over. He peeked inside, not expecting to find anything and wasn't disappointed. Whoever had come down in the tiny craft had either survived or the bodies had been retrieved. It reminded him of the occasion he and Andy had escaped a Mogul ship on a lifeboat a couple of years ago and shivered at the memory of how close they'd come to not surviving that.

'I can see the division separating the two zones,' said one of the marines, snapping Ed out of his daydream.

'Okay, look for somewhere we can cut the wire past that point without being seen,' he said, crouching down to sneak a look through the dense foliage.

They moved silently down the wire about fifty metres, where a group of bushes was within a metre of the fence. Ed nodded at the marine, who checked there was no one within sight and no cameras overlooking, before stretching across the gap and snipping a hole in the mesh.

Again checking the coast was clear, Ed led the three of them by crawling through. Standing up on the inside, he pushed the wire back so it wasn't so obvious and made a scuff mark in the ground with his boot so they could find it again in a hurry.

'Let's saunter,' he said. 'Act as if we belong.'

'Do we split up?' asked one of the marines.

'Best not,' said Ed. 'Besides, you don't know what she looks like or speak the language.'

They spent the next twenty minutes wandering through the camp, checking each tent as they went. There were plenty of other people milling around, so much to Ed's relief they didn't seem out of place or receive any questioning glances.

'Shit,' Ed griped, after they'd checked all the tents, the recreation area and the canteen, to find no sign of Callon.

'Perhaps she didn't survive,' said one of the marines.

'Perhaps she didn't want to, considering her condition,' said the other.

'She didn't seem like a quitter to me,' said Ed, irritated by the negativity. 'Come on, we need to get out of here before our cover's blown.'

They turned and began making their way back towards the far side and their makeshift entrance. As they turned at the last row of tents, Ed saw two of the camp guards bending down and inspecting the gap in the fence. One of them began speaking on his communicator and gesticulating at the cut wire.

'Bollocks,' muttered Ed, as the three of them quickly spun around and nonchalantly snuck back out of sight and back into the assemblage of tents.

They turned at a shout behind them to witness four guards hurrying towards the main gate. Two opened the gates while the other two kept their weapons pointed inside the camp to discourage anyone considering a run for it.

An electric military truck whined inside before the gates were closed again. It was a bigger vehicle than the one Ed had stolen and had a tarpaulin-covered loading area on the back. It turned and backed up to the larger canteen tent, which seemed to double as an administration area.

One by one a collection of harried-looking people, including a couple of bedraggled and scowling Klatt military, were quickly escorted at gunpoint towards the rear section of the camp.

Ed stopped dead in his tracks as a very tired-looking female clambered down from the vehicle.

'Bloody hell, it's her,' he said, beginning to walk forward towards Callon as she joined the back of the queue.

'Wait,' called one of the marines.

But Ed hadn't heard him and began quickening his step.

'CALLON,' he shouted, as he began to run.

She turned at the sound of her name, but so did one of the

guards. He was young, inexperienced and nervous. Unfortunately, he was also unused to carrying a weapon and inadvertently had his finger on the trigger. The weapon discharged accidentally as he spun around. The bolt narrowly missed Ed and the marine directly behind him, and punched a sizeable hole in a tent behind them before hitting the perimeter fence in a shower of sparks.

The two marines with Ed, not realising it was a negligent discharge, went into full defensive mode, pulling hidden weapons from underneath their cloaks and dropped the guard and his colleague with two expertly aimed stun laser bolts.

There was a split second of disbelief from everyone in the area before complete panic and confusion ensued as people began running and screaming in all directions.

Ed sprinted up to Callon and hustled her back behind the truck for cover as several badly aimed laser bolts slapped into the ground around them.

'Why are they shooting at us?' Callon cried.

'They don't know who to blame for all this,' Ed said, peering around the corner of the truck to see where the two marines were.

'I thought it was those ugly lizardy things,' she said, clinging onto his arm for support.

'It's complicated,' Ed replied, as his two bodyguards backed around the corner, still firing their rifles from the shoulder.

The truck shuddered as several bolts smacked into it and the canvas top caught fire.

'Immediate evac,' called one of the marines. 'Get that gunship down here now. These guys aren't using stun settings like us.'

'Roger that,' came the call over Ed's earpiece. 'Three

minutes out.'

'Thankfully, they're not very good at aiming the fucking things,' called one of the marines, snapping a few shots around the front of the truck to discourage anyone from coming round that way.

The heat from the flames above them was getting a little uncomfortable and Ed was concerned they didn't have three minutes, as there wasn't any other cover besides the truck.

'Anything you can do from up there gratefully received,' he messaged to Andy.

'Tell the soldiers to lob a couple of grenades over the top of the truck,' came the reply.

They did as requested and Ed got Callon to cover her ears as the crack-crack of the two stun grenades detonated.

'That's discouraged them a bit,' messaged Andy.

The distinctive scream of antigravs in the distance reached Ed's ears and he breathed a sigh of relief. Peeking up through the windows of the cab he could see the gunship rapidly approaching. The camp guards were also glancing nervously in that direction too.

The gunship fired several rounds from its forward-mounted heavy lasers that zipped close overhead and caused several trees outside the wire to explode dramatically. This had the desired effect, making the guards think again about moving forward. They wisely decided to remain in cover and keep their heads down.

The antigrav scream became a bellow as the gunship dropped alarmingly quickly down the steep hillside. No one ever did know why the pilot hadn't noticed the sharp rocky outcrop near the base of the hill. But as he flared and turned abruptly, his rear struts struck the rock formation, flipping the gunship up over onto its nose and giving the pilot no chance to recover. It slammed into the hillside just outside the compound and exploded in a massive fireball, its ammunition increasing the ferocity of the detonation and blast wave that almost caused the truck to tip over on top of them.

'Ah, fuck no,' shouted Ed, as he witnessed their only means of escape and the lives of a whole detachment of marines wiped out.

'Now we're in a lot of shit,' said the nearest marine.

'Is the truck drivable?' called Andy from above, sounding a little worried now.

'It's on fucking fire,' replied Ed.

'But the cab isn't, is it?' he replied.

'The gates are shut though, and they're quite substantial,' said Ed, peering around the cab at them.

'Not for long…get in the truck.'

The asteri beam from above vaporised the gates and blinded them all as they bundled into the small space. They kept their heads down so the guards didn't realise what they were doing. When Ed's sight returned, he risked a peek across. Luckily, the guards seemed more concerned by the sudden lethal beam from above and the still exploding ordinance in the wreck of the gunship. They had wisely decided to stay in cover.

Ed pressed the drive icon he recognised from the smaller jeep, hoping it still had some form of drive left in it, even with the fire on the back and damage inflicted by many laser hits.

It lurched forwards with a loud groaning from behind. He steered it straight through where the gates had been, bumping and clanking across the circular melted patch of ground where the beam had impacted, turned right and headed straight into the trees.

39

———————

Salft Engineering Platform, the Exoplismoi system,
Milky Way

'WELL, Ed's going to be well impressed with us,' said Pol, sitting in the corner of the store room they'd been locked in after being escorted off the *Gabriel*. 'What a bunch of numpties we are!'

'Don't remind me,' moaned Linda. 'Have the new ship for ten minutes and we gift it to the biggest criminal in the galaxy.'

'At least we're still alive,' said Phil.

'For the time being,' Linda answered. 'She said we were still useful to her…but what for and for how long?'

'Driving lessons on the ship perhaps,' said Pol.

'I don't think so,' said Phil. 'She was able to pilot it into here without any problem, so I don't think it would be that.'

'We know she blames everything on Bache,' said Linda. 'Maybe we're going to be used as a lure for him.'

'Yeah, but he'll have the use of a *Katadromiko*,' said Phil. 'The *Gabriel's* powerful, but no match for one of those.'

'Maybe that's what she's after…another *Katadromiko*,' said Pol.

'She blew the last one up though,' said Phil, shrugging.

'I don't think she had much choice,' Linda interjected. 'I reckon the Klatt had had enough of her, they'd realised their interests were no longer on her agenda and were attempting to take the *28* for themselves.'

'In some ways she did the galaxy a favour then,' Phil added. 'Can you imagine what the Klatt would do if they were able to reverse engineer and build a fleet of those monsters?'

'I don't think she's after another cruiser,' said Linda. 'Wealth and revenge are the only two things that motivate that woman. She needs to lay low for a while and let the dust settle; that'd be difficult with a ship of that size. The *Gabriel*, however, is a different kettle of fish.'

'Where could she go?' asked Pol. 'She must be getting short of funds now.'

'Any number of worlds,' said Phil. 'We have to remember she was the head of the wealthiest dynasty in all of GDA space. Between her and her husband, I'm sure they squir-relled away vast sums on a hundred human planets.'

Rayl, who'd been lying unconscious on some packing material in a corner of the room where the guards had dumped her, suddenly sat up and glared at everyone.

'I'm going to kill that bastard,' she sniped through clenched teeth.

The other three recoiled in surprise. It was the first time

she'd come to and said anything since being removed from the autonurse.

'Kill who?' Linda asked, breaking the momentary silence.

Rayl snapped her eyes round to Linda and glowered. Linda couldn't remember Rayl ever looking so angry; this wasn't normally in her nature.

'My fucking husband of course,' she spat. 'He's to blame for all this…he's ruined my life.'

Another short pause ensued.

'Erm…Andrew has nothing to do with our situation, Rayl,' said Linda.

Rayl laughed.

'Typical of you to defend him,' she sneered. 'Probably slept with him too.'

'Rayl, that's a horrible thing to say,' said Pol, looking at Linda, her eyes wide.

Linda didn't take her eyes off Rayl before replying in a calm, poignant tone.

'Yes, I will defend him,' she said. 'Because he's my friend and no more than that. Probably something to do with me being gay,' she added.

'Yeah, so you say,' she said. 'I'm just not…'

Rails eyes glazed over and closed as she sank back onto the packing and went quiet and still.

'Bloody hell,' whispered Phil. 'What was all that about?'

'It must have been the knock on the head,' said Pol.

'I'm not so sure,' said Linda. 'Andy mentioned to me a few weeks ago that she was acting weird and becoming quite snappy and irritated by almost everything he did and said.'

'It could be stress-related,' said Pol. 'The last couple of years haven't been without a few worrying situations and I should know.'

'Mental health is the one thing an autonurse struggles with,' said Phil. 'We're going to have to keep an eye on her and keep her calm.'

'Can't an autonurse read her krypti or something and prescribe some sort of anti-depressants?' asked Linda. 'That's what happens on Earth when someone's having problems coping.'

'It could,' said Phil. 'But the side effects of those can sometimes be worse than the depression.'

The conversation ended as the door burst open and four guards entered carrying rifles. Salft wandered in behind and scowled at her four prisoners.

'What the hell is that black bubble sitting in one of the hangars?' she asked, centring her attention on Linda.

'Ah, yes,' Linda replied, the question taking her by surprise. 'It's some sort of water bubble, we think,' she said, thinking fast. 'We found it on an asteroid in the Medusa galaxy, we brought it back for study and to—'

The floor shook suddenly, cutting Linda off mid-sentence. A low boom sounded from somewhere distant in the facility. Salft and the four guards staggered, but managed to keep their balance.

'What the fuck was that?' Salft snapped, turning to glare at one of the guards.

A second explosion, this one a little closer, shook the room, causing the door to pop open and the lighting to dim.

The guard stared into space for a moment and spoke into his headset, his eyes widening at the response he received.

'The ship has just left, ma'am,' he said, avoiding eye contact with Salft.

'What ship?' she snarled.

'Er…their ship, ma'am,' he replied nervously, nodding at the prisoners.

'What d'you mean, left?' she shouted.

'It, err…fired on the main door mechanism and the main array, it's now exited the yard and jumped away, ma'am.'

Salft turned to go, then stopped and turned back again.

'How the fuck did you do that?' she demanded, singling Linda out again. 'You were completely shielded from the ship.'

'We didn't,' Linda replied. 'Nothing to do with us. And anyway, he said it's jumped and gone…perhaps you've pissed off some of your staff again?' she added, with a shrug and a slight smirk.

'Don't you get smart with me, Earth bitch,' Salft snapped, pointing accusingly. 'If I find this was you, you're all going for a cold walk.'

Salft spun on her heel and stormed out of the room, closely followed by her guards. When the door slammed shut, Pol was the first to speak.

'I'd forgotten about Oona,' she said. 'Could she have taken control of the ship?'

Linda thought about that for a moment before answering.

'She's smart,' she said. 'She'd obviously inked the fluid in her bubble so she couldn't be seen. I wouldn't have thought Cleo would've given her operational control though.'

'Someone on the ship certainly has,' said Phil. 'Let's hope whoever it is, is on our side.'

40

Military vehicle, Yiss, Medusa Merger Galaxy

ED CRASHED the truck through the woodland, avoiding the larger trees as best he could. He headed in the direction of the jeep, but the noise from the truck was getting louder and he noticed the power was beginning to drop off.

'Prepare to de-camp,' he shouted above the ever-worsening racket coming from the vehicle.

As smoke began to permeate the cab, he decided to call it a day and stop. They bundled out of the truck and led Callon in the direction of the smaller vehicle. The only problem being, when they reached where they'd left it, it wasn't there.

'Bollocks,' muttered Ed, glancing down at the tyre marks where it'd been turned around and driven off back towards the track.

'Thieving bastards,' grumbled one of the marines.

Ed gave him a questioning look.

'It was their vehicle,' he said, looking up at the hillside looming to their right. 'Come on, let's head for the higher ground.'

'ETA on the pickup?' the other marine called on his communicator.

'Approximately seventeen minutes,' came the quick reply. 'They're on the way down.'

'You are being pursued,' Andy said to Ed. 'Although you wrecked their only truck, they do have the jeep, but if you head up the hill, the terrain will be too dense and steep for that.'

'Already thought of that,' said Ed. 'Will the rescue ship be able to pinpoint us?'

'Yeah, the marines have personal locators for the pilot to lock on to.'

'I hope he's better than the last one,' Ed muttered between breaths as he laboured up the ever-steepening hillside, pushing Callon in front of him.

'I don't feel so well,' Callon said, panting from the exertion of the climb.

'Is it your illness?' asked Ed.

'No…all those people died just to rescue me.'

'That wasn't your fault, it was an accident,' replied Ed, giving her shoulder a squeeze. 'These things happen…you mustn't blame yourself for something you had no control over.'

'I still feel physically sick at the thought of it though,' she replied, stumbling on a protruding rock and falling to her knees.

'Up you come,' said Ed, hauling her upright again, just as a laser bolt whipped through the treetops above, showering them in twigs and leaves.

The marines both turned and loosed a blaze of fire back down through the foliage, deliberately aiming high as their weapons were now turned up to full power. The ploy seemed to work as the sound of crashing and shouting reached them as branches and treetops showered down on their pursuers, hopefully dampening their enthusiasm in the chase.

'Go left up there,' said one of the marines, pointing to a rocky outcrop. 'We could climb onto that high ledge and defend it until the ship gets here. There can't be many chasing us, as there weren't many there in the first place.'

'Good plan,' said Ed, steering Callon in the indicated direction.

When they reached the base of the climb, one of the marines stood behind a tree with his weapon in the shoulder covering them, as they would be exposed while ascending the rock face. It took a bit of scrambling, especially on the steeper parts. The other marine led the way, indicating hand and foot holds, followed by Callon and Ed.

The climb took about four minutes and as they clambered onto the relatively flat ledge sticking out about five metres from the cliff, Ed signalled to the marine below to follow them up.

He turned over and lay on his back for a moment, staring up, hoping he could see a fiery trail somewhere to signal their ride up to the cruiser was imminent. Seeing nothing, he turned over again and looked down at the marine climbing up to meet them.

The laser bolt aimed at the marine came out of the blue. Although it was too high and missed him, it dislodged a pile of rocks above him. He ducked in, head close to the rock face, as they rained down on him. Most rattled over him, but unfortunately one of the larger ones caught his right arm, dislodging his hold. He slipped and hung by one hand for a moment, while scrabbling with his feet to find some grip. None was forthcoming and he slipped and fell the fifteen metres back to the base of the climb.

The other marine had fired a volley of shots into the tree-tops below them in the rough direction the laser bolt had originated.

'Are you okay?' Ed shouted down.

'Broken leg I think,' came the reply.

'Shit,' Ed muttered, glancing across at the other marine, who muttered something under his breath and intensified his fire to cover his colleague.

Something caught Ed's attention in the sky to the south. A small black dot was growing gradually larger. He pointed at it.

'Is that our ride?' he asked.

Just as the other two looked up to follow his finger, it split into two.

'Nope,' said the marine. 'More bad news.'

'Oh, that's just fucking dandy,' said Ed. 'They're just bound to be military aren't they?'

'They're not going to be tourists on a day trip, no,' the marine grumbled. 'And up here we've no cover.'

'Can you see those?' Ed asked Andy.

'Yeah…d'you want me to advise them of their mortality?'

'Wouldn't do any harm, just try not to harm them too much – we are supposed to be the good guys, after all.'

'Roger dodge.'

The two dots had neared now and Ed could recognise them as some sort of helicopter. Ominous-looking dark pods hung under small winglets on each side of the craft, which pretty much confirmed they weren't domestic and unarmed.

Something extremely fast flashed horizontally across from the west and impacted with the leading helicopter. It exploded, wreckage dropping in an arc down into the forest where a further explosion signalled its total destruction. The other helicopter veered away dramatically, slowed and sunk down out of sight below the tree line.

'What part of "don't harm them" didn't you get?' Ed called to Andy.

'Wasn't us,' Andy replied, just as something sleek and fast thundered overhead and climbed abruptly, its sonic boom making Ed jump.

'Who and what the fuck is that?' he asked.

'It came in from the west,' said Andy. 'It seems there may be more than one opinion to our presence.'

'It's not likely to engage our taxi I hope?'

'No, he has his shields on max. Four minutes out, by the way. Is that other marine going to be able to get up to you?'

'No, he's broken his leg.'

'Clumsy twat.'

'Don't you let him hear you say that.'

'He's not going to be able to chase me though is he?'

'Just shut up and keep an eye on that fast jet and the other helicopter.'

'Roger roger.'

Ed shook his head and rolled his eyes.

'Problem?' Callon asked, noticing Ed's reaction.

'No, just a wanker upstairs,' he said, glancing skyward. 'I'll slap him later.'

'Must be talking about Andrew,' she said, with a smirk.

The sound of laser fire below snapped them out of their reverie. The marine with them sat up and fired into the trees again.

'Were the fuck's that transport?' he moaned. 'My sergeant's down there injured with no support.'

The sound of antigravs screaming above answered his question before Ed could say anything. They all looked up to see it dropping like a stone.

Ed winced, remembering that was exactly what the first one had done, but as the intensity of the engine noise reached a crescendo, a smaller than before troop carrier dropped in front of them. The pilot saw them and turned the ship around, bringing the lowering rear ramp close to the ledge. They didn't need to be prompted, as they were up and inside in seconds.

The marine hung onto the door frame as the pilot dropped the thirty metres down to ground level. He jumped down and laid some covering fire as the injured marine hopped over and up the ramp, the agony of this unwanted leg movement written all over his face.

Ed showed Callon how to strap in as the pilot closed the rear door and ripped skyward as fast as the carrier could manage, not bothering to worry about the sonic boom as it seemed no one else did around here.

Ed glanced down as he felt his hand being squeezed.

'Thank you,' said Callon.

She looked over at the marine lying on the deck as his colleague pumped him full of painkillers.

'You shouldn't have come back just for me though,' she said. 'A lot of people have got hurt.'

'I made a promise,' said Ed, returning the hand squeeze. 'I keep them.'

41

Salft Engineering Platform, the Exoplismoi system,
Milky Way

'OH, BLOODY HELL!' exclaimed Linda, after Salft and her entourage had left the room.

'We'll get it back,' said Pol.

'No,' said Linda, her eyes closed. 'Not the ship…my DOVI is working.'

'Must've been the second detonation that hit the array or something,' said Phil. 'It was probably destroyed so they couldn't track the ship, but they must have been using it to produce the shielding within the facility too.'

Linda signalled for Phil to join her as she got up and walked to the door.

'If there's a guard outside,' she whispered. 'We'll grab him and drag him inside.'

Phil grimaced but nodded as he stood to one side and

waited. Linda closed her eyes and concentrated on the lock mechanism. It clicked and unlocked, and she ripped it open before they both lunged out to find an empty corridor.

'Hmm,' Linda grunted. 'Must be short of staff.'

'I'm not surprised,' said Pol. 'She goes through employees faster than a brothel goes through tissues.'

They both turned and stared at Pol.

'Sorry,' she said, pulling a contrite expression.

'One of Andrew's?' Linda asked.

Pol nodded sheepishly.

'Do you know what a brothel is?' Linda asked.

She shook her head.

Phil, who looked a bit happier now he didn't have to engage in anything physical, smiled and peered up and down the passageway.

'Her ship must be on here somewhere,' he said.

'Yeah, but so is she,' said Linda. 'And she's probably quite attached to it, especially now.'

'Best bugger off in it before she does then,' said Pol.

'If the *Gabriel* destroyed the arrays, this platform might not be able to assess its position,' said Linda.

'Oh, shit,' said Phil, his eyes opening wide at the thought.

'Which means?' Pol asked, looking between the two of them.

'The station might be at risk of de-orbiting,' said Linda.

'Oh…yes…shit…indeed,' she said, turning to look at Rayl lying in the corner. 'Can someone give me a hand with her then?'

Rayl muttered incoherently as they picked her up and half carried, half dragged her with them. They went left, because they'd been brought in from the right, so they knew that way only led to the umbilical that was probably destroyed now.

The corridor passed several closed doors and went around a slight left-hand bend before reaching one more door on the right and what seemed like an elevator door at the end.

'Hmm, let's see where this goes,' said Linda, shutting her eyes and scanning around.

There was a sudden knocking on the door to the right that made them all jump.

'Hello,' said a voice. 'Is there someone there? We haven't had any food for ages.'

They looked at each other in surprise.

'Who are you?' Phil asked.

'What?' said the voice. 'Who are you then?'

'We were locked in the room down the corridor,' said Pol. 'What were you doing here?'

'We're the temporary crew,' the voice said. 'The GDA tasked us to look after the station until it could be sold.'

'Did a good job then,' said Phil.

'Says the man who was also locked in a cupboard,' the voice replied, sarcastically.

'Hmm, touché,' said Phil, as Linda rolled her eyes at him.

She quickly unlocked their door and opened it. She recoiled at the smell of body odour and stale farts. The man standing inside the door stepped back nervously. He needed a shave and was dressed in some sort of dishevelled grey uniform that needed a good wash and iron too.

'It's okay,' she said, holding her hands up in a placating manner. 'We were prisoners here too.'

'How did you get out then?' he asked, suspiciously.

'I was a locksmith in a past life,' she said quickly, hoping it would do.

Three other men and two women, similarly unwashed and down at heel, appeared in the background.

'They made us crap in a bucket in front of our colleagues,' one of the ladies said, cringing in the background. 'I've never been so embarrassed.'

'Better than getting spaced,' said Phil.

Linda kicked him.

'You're not female,' she growled at him. 'You have no idea.'

'You must know the layout of this platform,' said Pol, quickly changing the subject.

'Every bit of it,' said the first man. 'They said they were a marine detachment on an exercise. They had a GDA gunship and everything.'

'We know,' said Linda. 'D'you know where they've hidden it?'

'Yes,' they all said in unison.

'It's in the bottom hangar,' said the embarrassed girl. 'It only just fit too, it's only designed for shuttles.'

'Can you take us there?'

They all nodded.

'Won't it be guarded?' the man said.

'Most likely,' said Linda. 'But we'll need to create a diversion. Are there any weapons on the station?'

'The armoury,' said another male voice from the back. 'I was in charge of that. It's on level twelve.'

'What level is this?' Linda asked, stretching up to see who'd spoken.

'Forty-one,' came the collective of voices, as they all answered at once, but not in unison this time.

'Can you take us there first?' Phil asked this time.

The man in front pointed at the elevator doors.

'Come with us,' he said, pushing through.

'Hang on,' said Linda, holding her hands up above her head.

They all stopped and stared at her.

'If we meet any of them before we get weapons, rush them,' she said. 'There's a lot of us now and they're not expecting anyone to be loose on the station.'

She noticed a few nervous glances, but no one put up any argument.

The man placed his hand onto a flat panel set flush with the wall on the left side of the doors. It flashed once and turned red.

'Oh, shit,' he said. 'Locked out.'

'Hang on,' said Linda, closing her eyes.

The panel turned green and a whirring sound came from behind the doors.

'How did you do that?' he asked, looking at her strangely.

'Locksmithing secrets,' she said. 'Classified.'

'Yeah, right,' he said and looked as if he was about to question her further when the doors swished open.

'All aboard,' said Phil, ushering them inside and giving Linda a wink.

It was a squeeze with ten bodies inside, but it gave Phil's and Pol's arms a rest, as they didn't have to hold Rayl up.

'What's up with her?' one of them asked.

'Bang on the head,' said Pol.

'Level twelve,' the man said from the middle of the group.

The doors closed and Linda felt the floor drop away as the lift descended quickly.

'What will we see when the doors open?' Linda asked.

'A similar corridor,' a voice from the back said. 'The armoury is the third door down on the left.'

The doors swished open again only moments after he'd finished speaking. The passageway was empty and Linda sighed with relief, mostly because she was right at the front.

She did her magic locksmithing trick with the third door down, getting another suspicious glare from the lead man, and they quickly piled inside.

'I can't see anything missing,' the armourer said, after scanning the racks for a moment.

'They brought their own,' said Phil, helping Pol sit Rayl on a chair.

The six caretakers began arming themselves with everything they could carry.

'We're taking a small ship, not a planet,' said Linda.

'I'd rather we had too much than get out-gunned,' one of them said.

'Just make sure they're all set to stun,' Linda added. 'It's not their fault they're working for a psycho.'

'That's a point,' said one of the women. 'Who is that little girl they all kowtow to?'

'It's Ystolion Flast or Noilstoy Salft…or whatever she's calling herself today,' replied Linda.

They all stopped what they were doing and stared at Linda as if she'd lost her mind.

'Don't be so stupid,' said one of the men. 'Ystolion Flast would be a hundred and thirty odd by now and the Salft woman who owned this facility was middle-aged.'

'She stole an autonurse from the Theos,' said Pol. 'It was on this station somewhere.'

'That must be the strange alien machine hidden behind that false wall up in the posh apartment,' said one of the women.

'So the Salft woman was actually Flast,' one of them said, shaking his head and glancing around at his colleagues.

'It's an anagram,' said Linda. 'She was hiding here in plain sight for years, gradually reducing her age with the autonurse.'

'Fuck me,' said one of the men. 'If we'd known that, we'd have brought a battalion of marines with us.'

'We're private hire contracted by the insurance company,' said another. 'I bet the company had no idea who their client was either.'

'The GDA didn't tell you then?' said Phil, shaking his head.

'Nope,' two of them said, while they stuffed grenades in their pockets.

'Grenades?' asked Linda, staring with raised eyebrows.

'Stun,' one of them said. 'Frags aren't permitted in space.'

'That's a relief,' said Phil, inspecting one and pocketing it.

'Are we all ready?' Linda asked, receiving a collection of affirmative nods. 'Let's go find us a ship then.'

42

Katadromiko 21, *orbiting Yiss, Medusa Merger Galaxy*

CALLON and the marine with the broken leg were both rushed to the cruiser's central medical centre as soon as they disembarked in hangar 19. Captain Mye was waiting, her arms crossed and wearing a lour expression as Ed stepped off the small troop carrier.

'That proved expensive,' she grizzled, her expression unchanged.

'It was pilot error surely?' replied Ed, defensively. 'You can't hold me responsible for that.'

'I can't…no,' she said. 'But try telling that to my contingent of marines. They lost a lot of mates to save an alien girl with terminal cancer who might or might not make it. If I were you, I'd keep your head down for a while.'

She stalked off before he had a chance to reply. Andy entered the hangar as she exited. Ed noticed Andy's smile as he passed the Captain wasn't reciprocated and he rolled his eyes as he neared.

'We're not flavour of the month at the moment,' Andy said, pulling an awkward face.

'So it seems,' said Ed, sighing.

'Have you reminded her about picking up the surviving Vriix on our way home?'

'No chance, she's a little pissed at the moment. I thought it could wait until she's not so eggy.'

'Oona's not going to be very impressed if we sail by her surviving colleagues on our way home. I'm sure they could make space in one of the hangars if they really wanted to.'

'I have to go to the medical centre,' said Ed, looking contrite. 'Can you be brave and raise the subject with the Captain? She's not quite so mad at you.'

'Oh joy,' whinged Andy. 'You get to hold hands with the pretty girl and I get snapped at by captain grumpy pants.'

'Privileges of rank,' said Ed, patting Andy on the shoulder and quickly scooting off towards the hangar door.

'Thanks, pal, the beers are definitely on you later,' he called, scowling at Ed's speedy retreat.

Ed went straight to the main medical facility on deck 307. Callon had been put in a private side suite and was in the process of being connected up to the diagnosis computer.

An orderly pointed to a chair in the corner and Ed parked himself there.

'When will you know what we're dealing with?' Ed asked.

'When the Chief Medical Officer evaluates the data,' he said.

'Which is when?'

'Right now, Mr Virr,' said a short Dasonian man as he

strode in, dressed in a white ship suit with senior officer's epaulettes. 'Managed to lose one of our marine squads and a very expensive gunship, I understand,' he mooted, shaking his head and tutting.

Ed exhaled and counted to ten before answering.

'They managed that all on their own,' he replied, irritatedly. 'I had nothing to do with it.'

'Hmm,' grunted the officer. 'Just to rescue this dying local, then?'

'All the more reason to save her…then,' Ed replied, through gritted teeth, crossing his arms and glaring at the man. He noticed the medical orderly's eyes widen and presumed it wasn't a common occurrence to talk back to the Chief Medical Officer.

'Perhaps a little more respect is due when you're expecting me to save the young lady's life, Mr Virr.'

'It's Captain Virr and I'm here as a representative of the Admiral of the Fleet,' he said. 'If you want to continue with this stupid alpha male pissing contest, go right ahead, it's your career.'

The room went very quiet for a few moments, the faint humming of the medical equipment and barely perceptible hiss of the environmental vents the only sound.

'It's bloody quiet in 'ere,' said Andy, breaking the awkward silence as he strolled in, closely followed by the Captain.

'Captain, I'd like to make an official complaint about this man's lack of respect to senior officers,' blurted the Chief Medical Officer, pointing at Ed as soon as Mye was in the door.

The Captain glanced at Ed, who shrugged and shook his head slightly.

'Of course you can, Chief,' Mye replied, cheerily. 'But only if you're planning to spend the rest of your career as an orderly on some distant mining colony. Admiral of the Fleet Loftt doesn't take kindly to whiney jobsworth bullies picking on his close friends…your decision.'

Andy sniggered, then seemingly regretted it after getting a glare from everyone in the room.

The Captain, her face a picture of nonchalance, turned her attention back to Ed just as the lighting dimmed slightly.

'That was the first jump on the journey to the Vriix system. Andrew has reminded me of our obligation to save the sentient octopoid race from extinction and I completely agree. I'm currently having one of the larger hangars cleared to make room for their spheres.'

'Thank you, Captain,' said Ed. 'Have we helped out the population down below at all?'

'Well, my main obligation in a situation like this is to ensure none of the technology on the *28*'s wreck gets into the wrong hands. That job is complete, but I did send a few freighter-loads of supplies down as a goodwill gesture. We're really needed on Dasos first and foremost; we can come back here once everything's stable there.'

Ed didn't like the thought of abandoning this human colony for one day, let alone a few weeks, but he did understand the mitigating circumstances.

'Still no sign of the *Gabriel*, I presume?' he asked.

Mye shook her head.

'Prognosis, Chief?' Mye asked, turning back to the Chief Medical Officer and nodding at the patient.

'Erm, advanced gallbladder cancer, Captain,' he said, the aggression in his voice now gone.

'Her chances?'

'With immediate targeted programmed nano ingestive therapy, I would say about forty percent.'

'How long will that take?'

'A week or two.'

'Don't let us hold you up then,' said the Captain, and nodded for Ed and Andy to follow her.

'My apologies for that arrogant arse,' she said, once they were out of earshot.

'He blames me for the lost marines,' said Ed.

'It's not that at all,' said Mye, giving Ed a sideways glance. 'He's using that as an excuse to get at you personally.'

'Why? Have I come across him before?'

'No, I don't believe you would've. But, you see, he was dating a certain *Katadromiko* captain a few years ago.'

'Oh? Who?' Andy asked.

Ed halted in his tracks, causing the other two to stop suddenly and turn to face him.

'Quixia?' he said, questioningly.

Mye nodded.

'Who?' said Andy, his face a picture of confusion.

'Captain Fleoha Utz,' said Mye.

'Oh…her,' said Andy. 'Bloody hell, no wonder he hates you.'

'He's still convinced she didn't have anything to do with that awful crime and wasn't an enemy combatant,' she said.

'He managed to keep his job then,' said Andy.

'By the skin of his teeth,' she said. 'No one wanted him on their ship. Too much suspicion.'

'But you did,' said Ed.

'I kinda felt sorry for him,' she said. 'He doesn't do

himself any favours sometimes and I have to slap him down and remind him he's not in a position of power or influence.'

'I better give him a wide berth then.'

They continued on to the tube station, where they boarded a train for the officers' decks.

'What's the ETA for the Vriix planet?' Ed asked.

'Tomorrow third shift,' said Mye.

Andy's eyes met Ed's.

'Fancy a beverage or three?' he asked.

'Use the senior officers' mess,' said Mye. 'Less likely to bump into any disgruntled marines.'

'Just disgruntled doctors,' said Andy, grinning.

Nobody grinned back.

43

---

*Salft Engineering Platform, the Exoplismoi system,
Milky Way*

LINDA CALLED the elevator again and this time it took a little longer to arrive. When the doors did eventually slide apart, the interior wasn't empty. Two of Salft's guards stood with their backs to the open door with some sort of machine taking up the majority of the interior space. They turned with surprised expressions, but before they could react, they got the good news from two laser rifles.

The unconscious bodies were stripped of anything useful and locked in a cleaning cupboard.

'That's the alien machine from upstairs,' said one of the women, sticking her head in the elevator.

'It is too,' said Phil, running his hand over the top screen to clear a layer of dust.

'It'd be good to take that with us for Rayl,' said Linda.

'We can't get all of us in there with the machine as well,' said one of the men.

'Pull it out here,' said Phil. 'I'll stay with it and clean it up a bit while you take the ship.'

'What about Rayl?' said Pol.

'Lay her in it,' he said. 'I can push her around in it and as soon as it's on the ship, I can connect it up to the power supply.'

After leaving Rayl with Phil, Linda, Pol and the others descended in the elevator to one level before the hangar. The security team had told Linda that the doors opened directly into the hangar with little or no cover within easy reach. So, if the ship was guarded they'd be sitting ducks to anyone with a weapon at the ready. The emergency stairs on the other hand were off to one side and partly hidden behind some auto trundles stacked high with their supplies for a stay of indeterminate length.

The stairs were narrow and Linda was glad they didn't have to carry Rayl down them. The door at the bottom had a small glazed window and as Linda was in the lead, she slowly raised her head up and peeked over the bottom edge and into the hangar.

The gunship was still there, although she could only see the upper part of the hull. The pile of supplies a couple of metres inside did indeed block the view of the majority of the ship, including the airlock and rear ramp.

'At least it's still here,' she said.

'Are there any guards?' asked one of the men.

'We won't find that out until we go—'

Linda was cut off by some shouting in the hangar. Peering in again and to the left, in the direction of the elevator, her heart missed a beat. Phil was being pushed out by two more of Salft's goons at gunpoint, along with Rayl in the autonurse.

'Oh, shit,' she whispered. 'We need to go in right now.'

'Why?' asked one of the women.

'Phil's been caught and is being escorted at gunpoint,' she said. 'Just stun everything that moves except him.'

She pulled the door open and they quickly filed out one by one and hid behind the auto trundles.

'On three,' she said, holding up one finger, then two, then three.

All eight of them sprinted out, rifles in the shoulder. The firing started almost immediately, but luckily the two guards escorting Phil and the autonurse had their backs to them and they went down without knowing what hit them. The guard standing thirty metres away on the gunship's open ramp was a little bit more prepared. He whipped up a hand weapon and began returning fire as stun bolts thudded into everything around him.

Linda heard a scream to her left as she knelt and carefully targeted the guard, finally dropping him with her second shot. Even then it was only a glancing blow and he was able to crawl back inside the ship as the ramp began to close. She caught a glimpse of Salft sprinting across the internal cabin space and up the stairway to the cockpit.

'She's in there,' Linda shouted, jumping up again and sprinting for the ramp. She knew she wouldn't make it before it closed and veered off to the right. She fiddled with the power switch on her rifle as she went, setting it to full. Again kneeling, she aimed at the gunship's array on the underside of the vessel. The white hot bolt of energy flashed across the hangar and dissipated around the hull in a spectacular display of forked lightning.

'FUCK,' she screamed, realising Salft had managed to get the shields up in time. 'That bitch has a charmed existence,' she mumbled to herself, as several more full-power strikes from the others sparkled around the ship. She began to wonder why the antigravs hadn't spun up, then her eyes widened as she realised why.

'GET DOWN,' she yelled. 'EVERYBODY GET DOWN.'

She dived down and flattened herself on the hangar deck and attempted to cover her ears as a deafening dull clang like a cracked church bell being hit hard with a sledgehammer assaulted her eardrums. The shock wave of the gunship jumping within the confines of the hangar blew her sideways across the floor and she slammed into one of the auto trundles.

Linda wasn't entirely sure how long she lay there, hurting all over and waiting for the ringing in her ears to subside. She knew she was bruised from head to toe, but as she gradually worked her way around her body, she realised to her relief, nothing seemed broken. As soon as she was able, she lifted her head up and surveyed the state of the hangar.

Anything that hadn't been bolted down had been blown into the inner walls and a lot of ship servicing equipment lay broken or damaged around the perimeter. She was relieved to see Phil sitting, peering out from behind the autonurse.

'You okay?' she called, wincing as she rolled onto her knees.

'I had no idea a jumping ship was so loud,' he said, rubbing his ears.

'Why didn't the autonurse get damaged?' she said, pointing at all the smashed stuff lining the walls.

'I guessed what she was going to do as the antigravs were

shut down and engaged the maglock,' he replied. 'It also sheltered me from the void implosion.'

They both stood slowly and scanned around to find the others.

The scream Linda had heard early on had been one of the men hit by a full-power laser bolt from the guard on the ramp. He was very dead, a hole the size of a fist in his chest. Two of the others, a man and a woman, were also gone, their necks broken as they slammed into the hangar wall. The other three had fared better, but one had a broken arm and the other woman a broken collarbone, ankle and possible concussion. None of them, it seemed, had flattened themselves on the deck when Linda had shouted the warning.

They sat silently staring at Linda and Phil as they limped over and checked their dead colleagues.

'I did shout a warning,' Linda said, helping the woman with the broken collarbone and ankle to get up and hop over to sit on one of the auto trundles.

'I had no idea a ship could jump without being in space,' she said, grimacing through the pain.

'As you can see, it's possible…but not very healthy for those in the vicinity,' said Phil, as he pushed the autonurse over to a power outlet and plugged it in. 'Give me a hand lifting Rayl out of here,' he said. 'I think you're in need of a bit of remedial work straight away.'

The girl looked at the machine whirring away as it woke up, with Phil tapping away on its keypad.

'Is this thing safe?' she asked, hopping around it and eyeing it dubiously. 'It is old and alien after all.'

Phil smiled at the comment.

'It's a Theo-built machine,' he said. 'And I'm a Theo…

we have six of these on our starship and I've been operating them for centuries.'

'I thought Theos were imitation humans,' the man with the broken arm said.

Everyone looked at him as if he'd grown an extra head.

'Well, you know what I mean…manufactured,' he added.

'Would you like a spade?' said Linda. 'Then you can dig yourself a bigger hole.'

'It's okay,' said Phil, giving the man a wink. 'I've a thick skin, it's nothing I haven't heard before.'

He took the girl's good arm and helped her up and to lie in the machine.

'Do I look fake to you?' Phil asked, not bothering to look over his shoulder at the man.

'Err…no,' he said. 'Up to now, I had no idea you were a Theo…you're the first one I've ever met.'

'Remain absolutely still,' he said to the girl, now ignoring the man. 'I'll let you know when it's done.'

'Will it hurt?' she asked, apprehensively.

'Only if you move,' he said. 'So don't.'

She lay back and closed her eyes as Phil touched one last icon on the control panel. Not a lot happened for a moment before the machine's humming increased slightly and microscopic beams of blue light flashed around her shoulder and ankle.

'Oh,' she mumbled, after a couple of minutes, and the machine went quieter again.

'Right, out you pop,' said Phil. 'Time for your mate to have a play.'

'Am I done?' she asked suspiciously, still not daring to move.

'Yep,' said Phil. 'Although, light duties for a day or so… let the new bone harden.'

'That's amazing,' she said, climbing out and flexing her arm and ankle.

'Next,' said Phil, raising his eyebrows at the man with the broken arm.

A siren together with red flashing lights stopped everyone in their tracks.

'What's that?' Pol asked, staring at the man who hadn't been injured.

'Shit…it's the master alarm,' he said, making for the elevator. 'We need to get to the central control room, quickly.'

'I'll come with you,' said the newly repaired girl, following him.

'I'll come too,' said Linda, glancing at Phil and Pol. 'You two stay and fix him. Follow us up as soon as he's cooked.'

'I have a bad feeling about this,' called Phil, as Linda strode away. He peered nervously up at the red flashing lights before turning back and helping the injured man up into the autonurse.

44

Katadromiko 21, *Vriix system, Medusa Merger Galaxy*

'HOW CAN THEY NOT BE HERE?' Ed demanded, as everyone on the bridge stared at the vast holomap above them.

Katadromiko 21 had jumped into the Vriix system some thirty minutes ago and powered her way over to the dead dry planet and its long-dried-up oceans the Vriix had once habitated for thousands of rotations. The ship's powerful arrays scanned everything within half a light year, finding no signs of life.

'Could they have given up waiting and jumped away, looking for a new home?' asked Mye, looking down at Ed from the captain's raised dais.

'They didn't have jump technology,' said Andy. 'Even at maximum their bubble ships couldn't have got even halfway across their system in that length of time.'

'Then they're here somewhere,' said Ed. 'They just have to be…unless someone else has picked them up.'

'Who else knew about them?' Mye asked.

'Well, only Salft as far as we know, and she only had a gunship,' said Andy.

'Captain,' a voice called from the rear of the room.

Mye turned and lifted her chin at the officer as a signal to speak.

'Erm…I'm getting some peculiar readings from the surface of the planet,' he said.

'Explain?' said Mye.

The officer pointed at the holomap as he panned the ship's huge cameras in on an area of barren desert below.

'The planet's been dry for many millennia,' he said. 'But I'm getting small areas of moisture dotted around the surface that really shouldn't be here after all this time.'

The image above them displayed a circular concave discolouration in the dry surface. Excreter lines stretching out from the zone displayed evidence of an impact of some kind.

'Oh crap,' said Ed. 'I hope that isn't what I think it is.'

'And what's that?' asked Mye, turning back to him.

'They've suicided,' said Andy, dolefully.

'I promised them I'd be back,' said Ed, his shoulders slumping. 'What are we going to tell Oona?'

'Wait,' came a call from Ed's right.

They all turned to find another of the array operators, her arm in the air and her face glued to her screen.

'What have you got, Bern?' Mye asked.

'One of the larger asteroids, Captain,' she said. 'I think something just peeked out…the rock here is very dense and our scans can't penetrate into it very far.'

'Give the location to the navigator and take us there,' Mye ordered.

All eyes were on the holomap as the giant vessel negotiated its way into the multitude of asteroids orbiting the planet, creating the occasional sparkle on the ship's shields as they bumped into some of the smaller inconsequential rocks. Everything was concentrated on the asteroid in question now and it soon became apparent there was an opening on one side they hadn't been able to see or scan inside.

'There, sir,' said the officer, panning a camera into the deep crevasse.

'You have the language file I gave you,' said Ed. 'Can you patch me in so I can flash some dialogue into that hole?'

The captain pointed at one of the communication officers and nodded. He tapped a few icons for a moment before nodding at Ed.

'This is Edward Virr, I've returned as promised with a bigger vessel to take you to a new ocean planet, please respond.'

There was a short delay before a reply came.

'You're too late.'

'Why d'you say that?' Ed asked.

No reply came for a few moments.

'I can push a tractor beam in there and pull it out, sir,' said a voice from Ed's left.

'No you bloody won't,' said Andy, turning to face the speaker and giving him a glare.

'They're all dead,' came the eventual reply.

'What happened?'

'They didn't believe you would return.'

'You did.'

'Not really…I'm just a coward.'

'Are you alone?'

'There's three of us.'

'Plus your colleague on my ship, that makes four. More than enough to restart somewhere new and beautiful.'

'It's not worth it…it'll take forever.'

'The universe will wait. It'll be here for a while yet,' said Ed. 'Just think of the advances your race has made over the millennia. You'll be starting out with all that and more that we can provide. You won't be alone either.'

'What's in it for you?'

'To not witness a tragedy,' he said. 'We're explorers and live for the days we can meet and learn from other amazing species such as yourselves. It's very rare to find another sentient race that isn't humanoid. I'll also have a new friend…if you'll let me.'

'Would we get to choose our new home?'

'Purely ocean planets are rare, but yes, we wouldn't place you somewhere you didn't like.'

'I think I might like that.'

'Does that mean you'll come with us as our guest?'

There was a slight pause again and Ed held his breath.

'Yes.'

'I'll come with you too,' coloured a new voice.

'Me as well,' said a third.

Ed puffed his cheeks out and exhaled a sigh of relief.

'That's wonderful news and thank you for trusting in me, I won't let you down.'

'Where do we go?'

'There's a hangar opening on our port side,' he said, unable to keep the grin off his face. 'Enter slowly through the atmosphere barrier and you'll find you get pulled down to the floor by the ship's internal gravity. Don't worry when your sphere flattens slightly, it's quite normal and don't be surprised about the size of the hangar; we were expecting a lot more of you. I'll be there to welcome you personally.'

All eyes on the bridge were glued to the hole in the asteroid. They didn't have to wait long as three spheres slowly emerged and made their way towards the huge cruiser, expertly dodging around the smaller rocks.

'How the hell do those things move about?' said Mye. 'I can't see any kind of drive motor at all.'

Ed shrugged and turned towards the main bridge door. As he made his way across the room, he noticed there seemed to be a newfound respect in people's eyes that hadn't been there when he'd entered.

'I think we're going to learn a lot about fluid dynamics from these guys,' said Andy, following Ed. 'There's some weird physics going on in those things.'

They didn't have to wait long after they'd arrived for the three Vriix spheres to buzz through the atmosphere barrier together and immediately squish down onto the deck floor. The hangar foreman picked each one up gently with the internal tractor beams and positioned them at the back of the large room, next to one of the exits.

Once they were in position, Ed and Andy walked over and placed a light panel that resembled a large A-frame in front of the spheres. Then Andy signalled for the hangar foreman to dim the lights a little. He'd designed the portable translator and got the engineering department to knock it up while they were on the way here.

'Welcome to *Katadromiko 21*,' said Ed, the panel translating the words into light and colour.

Three octopods floated over and peered at them through their peculiar fluidic hulls.

'You are our guests,' said Ed. 'If there's anything you need, just ask.'

'Will the journey take long?' one of them flashed. 'We use the nutrient in the fluid a lot quicker when we're awake and our hulls don't absorb more when we're out of our starlight.'

'I don't know how you measure time,' said Ed, rubbing his chin in thought. 'But it will be a lot less time than you've just had to wait for me to come back.'

'That is quite acceptable…we will rest now.'

45

Salft Engineering Platform, the Exoplismoi system,
Milky Way

THE ELEVATOR TOOK them up to the control room on level 52. It was obvious things had gone badly awry as soon as they entered. All the screens that would normally display the station's position in orbit were blank, but the screens showing camera views were working.

Linda stopped in the middle of the room and saw to her horror that the station was in a slow lazy lengthwise spin with the huge red planet of Sidero passing by every thirty seconds or so.

'Oh shit,' said the young girl. 'We must be so out of position.'

She dived into a chair and started tapping away on a control panel, muttering under her breath every few seconds.

'Are we out of orbit?' Linda asked.

'It's hard to tell,' she said. 'We need to reverse this spin first. Ghent, can you see if the manoeuvring jets are operational, I'm getting nothing from the array.'

'Yep,' he said, sliding into a seat on the other side of the room that had what Linda thought looked like two old-style fighter jet joysticks built into its arms.

Linda detected movement through her feet as he began manipulating them and watched on the screens as the spin slowly began to reduce.

'We're much lower,' he said, giving his colleague a nervous glance. 'The planet's bigger in the screens than it used to be.'

'Can you get us back up?' she asked.

'No chance,' he said. 'We'd need the jets on full and about a dozen tractor tugs to do that. We're way too low to do it ourselves.'

'So you're saying this whole facility is doomed?' she said, looking very scared now. 'Can't we call for help?'

'The nearest platform with tugs of the size we need is a couple of hours' flight away. They're powerful, but not very fast.'

'How much time have we got?' Linda asked.

'Hard to gauge it, but a rough guess would be an hour or two,' he said.

'Best get everyone in a lifeboat then,' said Linda. 'Where are they?'

'There are three,' the girl said. 'One over there for the control room staff, one down in the accommodation level and one on the side of that hangar we were in.'

'Only three for a station this big?' Linda inquired.

'It's an automated yard,' she said. 'There never were many people on here.'

Linda looked around the outer wall and found an arrow signalling the direction to the control room lifeboat. She followed it to the small round airlock and peered through the glass porthole.

'This one's not there,' she said, glancing back at the girl.

'What?' she said, quickly hitting some icons on her screen. 'Oh fuck,' she said, a few seconds later. 'They've been jettisoned.'

'What…all three?' said the man.

'Uh, huh,' the girl mumbled, her head in her hands.

'Who the hell left the station on those?' Linda asked.

'That's just it,' said the girl, lifting her head up and staring at Linda teary-eyed. 'It's recorded here that they were jettisoned empty just after your ship disappeared.'

Linda's shoulders slumped as she groaned. She stared up at the ceiling for a moment before glancing back at the screens showing the massive planet looming large.

'She was cleaning house,' she mumbled, more to herself than anyone else.

'How d'you mean?' asked the girl, overhearing the comment.

'The prize had gone,' Linda said. 'She had no more business here, so decided to cut her losses, grab the autonurse and move on.'

'Making sure no one here survived,' said the man. 'That murdering bitch.'

'It's her middle name,' said Linda, glancing around at the other consoles. 'Can we put out a distress call?'

'Not without an array,' said the girl.

'Are there any other vessels hidden away on this thing?'

'No,' came the answer from both of them in stereo.

'Shit,' she said out loud. 'How the fuck do we get off this thing before it becomes an inferno… Think, Linda, think.'

She looked at the camera shots from inside the cavernous construction bay.

'What about those?' she said, pointing at the maintenance and construction tugs hanging lifeless in their parking bays.

'They're unmanned drones,' the girl said, shaking her head.

'That's actually not completely true,' said the man, rubbing his chin in thought and turning to stare at the same screen. 'They do have a small cockpit for intricate manual jobs. My father was a maintenance engineer on Stathmos Vasi station and used to operate similar machines. He taught me how to fly in one by sitting me on his knee.'

'So, you could get two people in one of those?' Linda said, looking at him questioningly.

'It's a squeeze and I was only ten at the time,' he said. 'But yeah, you probably could if your life depended on it.'

'Well, it does…come on,' said Linda, heading for the door. 'That's our way off this thing before it becomes a fireball.'

'I can't fly anything,' cried the girl, running to catch up with her.

'You can sit on my knee,' said the man, smirking, as they hurried towards the elevator.

'No bloody way,' she said. 'I'd rather die in an inferno.'

Linda rolled her eyes and thought it didn't matter where you were in the galaxy, men were always the same.

'You can go with me or Pol,' she said, placing her hand on the girl's shoulder.

The girl jumped back and glared at Linda.

'It's okay,' said Linda, holding her hands up in a placating manner.

The girl burst into tears.

'I don't want to die,' she wailed, collapsing into Linda's arms.

'You're not going to,' Linda whispered as the elevator doors opened. She pushed the girl inside, the man followed and stared at the wall, seemingly still a little miffed by his colleague's earlier comment.

They found the other man was already out of the autonurse when they exited back down on the hangar deck. He was flexing his arm with an incredulous expression.

'Are we all safe now?' he asked, hopefully.

'No,' said the other man. 'We're dropping out of orbit and we've gotta get off quickly.'

'Lifeboats then.'

His eyes widened as his colleague shook his head.

'They've been jettisoned.'

'Who the hell did that?' said Phil, looking over from the autonurse.

'Guess,' said Linda.

'Oh…her again,' he grumbled.

She nodded.

'There's no other way off though, is there?' he said, stopping what he was doing and staring nervously.

Linda smiled and pointed at the other man.

'This man knows a way,' she said, turning to face him. 'Take us there…and we'll need a speed reader's lesson on the controls.'

'This way,' he said. 'It's a bit of a walk, so we'll need to run.'

46

Katadromiko 21, *Ancients' gateway, Medusa Merger Galaxy*

THE BEHEMOTH CRUISER had headed straight for the galactic gateway after leaving Vriix and entered the triple moon triangle after slowing to a few hundred kilometres an hour.

Ed and Andy were both on the bridge to watch as they reappeared in the Milky Way. This time it was a destroyer there to welcome them.

'Welcome home, Captain Mye,' said a female voice as soon as they materialised. 'This is Captain Jess'kin of the destroyer *Viaios*.'

'Good evening, Captain,' replied Mye. 'I was expecting the *Katadromiko 7* to be welcoming us back.'

'Admiral Loftt recalled the 7 to Dasos to aid in the recovery programme,' she replied. 'So, lucky us got this prodigious posting.'

Mye smiled a rare smile and slid back into the captain's chair.

'Has there been any sign of the *Gabriel* since we've been gone?' Mye asked.

There was a pause as Jess'kin glanced down at her screen for a moment.

'The last report I have of the starship *Gabriel* is it arrived in the Prasinos system a few days ago. Current whereabouts unknown as I haven't had an up-to-date report for a while now.'

'At least we know they're okay and home,' said Andy, cheerfully.

'Thank you, *Viaios*,' said Mye. 'We will continue directly on to Dasos. *K21* out.'

'Safe travels,' replied Jess'kin. '*Viaios* out.'

'We need to start thinking about potential homes for the Vriix now we're here,' said Ed. 'Do we have a list of ocean planets that'd be suitable?'

'A list?' Mye said, giving Ed a questioning look. 'If you call two planets a list, then yes.'

'Two's better than none,' said Andy. 'Show us.'

Mye touched at the icons hanging in the air in front of her, before looking up at the holomap above. A blue predominantly ocean planet expanded into view and sat there slowly rotating.

'Wow,' said Andy. 'Where's that?'

'It doesn't have a permanent name, just a designation number,' said Mye. 'It's been available for settlement for hundreds of years.'

'What's wrong with it then?' Ed asked.

'There's actually nothing wrong with the planet at all. It's in a young system, a stable yellow dwarf star and a habitable climate. It's just the landmass is only six point four percent of the surface, which doesn't make it viable for a human settlement. A few have tried over time, but soon give up as there's just not enough arable land to grow enough food to feed a growing population. It's very rocky and the storms that blow in from the ocean flatten anything you do manage to grow.'

'What about fish?' asked Andy. 'There must be plenty of those to go round.'

'Yeah…but you soon get sick of eating it every single day.'

'You seem to know a lot about it,' said Ed, turning away from the hologram to stare at Mye.

'Ah…I knew someone in a past life that went there,' she said, looking nostalgic for a moment.

Ed noticed the slight change in Mye's demeanour as she spoke.

'Happy memories eh?' he said.

'Not particularly,' she retorted, snapping straight back into her professional captain's persona.

'Are we going there now?' Andy asked.

'No,' said Mye. 'I can't authorise a resettlement myself. It has to go before the council first.'

Ed approached the captain's chair and crouched down next to her.

'Those that survived the attack might be a little busy at the moment,' Ed whispered, so none of the bridge crew could overhear. 'If we were to transfer the Vriix onto the *Gabriel*, this conversation never happened and you're in the clear. All I need is the planet's location.'

Mye stared out across the bridge, her expression unchanging.

'Where's your ship likely to be?' she asked, quietly.

'Knowing Linda as I do, probably helping Bache with the mess at Dasos.'

'Hmm…I was kinda hoping to avoid going there. Too much scrutiny.'

'I'll contact Linda as we near and we can rendezvous somewhere private and you can legitimately say it was to transfer myself and Andy back to our own ship.'

Mye continued staring forward and nodded slightly.

'On your head be it,' she said. 'If this ever comes to light, I will state I informed you to get council authorisation first.'

'Absolutely,' said Ed. 'I'd never expect you to risk your career for us.'

'I'll call for you when we're a few hours out,' she said, glancing at him out of the corner of her eye.

Ed took the hint and stood. He grabbed Andy by the arm and steered him towards the main doors.

'Has something just been hatched?' Andy asked, as they made their way towards the tube station.

Forty-two hours later, Ed was woken by a call from the bridge. He quickly dressed and made his way there without disturbing Andy.

'Your ship isn't in the Prasinos system,' said Mye, as Ed walked through to the centre of the bridge.

'It could be cloaked,' he said.

'No…Loftt sent them to get the construction plans for the Klatt octaship from the Salft yard.'

'How d'you know that?'

'Heard it from an old friend,' she said.

Ed looked at her, hoping she'd expand on who it was, but soon realised she had no intention of revealing her source.

'Wasn't that in the Exoplismoi system?' he asked. 'I can't remember what the big red planet was called with all the shipyards above.'

'Sidero,' said Mye.

'That's the one,' said Ed. 'We better go there then.'

Mye glared down at him from the captain's raised dais.

'You giving me orders on my own ship, Virr?' she asked, sarcastically.

'Sorry…no…oops.' He pulled his best face of contrition and stared at a spot on the floor. 'Erm…what I meant to say was, would it be at all possible to go there?'

'In a word…no,' said Mye. 'But saying that, I have been given authorisation to lend you a shuttle so you and Faux can go there and liaise with your vessel.'

'Oh, right…okay,' said Ed. 'From the same old friend, I take it?'

'The shuttle comes back,' said Mye, keeping her gaze on him and ignoring his deliberate slight. 'It's on my inventory, which you've already managed to deplete somewhat,' she added, with added emphasis on the last word.

Ed detected a few sniggers from the crew behind him.

'Thank you, Captain…it'll be returned, I promise,' he said and scuttled off to wake Andy before the conversation got any more sarcastic.

47

*Salft Engineering Platform, the Exoplismoi system,
Milky Way*

THEY REACHED the construction tugs after a ten-minute jog
around the central yard and then up ten floors on a staircase.

Linda, like the others, arrived well out of breath at the tug
charging bays. There were twenty-eight tugs in all and the
group had to pass through an interior airlock onto the lower
of two gantries. Phil and Pol carried Rayl through onto the
gantry while the man they called Ghent entered a code into a
small panel on the back of the first tug in the line.

A small hatch opened, whirring upwards. Inside was one
seat and two joysticks similar to the ones that controlled the
position of the yard.

'You weren't kidding when you said it was cramped,' said
Linda, peering inside. 'I've seen more spacious coffins.'

'Don't say that,' said Phil. 'I hate confined spaces at the best of times.'

'Sorry,' said Linda, giving them a hand to post Rayl through the small opening and sit her in the seat.

'Okay,' said Ghent. 'The right-hand stick is purely for the manipulator arm, the left-hand one controls your direction and speed along with the foot pedals. If you find yourself out of control, release everything and the tug will come to an abrupt standstill, so don't travel too close. Whoever is piloting, wear the headset and I'll lead and talk to you while we're in transit.'

'Where are you planning on going?' asked Pol.

'The nearest other yard,' he said. 'It's the Cornhilder facility.'

'How far away is that?' asked Phil.

'Four and a half thousand kilometres.'

'Fuck…really,' said Linda, her nervous gaze meeting Phil's similar look.

'They're all fully gassed up and I'm planning on using one third of our propellant in accelerating, leaving a third for braking at the other end and the final third for manoeuvring and slight course adjustments.'

'How long d'you think it will take?' asked Phil, not looking much happier.

'A few hours,' he said. 'We're already much lower than them and it gets worse every minute we wait.'

'Okay. Pol, you go with the lady here, and I'll look after Rayl. Phil, you go with the other man here – sorry, I don't know either of your names – and Ghent, you drew the long straw as leader and get one to yourself, we'll all follow you.'

'Drew a what?' he called, as he went down the line opening three other tugs.

'Sorry, Earth term,' said Linda. 'It means you won and get a tug to yourself.'

'Oh, great,' he moaned, quietly to himself. 'I get to die alone.'

'What was that?' asked Phil, his face creased in worry.

'Stop worrying, Phil,' called Linda, as she climbed inside her tug and sat carefully in Rayl's lap. 'Just follow along behind me and go sparing with the propellant.'

Phil didn't answer, but looking through the front bubble screen, she could see him settling into the tug next door with the other guy and familiarising himself with the controls.

'Is everybody sealed and set?' asked Ghent a few moments later, after patching all four intercoms together.

Getting three affirmatives, he opened the outer airlock door, situated below and to their right. It was about ten metres in diameter and just big enough for the tugs to fly through one at a time. Once it had retracted fully, he released his clamps and jetted forward a few metres and turned to face them.

'One to release at a time and make sure they're completely through and clear of the airlock before the next releases,' he called. 'Is that clear?'

On receiving another three affirmatives, he turned and made his way down and out. Linda, next in line, released and accelerated forward a little too abruptly and had to release the joystick to avoid hitting the wall in front.

'Go easy on the stick,' she said. 'They're a little sensitive.'

It took a few minutes to get everyone outside the airlock. Pol had caught the door surround on her exit, which had spun her around. She quickly gathered herself, checked the rotation and brought the tiny ship under control. They then lined up behind Ghent and faced forward towards the distant gaping hole where the giant doors had been.

A big problem immediately became obvious, as it wasn't just the blackness of space now visible outside. A trail of smoke and flaming debris began snaking away behind the station.

'Oh, shit no,' shouted Phil. 'We're already too low, we're in the upper atmosphere.'

'Ghent, we're too late,' Linda called. 'We exit now, we'll burn up.'

'Ancients save us,' he mumbled.

48

GDA shuttle, en route to the Exoplismoi system, Milky Way

ED SAT STARING at the small holomap, checking their emergence co-ordinates were correct as Andy snored quietly in the co-pilot's seat. He powered the small ship onwards towards the next jump zone and again shifted position in the uncomfortable seat.

Captain Mye had had the last laugh and given them probably the oldest shuttle in her inventory. In fact, he didn't think it was a GDA vehicle at all. It was a strange boxy design and reminded Ed of an old-shape American campervan. It certainly operated okay, but the heat shielding on the underside was badly scarred from multiple planetary insertions and the general state was shabby to say the least.

There was a strange odour in the cockpit and the alma drive, although operating normally, made a peculiar buzzing sound.

'Are we there yet?' said Andy in a childish voice as he woke and stretched.

'One more jump,' said Ed. 'That is if this heap of shite holds together for that long.'

Andy stood up grimacing and rubbing his backside.

'What is it with these seats?' he moaned. 'It's like they're hewn out of solid granite, they're so fucking hard.'

'This thing was probably the marines' idea,' said Ed, having to shift his seating position again.

'Hmm,' grunted Andy. 'I forgot to ask, how was Callon when you last saw her?'

'Still sedated,' he replied, shrugging. 'Doctor grumpy pants was his usual unhelpful self and refused to give me any real update.'

'He's such a tosser,' said Andy, wincing as he sat down again. 'He has the bedside manner of a flying brick.'

'That's on a good day,' said Ed, forcing a half smile.

Andy noticed they were approaching the jump in zone for the Exoplismoi system.

'I'll be so glad to see my bed on the *Gabriel* again tonight,' he said.

'Same here,' Ed agreed, touching the jump icon and watching the holomap as it changed to the new location.

It lit up with countless ship movements around the large red planet of Sidero and Ed scanned the region for the *Gabriel*.

'Hmm,' he grunted, when nothing showed up. 'Must be cloaked somewhere.'

'We'd better go and ask at the old Salft yard,' said Andy. 'They might've been and gone.'

'That's weird,' Ed mumbled, powering the ship towards Sidero.

'What is?'

'It's not where it's supposed to be.'

'Has it been moved or something?' Andy asked.

'If it had, its identification beacon would show up somewhere else.'

'That's a big dust storm on the planet,' said Andy, glancing at Sidero as it grew bigger as Ed panned in.

Calling on an open band, Ed asked if anyone knew the whereabouts of the Salft yard.

They received no answer for a minute or so until something happened that wasn't what they were expecting. Three Sidero security gunships jumped in around them and grabbed hold of them with their tractor beams.

'Sidero security police,' a confident male voice said, booming over the cockpit speakers. 'You are being detained under emergency directorate 178a. Your ship's drive systems have been neutralised. You will be escorted to an undisclosed location and questioned. Once inside the hangar, please power down and open the airlock.'

'That might be the reason we can't see the *Gabriel*…it's cloaked,' said Andy.

'It's certainly a weird reaction for a shipyard location request,' said Ed, taking his hands off the control panel and crossing his arms. 'We'd better just comply and see what the hell's going on.'

Their holomap went dark too, leaving only the view from the front screen, which didn't show much until they approached a space station of some kind. They were whisked inside a hangar, their struts deployed and they were dumped down heavily on the deck.

'Bloody hell,' exclaimed Andy. 'I'm glad it's not my ship; that must've bent the struts.'

'I won't tell Mye if you don't,' said Ed, removing the fail-safes on the airlock, enabling him to open both at the same time.

As soon as it opened, four personnel marched in wearing full marine issue armour with arm weapons deployed.

'Identify yourselves,' one of them said threateningly, the suit's electronic voice making him sound like a robot.

'Edward Virr and Andrew Faux,' said Ed. 'Acting on behalf of Admiral of the Fleet Loftt.'

'Of course you are,' he said. 'And I'm the president. If you were here on behalf of the Admiral, you wouldn't be flying this heap of crap.'

'The Admiral of the Fleet's name isn't Loftt either,' said another.

'After what happened on Dasos, he is, and this beautiful yacht is what was available,' said Andy. Reclining back on his uncomfortable seat, he laced his fingers behind his head and closed his eyes. He guessed Ed would be taking the two on the right, so he concentrated his DOVI on the left two motorised marines' armoured suits and shut them down.

He'd been right. He opened his eyes again just as Ed stood up, dodged around the now frozen and completely silent suits and exited the ship. Andy followed close on his heels and stopped temporarily to activate the manual airlock close toggle.

The hangar wasn't large as hangars go and only contained a couple of other sleek black vessels parked against the back wall.

'We should take back one of those instead,' said Andy. 'Captain Mye might love us again.'

'The marines won't when they find out what we did to their mates here,' said Ed.

Andy looked back over his shoulder.

'They can still breathe and everything can't they?' he asked.

'Ah, yeah…I think so,' said Ed and walked on, grinning.

Andy took another look back at the old shuttle, shrugged, and trotted after Ed.

There didn't seem to be anyone else in the hangar, or so they thought, until a man in a dirty pair of overalls stepped out of an office and stared at them.

'Is it okay to continue now?' he asked.

'Why d'you ask?' said Ed.

'Well, the marines said to stay in my office until they had declared the area safe.'

'Ah, right,' said Andy.

'Then it is,' said Ed, smiling.

'Right,' he said, not looking convinced and peering around them, back towards the old shuttle. 'Where are they?'

'Taking a break,' said Andy.

'They've had a busy morning,' said Ed. 'I wouldn't disturb them if I were you.'

'They get a bit grumpy when they're tired,' Andy added, as they nonchalantly strolled off and exited the hangar.

'We should've asked him where the control centre is,' said Ed, as they found an elevator door with no obvious way to call it. Closing his eyes, Ed roamed around until he discovered everything on this station was operated by a skin implant if you were an employee and by wrist bands if you were a visitor. He downloaded the required file into his database and sent one to Andy, who did the same.

Ten seconds later the doors swished apart, only the elevator car wasn't empty. A tall man, wearing a blue suit ironed to within an inch of its life, stood staring at them, his shockingly close-together eyes glaring out from under the peak of a rather officious cap that matched the suit.

'Who are you two?' he demanded in a voice that was strangely high-pitched.

It made Andy laugh out loud, which got him a nudge in the ribs from Ed. A loud clumping and whining behind them got their attention and they both turned.

The four armoured marines had rounded the corner some thirty metres back at a steady trot. Their body language suggested they weren't in the best of moods.

'Must've rebooted the suits,' Andy said and pushed his way inside the car.

Ed followed, quickly selecting several floors above. He could hear the electronic voices of the marines shouting at them as the doors closed.

The suited man in the elevator made a move to unholster his weapon. Andy chopped down on his arm and brought his fist up again under the man's chin. The officer staggered back as the uppercut stunned him for a moment and his cap hit the ceiling, allowing Ed to grab the pistol.

He pointed it at the man's midriff and raised his eyebrows.

'Perhaps you'd like to tell me what you've done with the Salft platform?' he asked.

'What we've done?' he answered, in his squeaky voice. 'For fuck's sake, don't you know? Five hours ago, it dropped out of orbit and impacted the surface of Sidero at over twenty thousand kilometres per hour. The resulting quake collapsed three mines, killing hundreds and trapping even more. The dust cloud it created has grounded all rescue flights into the zone. It's a fucking nightmare.'

'That was the dust storm I saw,' said Andy, as the doors opened again.

'Out,' said Ed, prodding the man with the weapon.

'I'm head of security here,' he moaned. 'You're supposed to do what I say.'

'Get out,' said Andy, giving the man a resounding shove. He turned and glared at Andy while flexing his jaw and rubbing his chin.

They found themselves in a shorter corridor than before, with several doors on each side. Andy kept trying them until finally one opened. It was a small four-room apartment. Andy quickly checked the other rooms to make sure they were empty.

'Right,' said Ed, pointing at the couch. 'Sit there and explain exactly why you thought it wise to try and arrest two representatives of the GDA Council. The Admiral of the Fleet sent my ship to find the plans for that secretly built Klatt ship on the Salft yard, to aid in the reversal of the climate disaster on Dasos.'

'I didn't know that,' the security man said, his eyes flicking between them.

'I want you to tell me exactly what happened on that yard over the last twenty-four hours,' said Ed.

The man stared at Ed for a few moments, before maybe deciding that what he knew wasn't exactly classified information.

'A few hours ago, a vessel appeared in system and entered the Salft platform.'

'How big?' Andy asked.

'Ah…erm…a few hundred metres, I think. It was a new design. Theo, I think.'

Ed and Andy's eyes met.

'What happened then?'

'The doors closed behind it as it was tractored in.'

'It was pulled in by a tractor beam?' Andy asked.

He nodded.

'It was quiet for around an hour before two explosions came from the yard. One blew the huge doors off. The Theo ship emerged, destroyed the array and immediately jumped.'

Andy exhaled noisily.

'That's a relief,' he said. 'At least we know the *Gabriel* wasn't in it when it went down and they got away safely.'

'That ship was the *Gabriel*?' the officer asked, his eyes wide now. 'What…Edward Virr's ship?'

'Correct,' said Ed. 'So, you finally know who I am.'

'Oh, shit,' he said. 'Have I just tried to arrest the most famous man in the galaxy?'

He retrieved a tablet from a side pocket and after tapping on it for a few moments, held it up and scanned Ed.

'Shit,' he mumbled. 'You are too.'

The door slammed off its hinges and four seriously pissed off armoured marines clumped through with weapons raised, their electronic voices screaming for them to lie on the floor.

The Chief instantly stood up and put himself in front of the marines.

'STOP,' he shouted, holding his palms out in front.

Ed felt a surge of relief when they did and it went silent for a moment, all except for the high-pitched whining of the suit servos.

'These are the occupants of the old shuttle you sent us to arrest,' the lead marine stated. 'They attacked us when we entered their ship.'

The Chief looked the marines up and down for a moment, before turning and pointing at Ed and Andy.

'These two unarmed men attacked the four of you did they?' he asked, sarcastically. 'I don't see much damage.'

'They deactivated our armour, sir.'

'Did they now?' he said, raising his eyebrows and chuckling. 'What with?'

'We don't know, sir.'

'Well, they're my guests now,' he said, pointing at the door. 'Off you trot…and I want a report on how four of my supposed badass armoured marines were decommissioned in seconds by two unarmed civilians.'

'Yes, sir.'

'And fix that fucking door too.'

He turned back to them and waved a hand at the seating.

'Sit down, gentlemen. I apologise for the overreaction of my grunts. If it's any consolation, I didn't send them to arrest you, just to question you about the Salft yard. Normally, a couple of security guards would've been there to meet you, but they're all down on the surface involved in the rescue mission.'

'Handy in a war, but not for delicate negotiations,' said Andy, smiling for the first time in a while.

'Indeed,' said the Chief. 'Now, where were we?'

'The *Gabriel* jumping away after the explosions,' said Ed.

'That's right,' said the Chief, shaking his head. 'When the first explosion happened all eyes were suddenly on that yard. Our array scanned everything that happened. Including the Theo vessel as it emerged.'

'If the shields were up, you wouldn't have seen much,' said Andy.

'That's just it,' he said. 'Its shields were down and we were able to conduct a complete scan of the ship.'

'And?' said Ed.

'It was unmanned…there was no one aboard, except for one peculiar life sign in one of the hangars,' he said, sitting back on his seat.

'Oona,' said Andy.

'Yeah,' said Ed. 'But where are the girls and Phil?'

'Cleo would never abandon them,' stated Andy.

'No,' said Ed. 'She can't jump the ship without permission, unless it's to save the lives of the crew…something strange happened on that yard.'

'A second jump was detected too, less than an hour later,' the Chief said.

'What ship was it this time?' Ed asked.

'We don't know. This one was shielded, and the weird thing was, it jumped from inside the yard's hangar.'

'Bloody hell,' said Andy. 'They were in a hurry.'

'Have you got footage of the Salft yard going down?' Ed asked, turning to the Chief.

'From several angles,' he said. 'Come with me to the control centre and I'll show you.'

49

Salft Engineering Platform, the Exoplismoi system,

Milky Way

'I DON'T KNOW what to do…I don't know what to do,' Ghent
kept repeating.

'Ghent,' called Linda.

'I don't know what to do,' he muttered again.

'GHENT,' she shouted this time.

'Yeah…w…what?' he mumbled in return.

'Do these tugs have an antigrav drive?' she asked, trying
to remain calm.

'Er…yeah.'

'Where?'

'It's the blue switch under the hinged cover on your top
right panel,' he said. 'Ah…I see where you're going with this.
Once it's activated, use the same controller. We'll be dropping very fast, I don't know if—'

'Okay, everyone,' she said, drowning him out. 'Spread out so we don't collide, activate your drive and as soon as the fire reduces out the back, I'll say go and we all give it the full beans upwards. Try and avoid each other and land reasonably close together.'

'How do I activate the landing struts?' asked Phil.

'There aren't any fitted if they're for use on a space station,' said Ghent. 'But I don't think we'll slow—'

'Shut up, Ghent,' said Linda. 'If everyone's ready, spread out.'

The four tugs jetted sideways and faced the back of the yard, Linda flicked up the switch cover and pulled the blue toggle down. Immediately the comforting whine of an anti-grav began to spool up somewhere beneath her.

Looking out front, she could see some larger flaming lumps of the station trailing away as they peeled off the superstructure on the outside of the station.

As she watched, the fire, sparks and black smoke seemed to be receding. She patted Rayl's leg and took a deep breath.

'Ready, everyone…let's do it, good luck. Three, two, one, GO.'

The four tiny vessels shot upwards and out the gaping opening at the back of the station as though they'd been fired from a gun.

Linda realised she'd forgotten to warn people about the lumps of debris following close behind and scooted right to avoid the worst of it. She still heard a couple of cracks as small stuff ricocheted off the manipulator arms hanging off the front of the tug.

With the joystick rammed forward, she held her breath. There was no way of knowing what speed she was doing as the craft wasn't fitted with anything that would tell her. She tightened the harness around herself and Rayl and tried to peek out the side of the screen. Sky both sides reassured her the tug still had some height. She was loath to turn the craft around and face the ground, as that would cost braking time, which might become critical in the next few minutes.

A small tuft of cloud flashed by which reminded her she still carried some considerable speed. The scream of the small antigrav motor began to change pitch and get louder as the atmosphere became thicker. She noticed a crimson reflection coming off the underside of the manipulator arms and knew this was from the planet's red surface.

She tilted the joystick to the left slightly and peered out the side again. This time she saw a horizon with mountainous peaks and realised she had to turn the thing around to avoid hitting a mountain top. She quickly spun the tug on its axis and yanked the stick back the other way, and breathed a sigh of relief when a flat red desert swung into view. She thought her speed was still too high, but at least now she could flatten out the trajectory of her crash landing, theoretically ensuring it became a little more survivable.

Thinking quickly, she decided that landing on the manipulator arms was a better idea than on its back, as that might damage the only way out of the thing. If there was a fire, it didn't bear thinking about. Surviving the atmospheric insertion in a vehicle not designed for one and then dying in a fire inches from safety would be incredibly stupid.

A massive detonation off to her left made her jump, until she realised it was the remains of the station ploughing into the surface at many thousands of kilometres an hour. She knew she had to ignore it and concentrate on surviving her own crash.

The red dust was coming up rapidly now, so she manipulated the craft into a gentle curve. The antigrav changed pitch again and developed an ever-increasing rattle.

'Don't you give up on me now, you bastard,' she griped through gritted teeth. 'Come on, pull up, pull up.'

The ground rushed up all of a sudden, the rattling increased and right at the last moment she pushed the manipulator arms right out in front in a vain attempt to absorb some of the impact.

When it came, it was sudden, astoundingly shocking and the harness almost dislocated her arms at the shoulders. An unexpected explosion in the confined cockpit caused something to hit her in the face, before the craft began to roll along the surface, the resulting g-force of the rotation rendering her unconscious.

When she came around, she didn't know how long she'd been out, but her immediate worry was the smell. The reek of burning plastic and electrics scared the life out of her, and the thought of being trapped encouraged her to get a move on.

Releasing the harness, she yelped at the pain in her arms and after checking Rayl was still breathing, she turned and attempted to open the hatch behind them. It was twisted and completely jammed, and then she realised the craft was partially lying on it anyway, which would prevent it from opening in the first place.

A breeze on her face caused her to turn back to the front and discover the screen had smashed, which explained the explosion just before she passed out. It was a narrow gap, but just about wide enough to squeeze through.

'A couple more chocolate fudge cakes and I'd have been

screwed,' she said to herself, as she wiggled her way out, dragging Rayl with her.

Once out, she laid Rayl against the back of the tug, stood up and looked around. It was very warm, the system's star was high in the sky and a light breeze was coming from the opposite direction to the main crash site. The resulting mushroom cloud from the impact now reminded Linda of a nuclear detonation, and she was glad they were upwind of all that dust.

There was no sign of any of the other three tugs, and apart from the main crash site there was nothing on the horizon for many kilometres in any direction. She felt out with her DOVI, but found nothing there either.

'Bollocks,' she muttered, slumping down next to Rayl. 'Fucking ironic after surviving all that only to die here of dehydration.'

'Order a drink from the bar,' mumbled Rayl, her eyes suddenly opening wide. She glanced around at all the red sand. 'Are we on holiday?'

50

Sidero Station, Exoplismoi system, Milky Way

'WHO WAS IN THE LIFEBOATS? And did they get down okay?' asked Ed, as he watched the three tiny escape craft drift away from the station just after it fell out of orbit.

'The lifeboats performed perfectly,' said the Chief. 'Landed together and reasonably close to a populated area too. Only problem being, when the rescue team got there fifteen minutes later, they were all empty.'

'What?' said Ed. 'Are you sure? Perhaps they'd all wandered off somewhere before the team arrived.'

'Where to? It was about an hour's walk to the mining encampment and we scanned the entire desert for life signs only twenty minutes after they landed.'

'That's weird,' said Andy. 'I mean, who would jettison the lifeboats…for what possible reason would you do that?'

'To ensure no one survived,' said Ed. 'And cover their arse before jumping away from inside the hangar.'

'Who the hell would do something so inhumane?' asked the Chief, looking at the two of them strangely.

'Would you like a list?' said Andy.

'My money's on Ystolion Flast,' said Ed.

'Flast?' the Chief spluttered incredulously while shaking his head. 'She'd be two hundred fucking years old, surely?'

Both Ed and Andy shook their heads slowly in return.

'She stole a Theo autonurse and gradually reduced her age,' said Andy, pointing at the planet crash site on a nearby screen. 'It was on that station, because Flast became Salft.'

'Ah, shit…really?' said the Chief, slumping into a chair. 'You mean, Flast was right under my nose all that time? D'you know what the reward was for her capture? I could've retired years ago. I could've used the autonurse too, to sort my damaged vocal cords out.'

'Don't sweat it,' said Ed. 'She's outwitted us many times and annoyingly seems to have done it again.'

Andy glanced back up at the large screen showing the frozen image of the Salft yard.

'Did any other vessel fly off the station before it fell?' he asked.

'Not that we saw,' he said. 'But at the time we were trying to gauge where it would impact and warn those below.'

'Can we see the replay of it dropping into the atmosphere?'

The Chief nodded at one of the control room operators and the footage continued.

'Ah, crap…look at that thing,' said Andy, as they watched the leading edge of the yard turn crimson and quickly become enveloped in fire.

Lumps of infrastructure big and small peeled off and a thousand fire trails streamed behind as the huge station dropped towards the surface, the dark gaping hole of its yard entrance facing back into space.

It was just as the blackened, smoking hulk had dropped into the lower atmosphere that Andy suddenly recoiled and pointed at the screen.

'STOP,' he shouted. 'Go back a bit and replay it in slow motion.'

The operator did as he requested and the footage began again, this time much slower.

'STOP,' Andy said again, and the image froze once more.

'What've you seen?' Ed asked, squinting at the image.

Andy walked over and pointed at several tiny, faint objects ejecting from inside the rear of the yard.

'What are those?' he asked. 'There's four of them…can we pan in on them?'

The operator nodded.

'We'll lose picture quality the further we go in,' he said, as he manipulated the depth and focus. One of the objects became larger and fuzzier, until finally it became just a pixelated smudge.

The operator reversed the pan and pulled back again slowly frame by frame, to a point where it became a solid object again.

A voice from the right-hand side of the room broke the silence, causing them all to turn.

'It's a tug,' the man said. 'I'm pretty sure of it…I used to operate them on the Desgran yard.'

'Wow,' said Ed. 'So, we've got four tugs shooting out the back of the thing at just the right moment to avoid burning up.'

'I take it those things have an antigrav drive?' Andy asked, looking at the man.

'They do, sir,' came the reply.

'Would it be powerful enough to slow the thing sufficiently?' asked Ed.

The man shrugged.

'No idea, sir.'

When the operator continued the footage, the four dots disappeared off the screen as the cameras continued to follow the main wreck.

'We need to find out where those things landed,' said Ed, turning to the Chief.

'Or crashed,' said Andy.

Everyone in the room turned towards him.

'They might be injured,' he said, shrugging. 'And if it had been me, I would have veered well away from the main crash site and come in at an angle to reduce the severity of the impact…so we need to search a very wide area.'

'He's right,' said Ed.

'They don't have landing struts either,' said the man who used to operate them. 'They're designed to operate in space or in gravitational hangars.'

'Okay,' said the Chief. 'We're looking for four crash sites of some kind. It could be they managed to slow down enough and just fell over on landing, or they came in at speed and left a track in the desert floor, or a mixture of both. Whatever it is, it's imperative we find them. If the people in those tugs have survived, they will know what really happened on that station.'

Ed and Andy exchanged a worried glance.

'There's debris impact zones all over, sir,' came a voice from their right.

'I know,' he said. 'All of you take a zone each and just go through them one at a time. No one takes a break until we find them.'

'We might go down there and scan around on the ground,' said Ed. 'Better than sitting on our arses here and waiting.'

'Okay,' said the Chief, nodding. 'Remember to stay well out of those dust clouds though, that stuff eats antigrav drives. Otherwise you'll create another crash site.'

'We will,' said Andy, as they made for the door.

'Tell you what,' said the Chief, following them. 'You take one of our shuttles. That shitbox you arrived in has already done too many insertions, it's an accident waiting to happen just parked.'

Andy chuckled at the man's sense of humour and began to regret punching him in the face earlier.

51

Northern desert, Sidero, the Exoplismoi system, Milky Way

LINDA THOUGHT after a short conversation that Rayl seemed to be a little more herself. The sedation the autonurse had administered appeared to have let her brain recover somewhat from the trauma of the knock.

Rayl had no knowledge of the past few days, which Linda thought was probably a good thing and she wasn't about to tell her much either. Her main problem now was, do they stay put and wait for help, or walk and try to find some?

She remembered a holiday in Australia, driving out in the bush. They'd been told if you broke down to always stay with the vehicle. There was also however a niggling thought that here they weren't on a track of any kind and if no one had detected the crash, then the chances of someone coming along were next to none.

It was now dusk and beginning to get dark, and the

temperature was dropping. She had nothing to light a fire with – or burn on a fire, for that matter. She decided to wait until the morning to make the decision. The risk of fire in the wreck itself seemed to have diminished as all the earlier buzzing and whirring had gone quiet now and the worst of the burning electrics smell had dissipated.

They climbed back inside, reasoning it would be a little warmer and they didn't know if any carnivorous fauna, indigenous to the area, roamed the desert at night.

Linda snuggled down next to Rayl in the cramped cockpit. She was glad she'd kept the laser pistol close at hand through everything as she checked it was set on heavy stun and slowly closed her eyes and soon fell asleep.

It was having the weapon snatched from her grasp that woke her. The noise of the approaching vehicle and the crunch of boots in the dry sand certainly hadn't.

She jerked back to find a masked face staring at her in the flickering shadows of the vehicle's headlights.

'Out,' the figure demanded, indicating as much with the muzzle of his own weapon.

'Have you come to rescue us?' asked Rayl, having been woken by his single word.

He laughed.

'Not exactly the term I would've used,' he said.

'Have you any water?' Linda asked, as she climbed out.

'Want something from us now, do you, Gidda?' said one of the others, also wearing some sort of matt black ski-mask.

He shoved her towards the vehicle by her arm. She

grunted as it reawakened the pain in her shoulder from the crash impact.

'What's a Gidda?' asked Rayl, stumbling along behind Linda.

There were four of them, all wearing similar masks, one driving the vehicle and three others, who all laughed at Rayl's question, but not one of them gave her an answer.

'Are you from one of the mining companies?' Linda asked, as they were bundled into the back of the vehicle, which shot away as soon as they were all aboard, its wheels spinning in the crusty red sand.

'Are you being deliberately obtuse, or are you really that naive?' one of them mumbled.

'Thirty seconds,' came a shout from the driver, stopping Linda questioning the man about what he meant by that.

'Will we make it?' another of the men asked the driver.

'It's going to be close,' the reply came as the little truck screamed across the flat expanse.

They were all jolted forward as the driver savagely hit the brakes. Linda glanced forward and through the front screen. The headlights showed a lump of still smouldering debris sticking out of the ground dead ahead. The vehicle skidded to a stop right next to it.

'Nobody move,' called the driver, as all four men sat stock still and stared forward.

A continuous alarm began singing out in the front somewhere. It reminded Linda of a missile lock siren from her fighter jet days.

'What the hell is that?' she asked.

'Shut up and don't move,' one of them growled through gritted teeth.

'It's longer than normal,' one of them said, as the siren continued its wail.

'Have they spotted us?' another said, sounding nervous.

'Spotted by who?' Rayl asked.

'Shut the fuck up,' was the only answer she got.

The siren ceased as abruptly as it had started.

'They're spending more time inspecting the debris sites for survivors,' said the driver.

'D'you think they detected us?' asked the man sitting next to Rayl.

'The roof shield would have disguised our life signs,' came the reply, as the driver engaged the drive again, the electric vehicle wheels spinning as the small truck launched off into the darkness once more.

Linda had given up asking questions and every time a reflection from the headlights flashed across Rayl's face, she noticed her eyes were closed.

They'd been rushing across the barren featureless redness for about twenty minutes when Linda heard the whine of the motor change pitch suddenly as the truck tilted forward slightly. She stretched up and looked forward again to see they'd entered some sort of cave, but without slowing to any degree. She gripped hold of the seat arms, her knuckles going white, as the vehicle thundered deeper through the narrow rough passageway at what seemed like a suicidal velocity.

She was pushed forward again as finally the driver mashed the brakes, turned abruptly left and stopped at a set of steel doors.

'Everybody out,' he said. 'Take the assets below, while I report to Faiten.'

'Are we going out again tonight?' asked one of the men,

as they prodded Linda and Rayl off the back of the truck and towards the giant doors.

'Too risky,' the driver said. 'They're paying this area a lot of attention at the moment.'

'Do we put these two with the others?'

Linda's ears pricked up at that question.

'No, keep them separate.'

The huge doors rumbled open and they were escorted in at gunpoint. It wasn't what Linda was expecting. They were in a huge metal box, big enough to get a large truck inside. It was a bit rusty round the edges and she could see scars along the sides scraped by large vehicles, probably over many years.

The doors rumbled shut again and Linda expected the far end to open, similar to an airlock. When the whole thing began to descend, with a lot of clanking and scraping, she realised it was an immense elevator. It rattled downward for several minutes and, being fully enclosed, she had no idea how deep they were being taken.

'Is this one of the mines?' she asked, getting eye contact with one of their captors.

She got no answer, but could tell by the way he rolled his eyes and the slight shake of his head, he thought the question was totally stupid.

The elevator shuddered to a knee-jarring halt. The far side did indeed then open, but what was slowly revealed as the huge steel monolithic doors rumbled apart shocked Linda so much, all the hairs on the back of her neck stood up.

An empty underground cavern, the size of a large city, stretched away into the distance, so enormous she struggled to see the far side. It was warm down here too and a light mist hung up close to the ceiling, obscuring whatever it was that lit the huge space to a dull red glow.

Linda was prodded on out of the elevator and towards a waiting cart similar in design to a golf trolley on Earth. Rayl followed Linda, not really paying attention to anything around her, a neutral expression on her face.

Yesterday, after they'd survived the crash and Rayl had awoken, Linda had been reassured that the old Rayl was returning. But now, this version had her concerned again.

The trolley whizzed them around the outside of the colossal chamber, turning suddenly left through a small opening in the rock face, down a narrow passage, before turning sharp right and pulling up sharply. A bunch of what looked like prefabricated buildings had been constructed into the side cave. Linda presumed they would've been site offices at a time when the mine was operational.

A door was opened and they were ushered from the cart and inside a windowless box. Just before the door was slammed shut and the mechanical lock rattled, Linda heard a voice she recognised shouting from an adjacent room.

'Oi…shit heads, what about some fucking food, we're starv…'

She smiled, as she helped Rayl to sit down on one of three uncomfortable-looking camp beds.

'That was Pol,' she said to Rayl.

'Four-armed freak,' mumbled Rayl, as she lay down and closed her eyes.

Linda slumped down dejectedly onto one of the other beds and shook her head.

'Bollocks,' she mumbled to herself. 'Out of the frying pan…'

52

———

Sidero Station, Exoplismoi system, Milky Way

THE CHIEF TOOK Ed and Andy back down to the hangar where their old shuttle was parked. He passed it by with raised eyebrows and glanced back at them.

'Tell me you didn't choose to fly that thing?' he said with a wry smile and walked on to one of the black craft parked against the back wall. 'You can use one of these.'

'I saw these earlier,' said Andy. 'What are they?'

'They were a prototype and custom-built ship made in the old Grenselhuit yard,' he replied. 'They couldn't pay their security bill a couple of years ago and we took these in lieu. They were going to pay us the money, then they'd get the ships back. The company folded so we kept them. I'd use one myself, but I can't fly. They told me they were being built for the company's owner and his wife.'

Both the small airlock hatches slid to the left and disappeared inside their bulkheads, revealing a small sleek cabin.

'Wow, look at this, Ed,' said Andy, climbing the three steps and sticking his head inside. 'It's like a Lamborghini in 'ere.'

Ed clambered in and had to admit Andy was right. The ceiling was low and the two front bucket-type seats were covered in some kind of blue stitched leather material with white piping. The rest of the interior was colour coordinated, with blue back-lit, contoured control panels that motored back to surround you and then tilt up towards you.

'Cloaking?' Andy asked.

'Yep,' said the Chief. 'This as well,' he added, touching an icon on one of the screens.

A whining came from outside and Ed, being at the back, stuck his head back outside to find a rather chunky laser cannon had dropped down from the small winglet just behind the airlock.

'One on both sides?' he asked.

'Uh huh,' nodded the Chief. 'They tell me the controls are standard GDA configuration, so you can fly it with a regular POK.'

'Cool,' said Andy, sliding into one of the seats. 'It's got a really advanced array too,' he added, as he activated some of the array's screens.

'Just make sure you bring it back,' said the Chief. 'Don't be leaving it unattended anywhere or the Kakous will have it away in seconds.'

'The Kakous?' Ed asked, raising his eyebrows.

'Subsurface bandits,' he replied. 'I suppose you wouldn't know if you hadn't been here before. They're disgruntled ex-employees of mining companies, having been sacked or made redundant, that sort of thing. Mining companies down there come and go and always leave a few residuals.'

'How do they survive?' asked Andy, looking over his shoulder.

'Theft,' he said. 'Pinch kit from one company and sell it cheap to another. They've occasionally been known to kidnap personnel for ransom.'

They all turned to the airlock as the sound of boots running across the hangar got their attention. A sightly out of breath girl Ed recognised from the control room stuck her head in the cockpit.

'We've found one of the tugs, Chief,' she said.

'Did it land safely?' Ed asked.

She winced before speaking.

'Don't know about safely,' she said. 'The skid marks are over a kilometre long, so it went down at some velocity.'

'Life signs?' Andy asked.

'None,' she said. 'But there are no bodies inside the wreck either.'

Ed turned back to Andy.

'They could've climbed out and gone to find help,' Ed said, trying to appear positive.

'We need to get down there,' said Andy, turning back to the control panel and sparking the antigravs into life.

The Chief took the hint and squeezed past Ed, but before he climbed out, he turned.

'Hang on just a moment,' he said. 'I've got something you might need.'

He jumped down the steps and trotted over to a grey steel cabinet on the back wall. He fed a code into a keypad on the front of it and opened the door. Quickly returning to the ship, he passed two marine issue laser rifles and a couple of special operations ration packs up to Ed.

'The Kakous are armed and you might need something with a bit more discouragement than your stun pistols.'

'Thanks, Chief,' said Ed. 'What's your name by the way?'

'Stratton,' he said. 'Coll Stratton. Tell me, is Bache Loft really the new Admiral of the Fleet?'

They both nodded.

'Hmm,' he said, looking wistful. 'I worked with him in the early days when I was a navigator in the navy.'

Ed closed the two airlock doors and reset the fail-safes, just managing to slide into the second seat as Andy lifted the small craft up and retracted the struts.

'This is really nice,' he said, as it fizzed through the atmosphere shield and out into space. The tiny ship turned and the cockpit lit up with a soft red glow as Sidero slid into view.

The co-ordinates of the tug landing site pinged onto the nav screen. Ed selected it as Andy activated the shields and instigated the auto insertion to take them there.

Ed was glad the seats were comfortable, as the small craft got bounced around quite a bit when the atmosphere began biting into the heat shielding underneath. Once deep enough, the nose dropped and the enormous dust storm spreading north from around the crash site filled half the screen. Andy took the ship off auto and turned south and upwind to avoid it.

'I'll keep the speed on for a while,' he said, pointing. 'The crash site's over near that mountain range.'

'No life signs in the vicinity,' said Ed. 'Plenty of heat signatures dotted around, but no people.'

The planet was large and distances considerable, so it still took thirty-six minutes to get there, even at many times the speed of sound.

Ed was out of his seat as Andy crunched the struts down into the red sand. He grabbed one of the rifles just in case the readings had been wrong and opened both airlock doors. The early morning chill made him shiver as he jumped down and approached the badly damaged tug. It had ended up lying on its front, the remains of mechanical arms buried in the dust and the rear hatch hanging open.

He peered inside. It was empty as he'd expected and he noticed the harnesses were hanging outwards off the seat, discarded by whoever had piloted the thing down.

'There's no blood or anything,' he said, as Andy looked over his shoulder.

They both turned and inspected the surrounding area for any kind of trail.

'Vehicle tracks,' said Andy, pointing and striding off to the left. 'It must've stopped here and wheel spun off in that direction.'

He nodded in the direction of the mountains. Ed stared at the soaring peaks in the near distance and glanced down at the tracks coming from and going back in that direction.

'I think we know where we're going next then,' he said, patting Andy on the shoulder.

They both turned and four minutes later, shielded and cloaked, they skimmed across the surface, just high enough to avoid kicking up a dust trail and giving away their existence and trajectory.

As they neared the strange rock formations suddenly sprouting from the flatness of the desert, they noticed a few derelict buildings and several more vehicle tracks coming in from multiple directions. They all however joined as one and disappeared inside a vehicle-sized opening at the base of the rock face.

'Small as we are, we can't fly in there,' said Andy, glancing sideways at Ed.

'No, you're right,' Ed agreed. 'From now on, I think we're on foot.'

53

Mining cavern, Sidero, the Exoplismoi system, Milky Way

LINDA ALMOST JUMPED out of her skin, as what she'd thought was an old pile of rags on the furthest away of the dozen or so camp beds suddenly sat up and stared at her.

'*Calez ton ver,*' the rather dishevelled and nervous-looking woman blurted.

'D'you speak Ellinka?' Linda asked, trying to sound calm, although her heart rate had soared.

'Little,' she replied, holding her thumb and forefinger close together.

'What's your name?'

'Had'qar,' she said, pointing at herself, before turning her finger towards Linda. 'Name?'

'Linda. How long have you been here?'

'Very long,' Had'qar said, nodding. 'Ransom for Kakous, yes.'

That one word explained a lot to Linda, as she realised what all this might be about. She closed her eyes and questioned her DOVI's database of information. Inputting Sidero and Kakous, the immediate response explained the remainder. She was being held for ransom by anti-GDA rebels hiding in deserted mines on Sidero.

'Yes,' she answered, rolling her eyes and smiling at Had'qar. 'Ransom.'

Some of the fear in the woman's face dissipated as her mouth creased in a half smile in return. She glanced over at Rayl.

'Unwell,' she said, the smile becoming a grimace as she continued to stare at Rayl.

'Yes, she is unwell,' said Linda. 'How did you know?'

'Jensetten,' she said, pointing at herself again. 'Odour.'

This confused Linda until she questioned the meaning of Jensetten. The database came back with *humanoids from the planet Jens, heightened senses, sometimes can detect your thoughts and especially the sense of smell.*

'Ah,' said Linda, looking back at her and tapping her nose.

Had'qar nodded and the shy smile returned again. She pointed at her shoulders and then at Linda.

'Arms unwell,' she said, raising her eyebrows. 'Kakous hit?'

Linda was amazed she could detect even her sore shoulders.

'No,' she replied. 'Ship crash.'

'Oh,' she said, staring intently. 'You concern for other.'

Linda nodded, but failed to keep the anxiety off her face.

She held up three fingers.

'Others,' she said, pointing to the room next door. 'Arrive.'

'Three others arrive before me?' Linda asked.

'*Ako*,' she said, nodding.

Linda presumed this was Jensetten for "yes."

'Are you sure it was just three?' she asked.

'*Ako*.'

Had'qar must have sensed Linda's disappointment, as her expression turned melancholic again.

'Missing friend?' she said.

'*Ako*,' said Linda.

'GDA find,' she replied quickly, tilting her head to one side. 'Kakous not.'

'I hope so,' said Linda. 'Anyway…why have you been here so long?'

'No pay.'

'Who, no pay?' she asked.

'Ancestor.'

'Which one…father? Mother?'

'Er…father?' she said, staring at Linda questioningly. 'Possible.'

'Why not pay?'

Had'qar shrugged and looked away, seemingly embarrassed at the question.

'H'mm,' Linda grunted, chewing on her lip. 'When we leave…you come with us,' she said, smiling again.

Had'qar snorted and shook her head as if Linda had said something ridiculous.

'Human appear…human go. Had'qar stay,' she said, tilting her head to one side again.

Noise from outside the door followed by a rattling of the lock had them both turning in that direction.

Two of the men from before stepped inside as the door opened, their rifles leading the way.

'You two come with us,' one of them said, pointing at Rayl and Linda.

Linda took her time so she could concentrate on neutralising their weapons. She could also see another one of them sitting in the driver's seat of the buggy outside. He didn't seem to have a weapon to hand, so she decided to leave him until last.

Walking up to the leading guard, she stopped and turned to face Rayl, who was sitting up on the bunk and looking confused.

'Come on, Rayl,' she said, extending her arm as if to beckon to her. What she actually did was recall a bit of the karate she had studied as an air force recruit many years ago. Her arm lanced back, her elbow hitting the man square on the nose with a crack as it broke and he dropped like brick. The other guard surged forward, bringing his weapon into the shoulder, but finding it wasn't working. He slowed slightly and pulled out Linda's pistol from behind his back.

Linda hadn't hesitated after downing the first man and had closed the gap. As he raised the pistol, she pushed the barrel up with her left hand and chopped down on his forearm with her right, head butting him at the same time.

As he staggered back, she reversed the pistol and hit him with a heavy stun bolt square in the chest. His legs went from under him and he joined his colleague on the floor. She stuck her head out the door to find the driver staring at her with wide eyes. The pistol was brought up again, this time with a double-handed grip, and the driver fell out of the cart unconscious after two bolts hit him in the side and the arm.

Linda heard Had'qar gasp, but before she could turn, the

first guard, with blood pouring from his nose, barrelled into her, knocking her off her feet as he came down on top of her. Her shoulders screamed as she tried to roll him off. He was having none of it. She could see the anger in his eyes as he twisted the weapon out of her hands and turned it towards her face. She gritted her teeth and tried to keep the barrel pointed away from her, but he was too strong and gradually as her strength faded it slowly turned around to face her. She instinctively closed her eyes and waited for the lights to go out.

The thump when it came jolted her whole body and her shoulders screamed their disapproval once more. Realising she was still conscious, she opened her eyes to find Had'qar standing over her holding one of the guard's rifles by the barrel. The guard was still half on top of her and out cold where he'd been crowned with his own weapon.

'Lovely, good,' said Had'qar, grinning.

'Lovely, good, indeed,' said Linda, pushing the heavy man off her. 'That was brilliant,' she said, giving Had'qar a kiss on the cheek.

Had'qar beamed.

'Revimge,' she said, giving the guard a final kick.

'Revenge,' said Linda. 'It's pronounced, revenge.'

'That was cool,' said Rayl, standing in the doorway. 'She hit him on the head with a gun…she's in the gang.'

Linda rolled her eyes and flexed her sore shoulders.

'Come on,' she said. 'Let's release the others and get the hell out of—'

She spun around as the sound of electric carts entering the small cavern interrupted her. Two more carts had entered, both containing four armed occupants, and they weren't looking best pleased.

54

———————

Mining cavern, Sidero, the Exoplismoi system, Milky Way

ED AND ANDY entered the mine after landing and leaving the black ship secured and cloaked half a kilometre away right under the cliff face, as it was less likely to get run into there.

'Coll would kill us if they find it,' Andy said, looking over his shoulder.

'Do you want to come in here on your own then?' asked Ed, staring off into the blackness.

'Not really, although I did it once before to save your sorry arse,' he said. 'You know I hate enclosed spaces.'

'If our crew are in here, I'm getting them out,' said Ed, illuminating the light attached to the barrel of the rifle Coll had given him.

Andy did the same and remained quiet as they moved as fast as the small lights allowed them to. After a few minutes, the cave ended with two huge metal doors on the left. They both swung their lights around the sides looking for something to indicate what opened them.

'Must be remotely operated,' said Andy. 'Hang on, it's my turn today.'

He shut his eyes and had a feel around with his DOVI. Opening them again, he pointed up in the right-hand corner.

'There's a receiver up there,' he said. 'Give me a second to run through the permutations.'

Ed knew when he'd succeeded, as a low rumble sounded from within, followed by a high-pitched whining.

They looked at each other smiling and both said, 'Elevator,' at the same time.

'Get back in the shadows, just in case,' said Ed, moving to the right of the door, crouching down and turning his light off.

Andy did the same. Complete and absolute blackness enveloped them.

'Fuck me, it's dark,' Andy moaned.

'Shhh,' hissed Ed. 'Sound amplifies and echoes in here.'

The whining changed pitch as the elevator neared, before cutting out altogether. A sliver of light had crawled up behind the doors where they met in the middle and now provided a tiny triangle of light across the floor of the cave.

They both held their breath as a moment of silence ensued. Ed held up his hand in the gloom as he sensed Andy was about to say something.

They both jumped and squinted as a deep *boom* echoed around them and the cave was suddenly flooded with white light from inside the giant elevator. The doors powered away from each other, revealing an empty interior.

'Shit, it's big,' said Andy, blinking and trying to adjust his eyes to the brightness within.

'Big enough for ore trucks,' said Ed, squinting around at the interior. 'They must've had automated trucks; there's no button for a driver to press or anything.'

As he spoke, the doors began rumbling together again.

'No backing out now,' said Andy. 'Bottom floor for menswear and electricals.'

As the giant elevator began clanking its way down, Ed walked to the far end.

'It looks as if it's a door this end too,' he said. 'This will be the one that opens at the bottom.'

'How d'you figure that?'

'The ore trucks would need to drive straight out. Reversing would be a bit of a faff.'

'Give that man a bonus,' said Andy, looking the door up and down. 'We should be at opposite sides when it opens. Just in case Roger the rebel is waiting at the bottom.'

Ed nodded and smirked at Andy's comment as they took up positions either side of the door.

'It'll be funny if it is the other door,' called Andy, as he pushed himself flush with the huge door frame.

Ed grunted as the elevator stopped abruptly and he breathed a sigh of relief as the big door, just inches away from him, began to rumble open.

Andy, impatient to wait, trotted forward to peek around his door and walked slowly backwards with it as it opened.

'Fuck me,' he said. 'You could get a small planet in there.'

He stretched his neck around the door, looking left and right.

'We're clear,' he said, giving Ed the thumbs up.

They both scooted in and stepped sideways, concealing themselves in the shadows either side of the door.

'Bloody hell,' Ed mumbled to himself, as he witnessed the sheer magnitude of the cavern.

'This is mining on a Herculean scale,' said Andy, wandering over, having realised they were completely alone.

They both ducked as something big and black flapped overhead, disappearing into the rock face above.

'That was big too,' said Andy, searching around above them nervously.

'Everything about this planet is big,' said Ed, examining the ground around them. 'For all we know it could be in its Jurassic period.'

'Oh joy,' said Andy, glancing at his rifle. 'D'you think heavy stun would work against a pterodactyl?'

'Tracks,' said Ed, ignoring Andy's question and pointing at the ground. 'Small vehicle going that way and following the wall.'

He trudged off following the tracks, leaving Andy trailing along behind continually looking up over his shoulder.

A few minutes later, Ed stopped and pointed again.

'It's going into a cleft in the wall,' he said.

They both approached slowly and peered around the corner.

'Is that laser fire?' Andy asked, the noise distant but recognisable.

'Come on,' said Ed. 'Someone might need help.'

They moved with more purpose now, one on the left and one on the right as they traversed the narrow passage. About two hundred metres in the cave went sharp right. Ed waved at Andy to slow down, as the weapons fire was considerably louder now and the odd laser bolt zipped out from around the corner and into the wall on the bend.

'Whoever it is, isn't using a lethal setting,' said Andy,

pointing at the shots dissipating into the rock and not burning a hole.

Ed crept up and knelt down before peering around the corner as low down as he could, to avoid getting a stun bolt in the face. He could see two four-seater buggies, a couple of bodies lying face down and a few other men sheltering behind the vehicles, snatching shots towards a prefab building with another of the buggies parked outside.

'Can you see who they're firing at?' asked Andy, grabbing the odd glimpse around the corner above him.

'A girl in the building, by the look of it,' said Ed. 'I don't recognise her, but there's someone else behind the cart who's remaining completely hidde— Oh shit.'

'Oh, shit what?'

'It's Linda.'

'Are you sure?'

'Yeah.'

'How many attackers are there?'

'Err, six…I think.'

'You take the three on the right and I'll do the left ones.'

'Okay, we have the element of surprise: don't miss, make every shot a hit,' said Ed, rechecking his weapon was set on heavy stun. 'Ready…go.'

They both stepped out and took five paces before Andy decided they were close enough and began the turkey shoot. All six went down within about four seconds; only one got a shot off as Ed missed with his third shot. The attacker's shot was snatched though and zipped way over their heads, impacting the wall behind.

The girl in the doorway took a shot at them, before Linda jumped up and shouted at her to stop. The bolt luckily hit one of the carts.

The two boys sprinted over to Linda and hugged her within an inch of her life.

'We need to get out of here,' she said. 'There could be many more on the way.'

'Are the others with you?' Andy asked, as Had'qar walked over, eyeing the unconscious bodies warily.

'Rayl's in there,' said Linda, pointing to one of the rooms.

Andy turned and ran in that direction.

'She's not very well,' called Linda, as he disappeared inside the room. 'I think Pol's in this one,' she added, walking over, adjusting her rifle to full power and melting the lock.

Ed wrenched the door open to find Pol with a black eye, beaming at him and immediately falling into his arms. The other girl peered out from behind her and like Had'qar, surveyed the unconscious bodies strewn around the small cavern with trepidation.

'What happened to your eye?' he asked, inspecting it closely.

'Is it bruised?' Pol asked. 'I banged it on one of the control arms trying to land the tug.'

'Where's Phil?' Ed asked, looking over her shoulder and into the rooms. 'Is he still on the *Gabriel*?'

'He was in another of the tugs,' said Pol. 'And we have no idea what happened to the *Gabriel*, it blew its way out of the yard and jumped.'

'Was it Salft?'

'No, she was with us at the time and escaped in the gunship from the *28*.'

'Must've been Cleo,' said Ed. 'But why did she leave?'

'It wasn't her,' said Linda. 'Salft had the Theo codes to take the ship and shut down Cleo.'

'Well, someone was operating the ship,' said Ed. 'What about Oona?'

'We really have no idea,' said Linda. 'When Salft took control of it, we were escorted off and locked up on the station. The *Gabriel* left without her – she was livid. We presumed it must've been disgruntled employees of hers. She'd already had a mutiny on the *28* by the Klatt, causing her to scuttle it over a populated planet.'

'We know,' said Ed. 'We witnessed the mess she left behind and the Klatt are being blamed. The *Gabriel* wasn't taken by anyone as far as we know, because the Sidero security station scanned the ship before it jumped and reported no human life aboard.'

Raised voices caught their attention. Everybody turned to see Andy ducking out of the other room as one of the beds clattered into the door frame behind him.

'What on Earth did you do?' Ed asked.

Andy shrugged and looked nervously over his shoulder.

'Fucked if I know,' he said. 'She's having a go at me for little insignificant things that happened up to two years ago.'

'She was knocked unconscious a few days ago,' said Pol. 'Been acting and saying strange things since.'

'Phil had her in the autonurse for a while,' said Linda. 'He wasn't that confident with it being able to do much about a concussion.'

'Is that what he thought it was?' asked Andy. 'I've never known her so angry over nothing.'

'Whatever it is, she needs complete rest,' said Linda. 'We need to get her home and away from all this crap.'

'Okay,' said Ed. 'We just need to find Phil and we can get out of here.'

'Can Had'qar come with us?' asked Linda. 'She's been held down here for ransom for ages.'

'Absolutely,' said Ed. 'It'll be a bit of a squeeze in the shuttle we're using, but she's more than welcome to come along.'

Her face lit up with a smile, but adopted a contrite expression as both Ed and Andy turned to face her.

'I'm sorry I fired at you,' she said, cringing slightly. 'I didn't know you were on our side.'

'Don't sweat it, pretty one,' said Andy. 'You weren't to know.'

'I might have bloody known,' growled Rayl, standing in the doorway. 'Turn my back for a single minute and you're already trying to fuck another girl.'

She launched herself out the doorway straight at Andy. Linda and Pol intercepted her before she could attack him and held her arms. She continued to curse and swear at him until finally, her eyes slid up into her head and the girls caught her as she passed out, laying her down gently on the ground.

'I have no idea what to do,' Andy said, getting sympathetic looks from the others. 'It's as though she's a different person all of a sudden.'

'It'll just take time,' said Ed, laying his hand on his shoulder.

'Riss will need to come too,' said Pol, changing the subject and pointing to the other girl sitting on the doorstep to their room. 'She was one of the security team looking after the Salft yard. There are two more of them somewhere on the surface, Ghent and another man we don't know the name of, along with Phil of course.'

'Okay,' said Ed, smirking at Andy.

'It's going to be a bit snug in the Lamborghini,' said Andy, with a wry smile.

Linda gave Ed a quizzical glance and raised her eyebrows.

'You'll see,' he said, walking over to one of the carts and inspecting it.

55

Mining cavern, Sidero, the Exoplismoi system, Milky Way

TWO OF THE buggies were still operational and after moving all the unconscious bodies into the recovery position, they motored back to the elevator. This time they drove the carts straight in and Andy used his DOVI to reactivate the system.

Driving straight out again at the top of the elevator, they moved as quickly as the weak headlights would allow, back through the wide tunnel and out squinting into Sidero's daylight.

Ed, who was driving the lead cart, slammed the brakes on suddenly, causing Andy driving behind to bump into him.

'Hey…less of the fucking brake testing…oh, shit.'

A half circle of military-style trucks, a type Linda and Pol knew well, were lined up closing the exit to the cave. More than a hundred Kakous were positioned in and around the vehicles, all pointing laser rifles at the two carts.

Nobody moved for a few seconds and as the dust settled around the buggies, one man stepped down from the most central truck.

He was dressed in some form of military fatigues, with creases so sharp they could carve a joint, a sand-coloured beret, and he carried a military pace stick under his right arm. He swaggered forward a few paces and glared at the occupants of the carts.

'Who's he think he is, Montgomery?' Ed heard Andy mutter and struggled not to snigger.

'DADDY,' screamed Had'qar, and before anyone could stop her, she jumped down and sprinted towards him.

Ed noticed a flicker of annoyance wash across the man's face, but it was soon gone as she approached and he scooped her up in an embrace. He stared straight forward as she clung onto him and Ed realised there was something slightly awry with this man's reaction.

'These are my friends,' he heard her say, pointing back at them. 'They helped me escape.'

'Did they now?' he said with a straight uncaring face. 'You go back there and jump aboard my truck.'

'I'll go and get my friends first,' she said, turning and smiling at Ed. 'You can tell these men to put down their guns, all the stupid Kakous morons are unconscious down in the mine.'

'Had'qar, get on the truck now,' he ordered, staring at her.

She seemed puzzled by his tone of voice and started walking slowly towards her father's truck. Suddenly as she drew level with the line of men, she stopped and stared at one of them. She must have recognised him, as before anyone could stop her, she punched the man square in the face. Ed heard his nose break, even from where he was. The man dropped his weapon and pulled his hands up to his face, now pouring blood. She snatched up the weapon, turned it on him and fired from point-blank range. Whether she knew it was set on full power, or thought it was on stun like the weapon she was previously firing, no one ever knew. The man flew back, a hole the size of a fist punched through his chest. The bolt carried on into the battery unit of the truck behind and exploded.

Bits of truck and men flew in all directions. The beret-wearing leader was blown onto his face, with burning debris landing all around him.

Everyone on the buggies dived out and down behind them. It was at this moment Ed heard the unmistakable howl of an antigrav drive. He peered over at Andy, who had his eyes closed and was seemingly remote flying the black shuttle.

Dust whipped up around them as it swooped in, uncloaked, and landed between them and the line of trucks. Both its laser cannons were lowered and as he watched, Andy swivelled the ship to the left and fired on the two outermost trucks, turning them into fireballs, and then the same to the right, ensuring Had'qar was not targeted.

Some of the men returned fire that was just absorbed by the ship's shields, but most were pulling back as fast as they could go and legging it into the desert.

Their leader – quite how he managed it, no one knew – suddenly appeared around the left-hand side of the shuttle, his face a picture of rage as he lined up a pistol on the small group cowering behind the buggies.

'You were worth a lot of money to me, Virr,' he shouted. 'But now you and your friends will have to die.'

Ed sprinted right, trying to lead the weapon away from his

friends. The first bolt just clipped his arm, spinning him around and into the red dust. He glanced back to see a face full of anger and a two-handed grip on the pistol, and knew the man wouldn't miss this time. A quick glance back to the others and Linda was holding a screaming Pol in her arms, a look of absolute horror on her face.

He heard the laser weapon fire and thought it a bit weird – they always said you never hear the shot that kills you, as the round or bolt travels faster than sound. Then he realised nothing had hit him and he looked back again. The leader was standing oddly, looking down confused, as a large section of his chest had just vaporised. He snarled and attempted to lift the weapon in Ed's direction again, and this time the left side of his skull exploded and he dropped like a rock.

Ed was wondering who'd saved his life, just as Had'qar staggered from behind the now landed shuttle, the rifle still at her shoulder and a look of shock on her face.

He forced himself up and, holding his bleeding arm, ran over to her and held her in his good arm as she collapsed to her knees.

'It was him all along,' she whispered, as he knelt with her. 'He was my captor, my own father.' She looked up at Ed, tears welling in her eyes. 'Is everyone all right?'

Ed looked over to see all of them, emerging slowly and unhurt from behind the carts.

'Yes they are,' he said. 'Thanks to you.'

She managed a half smile before her head slumped onto his shoulder. It was at this point he realised a very large chunk of shrapnel from the first explosion was embedded in her side and she'd been slowly bleeding out.

'Oh, fuck no,' he whispered, as he bowed his head forward into her hair and cried.

56

Northern desert, Sidero, the Exoplismoi system, Milky Way

IT HAD BEEN, as Andy had predicted, extremely snug in the shuttle on the ascent back up to Sidero Station. Most had just sat on the floor behind the two front seats. Ed had given up his seat so Rayl could lie comfortably and have some support for her head.

They'd found a tarpaulin on one of the wrecked trucks and Ed had wrapped Had'qar's body and gently laid it in the corner of the cockpit. He'd been very quiet since the battle had ended. No one was celebrating the victory and a sombre mood had descended over the group; even Andy had refrained from his usual jocular disposition out of respect for the young girl who'd given her life to save theirs.

Everyone sat immersed in their own thoughts as the small shuttle screamed its way back up into orbit.

Coll was waiting in the hangar as they arrived and had

some staff ready to receive the body and take it to the medical centre's small morgue.

'We need to find the rest of her family,' said Ed, watching as she was wheeled away on a medical trolley.

'Her father was one of the most senior mines inspectors,' said Coll. 'I can't believe he was the leader of the Kakous all along. No wonder they were always one step ahead of us. His wife and Had'qar's mother worked as an administrator on one of the yards.'

'Worked?' Ed repeated.

Coll nodded slowly and looked at the floor.

'She was killed in a freak airlock accident many years ago when Had'qar was very young. The Major didn't want to give up his job to look after her or for her to be looked after by the system. He just took her along on all his assignments and home tutored her.'

'He was a major?'

'Retired Thadonion marine.'

'The accident must've affected him more than he let on,' said Ed, nodding to Andy as he passed by with Rayl on another trolley. 'Do we have any more news on the other two tugs? We're still three people unaccounted for and one of them is a crew member of ours.'

'Sorry, no,' the Chief said, turning as the sound of another ship buzzing through the atmosphere shield and the sudden scream of its antigrav caught their attention.

'Who's this?' Ed shouted above the noise.

Coll shrugged.

'No idea,' he replied, having to shout into Ed's ear. 'Judging by how dirty it is, it's from one of the mines below.'

The red-stained boxy personnel carrier turned and clumped down on its struts. The racket from its motors receded down to a low grumble and a side airlock motored up into its housing.

A rather dishevelled man stood in the doorway and waited for the steps to power down to the deck before he limped down.

Ed took a sharp intake of breath and lunged forward as a second man appeared. It was Phil. He was wrapped in a blanket, his face and hair stained red, and he grimaced as he hobbled down the steps. He managed a lopsided grin as he recognised Ed, who ran up and enveloped him in a hug. Ed grimaced as Phil squeezed his bandaged arm.

'Have you found the others? Are they safe?' Phil asked.

'Yes,' said Ed. 'Everyone's alive and now accounted for; you're the last of our crew.'

'Oh, thank the Ancients,' he said, sighing with relief.

'We've been so worried about you,' said Ed. 'We couldn't find your tug.'

'Hmm,' he grunted. 'It wasn't one of my best landings. The sand was very soft and we ended up almost completely buried. It took us hours to get out of the thing and then we had to walk bloody miles to the nearest mine workings.'

'Well, you're here and you're safe now.'

'Have we found the *Gabriel* yet?'

'I'm afraid not.'

'Shit…Prota won't be very pleased. We've only had the ship ten minutes and we've lost it already.'

'We don't have to tell him if we get it back again.'

'No, I suppose not.'

'This is Coll,' said Ed, as the Chief sauntered over and joined them. 'He runs the station.'

The two men greeted each other as Ed glanced at the two sleek black shuttles parked side by side.

'How much do those shuttles owe the station by the way?' Ed asked.

'Er…just under fifteen million GDA credits,' replied Coll. 'Like I'm ever going to see that. They're not a recognised model and they're just too small.'

'How about I offer you twenty million for the pair?' said Ed, raising his eyebrows.

Coll stared at him for a second.

'But that's over five million more than we need,' he said, looking puzzled.

'Finder's fee. It'd give you a nice retirement, wouldn't it?'

Coll opened his mouth, closed it again, had a quick look at the two ships and looked back at Ed.

'Really?'

'Really,' said Ed. 'If you give me the details of the two accounts, I'll transfer the funds right now, but with one condition.'

'Which is?'

'You organise for Had'qar's body to be returned to her relations on her home planet.'

'That's it?'

'That's it.'

'Fuck…yeah. It's a deal,' said Coll, whipping out his tablet, his hands shaking with anticipation.

The three-ship convoy back to Dasos went without a hitch. Ed and Andy took the new black shuttles, leaving Phil to fly the old bus. He'd recovered quickly after a good scrub up and twelve hours' sleep and Ed knew he was back to his usual self, especially when he started moaning about the state of the old shuttle he had to fly.

They landed back inside the *K21* to find Captain Mye waiting for them in the hangar.

'No *Gabriel*?' she asked, as they all disembarked.

Ed shook his head and Phil winced.

'Disappeared,' said Ed. 'No one seems to know where, how or why.'

'Or who with for that matter,' said Phil.

'It'll be that crazy sentient box of sparks running riot again,' said Mye, rolling her eyes.

'I'm told she was offline at the time,' said Ed.

'You'd be court martialed if you mislaid your ship in this navy,' she said, glancing at the two new shuttles. 'And what the hell are they?' she asked. 'Our database has no record of that ship designation at all.'

'Our new runabouts,' said Andy, strolling over. 'With a little sting in the tail.'

He closed his eyes and four heavy-duty laser cannons whirred down from their hidden housings.

'Oh…that is cool,' said Mye. 'Don't show those to Bache or he'll want one.'

'I already do,' said a voice from behind them.

They all turned to find an unsmiling Admiral of the Fleet approaching.

'How the hell did you get aboard without me being informed?' asked Mye.

'Wizardry,' said Bache, without changing his expression.

Andy snorted a laugh, which earned him a glare from both Bache and Mye.

'I understand from Coll Stratton, you managed to park a

hundred million tonne shipyard on top of a mining region,' Bache added, his flinty expression unwavering.

'I think you'll find that was your old friend, Flast,' said Andy.

Bache flinched at the mention of the name.

'Am I to understand you not only lost your own ship but you let Flast escape from right under your nose?' he demanded, looking at both Linda and Ed with raised eyebrows.

They were disturbed by a crew member approaching. She saluted the officers present before addressing the Captain.

'Sorry to disturb you, ma'am, but there's a small shuttle that just jumped in system with someone who wants to see Captain Virr urgently.'

Mye nodded.

'Thank you, Lieutenant,' she said. 'Have all the safety protocols been addressed?'

'Yes, ma'am,' she said. 'It's a Theo-registered shuttle with one life sign aboard, en route from Paradeisos.'

Mye nodded again.

'Tractor the vessel into this hangar,' she said.

The junior officer acknowledged, saluted again and trotted off, while talking to the bridge.

'Oh, crap,' mumbled Phil, turning to grimace at Ed. 'From Paradeisos…now we're in serious shit if it's who I think it is.'

57

Katadromiko 21, *orbiting Dasos, Milky Way*

ED RECOGNISED the shuttle design as soon as it buzzed through the atmosphere shield. It was of similar configuration to the four they had on the *Gabriel*. The tractor beam operator skilfully turned the craft and deposited it at the far end of the hangar. Within seconds the side airlock slid silently up into the bulkhead, revealing a lone hunched figure wearing a long grey robe standing patiently, waiting for the steps to appear.

Ed heard Phil groan as it became obvious his prediction had been correct. Prota, the leader of the Theos and the man who had gifted them the *Gabriel*, made his way down the steps and walked quickly towards them.

'He doesn't look very happy,' said Andy, inching his way back so Ed was at the front.

'D'you think he knows?' asked Linda.

'Of course he knows,' said Phil. 'You can't hide anything from him.'

Prota approached Ed. The expression on his face suggested relief, rather than anger, Ed thought, but he was certainly no expert. He put on a friendly smile and hoped for the best.

'Edward…Edward,' said Prota, walking straight up to Ed and enveloping him in a hug. 'Thank the Ancients you're all safe. We were so worried when the empty ship came home, with its database and Cleo erased.'

'Came home?' Ed repeated. 'You mean the *Gabriel* is with you?'

'Absolutely,' he said. 'And with a rather confused and seemingly friendly octopod in one of the hangars.'

'Who flew it to Paradeisos?' Pol was the first to ask the obvious question.

'Programming,' said Prota. 'All our ships have a default setting, that if all the regular crew are no longer on the ship and the sentient embryo is offline for whatever reason the ship will automatically make its way back to a designated orbit around Paradeisos.'

'Ah…thank heavens for that,' said Ed. 'I was beginning to fear the worst.'

'Have we really lost Cleo?' asked Linda.

'I fear so,' said Prota. 'Unless you or she had a remote backup somewhere we don't know about. My engineers ran a complete database recovery program to no avail, I'm afraid.'

'Oh no,' said Phil. 'That's catastrophic.'

'She's irreplaceable,' said Linda, staring at the floor.

'We can provide you with another embryo,' said Prota.

'Just won't be the same,' said Andy, gloomily. 'I'm going

to the medical centre to check on Rayl,' he added, turning and making for the rear hangar door.

'I'm going there too to check on Callon,' said Ed. 'Phil, Linda, Pol, can you stay with Prota? We need to organise getting all of us to Paradeisos as soon as possible.'

'I'm glad the mystery of your missing ship is resolved,' said Bache, walking with Ed to the tube station. 'I'll come with you to meet this girl that cost me a detachment of marines.'

Ed flinched.

'Don't worry…I know from Mye that you've already had enough crap over that,' said Bache.

'I made Callon a promise,' said Ed, without looking up from the floor.

'I know… You're like me, when you promise something, you move mountains to ensure it happens.'

Ed nodded.

'It was an unfortunate accident.'

'I know,' said Bache. 'Pilot error. I watched the replay and to be honest, after what's gone on here over the last few weeks, it pales into insignificance. But obviously not for the families involved. I have to write my report.'

'More people who'll hate me,' said Ed, sighing.

'You won't be mentioned,' he said. 'They were on a humanitarian mission to save lives after the *K28* disaster, which is one hundred percent true.'

Ed nodded again and patted Bache on the shoulder.

'Thank you,' he said, looking up again. 'Erm…has any decision been made as to the settlement of the Vriix?'

'We have a potential world in mind,' Bache said. 'But I just need the final nod from the President before I make it public and you can go ahead.'

They arrived at the tube station and boarded.

'Sorry we didn't get Flast,' said Ed.

'She's slippery isn't she?' said Bache, shrugging. 'Any idea where she went?'

'None,' answered Ed. 'Off to empty a secret bank account somewhere, I suspect, and plan more revenge attacks for you and me.'

Bache smiled for the first time.

'I understand Andrew had a little altercation with our security chief in Exoplismoi, who has suddenly decided to retire? Giving me the job of finding a replacement.'

'I don't think the two things are connected,' said Ed.

'No…I believe there are five million other reasons coming into play.'

Ed grimaced and gave Bache a contrite look.

'Are you going to hold that over me?'

'No, I knew it was coming and already had someone in mind anyway.'

'It's important isn't it?' said Ed. 'I mean…most of your naval vessels are built and serviced there. You have to have a team on site to police the comings and goings in the system.'

'Mmm, absolutely. Coll's been our rock there for years,' said Bache with a faraway look. 'He was a junior navigator on one of the *Katadromiko* cruisers when I was a recruit.'

The tube carriage pulled to a stop and they disembarked. Ed noticed a tall attractive woman staring at him as they turned right towards the main medical centre, but she averted her gaze as they passed. He was sure he'd met her before somewhere, but couldn't put his finger on it.

On entering the medical centre, they were steered into a side room where Callon was sat up in bed reading something on a tablet. An array of beeping and buzzing apparatus surrounded her and a male nurse busied himself on a control board built flush with the wall behind her.

She glanced up and beamed a smile at Ed and then a quizzical look at Bache.

'You look better,' Ed said, returning the smile.

'I'm told it's going okay,' she said. 'You might just've saved my life.'

'Don't tell him that – we'll never hear the last of it,' said Bache.

'This is Admiral of the Fleet Loftt,' said Ed, nodding at Bache.

'Admiral, eh?' she said, raising her eyebrows. 'Should've known that by the dazzling gleam off all that gold braid. You have friends in high places.'

'What's the current diagnosis?' Ed asked.

'Going reasonably well,' said the Chief Medical Officer, entering the room and giving Ed a disparaging glance. 'She needs rest to recover from the invasive treatment, Admiral,' he said to Bache, completely ignoring Ed.

'Well enough to travel?' Bache asked.

He turned and stared.

'Is this you asking or him?' he demanded, stabbing a finger at Ed.

'Answer the bloody question,' Bache growled. 'Remember who you're talking to.'

'Yes, sir, sorry, sir,' he stammered. 'She can travel so long as she's in a cabin resting.'

'Have me informed when she's ready to go,' Bache said, as both he and Ed nodded at her, smiled and left the room.

'Insolent wanker,' mumbled Bache, as they headed for the tube again.

Ed snorted and shook his head.

'Aren't you going in to see Rayl?' Bache asked, as they walked.

'Thought I'd give them a bit of privacy.'

'All's not rosy in the Faux household I hear.'

'You don't miss much.'

'It's part of my job description.'

Ed smirked.

'I think we should leave for Paradeisos in the morning, fetch the *Gabriel* and return to help you with the mess here,' he said.

'You guys take a break,' said Bache. 'I've got my finger on the pulse here, after all it's only one ship. Go to your island and sit on a beach for a while. Callon certainly needs it and it sounds like Rayl and Andy need a bit of together time and that's the best place to let that head injury repair.'

'Okay, if you're sure,' said Ed.

'I'll message you when I get the green light from the President about resettling the Vriix.'

'Thanks, I'll let Oona know what's happening. She doesn't know about the suicides yet.'

'That was unfortunate…if only they'd waited a little longer.'

When they arrived back in the hangar, Phil was still there showing Prota around the two new mini shuttles.

'Ah, Edward,' said Prota, digging around in a pocket and handing Ed a small data module. 'I nearly forgot…I don't know if it's of any use, but one of the shuttles in the *Gabriel*'s port hangar had had its data core sealed. I was kinda hoping Cleo had downloaded herself there, but I'm afraid there were only two files on it. One is the schematics for a ship I don't recognise and the other just contains one six word sentence I don't understand.'

'Ship schematics, you say?' said Bache, his eyes meeting Ed's. 'It can't be, surely?'

'Give me your tablet,' said Ed.

He plugged the module into Bache's personal tablet and opened both files. He looked at the first one and read the second. He grinned and showed the first to Bache.

'It must've been the last thing Cleo was able to do before being erased,' said Ed.

'The octaship design plans,' said Bache, his eyes widening. 'Thank the Ancients…d'you realise she must've given her life to save Dasos?' He grabbed the tablet and waved it over his head as he dashed for the door. 'Going to engineering,' he called before disappearing.

'I take it that's something you needed?' said Prota, looking between the door and the two remaining faces.

'Just a bit,' said Ed.

'What did the other file mean?'

Ed thought about the six words, and shrugged before recounting it.

'"On holiday, have my recommended pizza,"' he said. 'Any ideas?' he added, aiming the question at Phil.

'None whatsoever,' Phil replied. 'I'll have a think about it on the way to Paradeisos.'

58

The Gabriel, *en route to Panemorfi, in the Trelorus system,*
Milky Way

ED AWOKE to the sound of persistent knocking at his cabin door. Pol was snoring quietly beside him, nothing it seemed would wake her. They hadn't had much shut-eye on the flight from Dasos to Paradeisos; the small shuttle he flew didn't have cabins and they'd been forced to doze in the pilots' seats. He glanced at the time and realised they'd only been asleep for two hours. Slipping out of bed, he trudged moodily through to the cabin's lounge area and towards the door, requesting it to open.

'She's gone,' blurted Andy, walking straight in as the door evaporated. 'She's fucking gone.'

'Err…who's gone?' Ed asked, already fearing the answer.

Andy paced up and down, teary-eyed and wringing his hands.

'Rayl…she took one of the shuttles and left the ship,' he sobbed.

'Why…where to?' Ed asked, trying to shake the sleep and fatigue from his brain.

'I have no idea…she hasn't told me.'

'I thought she was in the autonurse,' said Ed.

'She was, but she persuaded Phil she was fine, went back to our cabin while I was on bridge duty and packed her stuff.'

'She's taken her belongings?'

'Yeah.'

'Oh shit.'

Ed stepped up and gave Andy a hug.

'She'll realise what she's done and be back,' he said. 'She knows where we'll be.'

'I dunno about that,' Andy said, flopping into an armchair. 'She's been different for a while, gradually getting more and more secretive, seems to think everyone's out to get her.'

'How d'you mean?'

'She hates the celebrity status being part of the *Gabriel* crew gives her.'

'I noticed she'd lost a bit of weight too,' said Ed, sitting opposite.

'She became obsessed by everything the holographic gym instructor said, exercising every day and following some awful diet that made her look undernourished…anorexic even. She never stopped talking about him and then suddenly getting Cleo to make her a load of sexy lingerie, which she'd hated and not seen the point in before.'

'That wasn't for your benefit then?'

'She didn't like me commenting on it, or saying how pretty she was in it.'

'But she was crazy in love with you…I heard her tell you on many occasions. You used to argue about who loved each other more.'

'She must've been lying…all she's been doing recently is criticise everything I say and do. We had everything in common, then suddenly, apparently, we didn't, but nothing had changed.'

'Where can she go? Perhaps Trigono Three?' said Ed, rubbing his chin in thought. 'But, on the other hand, she has no family to run back to and why does it have to be so clandestine?'

'I know…it makes me look like some sort of monster. I haven't looked at another girl since we met either. People are going to think I was knocking her about or something.'

'No, they're not, Andy,' said Ed, pointing at him. 'Everyone knows you're not that kind of person and you loved her unconditionally. No one will ever think that.'

'Think what?' said Pol, yawning as she joined them in the cabin lounge.

Ed and Andy glanced at each other and raised their eyebrows.

'What's going on?' she asked, obviously picking up on their reluctance to reply.

'Ah…well,' said Ed, clearing his throat. 'Rayl has left Andy and the ship.'

'What? When?'

'Couple of hours ago,' sniffed Andy.

'Stand up, Andrew,' she said, demandingly. 'You need a hug.'

'D'you want to cancel the trip to the island?' Ed asked, as his girlfriend squeezed the life out of his best friend.

'Nooo,' he squeaked, as Pol released him and he could

breathe again. 'You all need the break and if she needs space, I'd better let her have some. No matter how much I miss her.'

'Inconsiderate, selfish bitch,' said Pol, with her hands on her hips. 'How could she?'

'Hey…that's my wife you're talking about,' Andy moaned, glaring at Pol.

'You might not want to say it, but I do and I can. I think what she's done is cowardly and if she was here now, I'd say it to her face.'

'Do Phil and Linda know?' Ed asked.

Andy shook his head.

'Right…we all need some sleep. I suggest we reconvene in the morning when we reach Panemorfi. We'll tell them then. Andrew, you can have the couch here, if you can't face going back to an empty cabin.'

Andy forced a half smile, nodded, moved over to the sofa and lay down.

———————

The mood on the *Cartella* was sombre the next morning as they followed the fire trail of a small freighter down into Panemorfi's atmosphere. Ed had informed Linda and Phil of Rayl's departure and as expected they weren't best pleased. Andy had decided to remain on the *Gabriel* for a while to compose an encrypted message to Rayl and join the others later in the day.

'I can't believe she didn't have the courtesy to say good-bye,' griped Linda, as she piloted the small vessel. 'After everything we've done for her over the years, to just piss off like that.'

'We can't castigate her too much,' said Phil, sitting at the back of the cockpit. 'We really have no idea what mental state she was in. She may come out of it yet, not realising what she's done.'

'Perhaps one of us should've stayed with Andy,' said Pol, glancing pointedly at Ed.

'I tried,' replied Ed, holding his hands up in surrender. 'He wouldn't hear of it. I think he just wanted some alone time to get his head around what's happened.'

Linda brought the ship straight down over Theo island, the antigravs screaming their disapproval as she dropped the struts at the last minute and thudded the ship down onto the sand a little harder than necessary. Ed realised Linda was extremely pissed off and decided not to mention it.

While the others went to their beach cabins, Ed opened up the main building and ordered the semi-sentient island computer to do a full systems check. It read back the usual reports in its machine-like methodical way and it was one of the last figures that caused Ed's ears to prick up. Phil had approached at the same time and he heard it too.

'Ninety-one percent,' said Phil, staring incredulously at Ed. 'How can the main data core be at ninety-one percent capacity? It's normally only twenty or so.'

'I don't know,' said Ed. 'Did we do something wrong the last time we were here? Island, what's taking up the most storage on the data core?'

'*Food replication data bank, Edward,*' came the polite reply.

'Food?' repeated Phil. 'How can it be full of food?'

Ed thought for a moment, before holding up a forefinger as if something had just occurred to him.

'On holiday, have my recommended pizza,' he said, turning to get eye contact with Phil.

Phil's eyes lit up.

'Surely not,' he said.

Ed tilted his head to one side and smirked.

'D'you want to order or shall I?' he said.

'Oh, please let it be that simple,' Phil whispered.

'Island,' called Ed. 'What pizza choices do you have?'

'*Margarita…pepperoni…vegetable…meat feast or Cleopatra*,' came the reply.

'Fuck,' said Phil. 'Clever girl.'

Ed smiled at Phil's reply. He very rarely swore.

'Island…can we order a Cleopatra?' Ed asked and held his breath.

The first thing they noticed was the lights behind the bar dim slightly, then the holo-imprinted barmaid froze for a moment and the door locks clicked twice.

They both stared around, before turning back to each other.

'Has anything happened?' said Phil, his brow furrowing.

'It must've done,' said a familiar voice and a hazy holographic image of Cleo appeared in front of them. 'If you've activated this back-up of me, then something catastrophic has occurred.'

'Oh, Cleo,' said Ed, with a slight wobble to his voice. 'You beautiful girl.'

'Beautiful, my fucking arse,' she said, frowning. 'I'm mostly compressed and it hurts. I'm glad you brought the *Cartella* down here with you. It has a starship-sized data core that the shuttles don't. Can I have permission to download myself into its core?'

'Yes, yes. Do it,' Ed blurted, unable to keep the smile off his face. He looked up at Phil, who was grinning from ear to ear and he was sure he saw a tear run down his cheek.

They high five'd and danced a little jig, as they watched Cleo's hazy image blossom into the three-dimensional being they were accustomed to.

Ed was the first to dash over and give her a hug, closely followed by Phil.

'Am I to take it, for some reason I didn't make it?' she asked.

'No,' Ed and Phil both said in unison.

'We thought we'd lost you completely,' said Phil, this time wiping the tear from his eye.

'You guys,' she said, adopting a coy expression. 'Getting all emotional over a computer program.'

'That is something you'll never be,' said Ed. 'You're a full and irreplaceable member of the *Gabriel*'s crew and don't you ever forget that.'

She grinned and hugged them both again.

'Thanks, guys,' she said, adopting a slightly embarrassed expression. 'Now, is someone going to tell me what happened to me?'

59

———————

Theo Island, Panemorfi, Trelorus system, Milky Way

Ed lay in bed listening to the early morning squawking outside in the blue-tinged palm trees – although today, he did think they sounded louder than he remembered.

Opening his eyes, he was shocked to find himself staring at the sky. He lifted his head and glanced around. He was lying on the beach in his underwear, the palm trees containing the noisy birds just above and behind him.

He sat up and realised he couldn't see his cabin, or any of the other buildings for that matter. He thought about how much he'd had to drink the night before and quickly discounted that. It would take a lot more than three glasses of wine for him to lose his way home.

A sudden voice from behind him made him jump.

'Good morning, Edward.'

He leapt up and turned to find a very much alive and

smiling Xavier Lake sitting under one of the palm trees. He was wearing a white suit, with a white shirt, even a white tie and shoes. He took a sip from a bright red cocktail and regarded Ed with his blue soulless eyes.

'Lovely day for it,' Lake said, lifting his drink in Ed's direction. 'Would you like a drink?'

Ed stood still and stared at Lake, feeling a bit vulnerable dressed in only his underpants.

'We believed you were dead,' he said.

'That was and still is the intention.'

'I know you're not though.'

'Hmm…shame that,' Lake said, flicking his eyes skyward. 'Nice new ship, by the way. I noticed you'd buggered up the first one when I visited Earth recently.'

'What's with the silly suit?' Ed asked.

Lake looked down at himself.

'I seem to remember seeing Morgan Freeman wearing something similar when he was playing God in an old movie a few years ago.'

'Oh…so you think you're a god now?'

The beach disappeared, replaced by a snow blizzard. Ed felt his feet sink into several inches of snow and the bitter cold chilled him to the core. No sooner had he come to realise where he was, it changed again. This time he was standing on top of one of the giant pyramids, the city of Giza stretching away before him and the sun-baked stone burning his bare feet.

As quickly as it had begun, in a blink of an eye, he found himself back on the beach again.

'I do…because I am,' said Lake.

Ed stared at Lake and thought for a moment.

'The planet Yiss in the Medusa galaxy – was that your doing?' he asked.

'Very astute of you, Edward,' Lake replied, with a faraway look in his eyes, before taking a sip of his drink. 'I'm quite proud of that bit of world building. It was my first attempt by the way,' he added, boastfully.

'Bully for you,' said Ed. 'The fact that they spoke English with a home counties accent made me join the dots.'

'Hmm… It's a shame you have to die. Having smart people around when I'm constructing a new human race would be beneficial.'

'Where's your South American sidekick by the way? Couldn't he help you out?'

'Ah…Mr Herez,' said Lake, chuckling. 'He's living it up as a Mexican billionaire on St Lucia. The fact he has the intellect of an amoeba is the reason I no longer require his services. And talking of sidekicks, why's that foul-mouthed, alcoholic hanger-on of yours not with you?'

Ed rolled his eyes and shrugged.

'Family issues.'

'Hmm…I was hoping to get the two of you together, but no matter, he'll get his comeuppance when I destroy your ship.'

'What the hell is it you have against us, Lake? I seem to recollect you stealing my design for the jump drive and getting yourself in a right mess with the GDA, which wasn't our fault. I also seem to remember it was our uncovering of Captain Utz's identity and crimes that saved yours and Herez's lives. So, by my account you owe us.'

'You forget it was also you that insisted we were taken back to Earth and incarcerated in those lovely holiday camps on the west coast of America.'

'Yeah…for extortion and multiple murders; nothing serious at all, was it?'

'Ah, you see…you're just too honest for your own good, Eddie,' said Lake, exhaling noisily and having another sip of his drink. 'Which one of us is a god and which one is about to die? You get nowhere in this universe by being nice.'

'Who the hell was dumb enough to give an idiot like you these powers?' said Ed, thinking he'd had enough of this bullshit.

He expected Lake to come back at him hard for the insult, but he was surprised, as Lake just sat there completely still with a vacant expression on his face. Except, when he looked closer, he noticed Lake's body was actually shaking slightly.

'That dumb one would have been me,' said a female voice as she stepped out from behind one of the large palm trees.

Ed nearly jumped out of his skin.

'Bloody hell,' he stammered, taking a step back in surprise. 'Where the crap did you come from?' he asked, as the stunningly beautiful woman dressed in black and gold and resembling an Egyptian Pharaoh stepped into sight. 'Hang on a minute,' he said, pointing at her. 'I remember you…we've met before…wasn't that you in the Messier galaxy that accused me of killing your friends, and yes, it was you in the corridor near the medical centre on the *K21* yesterday. I knew I recognised you from somewhere.'

'Nothing wrong with your recall,' she said. 'Yes it was.'

'So, it's you that's to blame for this?' he asked, nodding at Lake.

'I have to admit it is,' she said, seemingly embarrassed by the fact.

'Your name is Nefer…something or other? What exactly are you then?'

'Neferuptah the Seventeen. I'm what's known locally as one of the Ancients.'

'It was your race that constructed the galactic gateways?'

'We did.'

'Why were you watching me yesterday?'

'I've been watching over you for a few days now.'

'Why?'

'I knew he'd come to find you. If nothing else, he's predictable.' She nodded at Lake, her expression hardening. 'He was a huge mistake I had to rectify before he did any more damage to the human races and I wanted to apologise to you.'

'I see…so, your race created some of us then?'

'Myself and my associates have created all of you over many millennia. Seeding suitable planets with human DNA, as you call it, on our travels throughout the universe. This little gathering you know as the GDA is just, to use one of your Earth terms, "the tip of the iceberg."'

Ed nodded, suddenly feeling rather undressed in front of one of the creators of the human race. He looked down at himself and looked back at her with a weak smile.

'Ah, yes,' she said. 'Spending time on your planet has taught me you do have some issues with being unrobed.'

She clicked her fingers and Ed found himself wearing the same clothes as he had on yesterday.

'Another thing it's given me,' she continued, 'is a reminder that I was a living, breathing, biological human too, once. Albeit many tens of thousands of your years ago. But all the same, I realise now I was getting a bit up myself.'

'You're a god, you're our creator,' said Ed. 'I think that does give you the authority to be a little aloof.'

'Don't kiss arse.'

'Sorry.'

Ed glanced at Lake. 'What are you going to do about him?'

'He escaped me once, I'm not underestimating him a second time.'

'Oh, where was that?'

'You call it the Oval Office.'

Ed's eyes widened.

'You caught up with him in the President's private office on Earth?'

'He went there to kill him too.'

'Wow…that was never in the news.'

'That's because he didn't succeed and your President didn't report it.'

Ed glanced at Lake again. 'You still haven't answered my question,' he said.

She sighed and waved a hand at the quivering white-suited figure. Ed was sure he saw a fleeting look of fear in Lake's eyes before he disappeared, replaced by a metre-long oval carapace. It was dark grey and pitted, as though it had had a hard life, and lay in the sand seemingly fizzing with energy.

'See you around, Captain,' she said, giving Ed a wink.

'Wait,' he said, quickly. 'Are we going to see you again? I've got so many more questions.'

'Ah…I might stick around for a while,' she said, glancing up and out to sea. 'I quite like this galaxy.'

Both Neferuptah and the carapace vanished and Ed found himself lying in bed in his little island cottage. Pol snorted in her sleep next to him. He snuggled up behind her and, closing his eyes, he said a little thank you to Neferuptah.

'You're welcome,' said a quiet whisper inside his head.

60

—————

Theo Island, Panemorfi, Trelorus system, Milky Way

'ED, WAKE UP,' shouted Pol.

'What's she want now?' said Ed, coming to with a start.

'What's who want?'

'Oh,' he said, sitting up. 'Sorry, I was dreaming.'

'Linda's at the door. There's a problem with Andy.'

Ed threw on a robe and hurried through to the cottage door, where Linda was waiting and wringing her hands with worry.

'You need to get up to the ship,' she said, before he had a chance to say anything.

'What's happened?'

'Andy's locked himself in an airlock with a bottle of vodka.'

'Oh, shit,' he said, turning and running to get his clothes.

As far as Ed was concerned, the shuttle trip up to the *Gabriel* had taken an age, although Linda had pulled out all the stops and it was only twenty-two minutes.

He dived out of the half-open door almost as the struts hit the hangar floor and waved at Cleo, who'd just completed her reload, to take him to his best friend.

'Get one of the shuttles around to the airlock and sit it right outside. I want its docking tube out and ready to seal around that door.'

'He said he'd vent the airlock if we tried that.'

'I'll distract him and give him other things to think about.'

'Okay, boss,' she said, pointing to the airlock at the end of the corridor and promptly disappearing.

'And Cleo,' he called, slowing his pace.

'Yes,' she said, reappearing.

'It's wonderful to have you home.'

'Thanks, boss.'

She vanished again as Ed approached the closed inner airlock door. He peered in through the small porthole window. He could see Andy sitting against the outer door, the safety cover pulled up off the manual airlock vent switch right above his head.

'Oi, toss bag,' he called. 'I was having a nice lie in.'

Linda, who'd just caught up with him, looked at him in horror.

'Fuck off, dick face,' came the muffled reply. 'You don't know what it's like.'

'Actually, I do,' said Ed. 'Steph dumped me, remember?'

'She wasn't your wife.'

'You can still love someone without that piece of paper you know…and I did.'

'You didn't show it.'

'Not in public, no.'

'It hurts so much.'

'Of course it does…true love doesn't go away, even if they have.'

Andy threw the half-empty bottle of vodka across the airlock. It smashed against the far wall.

'That fucking lying bitch,' Andy blurted, standing and kicking the outer door. 'She told me she loved me…she promised me…she said she loved me more than I loved her. She was lying all along.'

'I don't think that's true, Andy. What I do know is she's suffering from a severe concussion and I'm sure the girl you married is still in there somewhere.'

'You didn't hear the awful things she's said to me over the last few months. She says she hates her life, hates what we do, even hates her parents for putting her in this situation.'

'Give her time to recover,' said Ed. 'I'm sure she'll be back.'

'But could I ever trust her again, if she did?'

Ed didn't know what else he could say about the situation, so he thought he'd change the subject.

'Ample was asking where you were.'

'She's just a holographic barmaid, there's no comparison.'

'No…but like your friends standing out here worried sick, she's a good listener and she has a new ale she wants you to try.'

Ed noticed Andy's shoulders slump as his tear-streaked face turned to look at him through the porthole. He shook his head, stood up and stepped over to the uncovered airlock vent switch. Ed looked on in horror as Andy lifted his arm towards it.

'Andrew, you're my best friend…and I love you.'

'So do I,' shouted Linda.

His hand hovered near the switch for a moment, before he slapped the safety cover back down, kicked the door again and turned to enter a code into the inner airlock panel. Ed audibly breathed a sigh of relief, as did Linda next to him. Andy found himself enveloped in a tearful group hug as the door slid away.

———

Later that day, Andy watched as the star began setting below the horizon, far out on Theo Island's surrounding ocean. Linda was sat on the sand to his right and while Ed was at the bar getting fresh drinks, she asked Andy whether he wanted them to go find Rayl.

'My heart says yes, but my head knows it's probably not a good idea,' said Andy, shrugging and his head dropping. 'Really, I want to, but I know she'd go mad if I turned up and demanded an explanation.'

Their conversation was cut short as they both heard a sonic boom overhead that had them gazing skyward.

'There,' said Andy, pointing over to the east, as a small black dot against the red sky began growing at an alarming rate. 'Have we got guests coming for dinner?' he asked.

'Not as far as I know,' said Linda. 'Might be for another island.'

They both realised that was definitely not the case as the small vessel continued to fly straight at them.

'Island, is the resort shielding operational?' Linda shouted over her shoulder towards the main building.

'It is, Miss Linda,' came the short reply from the island's computer. 'I'm also getting a landing request from an Admiral Loftt.'

'What's he doing here?' asked Andy. 'Surely he hasn't time for a holiday at the moment too?'

'No,' said Linda, giving the island permission to allow the landing. 'It must be something important for him to leave Dasos at the moment.'

The small sleek private yacht had stopped to hover just outside the shield. Its antigravs screamed their disapproval at Panemorfi's gravity as it waited. Given permission to land, it side-slipped to the right, turned and dropped down next to the *Gabriel*'s two shuttles.

Andy and Linda jumped up and wandered over as the airlock powered up. Bache, still in uniform, bounded down the steps before they'd fully deployed.

'He doesn't look happy,' said Andy, as they approached each other.

'Sorry to disrupt your peace and quiet,' said Bache, through a forced smile. He pointed at the main building. 'Can we have a shielded conversation in there?'

'No problem,' said Linda, turning in that direction and putting her hand up to tell Ed to stay where he was as he exited the bar carrying a tray of drinks.

'Has something else bad happened?' Andy asked, as they went inside.

'I'll tell you when the shielding's back up,' he said, pointing at one of the tables.

Ed called Pol, who was resting in their cottage, and she quickly appeared.

'Where's Phil?' Bache asked.

'On the *Gabriel*,' Linda replied. 'He wanted to work with Cleo on changing the ship's coding, so it can't be borrowed again.'

Bache nodded and looked up.

'Are we private now?' he asked, nervously.

Linda couldn't ever remember Bache looking so rattled.

'We are,' she said. 'What the hell has happened?'

'I, we, have a big problem,' he said, glancing around at the four of them. 'I want you to listen to this.'

He produced his tablet and tapped away for a moment.

'This is a recording of a tight beam private communication shortly before the attack on Dasos,' he said, before touching the play icon.

All four of them listened intently as a male voice began speaking.

'*Are they all in place?*'

'*They are,*' answered a female voice.

'*You have one hour to get underground.*'

'*I'm on my way.*'

Ed exhaled noisily and shook his head as the recording finished. Everybody turned to stare at him.

'D'you know who they were?' Pol asked.

'I know who the male voice is,' he said, looking solemnly at Bache.

'I thought I did too,' admitted Bache. 'I just wanted you to confirm it.'

'Xavier Lake,' said Ed.

'You are fucking joking,' said Andy, as jaws hit the floor.

'Lake!' exclaimed Linda. 'But he's dead.'

Ed explained the happenings of the day before and the conversations with both Lake and Neferuptah.

'He came here…to kill you?' said Pol, her eyes wide. 'Why didn't you tell me?'

'Didn't want to worry you.'

'Wait a minute,' said Andy, looking at Bache. 'Who was he talking to? Who was the female voice?'

It was Bache's turn to exhale.

'Milne,' he said.

'What…the new President…Milne?' Linda asked, her eyes wide.

Bache nodded and sighed.

'Now you know what I mean by big problem,' he said.

'Holy crap,' said Ed, his head in his hands. 'The GDA is in serious trouble.'

'How did you get this recording?' Pol asked.

'Just by accident from someone who wants to remain anonymous,' Bache replied, in a tone that implied that information would not be forthcoming.

'D'you think she was in collusion with Flast too?' Linda asked, quickly changing the subject. 'As she's in the middle of this as well.'

'Can't rule it out,' said Bache. 'And I'm afraid this is where I ask for your help again. I know you're supposed to be on a well-earned break and if there was someone else I could ask, I would. It's ridiculous, I'm the Admiral of the Fleet and don't know who I can trust.'

'There's Captain Mye for one,' said Ed.

'Mye is an ex-girlfriend from years ago,' Bache replied, a little sheepishly.

'What difference does that make?' Linda asked.

'So was Milne,' he said, sitting back and crossing his arms.

'Oh…right,' she said.

'You do have a thing for powerful women, don't you?' Andy quipped.

'They weren't quite as powerful when I knew them,' Bache replied, giving Andy a withering stare.

'Anyway,' said Ed, quickly. 'How can we help?'

61

The Gabriel, *near Dasos, Prasinos system, Milky Way*

PUTTING THEIR HOLIDAY ON HOLD, the crew of the *Gabriel* had taken the ship back to the Prasinos system. Now cloaked and sitting in orbit around Kaelin, one of Dasos's two moons, their clandestine operation, instigated by Admiral Loftt, was about to begin.

'Is he in yet, Cleo?' Ed asked, as he stepped off the tube lift and onto the *Gabriel*'s bridge deck.

'It's taking Admiral Loftt a little longer than expected to get inside the remains of the Gerousia council chambers,' she replied, standing in the centre of the bridge underneath the holomap. 'It's quite a mess.'

'Well, let's hope the data core has survived – there's got to be something on there from the days preceding the attack.'

'The nano trail he's laying should provide us with a

connection before too long,' said Cleo. 'Then I'll attempt to download the contents before any breach is detected.'

'Bache didn't think any of the security measures would still be operational,' said Ed. 'But you never know…so be as quick as you can.'

'Oh…now that's unexpected,' said Cleo, her eyes wide as she turned to face Ed.

'What's that?' Ed asked, as he slid onto his control couch and met her stare.

'Someone's been there before and replaced the debris,' she said. 'There are occasional partial boot prints in the dust. Someone attempted to cover their tracks, but missed a few tell-tale signs.'

'Why would they do that?' Pol asked.

'For exactly the same reason as us,' replied Ed. 'They were either trying to gather evidence like us, or destroy it.'

'It's the latter,' said Cleo. 'The main data core has been sabotaged. I've just got in and there's nothing there. Oh… hang about!'

'What've you found?' Linda asked.

'Whoever it was, wasn't very tech savvy,' she said. 'The building's security was kept separate from the core and is partially intact. I just need to…oh, bugger.'

'What now?' Ed asked.

'It's booby trapped. Tell the Admiral to get out fast. I can't guarantee that whatever it is won't go off when I try to download the contents.'

Ed whispered to Bache what Cleo had discovered. The marine black ops team Bache had with him didn't know about the *Gabriel*, so they had to be discreet.

Cleo waited until Ed gave her the thumbs up and the group were clear of the building again before she attempted to disarm the trap. Once done, she spent a few minutes downloading the data.

'That was surprisingly easy,' she said, giving Ed a suspicious glance. 'The trap was quite amateur, almost as if it was supposed to be breached.'

'Best have a look at what was on there then,' said Ed. 'Are there any camera files?'

'Only one,' she said, pointing at the holomap.

A two-dimensional image of a man in dark clothing appeared clambering through to the data room, where Bache and the marines had just been. He connected a tablet up to a data portal and tapped away for a few moments, before doing the same thing to the security core.

'That camera was still working then,' said Andy. 'It certainly isn't now.'

They found out the reason for this moments later, as the figure pulled out a laser pistol, looked straight at the camera and pulled the trigger. Everyone on the bridge gasped as the image disappeared. Not at the laser shot, but at the recognisable face that looked straight into the lens as the weapon was discharged.

Everyone turned to look at Ed, as the face in the image had been unmistakably his.

'Something you haven't told us?' said Linda, her eyebrows raised.

'Cleo,' he said, seemingly unconcerned. 'Is there a date on this footage?'

'The day after the attack,' she said, nodding and grinning.

Ed grinned too.

'Nice try…whoever you are,' he said, gazing around at the others. 'I was still in the Medusa galaxy with Andrew on that day. But whoever superimposed my face onto this image most likely didn't know that. Or even if they did…didn't care.'

He turned back to focus on Cleo.

'Can you pop back in there and trip the booby trap, so that fake image is destroyed?' he asked.

'I can,' she said. 'But remember, it might not be the only one.'

'I know,' he said, rubbing his chin in thought. 'Can you pull the image apart and see if there's any way to find out whose face they superimposed mine onto?'

'Absolutely, darling,' said Cleo, vanishing from view.

'They might've found a doppelgänger,' said Andy. 'Or a clone.'

Cleo reappeared before Ed could reply and wagged her finger at Andy.

'No clones,' she said, turning and pointing up. 'It was cleverly done and well hidden, but here's your man.'

Ed groaned as a face he recognised appeared.

'Him again,' he said, rolling his eyes.

'It's that fucking demented Grupps arsehole,' groused Andy. 'I was hoping he'd buggered off and died somewhere.'

'Well, he's here somewhere,' said Ed. 'We need to get this information to Bache as soon as possible. He'll be a wealth of information if we can find him.'

'Why can't life be simple?' said Linda, throwing her arms in the air. 'At every turn there's another power-hungry shit head who wants to ruin your day.'

'Napoleon syndrome,' said Ed.

'Putin syndrome,' said Andy.

'What's that mean?' asked Pol, looking between the two of them.

'Short egotistic men with small dicks and delusions of grandeur,' said Linda. 'Earth's had a few of those in its past.'

'Ah…right…yep,' she said, nodding. 'My planet had those too.'

'I remember them well,' said Ed, smirking at her and getting a frown in return.

'Are we going straight to the rendezvous point now?' asked Cleo.

'Yeah, take us there,' said Ed, standing and looking up at the image of Grupps again. 'And get rid of that ugly mug too.'

62

———

The Gabriel, *outer belt, Prasinos system, Milky Way*

ADMIRAL LOFTT HAD MET them deep in the outer belt, several hundred million kilometres from Dasos. The thousands of ferrous metal asteroids out here made it next to impossible to be detected. They were all seated around a large table up in the blister lounge on the top deck of the *Gabriel*.

'Do you think you can find him without raising suspicions?' Ed asked, after showing Bache the image of Grupps wiping the data core in the damaged council building.

'He's a slippery little shit,' said Bache. 'He'll be difficult to find.'

'We could accidentally leak this footage to the Dasos media,' said Andy. 'That could make things a bit uncomfortable for him and he might break cover to make a run for it.'

'I have a better idea,' said Cleo, appearing in the room.

'How about we obtain footage of Grupps in a tell-all meeting with Milne?'

'They're too smart for that; they'd never actually meet in person,' said Bache, shrugging.

As they watched, Cleo's hologram morphed into Grupps and grinned.

'They would if he just walked in and demanded a meeting,' she said, now sounding like the man too.

'Bloody hell,' said Bache, his eyes wide. 'That's actually quite concerning. But the security around the President is extremely high and she would simply refuse to see you.'

'I understand she's conducting business at her home in Stattum Nye,' said Cleo, morphing back again.

'Yes, the risk from falling debris has declined to the odd bit here and there and most of it is so small it burns up anyway,' said Bache. 'So she's moved out of the bunker and into a bit more comfort.'

'Exactly,' said Cleo. 'If she was still in the bunker, I wouldn't have been able to get in. But now, her home security system's child's play for me and she has excellent quality holo projectors throughout the house.'

'You've already looked, haven't you?' asked Ed.

'Been there for several hours,' she said. 'Nice pad…you should buy it when it comes on the market shortly.'

'The gravity's shite and recently the weather's taken a bit of a downturn,' said Andy, shaking his head.

'We will need some way of getting the evidence out there once we've got it,' said Ed. 'I'm sure the media networks are going to need proof it's genuine before they stick their necks out.'

'I might have just the person for that,' said Bache, tapping away on his tablet. 'Can I have a tight communication beam to a Mr Stavri Venn on the Potamaki Peninsula on Dasos?'

'Who?' Linda asked, glancing at the holomap as a location on the coast around two hundred kilometres from Kentro City began flashing.

'An old friend,' said Bache, as Cleo secured the connection.

A slightly shaggy grey-haired old man appeared above them. His laughter lines creased as he smiled at the camera.

'My old friend, Bache,' he said. 'Or should I call you Admiral now?'

'Hello, Stavri,' replied Bache. 'It's been way too long I know, but I might just have an exclusive to the biggest news story in GDA history and wondered if you might be interested?'

'Well, judging how big the last one was, this must be good. I've taken more of a back seat in the organisation now, but if it's as big as you make out, I'm all ears.'

Bache spent the next ten minutes explaining the situation and what they planned to do. Stavri's eyes grew wider and wider as all the details about the last few days were relayed to him.

'Ancients preserve us,' he said, as Bache concluded. 'And you're absolutely sure about all of this?'

'One hundred percent,' said Bache.

'And one of the Ancients is here now?'

'Well, she was a couple of days ago.'

'What I'd give for that exclusive interview,' admitted Stavri, rubbing his chin and rolling his eyes. 'Okay,' he said, adopting a more serious expression. 'Get me that footage and it'll be out there and obviously all the other thousands of GDA networks will pick it up too. So, I'm praying you're right about this, it'd be the end for all of us if we'd got it wrong.'

'We haven't…I'll be in touch,' said Bache and cut the connection.

'Right, Cleo, let's go and hunt a president,' said Ed.

Early the next morning, the *Gabriel* sat uncloaked orbiting Dasos and to any casual observer, was helping in the space debris clean-up operation. One of its drones sat cloaked, five kilometres above Milne's house in the Stattum Nye region on the outskirts of Kentro City. It provided an extra stable platform for Cleo's hologram, thus avoiding any unplanned and unwanted glitches in her projection.

'Is everyone ready?' asked Ed, glancing round the bridge at the ring of expectant faces. Getting a nod from everyone, he turned to Cleo. 'Okay, let's do this,' he said to her as she morphed into Grupps. 'And don't forget the questions you need to ask Milne.'

'I'm a bloody computer, I'm hardly going to forget a few fucking questions,' growled Grupps, before sticking his tongue out and disappearing.

'That told you, ah, ha,' scoffed Andy.

'Ah,' said Ed. 'You're becoming annoying again…you must be feeling better.'

The holomap changed to a scene from Milne's home, which quickly ended the conversation. It showed a large office, with curtains drawn across four large floor-to-ceiling windows. A log fire created a rosy glow that flickered off the soft furnishings and the three people in the room. One was Milne, dressed smartly in a suit and standing with her back to the fire, warming her hands behind her back. The other two gentlemen were unfamiliar, but wore clothing that wasn't the kind usually seen on Dasos, so they presumed they were probably ambassadors from other worlds.

A door to the right opened and Grupps strolled in as if he owned the place. Leaving the door open, he stood to one side and raised his eyebrows at Milne.

Milne glared malevolently at him, before turning back to the other two and apologising.

'I'm so sorry, gentlemen, can we continue this discussion in a few minutes?' she said, ushering them to the open door. They left, giving Grupps a disapproving glance as they passed him.

As soon as the door closed, Grupps walked over to the fire and started warming his hands.

'What the fuck are you doing?' snapped Milne. 'You can't be seen here.'

Grupps completely ignored her comment, rested his hands on the warm mantle and with his back to her, spoke in a quiet menacing voice.

'She has a few more subjects that need to disappear,' he said. 'And before you answer, please remember who you're talking to.'

'You're kidding me,' Milne protested through gritted teeth. 'I've transferred all the funds she wanted, we've already had half the council disposed of, along with the majority of the senior naval officers, and she still expects me to dispose of more? She might be my aunt, but I'm not her fucking personal banker and assassin.'

The bridge on the *Gabriel* sat in stunned silence for a second, before Andy whistled through his teeth.

'Fuck me,' he said. 'She's Flast's niece.'

'Bache'll never believe it,' said Linda. 'And now we know where she gets some of her funding from.'

'All this time,' said Ed. 'Is it any wonder Flast's been able to evade the authorities for so long?'

'Whatever happened to due diligence when these people run for office?' asked Linda.

It went quiet again as they listened in to see if Milne would say any more to condemn herself.

'There is one in particular she would like removed today,' said Grupps, still warming his hands on the mantle before turning to scowl at Milne.

The President slumped into a chair behind a large wooden desk, crossed her arms and sighed.

'Who now?' she asked, through clenched teeth.

'Admiral Loftt,' whispered Grupps. 'I understand he'll be here for a meeting shortly. Make sure he doesn't leave this office alive.'

'I can't kill Loftt,' she said. 'He thinks I'm his friend; he's an asset to the cause.'

'Not to her he's not.'

'And where's my new navy? Lake promised me a new fleet in exchange for the defence satellite codes and now the bastard's nowhere to be found.'

'You should watch what you say about a living god, or the only ship you'll be receiving is a shuttle ride into the nearest black hole.'

Grupps wandered over to the desk and placed a laser pistol in front of Milne, before strolling back to the door. He looked over his shoulder as he grasped the handle.

'Loftt…today,' he growled and left the room.

Milne slumped in her seat, before grasping the pistol and

quickly secreting it under the desk. A sudden knock at the door made her jump.

'In,' she bellowed.

Admiral Loftt strolled in. He closed the door behind him, turned and smiled.

'Madam President,' he said, nodding his head in respect.

'Ah, Admiral,' she said. 'Come in, and can you leave your side arm on the table by the door please.'

Bache shrugged and drew his personal weapon. As soon as he had it in his hand, Milne raised her hidden weapon and shot him through the heart. With a look of absolute shock on his face and a fist-sized hole in the centre of his chest, he slumped back and was dead before his head hit the floor. Pressing the panic button under her desk, Milne remained seated and, with a sick feeling in her stomach, watched a pool of blood gradually swell from her friend's torso.

63

President Milne's office, Stattum Nye, Dasos, Milky Way

MILNE JUMPED AGAIN as two black-suited armed men unexpectedly entered her office. She still had the weapon in her hand, so she pointed it at them.

'Who the fuck are you?' she asked, the pistol shaking in her hand as she recognised the Skirmat Eagle insignia on their right arms. 'The Admiral just attempted a coup, he pulled a bloody weapon on me,' she stammered.

The stern expressions on the men's faces remained as they stared, but said nothing. They just shook their heads slowly.

'I don't think that's entirely true, Madam President,' called a voice from outside the door.

Milne's eyes almost bugged out of her head as Admiral Loftt stepped into the doorway and stared at her accusingly.

She opened her mouth to say something, then changed her mind and looked back down at the body on the floor. The massive chest wound vanished, as did the pool of blood that had been gradually increasing around the body. She gasped as the first Admiral Loftt stood up again and smiled at her, then morphed into a young woman wearing some sort of regal attire and promptly disappeared.

'Hologram,' she whispered, before looking up again and pointing the weapon at the Admiral for the second time. 'You just fucking set me up, Loftt,' she blurted, her voice louder this time.

'And you just murdered the Admiral of the Fleet in cold blood,' he said, stepping into the office for the first time and pointing at the floor where the body had been.

'You have no proof,' she said, her eyes hardening. 'There are no recording devices allowed in this room. It's checked by my security every day.'

She glanced at the door when she mentioned her security, presumably wondering where they were.

'They're having a little sleep,' Bache said, noticing her look.

He walked over to the fireplace and pointed to a tiny black mark on the mantle above the fire.

'Micro camera,' he said. 'Transmitting live, everything said and done in this room since Grupps placed it there.'

'Grupps was a hologram too?' she said, her voice getting a little shaky again.

'Uh, huh,' said Bache, nodding slowly.

'Transmitting where?'

'Live on all the major networks.'

Her face went white as she slumped back in her chair. Before anybody could do anything to stop her, she raised the pistol, pointed it at her head and pulled the trigger.

Nothing happened.

'Only had one shot in it,' said Bache. 'For safety reasons. No coward's way out for you.'

Milne smiled a half smile and threw the pistol at them. While they ducked and flinched at the flying weapon, she opened a drawer, retrieved another pistol and fired a laser bolt through her skull.

———

The political ramifications went on for a very long time, with over sixteen hundred human worlds pointing the finger and wanting answers. Many of them had lost their ambassadors, along with their president, naval officers and vessels they had financed, and were rightfully demanding indemnification. Some were even asking for Admiral Loftt to be prosecuted as he must have been involved. After all, he had been brought out of retirement and promoted to the most powerful job in the navy by the most corrupt and murderous president in the history of the GDA.

Common sense prevailed as it was quickly pointed out that it was he who had brought about the sting that had uncovered Milne's treachery and if not for him, she would've most certainly got away with it.

The voting in of a new president, and indeed the complete Inner Gerousia Council, got underway. It was expected to take several months, with almost all the human worlds fronting candidates.

The scientists worked hard at reverse engineering the beam technology from the Klatt octaship that Admiral Loftt had also advocated. They came up with a reseeding procedure that, although a lengthy process, would over time return Dasos's climate to a more temperate one.

The rebuilding of the planet's destroyed infrastructure began in earnest, some of which was financed by the funds from the frozen then seized Salft accounts. All the military shipyards were at capacity replacing the lost vessels and all surviving ships remained close to the Prasinos system until the planet's defence satellites could be replaced. Also heavily depleted, they couldn't rule out the surviving Klatt navy taking advantage while they were militarily compromised.

The search for Ystolion Flast and the transferred trillions of credits went nowhere and as before, both disappeared into the depths of galactic space.

Admiral Loftt spent many days interviewing, appointing and promoting, creating a new naval command structure, mostly from people he knew from his thirty-eight years in the organisation.

He did find time, however, to spare a single heavy freighter and load it to the roof with supplies, most of which were sponsored by Prota and the Theo population of Paradeisos, to be sent through the gateway to Yiss.

64

Theo Island, Panemorfi, Trelorus system, Milky Way

THE HEAVY FREIGHTER dropped down about a hundred metres off the south side of Theo Island and hovered a couple of metres above the ocean, its antigravs churning the surface as if it were boiling.

Everybody watched from the beach as the ship's huge rear door slowly hinged down and four Vriix spheres rolled out and splashed into the ocean. The screaming antigravs reached a crescendo of pitch as the ship lifted away upwards, gradually climbing higher and higher until it vanished into the haze of Panemorfi's early morning sky on its way back to *Katadromiko 21*.

'You explained that this is a temporary home for them, didn't you?' Bache asked, turning to Ed.

'I did,' he replied. 'Do we have a timescale for that? They did ask.'

'The boffins have said the ocean on TX187302 should have reached a liveable temperature for them in about four years. They're using the same technology as on Dasos to raise it up.'

'I'll let them know,' Ed said, slipping out of his flip-flops and wading into the sea.

He checked the communication band around his wrist was working and stopped about thirty metres out when the water was up to his chest.

The spheres floated about half in and half out of the water and seemed to have joined themselves together.

Ed felt the water swirl around his legs, which unsettled him slightly, but he thought it best if he remained completely still. Something large and dark loomed in the water directly in front of him and he found himself holding his breath.

The Vriix's torso and four of its tentacles raised up, its single eye observing him and the island behind.

'You are an honourable human,' coloured Oona, Ed's wrist band translating the multitude of colours into Ellinka.

For the first time Ed could witness the true size of a Vriix. It had always been difficult to judge with the distorting effect of the sphere. Oona was standing on the bottom with four of her tentacles and was about as tall as Ed's shoulder.

He reached out a hand and Oona responded by wrapping a tentacle gently around it.

'Thank you for trusting us and being our friend,' Ed replied. 'This will be your temporary home for around four of our years. I hope it's all right and warm enough.'

'A little more saline than we're used to, but it's fine temperature-wise,' she said. 'We'll attach and live in our spheres on the ocean floor just off this strange raised area.'

'It's called an island and this one's ours and we're here

about twice a year. Remember what I said about avoiding other humans too?'

'They can be arsehole fuckwits.'

'You've been talking to Andrew, haven't you?'

'That was Pol.'

Ed chuckled and looked over his shoulder at the small group on the beach.

'I'll have to have a word with her about defaming my race,' he said, squeezing her tentacle gently. 'Take care, Oona, and we'll see you soon.'

'Be well, Edward, and thank you.'

With a whoosh of water against Ed's legs she was gone. Looking up, he noticed the spheres were much lower in the water now and would soon be gone. He nodded, turned and waded back to his friends.

Two weeks later, Ed, Andy, Pol and Phil were sat on red leather Chesterfields sipping mulled wine in front of an inglenook fireplace so big you could seat six people inside it. Ed had indeed bought a castle on the Somerset coast. It was December and a huge fire was the only way to heat the main hall – with its criss-cross of thousand-year-old oak beams forty feet above, it was a big space. One end of the hall was completely taken up by an immense multi-panelled stained-glass window where sunlight streamed in, creating a multitude of sparking coloured patterns around the walls and stone floor. Two black greyhounds, Ripley and Willow, snored lightly on an old sofa to the left of the fireplace.

'This really is the dog's nuts, this place,' said Andy,

looking over his shoulder at the old oak furniture and tapestries adorning the walls. 'Or have I already said that?'

'About four times now,' said Pol, grinning.

They all glanced back as a shadow passed by the big window and they heard the unmistakable sound of antigravs spooling their disapproval as a ship landed outside.

'Expecting anyone?' Phil asked.

'Might be Linda,' replied Ed. 'Although she was supposed to be visiting relations in Minnesota this week. Whoever it is better not have landed on my new lawn.'

He jumped up and made his way through two more rooms and a twenty-metre-long corridor to the front entrance. Heaving the thick eight-foot-tall door open, he was pleased to see whoever it was had landed a GDA-badged military issue shuttle on the large gravelled courtyard area.

Ed smiled as he saw Admiral Loftt in the airlock along with two others, Captain Mye and Callon. He ran forward and hugged a rather surprised Callon.

'Doctor gave her the all-clear a couple of days ago,' said Bache. 'Now she's become a galactic vagrant.'

'No, she hasn't,' said Ed. 'She has a home here for as long as she wants.'

Callon appeared a little embarrassed, but beamed a smile anyway.

'Thank you,' she whispered. 'You really are a man of your word.'

'That seems to be trending at the moment, doesn't it?' said Mye, tapping away on her tablet. 'Which reminds me, my crew would like to apologise for the way they treated you and Andrew recently. We have a few cases of Euphoria beer from Regg'taa on board as a recompense.'

The ramp at the rear of the shuttle lowered to show four auto trundles loaded up with dozens of cases of beer.

'Looking at the size of your new lodgings, you might just have room for it,' said Bache, gazing up at the battlements and turrets looming above them.

'Wow,' said Andy, strolling up behind them. 'There's enough beer there to last me a good couple of weeks.'

Bache shook his head as Ed noticed Callon shiver with the cold.

'Come in, you guys,' he said. 'Come and get warm by the fire.'

'You timed your visit well,' said Ed, as they trooped inside. 'I've only just returned from a meeting with the new American president, who I think you already know?'

'Ah, yes,' said Bache, nodding. 'James Rucker, we're old mates. I seem to remember having a few beers with him at one of your favourite pubs a few years ago.'

Ed glanced at Bache and smirked.

'Just after you threatened to push his space station into the atmosphere, if I remember correctly,' said Ed, as they entered the main hall.

'Ah…the good old days…Ancients alive,' gasped Bache, stopping suddenly and glancing around the huge room, his eyes wide with surprise. 'How old is this bloody place?'

'A thousand years,' said Ed, proudly.

'Amazing,' Bache said, thoughtfully. 'The GDA was a completely different animal in those days.'

'You were just a junior lieutenant then weren't you?' joked Andy, overhearing the conversation.

'Cheeky bastard,' said Bache, turning to glare at Mye, sniggering behind him.

An immaculately dressed waiter entered and offered the visitors glasses of mulled wine.

Bache raised his eyebrows at Ed.

'You have staff now?' he asked.

'They kinda came with the place and live on the estate,' Ed replied, shrugging as Pol and Phil shook hands with the newcomers. 'I promised them continued employment all the time I was here.'

'Any news of Flast or that bastard Grupps?' Pol asked, changing the subject.

'No,' grumbled Bache, a cloud passing across his face. 'Although she no longer has a Theo autonurse, so that will piss her off. The good news is we retrieved her DNA from the autonurse she stole.'

'I thought that went down with the station,' said Ed.

'It did,' said Bache. 'But the investigators went through the wreck on Sidero with a fine-toothed comb and it seems the Theos make those things to last. Okay, it was smashed and would never operate again, but the internal core was retrievable and readable. If she enters any GDA world that has bio scanning technology, flags will go up and we'll be notified straight away.'

'Good, she probably won't know that,' said Ed. 'Nothing on Grupps?'

'Nothing at all...he's a bit of an enigma to be honest. No one seems to know what world he's from or have anything on him whatsoever.'

'We'll get the bastard one day,' said Andy.

'How much had Milne transferred to Flast from the GDA accounts?' Phil asked.

'We're not completely sure,' said Bache, sighing. 'But,

it's in the trillions unfortunately. We could really do with those funds right now.'

'Have the Klatt shown themselves recently?' Ed asked.

'Thankfully, no,' said Bache, rolling his eyes. 'We believe they're doing the same as us and licking their wounds and rebuilding.'

'Let's hope they're not rebuilding too well, or quickly,' said Ed.

Bache nodded and looked at Andy.

'How are you bearing up after your personal disaster, Andrew?'

Andy shrugged and adopted a pensive expression.

'Every day I wake up and the pain is a little less.'

Bache nodded and rubbed his chin.

'I feel I should let you know…Rayl has applied as an officer cadet.'

'With the GDA navy?' Andy asked.

Bache nodded again.

'Are you going to accept the application?'

'That's down to the recruitment committee,' replied Bache.

Andy stared at him questioningly.

Bache sighed and averted his gaze.

'Most likely,' he said.

This time it was Andy's turn to nod.

'I'm going for a walk,' he said, standing and heading for the door.

Ed gave Phil a look and nodded towards Andy.

'I'll come with you,' said Phil, getting Ed's hint and quickly following. 'The pub's open up the road and it's my round.'

Bache smiled at Ed.

'Give him time,' Bache said. 'It's the best healer.'

'I know,' said Ed. 'I've made a decision not to venture out again until he's right.'

'And that's the right decision. Call me when you're ready…I'm sure I'll have something for you to do. Now, is there any more of this delicious hot wine?'

EPILOGUE

The special operations room, White House, Washington,
Earth

Prsident Rucker sat at a large rectangular table with several senior military figures. It was the end of his first month in office. The operation they were watching on four screens at the end of the room had been sanctioned after information brought to him by Edward Virr a couple of weeks ago.

The blurry images on the screens suddenly became clearer as the four-man navy SEAL fire team emerged from the Caribbean. Silently removing and stowing their diving apparatus amongst the rocks, donning their night vision goggles and checking their weapons, they made their way stealthily up towards a huge white villa looming high above on the clifftop.

It was three thirty in the morning and the two armed

guards supposedly patrolling the grounds were sitting on pool loungers. One of them was asleep and the other was smoking and watching a video on his phone. The sound from whatever he was watching, although low, made it easy for the team. Neither man knew who or what had killed them.

They'd studied plans of the villa for over a week and knew exactly where the best point of entry was for the master suite. Unbeknown to the house owner, the security system had been remotely cracked and deactivated by military hackers aboard the USS *James* just three miles off the coast.

The side door lock took two minutes to breach and the team were inside. Moving to the back staff staircase that led from the kitchens to the upstairs apartments, they ascended to the second floor, emerging nine feet from the large double doors they wanted.

They were expecting another guard here, sitting outside the apartment. Only he wasn't there. His chair was there though. The lead SEAL laid his hand on the seat and found it still warm. Their heads snapped around as a toilet flushed at the far end of the corridor, some twenty metres away. Training kicked in and the rearmost team member sprinted down towards the toilet door with his weapon in the shoulder.

The guard emerged from behind the bathroom door, his eyes going wide at the black figure lunging toward him. The weapon clacked once and a neat hole appeared in the guard's forehead, curtailing any shouted warning. The SEAL dropped his weapon onto its harness and grabbed the man, lowering him back and down into the bathroom behind. Closing the door again, he quickly rejoined his colleagues as they silently pushed open the right-hand of the two master suite doors. They knew from the plans that the small anteroom they were in led to two other doors. One was an office and the other the bedroom. One of the SEALs remained here and watched the corridor.

The bedroom door was unlocked, which saved them time. As the three SEALs entered without a sound, they found the room was larger than they had expected. A huge white four-poster bed stood against the far wall, between two floor-to-ceiling windows. The bed frame was draped with a light blue fishing net-style material and swayed slightly in the breeze created by a big ceiling fan turning lazily above.

Three naked figures lay asleep on the bed: two tall thin white females and a shorter darker-skinned man.

One of the SEALs knelt down silently next to the man, allowing his camera to get a good image of his features. Seconds later he got a faint whisper in his earpiece.

'Identity confirmed,' was all that was said.

He stood up again and nodded at the others. Instantly, two of the men grabbed the girls, dragging them off the bed and clamping hands over their mouths to reduce any screaming to a minimum. Three clacks sounded as the fourth SEAL put two rounds in the man's skull and another in his chest.

The girls, now wide awake and terrified, were gagged and zip tied to a heated towel rail in the bathroom. The leader dropped a folder of information on the bed next to the dead man before the team beat a hasty retreat back the way they'd come and down the narrow steps to the rocky shore. Two minutes later, they slipped back under the early morning Caribbean swell.

The following day, the St Lucia police, responding to a panicky call from the housemaid, discovered four murders had taken place the previous night: three ex-military Colombians working as security guards and Juan Mateos the house owner, a Mexican billionaire.

After a lengthy and, according to the local chief of police, exhaustive, investigation, it was discovered the house owner hadn't been Mexican at all, but in fact also Colombian and none other than the infamous escaped criminal Floyd Herez.

A MESSAGE FROM THE AUTHOR

I wanted to say a huge thank you for choosing to read *The Medusa Fold*. I sincerely hope you enjoyed the sixth adventure in the *Fold* series.

If you did enjoy this novel, it'd be fantastic if you could write a review. It doesn't have to be long, just a few words, but it is the best way for me to help new readers discover my writing for the first time. I use the best and most imaginative reviews in my marketing too.

If you'd like to stay up to date with what's going on, you're welcome to join my reader group at my website www.nickadamsbooks.com and receive a bi-monthly newsletter, advance notice of new releases and cover reveals. I will never share your email address and you can unsubscribe at any time.

You can also contact me via Facebook, Instagram, Twitter, or by email. I love hearing from readers – I read every message and try to reply to everyone personally.

Thanks again for your support.
Nick Adams